GRAPESHOT AND DEMONS

VINCENT P. SCULLY

ISBN: 1480285307
ISBN 13: 9781480285309

ART BY ROBERT CALDWELL

A.	Mizen Topgallant	K.	Main Topmast Staysail
B.	Mizen Topsail	L.	Fore Royal
C.	Spanker	M.	Fore Topgallant
D.	Main Royal	N.	Fore Topsail
E.	Main Topgallant	O.	Fore Course
F.	Mizen T'gallant Staysail	P.	Fore Topmast Staysail
G.	Main Topsail	Q.	Inner Jib
H.	Main Course	R.	Outer Flying Jib
I.	Main T'gallant Staysail	S.	Spritsail
J.	Middle Staysail		

1.	Taffrail & Lanterns	11.	Waist
2.	Stern & Quarter-galleries	12.	Gripe & Cutwater
3.	Poop Deck/Great Cabins Under	13.	Figurehead & Beakhead Rails
4.	Rudder & Transom Post	14.	Bow Sprit
5.	Quarterdeck	15.	Jib Boom
6.	Mizen Chains & Stays	16.	Foc's'le & Anchor Cat-heads
7.	Main Chains & Stays	17.	Cro'jack Yard
8.	Boarding Battens/Entry Port	18.	Top Platforms
9.	Shrouds & Ratlines	19.	Cross-Trees
10.	Fore Chains & Stays	20.	Spanker Gaff

L'Académie d'Escrime de Paris
1807 Fencing Manual
English Translation

Valid Target Areas of the Body

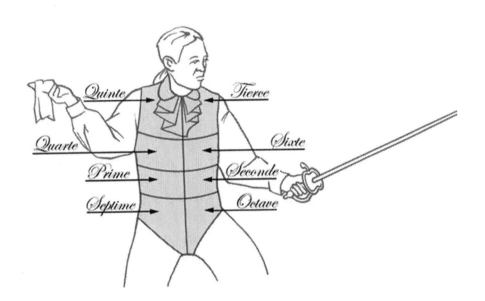

L'Académie d'Escrime de Paris
1807 Fencing Manual
English Translation

Parries
Prime (first position)
Lower right, palm down, tip down, cross body
Seconde (second position)
Lower left, palm down, tip down, straight out
Tierce (third position)
Upper left, palm down, tip up, straight out
Quarte (fourth position)
Upper right, palm down, tip up, cross body
Quinte (fifth position)
Upper right, palm down, tip down, cross body
Sixte (sixth position)
Upper left, palm up, tip up, straight out
Septime (seventh position)
Lower right, palm up, tip down, cross body
Octave (eighth position)
Lower left, palm up, tip up, straight out

L'Académie d'Escrime de Paris
1807 Fencing Manual
English Translation

Glossary of Fencing Terms

Attack. An extension of the point to threaten a valid target area.

Balestra. A forward jump that starts with the attacker pushing off the back leg as if lunging, but ends with the rear leg recovered forward to replace the attacker in the on-guard position.

Compound attack. An attack with feints to different lines.

Corps à corps. The act of two fencers coming together in bodily contact, at which time the director will halt the action.

Coupe. An attack that first lifts the blade over the opponent's blade and then returns to a line of attack.

Disengage. Dropping the point to avoid a parry or to change the line of attack.

Double. An attack that makes a complete circle around the opponent's blade.

Feint. An offensive movement to provoke a reaction to open a line of attack.

Invitation. Intentionally opening a line for the opponent to attack.

Lines. The eight numbered valid target areas of the body.

Lunge. An attack using the back foot to push the attacker forward to land in a stretch, with the rear leg extending straight back and the front knee directly over the front foot.

On guard. The neutral stance of the fencer from which offensive or defensive actions can be taken.

Parry. A defensive movement of the blade to deflect an attack.

Passé. An attack that passes the target without hitting.

Riposte. A counterattack after a successful parry.

Salute. A gesture of respect to one's opponent at the beginning of a bout, performed by extending the point toward the opponent, kissing the guard, then finishing with a downward cut.

Take the blade. A controlling press on the opponent's blade.

Touch. The declaration of a valid hit.

HMS *Righteous*
Officers
Rodney Wyckham, Captain
Pierce Rawlins, First Lieutenant
James Clifton, Second Lieutenant
Thomas Sorenson, Third Lieutenant
James Gregory, Fourth Lieutenant
Charles Moore, Senior Midshipman
Malcolm Donnelson, Captain of Marines
Warrants
Robert Greaves, Chief Bosun
Harvey Rames, Ship's Purser
Franklin Jones, Ship's Carpenter
Daniel Shroeder, Surgeon

HMS *Zeus*
William Jarvis, Admiral of the Red
Sean O'Neal, Flag Captain
Alexander Terhughes, First Lieutenant
Terrence Warren, Fleet Captain of Marines
Arnold Burgess, Fleet Surgeon

HMS *Hedgehog*
Harris Grimwald, Captain

HMS *Vesuvius*
Winston Randolph, Captain

HMS *Scamp*
Martin Hamilton, Commander

HMS *Gnat*
Robert Wallingford, Commander

TABLE OF CONTENTS

1

THE ENGLISH CHANNEL OFF
USHANT, 1814

At the sound of the shuddering crash, he bolted upright in his swaying bunk, almost hitting his head on one of the quarterdeck beams. He recognized immediately what was happening, one of the worst fears of a Royal Navy officer. It wasn't the gale's dangerously large waves breaking over the bow or thunder directly over the ship—Post Captain Rodney Wyckham of HMS *Righteous* would sleep peacefully through those events. It was the sound of one of the waist's eighteen-pound long guns, almost two tons of cast iron and heavy wooden naval carriage, broken loose from its bowsing cables and careening about the ship in the middle of a half gale.

"Sah!" The loud bang of his marine sentry's brass-wrapped musket stock on the floor was nothing compared to the wood-splintering crashes from above.

"Mr. Moore, sah!" the sentry barked out, letting him know the teenage midshipman was at the door to the captain's quarters.

"Yes, yes, come!" Wyckham spat out as he reached for his shoes.

"Lieu...lieutenant Ra...Rawlins's compliments, sir, and...and... there's..."

Wyckham cut the stuttering boy short. This was no time to mollycoddle this shy "young gentleman," who Wyckham doubted would ever make lieutenant.

"Thank you, Mr. Moore. I'm under way. Has the watch been called?" Wyckham might have slept through the bosun's pipes.

"Aye, s...sir. C...coming up now, s...sir."

Wyckham threw on a weather coat and sprang up the stern gallery as the entire ship shook sickeningly from an even louder impact. He recognized the squawk of foot-thick oak bulwarks being ripped apart. A loose gun could cause far more damage than even hits from the largest of French artillery. If it fell down an open hatch, it could even go right through the hull and sink the ship. *Bloody hell!*

The captain emerged onto the ship's waist just as *Righteous*'s bow rose up on a large wave, and there it was, the cave-like maw of the gun's muzzle flying toward him, almost in his face—with *almost* about to be eliminated from the scene's description. Time froze as he stared into the huge black hole, like the gaping entrance to hell itself: very dark, deep, and empty, and about to crush him against the stern gallery.

But he wasn't going to hell just yet if he could help it. Wyckham grabbed the gallery post and spun to his right just as the eight-foot gun barrel blasted through the entryway. He ducked into the corner by an arms locker to avoid the thick splinters that exploded all around, his heavy pea coat protecting his body. Only his right hand was exposed, and that took a beating.

The stern rose as *Righteous* rolled down the steep backside of the wave, causing the gun to reverse itself and accelerate back across the deck toward the forecastle, intent on additional destruction. Several hands coming up from below scattered, but one old tar got hit by the gun's left truck and went rolling across the deck with a deep grunt.

Goddamn unbelievable! Here he was, just a half day from Portsmouth harbor, and his career was about to be ruined. The voyage's successful capture of a notorious Yankee privateer would mean nothing at Admiralty if his ship destroyed itself in the English Channel. He'd most likely face a court-martial, lose his ship, and be on half pay forever. He could envision his father's enraged ranting about disgracing the family name, just as he was about to be admitted to Lords.

What's more, his older brother, Chauncey, would use the incident to push the old man to further disinherit the younger son. Wyckham always simmered at the thought of his older brother. While *he* was standing up to French and Yankee broadsides, fighting for his country, Chauncey spent his time gadflying about the London clubs, doing nothing but basking in the glow of the Wyckham family name. Yet his father always favoured Chauncey, the firstborn but useless son, ignoring his younger son who had pursued a noble career in the navy. The only comment his father ever made about Rodney's naval accomplishments was to observe that now his son swore like a common deckhand.

He'd better get this cannon tied up before it wrecked his career along with his ship. Crewmen were trying to get a rope around the gun, but it kept bouncing around the gun deck in the roiling seas. They needed to steady the deck quickly to get this gun bowsed back down. "Mr. Clifton, back the storm jibs. Put the ship in irons."

"Been trying, Captain. Can't get them around! It's blowing too hard!" his second lieutenant bellowed back from the forecastle.

Wyckham scanned the ship's trim, looking for a way to get the bow just a bit into the wind so the two storm jibs on the bowsprit could be brought around. "Let go spritsail! Lieutenant Rawlins, loose the spanker!"

His first lieutenant on the quarterdeck jumped to get some hands to let fly the spanker. With less weather helm on both bow and stern, maybe the jibs could be hauled across the foremast to stall the ship. "Now haul away, Mr. Moore!"

A group of foredeck hands leaned into the wind and strained on the forward sheets. Slowly the triangular jibs pulled tightly across the foremast, the ship turning to lee. The main gun deck started to level, and, most importantly, it steadied up.

"Ropes now, lads!" A dozen hands were now able to surround the still rolling gun, trying to get a rope under the muzzle. After the gun rolled over a couple of ropes, a third attempt stayed in place long enough for the men to pull the gun up to the bulwarks. There, another group quickly bowsed it down, breech first, where it would await calmer seas to be returned to its own gunport.

Rodney Wyckham, at twenty-eight years old the youngest post captain in the Royal Navy, had just avoided a career-changing catastrophe. He untied the black ribbon from around his chestnut hair and wiped sweat and salt spray from his prematurely weathered face, sighing in relief. The half-dozen wood splinters sticking out of his right hand were a minor inconvenience compared to what that gun might have done.

"Well done, you stout fellows there on that rope." Wyckham approached the bosun, Greaves, who was at the quarterdeck gallery. "Mr. Greaves, my compliments, and an extra grog ration for those hands and you as well."

Wyckham always made sure to hand out rewards for anything done right. After months at sea, his crew was now well motivated and trained. Greaves nodded in understanding. Even he had changed his ways and no longer pressed for harsh discipline. There had been only one flogging aboard *Righteous* during the entire voyage.

Wyckham surveyed the damage, and it wasn't pretty. Besides extensive damage to the scantlings on both sides, the quarterdeck gallery was now just kindling for the cook's fires, and a starboard gun had been hit and dismounted. But it was all repairable; Wyckham was even optimistic about getting most of it straightened out before they made port.

Hopefully, another result of the gun running amuck was also fixable. "Mr. Moore, my respects to Mr. Shroeder and report back on the state of any wounded."

Wyckham had seen at least one hand taken below to the orlop to be administered to by Shroeder, his Prussian surgeon. Any fatalities from a loose gun would be a blot on Wyckham's record, not to mention the sorrow and guilt he would feel on those lonely nights in his cot.

Wyckham's second lieutenant, James Clifton, a lean thirty-two-year-old with sandy hair, stepped up. "Only one, sir. Ordinary Seaman

Miller. Mr. Shroeder reports that he has two cracked ribs but no inside damage and should be fit for duty in a few weeks."

"Thank you, Mr. Clifton." Again, the crew's efficiency surprised even Wyckham. But there was one blemish on the ship's crew from the incident that needed to be addressed. The gun captain of the loose gun who had let it break free would have to face harsh discipline.

Before he could attend to that, someone yelled at him from below decks. "Well done, Captain!" It was their Yankee prisoner, James Harrison, the privateer they had captured off the Chesapeake and were taking back to England for a public trial and hanging. He was quite feared in England for his foray into the Irish Sea, where he'd taken many prizes and sacked several villages along both the Irish and Scottish coasts. The American was now imprisoned in the brig below, speaking up through a grating. "Though I can't say I ever had a gun loose on any ship of mine. Of course, my sailors were always competent volunteers, not ignorant landsmen pressed into service. Mine were real sailors, dedicated to ridding the seas of the British ships that impress any man off any ship they come across like it's their goddamn right. But I understand. All you highborn British officers have to keep your navy fully manned. King George's purse might suffer if you couldn't sail about and establish new British colonies, despite the objections of their current residents."

"As always, your comments are so well appreciated, Captain Harrison," snorted Wyckham. "I'm sure the judges in London will also be delighted by your rants against the Crown and will throw you quite a ball in Tyburn Square. I will certainly be there to watch you dance. You'll definitely be very light on your feet, dangling on the end of a rope."

He walked off to determine responsibility for the loose gun before the American could come up with a riposte. Lieutenant Rawlins was standing near the quarterdeck stairs. "Mr. Rawlins, a moment?" His first lieutenant, twenty-seven years old and a lifelong friend, gave some final directions to the watch and approached. Like Wyckham, his weathered face made him look much older, but Wyckham knew his age and many other details of the young squire's life. They had grown up together and attended the Haversham School before signing on with the Royal Navy.

"May I ask whose gun that was dancing jigs across our gun deck?" Pierce Rawlins's smug expression confirmed what Wyckham had been suspecting.

"The gun captain on the larboard third eighteen is Crawford, sir."

Peter Crawford was a seasoned hand who had been a thorn in ship's discipline, repeatedly reported for drunkenness, the only crewman on the entire voyage who had been flogged after he argued with a midshipman. Lieutenant Rawlins had often pressed for his demotion back to Ordinary, but Crawford's gun repeatedly was the most accurate at live gun drills, and he was popular with his gun crew for winning them the resulting extra grog rations. And Wyckham had felt for the man. In his late thirties, he probably couldn't change his ways, and besides that, he was helpful when sober and a good mentor for the younger hands. But he wasn't feeling any warm thoughts about the man right now. "Christ, it seems I should have taken your advice, Mr. Rawlins. Have him see me in my quarters. In an instant!"

Wyckham noticed the ship's carpenter, Jones, surveying the damage. "A report as soon as you can, Mr. Jones. I don't want this ship going into Portsmouth looking like a beat-up Thames barge."

As the captain turned to climb over the wreckage to his quarters below, Midshipman Moore came running up from the forecastle where he had been supervising the removal of some wreckage forward.

"C...captain, sir, s...signal from *Vesuvius*, r...relayed from the f... flag, sir. 'Enemy squadron north-northwest,' s...sir."

Enemy squadron? Had Admiral Jarvis gone completely mad? They were in the channel, for God's sake. Any sail sighted would be English; this enemy squadron was probably just a merchant convoy headed for the London docks. No Frenchmen had dared the channel for over a year; they hadn't been out since Nelson removed their hides at Trafalgar. Though the war was on again, thanks to the idiots in the War Office who had managed to let Napoleon escape from Elba just three weeks ago, the French navy was still blockaded in harbor at Brest.

Moore lowered his Royal Navy telescope and approached him again.

"S...sir, another s...signal from *Vesuvius,* our n...number, 'Need assistance'?"

"Thank you, Mr. Moore. Please acknowledge the first and decline the second."

Wyckham saw *Vesuvius* wearing about after dropping back to the tail of Jarvis's squadron to deliver the message to *Righteous. Vesuvius* was one of the bomb ketches (along with *Hedgehog*) that had been used in the failed attack on Fort McHenry in the current war with the new American nation. In addition, the squadron included the twenty-gun brigs *Gnat* and *Scamp,* and Jarvis's *Zeus,* an eighty-four-gun second-rate ship of the line.

Righteous, a thirty-eight-gun frigate and the fastest of the group, should have been the ship to investigate any strange sail, but she had fallen off her leeward screening position when she hauled her wind to deal with the loose gun. Wyckham could just imagine the dressing-down Jarvis would be giving him over that; the old admiral would relish every minute of it.

He turned back to First Lieutenant Rawlins. "Get her out of irons, Mr. Rawlins, and set course two points to loo'ard, thank you. And get a hand with a strong eye and a very sure foot aloft." During a half gale, no ship kept any lookouts aloft, but with the outside chance of an enemy in sight, he would have to risk it.

Now, where in hell was this enemy squadron? He was about to ask Moore for his glass, but up popped his steward, Larkin, with his own telescope, a fine piece made by Leica in Savoy. Wyckham put it to his eye, turned it to larboard, and focused to distance.

And saw the strangest formation of ships he had ever envisioned. There, about two miles off, strung out in a perfect line like the Scottish Guards marching into battle, were ten perfectly square, bright white sails. They were identical and stayed equally spaced apart, even in the rough seas, maintaining two cables' distance between each ship. He'd never seen the like, certainly not in the French navy. Possibly Neapolitan galleys visiting their British allies? Hell, no Italian ships could ever stay tight in any formation, much less put on this incredible display of ship handling.

Wyckham continued to stare in disbelief. As he watched, the sails grew in size at an impossible rate. These ships were moving at an unbelievable pace, in excess of twenty, maybe thirty knots, or even more? And these strange sails stayed perfectly vertical despite the storm. *Are they all roped together?*

He lowered his glass and then realized he had been staring with his mouth open, like a farmer visiting London for the first time. That just wouldn't do—captains in the Royal Navy had to look on top of matters at all times, no matter what the dangers or tasks to perform. He noticed all his lieutenants on the poopdeck studying the strange sails themselves.

He straightened up and clasped his hands behind his back in the normal captain's stance. "Gentlemen, does anyone here recognize these strange sails?" Mayhap his eyes were still bleary with sleep; the captain needed help on this one.

All three officers lowered their own glasses, their faces exhibiting similar looks of incredulity. His fourth, Gregory, a bright young squire's son from Winchester, moved closer to the quarterdeck. "Sir, I do not believe those are ships, but for the life of me, I cannot place those images anywhere in naval experience."

Not ships? Then what are they, in the middle of an ocean? Wyckham returned his glass to his eye. The sails, or whatever they were, were growing at a furious rate; they would be upon the ship in minutes! And coming into view were the other four ships in their squadron, seemingly moving together and making rapid leeway sideways toward the ten white squares. As he watched dumbfounded, *Gnat* approached one of the squares—stern first! It had dropped off to a starboard reach, its best point of sailing, yet it was moving backward toward the square like a leaf drawn to a waterfall. And then, like it was sinking, her bow rose up out of the water, and she disappeared into the glowing white square! *Christ, Gnat is gone! These squares are going to eat us all!*

But a captain needed to be calm in adversity. "Helmsman, fall off four points to starboard. Mr. Rawlins, hands aloft to set all plain sail. Like rabbits now."

His stomach clenched and churned as he watched the hands scurry aloft. Most of them had been cleaning up the gun deck and hadn't seen what had happened to *Gnat*. But at least a few had, and those on the deck were starting to babble about it to their mates. Still, they were going about their work—thank God for naval discipline. It would take them around two minutes to get *Righteous* back under way, and at least five more to get her to a decent speed. Wyckham had a gut-twisting fear that they would be falling into one of these holes well before then.

His fear increased as he looked back to see the square getting closer, the other four ships moving speedily backward toward the line of...what? Hellholes? That's what they seemed to be, ready to devour whole ships and their crews. *Zeus* was about five cables off, sideways to the current, making leeway very quickly now, like a rowboat caught in river rapids. The gigantic size of these things was now clear—they were ten times the size of *Zeus*, one of the largest vessels in the world! Finally, *Zeus* reached the brim of the third square from the line's end. Her masts went upright from the starboard tack she was on, then continued over to leeward as the ship broached and fell sideways into the glowing square. Wyckham saw the ship actually drop down out of sight once it entered the hole, amid clouds of spray as sea water spilled over the ship.

Good God! He had just watched six hundred and fifty sailors, marines, and officers, some of them friends whom Wyckham had known for years, all plunge to what must be their deaths.

Reeling, he reached out for a ratline to steady himself. He had just witnessed the fate that *Righteous* would soon meet if they couldn't pull away. But the growing size of the last square in the line showed that the crew's best effort was not enough, and in a few seconds, it would be their turn to go over a gigantic waterfall.

But how far were they to drop? Maybe just a few feet? Could the ship survive? *Get her ready, for Christ's sake!* He spun to the helmsman. "Helm over to nor'nor'west! Now!" The ship would head towards the square and enter it bows on, the best way to take any wave. Wyckham turned back toward the main deck and stepped up to the quarterdeck rail.

"Lads, lads! Listen to me!" *Stay calm and carry on, Wyckham. Put them at ease.* "In less than a minute, this ship will enter whatever that thing is on our beam, and *Righteous* will be taking a bit of a drop, like when you depart a lock in one of those French canals, and the crapaud locksman drops you too soon. So, unless you fancy a swim, grab right now to anything handy that's strong enough to keep you on board. All midshipmen will run below right now and warn everyone to prepare for a big wave, make sure you advise all three decks. Go! Now!"

The six boys sprang for the gangways as officers prodded everyone on deck to get moving toward something solid—guns, stays, ratlines, any stout piece of woodwork.

Their new course had them approaching the falls quite quickly. Their speed was increasing, and the waters about the ship were getting quite loud as the currents rushed toward the mystical door ahead. Wyckham didn't want the fast current to catch his stern on the way in and breach *Righteous* as well.

"Helm, drop off to due west." It was time to get *Righteous* pointed directly at the falls' head. "Everyone, brace yourselves!"

The helmsman spun the wheel futilely. The ship had no steerageway in the surging current, but as the waters sped up, they turned *Righteous* dead onto the square, as Wyckham had hoped. He could see the last crewmembers getting low and holding on.

The captain stared through the hole ahead and was astonished to see sunlight and a clear blue sky with some puffy clouds. *Good God, sunlight? Apparently hell has good weather.* Then they went over the edge.

The bow fell away, revealing a calm sea fifty feet below with land in the distance, all brightly lit up, like a scene from the Caribbean sugar islands. When the quarterdeck started to drop from under his feet, Wyckham suddenly realized it was his turn to grab onto something, and he'd better do it right quick. He clasped his hands through the wheel's spokes as helmsmen did in a large wave and held on for his life as *Righteous* briefly fell through space. It splashed into the sea below, ten feet of green water breaking over the bow. The impact threw Wyckham's feet sideways, but he had held on! Tons of water washed down the main deck, but quickly went out the scuppers as the bow rose smartly.

Damn my eyes, if the ship hasn't survived! Some of the hands were rolling about the deck, but it looked like most had held on. However, a call up forward dashed his relief. "*Righteous*, man overboard!" That call quickly spurred every crewman to the gunwales to look for crewmen in the water.

Most sailors could not swim and only had a few moments to be rescued before they went under. Wyckham saw Midshipman Moore throwing a wood grating to a figure calmly bobbing to starboard, right below the bow, in calm seas. Thank God, whoever it was could actually swim. The sailor made two quick strokes and hauled himself up on the grating as hands threw him lines. Wyckham scanned the waters but saw no others. However, some hands were slow getting up—clearly they had some wounded. He was about to send somebody below to fetch the surgeon, but he saw Lieutenant Rawlins already organizing help to get the wounded below.

The crew of the *Righteous* had been together for over two years, and it was the best crew Wyckham had ever been a part of. Unlike most crews, there were very few pressed hands. Most had volunteered to serve under Captain "Prize Bounty" Wyckham, his nickname in all the Portsmouth taverns due to his success at taking three valuable French prizes during a Mediterranean cruise four years ago. Now the crew's cohesion and training were clear. Here they were, in some complete unknown, and the first thought of everyone was to follow navy routine, just as they were trained to do.

So where the hell were they? The captain shifted his gaze about and slowly surveyed a complete circle about the ship. Off the stern, the ten gates to this unknown sea floated above them like Parisian hot air balloons, torrents of water pouring out of them to the calm sea below. It reminded him of the giant falls he'd seen in Africa years ago during a land attack against slavers. As he watched, the two bombs, first *Hedgehog*, then *Vesuvius*, appeared bows on in two different gates and slowly fell into the sea astern of *Righteous*. Apparently, they had seen *Righteous* avoid breaching by getting in line with the current and they, too, had come through bows on. Although both lost some rigging with the impact of the fall, the ships had survived.

But *Zeus* had not been so fortunate. There she was about a mile off, swamped, her larboard gunwales in the water and all three topmasts broken off and trailing the ship. Many hands were in the water, but Wyckham saw no efforts to assist them. The rest of the crew must be in bad shape to let their mates drown. Ominously, there was no sign of *Gnat*, but he could see *Scamp*, seemingly whole, wearing ship to come to the flagship's aid. He'd better do the same.

The moderate breeze was blowing fair for a quick run down to the swamped flagship. He looked over at the binnacle compass to get a heading for *Zeus*, but the needle was slowly drifting in circles. Must be damaged.

"Helm, make for the flagship. Mr. Rawlins, prepare all boats to assist *Zeus*. We will be trying to take her hands aboard quick. If any drown, the admiral's blame will most certainly fall upon *Righteous*. And get a hand in the chains with a lead, let's make sure there's enough water below us." For all he knew this was a shallow bay with sandbars all over the place.

Rawlins nodded and headed forward bellowing for the bosun, Greaves. Within a few moments, a sailor was hanging from the bow's anchor chains, throwing a lead weight on a rope to sound out the water depth. After his first cast the man shouted out, "No bottom wif 'iss line." So there was one less thing to worry about here.

As *Righteous* dropped off to starboard, Lieutenant Clifton approached the quarterdeck with a dripping wet crewman, the fellow just pulled from the water.

"Captain, Topman James here. He was in the crosstrees on lookout and reports seeing a group of very large fish heading right toward *Zeus* before he fell. Says they were quite big, sir."

Now what? Did this sea have sharks? If so, they'd surely be attracted to all the thrashing of *Zeus*'s crew in the water. Best to be prepared for that possibility.

"Captain Donnelson." The marine captain approached from where he'd been standing with the other officers. They'd all been watching their captain. Wyckham realized he'd better look calm and in control. He couldn't let his shipmates know the inner doubts he had about his own ability to lead them in this completely unknown place.

"My respects, Captain, and may I ask that you take your best marksmen and place them in the crosstrees with whatever rifles we have? It seems some nasty fishies are headed toward *Zeus,* apparently planning to dine on the flagship's crewmen in the water. Maybe your men can turn the tables, and instead we'll be having fresh shark for our own breakfast, hey?"

His lightness in the face of unknown adversity seemed to calm the other officers. The Scottish marine captain smirked, nodded his understanding with a quick, "Aye, sir," and called out to his sergeants. Several men in full kit headed below to get the excellent Pennsylvania rifles they'd taken from some Yanks at the burning of Washington last year.

Topman James approached, shaking his head. "Sor, if'n I may, what I saw warn't no sharks, sor. Big as 'owses they was, sor, an' they gots arms an' legs an' swims jus' like I do, sor."

Christ, big as houses? Wyckham snapped his glass out and scanned the horizon. There they were, about a mile off the leeward bow: two dozen or so very large creatures splashing toward *Zeus.* He couldn't make out much detail, but he could see long arms with webbed hands milling the water in overhead strokes. *Christ almighty, this place was just full of surprises.* Again, the empty feeling hit his gut. *Is this really hell?* Never before had he felt so alone and unprepared.

Christ, Wyckham, get prepared! Get your hand around this like any other scrape you've been in! Righteous *is a British thirty-eight-gun frigate and for goddamn sure can deal with any hell-spawned creatures in whatever place we're in!*

He grabbed a speaking trumpet, turned back to his assembled officers, and bellowed as loudly as he could so the whole ship could hear.

"Gentlemen, beat to quarters! *Righteous* will clear for action!"

Drums sounded, bosuns' pipes whistled, lieutenants called out orders, and every crewman jumped to his duty. Gun crews moved to unbowse their guns, loblolly boys scurried below to fetch cartridges and shot, and all of *Righteous*'s forty marines came up from below, struggling into their full red kits and priming their muskets. Pails of water were placed by the guns for swabbing out the barrels after each shot, and slow matches were lit in case the flintlock strikers failed. Boarding nets were strung above the decks. Arms lockers were opened so their muskets, pistols, cutlasses, and pikes could be distributed among the crew. Gunports banged open as all the ship's great guns were loaded and run out. Even the cook, Stuart, came up on deck, waving a massive meat cleaver, his preferred weapon for a deck fight.

Wyckham's valet, Larkin, came up from below with his pistols. They were from Nock's of London, rifled and vastly more accurate than standard-issue Navy Sea Pattern pistols. He also handed Wyckham his small sword, an ornate but well-balanced weapon he had taken from a Moroccan slaver he'd put out of business. Larkin strapped the sword's frog on the captain's belt as Wyckham tucked the pistols into his sash.

Wyckham then put the glass back up to his eye, checking on the beasts' progress. At the rate they were swimming, they were still a few minutes from *Zeus*, time enough for *Righteous* to get to the flagship first. He swung the glass to see *Zeus,* swamped and defenseless, both gunrows of her larboard battery almost submerged.

Then he watched dumbfounded as a giant monster climbed out of the water and onto *Zeus*'s main deck! One of them had gotten there already! It must have approached submerged—God knows how long it had held its breath. Or maybe these things could breathe underwater? It was huge, maybe thirty feet high. Wyckham could make out mottled brown fur, round bulging eyes, and damned if it didn't have some kind of decorated cloth about its head. Then Wyckham's own eyes stared in horror as the beast picked up a crewman from the deck like it was a child's doll, opened a gaping mouth filled with foot-long teeth, and popped the screaming sailor into his mouth like a hot chestnut! Then the monster grinned like a child enjoying a special treat!

It started to reach for another man but Wyckham couldn't watch. His knees sagged and he would have fallen had not his watchful steward, Larkin, put out his arm in support. He'd just seen a sailor eaten! Like in a Greek tragedy, only very real. But the revulsion started to ebb as Wyckham's anger took charge. *The goddamn thing just ate a British sailor!* Gentlemen like himself could participate in violent and brutal battles, but you still fought your enemy at a level of basic decency. *Some things are just not done, for God's sake! And one of those is eating your foe!*

In an energetic rage, he jumped out of Larkin's arm and down the quarterdeck stairs, shouting as he ran forward.

"Rawlins, get your best gunner forward on the bow chasers! Now!"

He sprang up onto the forecastle. *Righteous* mounted two "Long Nine" brass nine-pounders in the bow, the most accurate gun in the Royal Navy, used to disable a ship's rigging during a chase. He turned to see Lieutenant Rawlins, to his anger and disbelief, leading Seaman Peter Crawford up the forecastle stairs.

"Crawford! You bring me Crawford? Christ, is he even sober?"

Crawford nodded sheepishly. "Yessor, sober as a church mouse oy iz. Learned me ways oy 'ave, Cap'm, sor."

Wyckham doubted that. But there was no time to pick another gunner. "Seaman Crawford, I need you to put a ball in that rotting brute over there. Think you can do that?"

Crawford's face became grim. "Aye, sor, sea 'iss calm, I'll jes' skip a ball across, right up th' bugger's arse." Then he looked Wyckham right in the eye, and his voice changed to one of simmering determination. "I seen what ee's been doin' over there, sor. Be 'appy t' do it."

Wyckham was impressed with Crawford's sudden show of grit. He nodded. "All right then, shoot that big hellion over there, right quick." The seaman jumped to the leeward bow gun and spoke to the gun crew. "Got sum' gud balls 'n these two, Jack?"

The gun captain on the bowchasers had seen what was going on aboard Zeus and was in a shocked daze, but the presence of the captain jerked him back to his duties. "Aye, rolled em aroun' meself, Pete, round 'n' smooth as a babe's bum," Jack managed to respond. Gunners would usually roll round shot about the deck before loading. They'd pick the smoothest and roundest ones, the ones that rolled straight without thumping.

Crawford was already kneeling, sighting the gun with a handspike. With the triangular quoin pushed in under the breech, the barrel was depressed, and the shot would skip across the sea, removing the difficulty of setting elevation. While aiming the gun, Crawford licked his finger and held it up to get a feel for wind deflection. Then suddenly he stepped to the side of the gun and yanked the lanyard. The hammer struck the frizzen, the priming powder flashed, and a split second later the main powder charge ignited. The gun fired with an eruption of flame and a billowing smoke ring, leaping backward with a thunderous discharge, as the officers on the forecastle watched through their telescopes for the shot's impact.

First, a splash two cables off, a second one just before *Zeus*'s main deck, then a shower of splinters exploded from the quarterdeck behind the grotesque creature. The ball had passed a few feet in front of the beast and struck the ship's great cabin.

"Bloody bugger moved," Crawford muttered as he jumped to sight the second gun.

Wyckham kept his eye on the beast. Now it had another man in its hand—damned if it wasn't Admiral Jarvis himself! Wyckham recognized the overdone gilded coat and heavily embroidered hat even at this distance. Jesus, it was going to eat the admiral!

But the beast had frozen momentarily, looking about for the cause of the first shot's impact. That was all Crawford needed and he yanked the second gun's cord. The nine-pounder blasted off, two more splashes, and then a red mist appeared about the monster's head as its jaw went spinning away in a spiral of blood. The apple-sized ball had struck the creature right at the base of its jaw. Truly a superb shot! *Breakfast time's over, bastard! Forever! Hard to eat a British sailor without a lower jaw, you filthy swine!*

It spun back into the water squealing like a pig at slaughter, dropping Jarvis unceremoniously on the main deck. So this thing felt pain like any other living being. *Humph. It may look and act like Satan himself, but it is certainly mortal.* Extending his telescope to close in on the creature, Wyckham could see the beast had stopped thrashing and now had its eyes settled right on *Righteous*. As he watched, he saw it had several circles in its retinas which were spinning strangely in opposite directions. The ridiculous movement reminded him of young Spanish men and women at night in a Madrid plaza, parading in opposite circles in their traditional mating ritual. He continued watching as one by one the circles came to a stop and the fiendish eyes locked still. Then the monster's eyelids narrowed in a look of pure hatred, seemingly focused right on him. Christ, this eyeball movement was nothing comical. *The evil demon's eyes work like a telescope and he's focused right on me!*

Suddenly the captain felt a penetrating cold in his chest, producing an almost overwhelming wave of panic from head to foot. Was this damned monster probing into his very soul? Could this demon conquer him from afar with just a magical stare? Wyckham turned his head away and gave it a shake, managing to clear his body of the dread and cold. He had a nasty feeling that, even as wounded as it was, he did not want to cross paths with this incredibly evil creature ever again.

He snapped his glass closed and turned back to the forecastle. "Crawford, it seems this fellow is absolutely beside himself now that he can no longer dine on his favourite victuals. Perhaps we should put him out of his misery?"

Crawford was already back behind the reloaded starboard gun. "Me thinkin' 'zackly, sor. Gots th' range o' im now." He tapped the gun's quoin out a bit to raise elevation, his wet finger in the air, waiting for the gun captain to finish priming the firelock. For a moment he froze in a rigid crouch, his left hand on the breech for steadiness, his right eye wide open, sighting down the gunbarrel. Then a sudden spin to his left, a yank of the lanyard, and the gun fired with another ear-splitting crash.

This time the first splash was further off, right in line with the big ogre's head. But just before the ball reached him, the thing suddenly ducked beneath the surface and the ball passed harmlessly over. *Well, bollocks if the damned thing hadn't figured out how artillery works right quick.* It immediately surfaced, let out an ugly roar, then turned to all its mates in the distance and screeched out to them. With answering roars, they all suddenly changed direction and made straight for the frigate!

Humph! Apparently this fight's just beginning. "Helm, fall off two points." *Righteous* needed to change course so its portside battery would bear on the approaching enemy horde. But as the ship turned the bowchasers were no longer aimed at the wounded demon, and Wyckham could only watch as the creature casually submerged, this time staying down, apparently swimming off under water. *Bastard got away, damn him.*

He turned to address the maindeck. "*Righteous*, I don't know where the hell we are, or what has happened to get us here. Hopefully, it will all become clear soon enough, and we'll set a course for England and home. But right now, it seems we're about to have some visitors, some very large local inhabitants who are about to attack this ship. Let's give them a warm welcome: first round shot, then a double load of grape. Just man your guns, and I'll get you out of this place soon enough."

Some crewmen nearby turned back to their guns, but most of the gun crews were staring in overwhelmed terror at the approaching monsters. Even this far off, the creatures' roaring was quite loud and fearsome. Many hands were yelling out in fear. He heard, "God's mercy, we're t' be eaten!" and "We're done fer! Armageddon's 'pon us!"

Seamen were an ignorant and superstitious lot, and panic was taking hold. They'd done remarkably well so far in following orders after being thrust into a mystical new world, but seeing a horde of giant hungry beasts approaching fast had broken their faith in all they knew. Even Royal Navy discipline broke down in the face of this new reality.

"*Righteous*, stick to your guns!" Wyckham bellowed as loud as he could. "This is still a Royal Navy ship! Any man found derelict of duty may be hanged!"

"That shite doan' figger 'ere 'n hell, Cap'm," a slumping crewman called out. It was Ordinary Seaman Evans, known for his large stature and distaste for officers. "You 'n' all th' off'cers be goners soon enough, same iz us. So no more bloody ord'r'n us aroun'." The tall Welshman waved his hand dismissively at Wyckham in disgust. Some crewmen were nodding agreement; others slumped to the deck in final despair. Wyckham searched his mind frantically for magical words to rally them, but he came up empty. He'd never been in a fight with giant demons; there was nothing he could say to calm the crew.

He'd lost them. They would all die horribly.

2

MUTINY AVERTED

"Wotsa matter, Evans? Can't bring yerself t' shoot these pretty li'l trolls?" It was Crawford, bounding down from the quarterdeck and walking briskly over to his gun on the main deck. "Remin' ye too much o' yer mum, does they?" Several hands smirked; one elbowed Evans.

Crawford slowly turned about, addressing several gun crews he knew. "Bloody hell, jes' shoot th' bloody bastards. Ye all saw wots I jes' did t' that firs' un wif only a wee nine-pounder. Wots ye think th' eighteens'll do t' em? An' eez big fookers iz comin' right t' us. Even blind ol' sods like ye can't miss. Fook em all, I sez." Disgusted, he shook his head at them, then knelt down behind his gun and started to aim it with the handspike.

The crew mostly stood still, eyes darting about, looking around undecided. Then some older hand in the back piped up. "Mr. Evans, I did see your mater back in Portsmouth; by God she does bear a very strong resemblance to that attractive green one there in the middle!" Loud guffaws rolled through the crew as Evans received some pats on the back and further comments on his mother's looks.

Wyckham looked for the source of the well-spoken jibe. It was a new hand, Landsman Thomas Obujimi, nicknamed "Sir Thomas" by the crew. He was an African, a slave *Righteous* had liberated in Virginia; both the British army and navy in America routinely offered freedom to any slave that would sign up. Obujimi had been educated and was managing a large plantation's mansion when a foraging party from *Righteous* offered him freedom if he'd join the Royal Navy. Even though he wasn't much of a sailor yet, the crew liked him and held him in high regard for his refined speech and keen wit. It was even rumored that he had been some kind of tribal prince in Africa before he was abducted by Arab slavers.

"Gentlemen," he continued in a dignified tone. "I have given my written promise to rid the seas of the king's enemies. Sadly, Mr. Evans, your mater here most certainly seems to be one. Her impending plan to eat Royal Navy persons definitely places her in that genus. So with my deepest apologies to you, my most worthy shipmate, I will now do my best to blast your dear mother into pieces." With that he grasped a rope for hauling out the nearest gun and asked, "Any of you gentlemen care to join me?"

Wyckham seized the moment. "Men, Crawford's right! When you lads hit them with your eighteen-pounders, it will be like the butchering at a country fair! No British ship can be bested by a bunch of fish! For God, king, and country! *Righteous*, follow Sir Thomas and get back to your guns!"

They were coming back! Their faces were grim. They knew they might be about to die, but that was a part of any sailor's life. To lighten their own fear, many continued japing about Evans while they sited their guns. "Looka th' size o' them teats on 'iz mum there! No wunner Evans grew so big!"

Lieutenants paced along the batteries, giving final instructions. "Quoins in. Skip your shots down to them. Just like a game of bowls on King George's lawn."

The captain turned back to the approaching monsters, which were roaring like giant savages, thrashing the water with their windmilling arms. They were about two cables off, less than six hundred yards, easily in range. *Lord, but they are distressingly loud. Time to start quieting these noisy banshees.*

"Lieutenant Clifton, you may fire when ready," he called out to the young lieutenant on the leeward battery.

"Wait for the downroll…" Clifton bellowed. The sea was fairly calm here, but there was a slight rolling motion to the ship's way. "Ready…fire!"

The sixteen guns on the leeward battery crashed out as one, their tongues of flame jetting through the billowing white smoke. These were big eighteen-pounders—ship smashers. The crash of the broad-side shook the whole ship as the guns danced back into their restraining ropes. Wyckham watched with elation from the quarterdeck above the smoke as the large balls skipped home, plowing into the massed creatures, throwing limbs and great chunks of meat flying through the air. Several balls struck with satisfying thuds as they went deep into flesh and bone, and the air was filled with the animals' whining screams. Wyckham was relieved to see that these demons too were quite mortal. *Thought you'd eat some more British sailors? Well, dine on some sweet hot revenge from HMS Righteous!*

"Well done, lads! Now double grape for our visitors!" As the smoke cleared, Wyckham saw that several creatures were dead in the water, but many of them had been untouched. Others, despite obvious wounds pumping blood, were still swimming madly toward them. *Many faults these creatures may have, but unfortunately cowardice is not among them,* Wyckham had to acknowledge with a grimace.

A ship's broadside firing all at once delivered quite a shock. He'd hoped that one broadside would send them all running, but they were still coming and moving fast. *Righteous* would get off one, maybe two more broadsides at most before they reached the ship. Most likely some of the creatures were going to make it through. And at close quarters, these angry beasts would be the devil to fight. He'd better figure out a way to repel the biggest boarders in naval history.

He called out to his captain of marines. "Captain Donnelson, I'd admire you get your best men on the swivels, load with double grape."

Righteous mounted fourteen swivel guns on its railings and up in its fighting tops, small cannons used for sweeping an enemy deck alongside or repelling boarders. Wyckham had a gnawing feeling in his gut that the marines' muskets would have no effect on these huge, charging beasts. Instead of the sailors manning them now, it would be better to get the marines with their superior gunnery skills on the swivels.

He then turned to his third lieutenant, who was manning the idle starboard battery. "Mr. Sorenson, be so good as to get your boarding nets down and mount them over those already on the leeward battery." Wyckham wanted additional hindrance to any giants trying to board his ship. "Make sure you cover the gaps between the ones there now. This instant, now!"

Sorenson barked orders, and his gun crews scurried up the ratlines to get the nets down as the leeward battery erupted again, this time in a rolling broadside of grapeshot. The sea around the monsters erupted in splashes ten feet high. Each gun had been loaded with two bundles of about twenty one-pound balls, stacked on a wooden disk and wrapped with netting around a dowel in their center. Their resemblance to a bunch of giant grapes gave the loads their name. A single ball could bring down an Indian war elephant, and the group in the water staggered as they were struck by most of the seven hundred balls discharged. At this range it was hard to miss, even with the spreading pattern grapeshot made as it left the guns' muzzles. Wyckham could see shreds of brown furry flesh flying through the air and heard more of their shrill squealing, almost unbearably loud this close.

"Well done, *Righteous*! Quickly now, one more and they're done!" He hoped he wasn't lying.

Momentarily stopped, several of the creatures in the back of the group climbed over their fellows' corpses and launched themselves toward the ship again, still roaring like hell and full of fight. Whether or not *Righteous* could get off another broadside in time might decide the matter; in just a few moments, the creatures would be too close for *Righteous*'s guns to aim low enough. And even if they did get off a third broadside, chances were that at least one or two would make it aboard, and that might be all it would take to get his entire crew killed and devoured. What else could he do to prepare the ship?

Wyckham saw Sorenson's men climbing back to the deck after stringing the extra boarding nets. "You lads there, grab some pikes in case we have some visitors needing a bit of a tickle." Pikes, which were eight-foot wooden spears with long steel points, might be more effective than muskets in a deck fight against these things.

Guns started firing individually or in small groups as some crews reloaded more quickly than others. Wyckham squinted through the smoke to see the result of the final volley. All seemed still. Had they done for them all?

Suddenly the water erupted just under the ship's lee. *The damn monsters had submerged as they got close to the ship! Christ, just the way the first bugger did it to* Zeus! The ship rolled with the weight of several huge beasts grabbing on and climbing up the lee side.

Crawford was standing behind his gun, watching his rammer Barrows about to ram another double load of grapeshot down the barrel before running the gun out. Suddenly *Righteous's* larboard rail dipped and his vision was filled with the huge face of one of the creatures climbing up, just on the other side of the boarding nets! It passed so close that it snapped off the handle of the rammer's eight foot ramrod protruding through the gunport. Barrows, a simple man, seemed unfazed by the presence of a giant demon but very concerned that he was now unable to do his job.

"Big lummox broke me ramrod!" he angrily stated and jabbed a thumb over his shoulder at the immense beast passing not three feet behind him. "Now oy canno' ram th' load 'ohm!"

Crawford shook his head, dumfounded. "Barrows, me thinks range will no' be a problem fer 'iss shot. Could ye jes' step back now?" A fellow crewman pulled Barrows back as Crawford jerked the lanyard and the big eighteen pounder fired off with another thunderous crack. Since the gun was still back from its gunport, the discharge blasted away several feet of the larboard railings, sending oak splinters the size of a man spinning into the beast along with forty balls of egg-size grapeshot. Crawford stepped to the side and watched with concern as the gun jumped back into its shortened runout and bounced around violently, but the stout cables held. Looking back at the demon, he immediately saw daylight through the smoke. *Bloody hell, blew th' thing 'n 'aff!* Sure enough, the giant no longer had a bottom half as it slid back down the side, a puzzled look on it face as it passed by and fell into the water.

Wyckham watched with relief as a second gun fired off, then another. Thank God, other gunners as well had held their fire awaiting targets! The animals in the water were below the guns' depression, but when they climbed up the side they went right over loaded guns. All three were blown into ribbons when double loads of grapeshot went right through them. They fell in pieces, burning wadding stuck to their skins, their mouths open but silent as they dropped from sight. Then suddenly two more appeared above the gundeck—the sly bastards had gone over the guns that had just fired!

Now Wyckham got a close look at their adversaries. They were truly the frightening visions of a child's worst nightmare. The beasts were nigh three stories tall and must have weighed five hundred stone apiece. Although their bodies were covered in matted, wet fur, their faces were hairless. They had bulging, bloodshot eyes the size of Mediterranean melons; their open mouths displayed teeth big as bayonets. Two browned tusks the size of dock pilings protruded from their lower jaws. And damned if they didn't sport huge, porcine noses, nostrils flaring and snorting. But most disconcerting of all were their small, pointed ears—maybe they really were demons, and Wyckham actually was sailing through hell?

With a roar, the two ripped apart the boarding nets, slashing them into tatters with the saber-like claws on their large, webbed fingers. But the moment spent dealing with the nets gave Donnelson's marines a still target, and all the ship's swivel guns opened up in a rolling volley. Each strike from the small cannons jerked the two huge beasts about like toy animals on a string. Between squeals of pain, they roared their defiance, but they were done for. After several seconds of steady bombardment they fell to the deck in growing pools of their own blood.

Silence. Was it over? Marines frantically reloaded swivels while a few seamen approached the ship's side to peer over.

For some it was a fatal mistake. Roaring like Satan himself, another huge demon leapt over the side and sprang through the shredded boarding nets. Flailing its long arms left and right, it swept crewmen into the air, bouncing them in gory ruin against masts and bulwarks or throwing them overboard. A dozen men must have died in a few seconds. Musketry rattled all across the deck, but the creature seemed unharmed. Wyckham watched some crewmen approach with pikes, but they too were swept away, grunting and crying out.

Then the creature froze. *Bloody hell, it's focused on me!* With one leap it was standing over Wyckham, cocking its hairy arm for a deadly blow.

Captain Wyckham steeled himself for death. What a way to go, mangled by a huge pig in some unknown sea. He thought of his father's disappointment that his son didn't die valiantly in a real naval battle. *Sorry to disappoint you again, Father.*

A huge crash exploded across the deck, knocking Wyckham down and blowing off his hat. But the long hairy arm about to crush him was also completely blown away, along with most of the attached beast.

Stunned and dizzy, Wyckham looked to his left, searching for the cause of his salvation. And there, next to a carronade on the forecastle, was a grinning Crawford, still holding the gun's lanyard.

Righteous mounted two twenty-four-pound carronades on the forecastle, short, heavy caliber guns known in the Royal Navy as *smashers*. While their range was short, they could devastate targets at close range with their heavy loads. Seaman Crawford had swiveled the larboard one around so it pointed inboard, then fired its load of almost one hundred balls of two inch grapeshot right into the monster's side. Aside from the demon's huge head, there was hardly a recognizable part of the creature left, just piles of meat strewn across the deck.

Wyckham was too groggy to speak. But he heard officers still working the gun crews. "Stay alert! Might be more of them." His man, Larkin, appeared by his side, helping him up, inquiring about his well-being. He nodded to show he was all right and then watched Crawford approach.

"Sorry oy wuz a li'l late wif th' carronade, sor. 'Ad t' wait fer me mates t' git out o' th' line o' fire. Did th' thing 'urt ye, Cap'm?"

"I'm...I'm fine, Crawford, thanks to your...timely...action." He saw the rest of the crew looking on anxiously; he waved and nodded to show he was unwounded. Cheering went up from the entire crew. "At's 'Prize Bounty' Wyckham fer ye! Luck's always wif em!" and "*Righteous* done fer 'em all, cap'm!"

He shook his head, still somewhat concussed from the carronade's charge passing so close. Sailors could be knocked senseless by the close passage of cannon shot in battle, and Crawford's blast had almost done that to him. *Get your wits back, man; you've a ship in action to command!* For all he knew, Lucifer himself might be climbing aboard next. He motioned for his first lieutenant, not yet trusting his voice. Wouldn't do to have the crew hear the captain's speech wavering.

A still-astonished Rawlins walked up, shaking his head in amazement, trying to make a report but not sure where to start.

"Well...that was a... close-run... thing," Wyckham managed to get out, finding it hard to get his thoughts organized. Were they still in this fight? "Ah, Rawlins. Have we...dispatched...them all?"

"All quiet now, sir, except for a few wounded ones in the water complaining about our hospitality. Some did swim away under the surface; we saw them popping up a few cables off. I count at least fourteen of them here dead or dying. Should I dispatch their wounded, sir?"

"Yes... for God's sake, please do so, Mr. Rawlins. At this time my head cannot bear their...constant...squealing." He gestured at the remains of the three monsters on deck. "And get all this..." he waved at the two giant corpses hanging in the boarding nets and the remains of the third demon scattered about the deck, "flotsam...over the side. But what's our bill?" Concern for *Righteous*'s crew had overcome his mental fuzziness.

"I don't have an exact count yet, but I believe we have lost eight with another dozen or so wounded, including Gunner's Mate Dawes, who sadly will not survive the day."

The butcher's bill was actually less than he had expected. Wyckham surveyed the carnage on the main deck. The wounded were being carried below to Shroeder in the orlop, some screaming in pain. There were clumps of flesh strewn about, mostly belonging to the obliterated creature, but some pieces were wrapped in bits of seaman's clothing. His head jerked in pain as a final swivel gun fired, ending the last ear-piercing squeals from the water below.

He walked toward the nearest beast's remains to examine his foe close up. It was pretty much shredded into unrecognizable chunks, though Wyckham could make out what must have been a heart and lungs. Damn if there weren't long, fleshy frills on its neck that looked like gills, too, and some very strange-looking, shiny globes dispersed throughout its body. He bent over to examine them more closely. Strange pulses of light like little bolts of lightning were flashing through these globes. What in hell were those things?

Dizziness threatened to overcome him, and he straightened up. "A sip t' clear yer 'ed, sir?" It was his steward, Larkin, with a cup of brandy from the decanter in his cabin. Wyckham sipped a little as Larkin fetched his bicorn hat from across the deck. The brandy's warmth was settling. *God bless Larkin. I'll need a clear head to figure out what to do next in this hellish place.* His mind had to settle into navy routine. First thing to do was to attend the wounded flagship. He looked up to see *Righteous* still on course for the stricken *Zeus*.

"Mr. Rawlins, signal to the flag, 'Will assist.' We will anchor a cable leeward of *Zeus*. Get my gig ready; I will be going over. And get the barge over the side as well. I expect we will be bringing over their wounded—their orlop must be flooded." There was no longer a need to use *Righteous*'s boats to rescue *Zeus*'s sailors from the water. Their time had run out.

The helmsman made for *Zeus* as hands went aloft to reduce sail. Wyckham turned away as crewmen bearing pikes pushed and prised the two dead demons hanging in the starboard nets over the side. Other crewmen, including the cook Stuart, gunner Crawford and the frustrated rammer Barrows, started cleaning the deck and throwing the scattered remains of the last creature overboard as well.

Accustomed to handling raw meat, Stuart picked up an armful of shredded flesh and headed to the side to throw it over. But just as he crouched to give it a heave, a tantalizing smell reached his nose. The meat in his arms had been seared by the hot grapeshot, and it smelled pretty damn good! Always scrounging for fresh food, Stuart ripped off a small piece of meat from a still-warm grapeshot hole and flipped it into his mouth. *By gar, it be roast pork! And tender 'z a tavern maid's lips!*

"Avast that!" he called to the dozen hands throwing the monster's parts over the side. He pointed at the two immense severed legs lying on the deck. "Grab 'ese two 'aunches 'ere 'n gets 'em below t' th' food locker. Quick!" Right now there were no officers or midshipmen on deck. "Doan let no off'ser see, 'n we'll 'ave fresh meat fer supper!"

The men stopped but just stared at Stuart, shocked by what he clearly planned to feed them. Barrows in particular looked terrified of eating what was surely the devil himself.

"Ye gots t'be looney, Stew Rat," said Barrows, using the nickname they'd made up for Stuart after one particularly unidentifiable meal. "Oy eats 'at n' oy'll grow 'orns n' a tail!"

"Ye fool!" Stuart wacked the giant smoking limb with his cleaver, ripped off a chunk and shoved it into Barrows's gaping mouth. "See fer yeself. It's no demon flesh! It's pork! "N richer than ye e'er et!"

One chew and the hungry simpleton's eyes went wide. With a changed mind he licked his chops and followed Stuart's directions to grab a hold onto one of the two haunches. The rest of the group joined him and the giant soon-to-be-hams were quickly manhandled below.

Righteous slowed to a crawl, swung alongside the flagship, and dropped her kedge anchor. Wyckham went unsteadily over the side into his gig, still clutching the precious brandy. He gulped the last of it down as his gig bumped up against the flagship's side. No one had hailed them as they approached, but he could hear angry shouting above.

A short climb brought him up to the angled maindeck. It seemed a bit more level than earlier; he could hear the ship's pumps at work. But no shrilling pipes welcomed him. No greeting party had assembled to line up and welcome a captain aboard, and Wyckham could see why. The deck was in chaos. Officers were trying to organize repairs, but some hands had gotten to the rum barrels and were yelling back, or just ignoring them. Men wounded when the ship had fallen were splayed about on the deck, moaning. Others were just rolling around crying like babies, begging for divine help. "Lord, Lord, save us f'm th' demons!" and "God, I'll go to choorch ever' Soonday, oy swears!"

Zeus's Flag Captain Sean O'Neal emerged bellowing from the quarterdeck stairs with a line of armed marines. O'Neal was a burly Irishman, about forty years old, ginger haired, with the weathered face of an old salt. Wyckham had served under him as a midshipman and knew him to be a smart, experienced, no-nonsense officer. During their time together, O'Neal had given him useful guidance in his naval career.

"Enough of this malarkey! All crewmen will rise to do their duty, or I'll take you to a grating right now, one by one, and flog your arses raw! Will you be first for the cat, Roberts?" He wound up his body and gave the seaman at his feet a pretty respectable kick, right in the ribs. Roberts's eyes went wide as his lungs emptied. He jumped up and knuckled his forehead in salute.

"Done with your whining? Get your gun crew below to the stern pumps." O'Neal addressed the deck as more marines emerged from below. "You hands think you're in hell? Any man shirking, I'll show him hell!" Roberts and his mates scurried below as O'Neal and his marines continued about the main deck. Soon their persuasive efforts had most of the crew moving to man pumps or haul in the spars and rigging hanging over the side. There was no sign of Admiral Jarvis.

O'Neal hadn't yet noticed that *Righteous*'s captain was on deck as Wyckham walked up behind his mentor. "Looks like you're having a jolly party here. Should I fetch your hands some more rum from *Righteous*?"

The flag captain angrily snapped his head around and then broke out in a broad grin as he recognized Wyckham. "By God, if it isn't our saviour himself!"

O'Neal turned to address the deck. "*Zeus*! Look here! It's Captain Wyckham of *Righteous*, who just saved our admiral from that creature!" O'Neal thought he'd found something positive to motivate his ship. But though the crew stopped what they were doing to look, no cheers went up, just some low mutters.

O'Neal continued. "And then he blew the rest of them to hell before they got to us!" That got a respectable cheer, the hands yelling out, "Thankee, *Righteous*!" and "Ye did fer em, *Righteous*!"

O'Neal barked out a few more orders, then took Wyckham's arm and motioned him over to the quarterdeck. This was the captain's sanctum where they would have privacy, and no one could approach uninvited. The two savvy captains looked at each other for a moment, both at a loss for words. Finally, Wyckham spoke up. "Well, I must say, an interesting day so far, what?"

O'Neal shook his head and pursed his lips, then smiled crookedly. "Yes, one might say that. What in God's name has happened to us? What waters are we in? But I don't know why I ask you. Your navigation skills were always quite lacking."

Wyckham smiled at the jovial mock. O'Neal knew the importance of a little humor when he needed to steady those about him, whether crewmen or officers.

"But Jesus, that was some damn fine shooting with your bow chasers," O'Neal congratulated Wyckham as he heartily clapped him on the back. "Saved this ship, you did. Now we can get things back in order. We lost a lot of crew overboard when the ship dropped in here, thanks to our brilliant admiral keeping the ship broadside to the falls. The rest of the crew just fell apart, wouldn't have been able to fight the ship against those beasts. Thank God that you came to our aid. Meanwhile the marines who were below didn't know what had happened, figured it was just the storm. They're now reminding the hands that their duty is the same in any place, even here. So we'll get things shipshape presently. But then to figure out how to get to familiar waters? I must confess that topic has me completely baffled."

Wyckham nodded in agreement. "Even Cook would be confounded to identify our whereabouts. I doubt God even knows what's happened to us. Well, my cutter is alongside. May we take some wounded back to *Righteous*? And I could spare you my carpenter; he's got our repairs well under way." The two captains continued discussing ships' repairs.

Finally, Wyckham asked the obvious question. "Should I report to Admiral Jarvis now?" Unsaid was that according to naval doctrine, the admiral's absence on deck in the present circumstances was absolutely unforgivable.

"Yaaas…Well, he's below in his cabin," said O'Neal. "He's still… ah…discomfited. After all, he did just barely avoid getting eaten by a giant demon."

O'Neal drew Wyckham further back on the quarterdeck and lowered his voice. "He's fallen apart, he has. Been raving away about God punishing us for our sins, Lucifer has us now, it's God's final reckoning, and so on."

All this didn't surprise Wyckham at all. Admiral Sir William Jarvis, Esquire, was one of the many officers in the Royal Navy who had advanced mainly due to family connections at Admiralty. Besides being incompetent, he was pompous and arrogant to all his subordinates except those that constantly showered him with praise and adulation. In recent years, he had turned fanatically to the church, always travelling with a chaplain and pushing all sorts of Anglican services on his crews. But most inexcusably, he was a coward. Wyckham had personally seen him avoid action on several occasions, even keeping his whole squadron out of the Battle of Camperdown.

"Our courageous admiral affected by such minor events? I don't believe it. Well, I'd better go see him now," said a resigned Wyckham. "Been aboard too long—don't need to give him another reason to spit on me again." The relationship between Wyckham and Jarvis was poor enough already; on one previous occasion Jarvis had become so furious that his flying spittle had sprayed Wyckham's face.

"Well, my friend, I fear you've given him that already. It seems your first shot at that big devil on our deck went right through his cabin. Did a bit of damage, it did." O'Neal paused and looked away as if he was checking the deck. "Actually, a great shot," he said with approval, trying to suppress a grin.

The first shot from *Righteous* had gone right through Jarvis's great cabin? Christ, that was all Wyckham needed to complete a perfect morning. Shaking his head and cursing under his breath, he made his way below with O'Neal and was announced into Jarvis's quarters.

Wyckham was used to flag cabins that were well appointed, but this one had always amazed him. There were marvelous woodcarvings everywhere: on Jarvis's chairs, his table, his desk, even on the mahogany moldings around the ceiling. The headboard of his bed was topped with flying cherubs, apparently blessing its saintly occupant. Many of those details had been gilded, so much so that the room reminded him of some baroque cathedral in France. And from the silver plates on the table to the velvet pillows strewn about the plush sofa, everything was of the highest quality.

However, this time, the scene was quite different. The center of the room was a splintered wreck. Broken china and bent plate were everywhere, and several stern windows were shattered. Crawford's first shot, which had missed the creature, had almost completely destroyed Jarvis's cabin. And worst of all, it had scored a direct hit on the finest piece in the room: a very large mahogany table that had been in the Jarvis family for centuries.

And there was Sir William Jarvis, Esquire. Damned if he wasn't kneeling at a wrecked altar, deep in prayer instead of being on deck. The admiral was short, in his late fifties, well past fleshy, with hanging jowls that shook when he spoke. As usual, he was dressed for a ball, with an ornate waistcoat, embroidered breeches, silk stockings, a lace cravat, and shoes shining like a mirror. His white wig was curled and powdered but hung a little sideways. Also in the room were Jarvis's steward and his Anglican minister.

O'Neal announced them a second time. Jarvis turned, saw Wyckham, and stood up angrily.

"You! The cause of all this! Why were you not on station to leeward to warn this squadron of the approaching danger? We could have made our escape, instead of being sucked into the bowels of hell itself!"

So much for gratitude for saving the man's life. "Had a gun loose, sir. Had to heave to get it tied down," Wyckham explained. It was like putting oil on a fire.

"A loose gun?" Jarvis's eyes bulged out even further. "Your crew doesn't even know how to properly bowse down a gun? Again, your incompetence and your inept crew beget trouble for all! Rest assured, Admiralty will hear about this!"

Then his eyes turned to slits as he conjured up other accusations. "But maybe nothing of the sort happened? Mayhap that's just your excuse for leaving the squadron to go looking for prizes, Captain "Prize Bounty" Wyckham?"

Good Lord, are there any crimes I haven't committed? Wyckham eyed the admiral with barely concealed distaste.

O'Neal stepped in to defend Wyckham. "Sir, under his command, *Righteous* came to this ship's defense and, most particularly, interceded on your personal behalf in a most timely manner."

"Yes, didn't he? It was almost miraculous, wasn't it? As if it were a play staged in Drury Lane, with the handsome young hero saving the day at the last moment!"

Jarvis's lower jaw jutted out, and he stepped toward Wyckham. *Christ, is he preparing to bite me?*

Jarvis spoke slowly through clenched teeth. "But it's quite clear to me what you did. Sinners cannot so easily fool a truly godly soul, Mr. Wyckham. You made a pact with Lucifer himself so you could get credit for saving an entire British squadron, didn't you? You'd be the new Nelson! And just for laughs, you put a ball right through my grandfather's Italian Renaissance table! It could have killed me! Thank God I was on deck saving the ship from that enormous demon."

His voice started to rise as his eyes squinted in simmering rage. "But Lucifer outwitted you, didn't he, Wyckham? He didn't tell you we'd all be left to rot here in hell, did he, Captain Wyckham? Didn't bother to tell you that little detail, did he, Captain 'Prize Bounty' Wyckham?"

Jesus, he is completely crazy. Wyckham took a step back to avoid the spittle spraying about from the admiral's frantic rant. Jarvis's valet stepped up, trying to settle things, as if such a ridiculous outburst was an everyday occurrence he routinely dealt with.

"Gentlemen, our surgeon said the admiral should take matters easily for a bit after what he's been through. Maybe you should return later after the admiral has completed his daily prayers for our salvation?"

The steward managed to get Jarvis back to the altar, giving Wyckham and O'Neal their chance to mutter a quick goodbye and take their leave. The minister hadn't moved a muscle. As they left the cabin, he was just standing there with an arrogant grin.

They returned to the quarterdeck for privacy and spoke in hushed tones. Wyckham was stunned. "Well, he's completely ass-over-teat. What's he plan to do to get us out of here—pray for a regiment of angels to appear and fly us all home? How long has he been like this?"

"It's that damn Anglican priest, DeGeorges, that he travels with," O'Neal said. "Jarvis doesn't eat a meal nor fart without his say-so. And now he's got the admiral believing all this is the final judgment and that all the sinners in his command will be sent to hell. I think Jarvis plans on just waiting to see the rest of the squadron burn in eternal punishment while the noble souls like himself go to heaven."

Wyckham leaned closer. What he was about to suggest could easily get him hanged. "Sean, you know what the right thing to do is. Jarvis is as daft as a bat in a church belfry. You need to get him declared unfit for duty and take command yourself. Not one of us here knows what we should do next, but you owe it to the whole squadron to make sure it has an able commander in our present unusual situation, don't you think?"

"Aye, don't you think I'm not wracking my brains trying to figure out how to pull that off. I've talked to our surgeon, but he's a country commoner, in awe of nobility. Getting him to write down in his log that our admiral has gone imbecile will take some time. He respects Jarvis's noble birth but is afraid of his patronage at Admiralty. I think it's best for us now to just start exploring this place we're in without getting Jarvis involved. He won't be leaving his altar anyway, so he won't have any idea what we're doing and probably doesn't care anyway. We'll just do it under the guise of foraging for fresh water and provisions. But let's get the entire squadron out looking to ascertain where we are and find the way home."

Wyckham agreed. It was the right course to pursue. But he did not doubt that problems with Jarvis would resurface at some point.

"Well, I'm on board with you for whatever you decide upon, Sean—you know that. May I offer my cabin aboard *Righteous* as a place for all the captains to meet? I don't expect we should all have a chat here right under the nose of that spying priest if we want to keep Jarvis out of things. And I've got some decent fresh fish aboard that I could have my cook fry up for us all."

"Yes, thank you, Rod. Let's meet aboard *Righteous*. It can be said that *Zeus* is still too much under repair. I'll signal when matters are settled enough here for me to take leave." O'Neal turned and faced the waist. "Bates!" O'Neal's steward scurried up, knuckling his forehead. "Ready three invitations to all captains and firsts for dinner aboard *Righteous* around eight bells, upon signal from *Zeus*. After my signature and seal, get them to my coxswain for rowing about the squadron."

A midshipman approached the quarterdeck. "Captain, signal from *Scamp*. 'Rescued Crew Aboard.'"

"Thank you, Mr. Hall." O'Neal nodded. "Good news, that!" Apparently, the little brig had plucked some of *Zeus*'s crew from the water. "Signal *Scamp* to anchor alee and transfer any fit hands back aboard *Zeus*, the wounded to *Righteous*. Also signal to all ships for any carpenters they can spare to repair aboard *Zeus* forthwith."

The midshipman scurried to the signaling lines. Wyckham pulled out his glass and looked out over the bay, seeing *Scamp* about a cable astern, with the two bomb ketches, *Vesuvius* and *Hedgehog*, about three miles off the bow and slowly beating back to the flag. They had fallen through one of the more distant squares and had apparently been carried away by the volume of water spilling down. *Scamp* appeared mostly shipshape; one topgallant spar was askew. The two bombs were too far off to see if they had any damage. There was still no sight of *Gnat*.

Then he surveyed what he could see of the land about them. It was very lush, green country, reminding him of the Indies, with puffy white clouds gathering above and some squalls in the distance. There were low hills, fairly steep in some places, with lots of rather large trees.

Closer to shore were many small islands and swampy coves. He could see waterfalls feeding the coves, some of them hundreds of feet high. Wyckham noticed several different varieties of birds nesting in the rocks along these falls. He couldn't make out any details, but he had a nasty feeling that they were going to be very different from the seabirds he was familiar with. Maybe just the first of some interesting fauna that they would soon be running into in this place? Hopefully, they would be friendlier than the pigs they had met—and with a different diet.

No matter the beauty, this was a place he needed to lead his ship out of. Wyckham called for his gig, made his farewells and returned to *Righteous*. For the next two hours, he supervised repairs, visited his wounded, and watched grimly as eight wrapped corpses, with round shot sewn into the canvas, were slid over the side. British warships in battle zones had no time for elaborate funerals.

He sat down in the wardroom with his four lieutenants—Rawlins, Clifton, Sorenson, and Gregory—to go over what he and O'Neal had discussed, though he glossed over Jarvis's condition. But mostly it was a counsel with his experienced officers to discuss the day's events. Of course, no one had any explanation for where they were or what had happened, but it did them all good to commiserate in their mutual astonishment. Lieutenants Sorenson and Clifton, not churchgoing men, did admit that they would be praying a lot more. Finally, Larkin informed them that dinner was ready; Wyckham had arranged for his officers and warrants to be served here in the wardroom before the rest of the other ship's officers arrived. He could use a bite himself right now; it certainly had been quite an active morning. Maybe after some decent food they would come up with some brilliant insight as to the next course of action.

But even before any drink arrived, Larkin returned and reported that boats from the entire squadron were heading toward *Righteous*. The two bomb ketches had arrived while they were below, and O'Neal had signaled for the captains to assemble early aboard *Righteous*. So much for a moment's respite. As each gig approached the ship, they were hailed by a crewman on watch, with the gig's coxswains holding up four fingers to indicate a captain coming aboard. The trilling of bosuns' pipes from the assembled side party greeted each as they climbed up and onto the deck.

Wyckham was familiar with all of them—the squadron had been together for three months. Captain Hamilton of *Scamp* was in his late twenties, fair haired and lean, with a reputation as a ladies' man. Grimwald of *Hedgehog* was in his late forties and balding, an expert with the two huge mortars on his ship. Randolf from *Vesuvius* was around twenty-five years old, quite young to command a bomb ketch, and rumored to be the beneficiary of extensive family patronage at Admiralty. Each captain brought his first lieutenant, as was British navy custom.

Standing right behind the side party, Wyckham welcomed them all aboard and directed them to his quarters below. As they headed toward the stern, an excited lookout called from the mainmast cross-trees. "Ahoy th' deck—more big squares 'n th' air!"

3

A RUDE GREETING FOR ALLIES

The floating squares had disappeared right after all the ships had fallen through. Apparently, they were back. *Bloody hell, now what?* It seemed there was never a dull moment in this place. "Where away?" Wyckham called out.

"Dead off th' bow, mebbe three miles," came the reply from above.

All the officers pulled out telescopes and scanned the air ahead of *Righteous*. Wyckham spotted the portals quickly; ten of them stretched out in a line about a thousand yards long, but with no water cascading down to the surface

O'Neal took charge. "Gentlemen, I suggest you all return to your ships at once and get them prepared for God knows what. Captain Wyckham, may I propose you hoist general signals, 'Captains returning' and 'Squadron beat to quarters'? We need to get this squadron to arms right quick."

"Aye, sir. Mr. Rawlins, beat to quarters."

Captains hailed their gigs as Wyckham called over Midshipman Moore and gave him the signaling instructions. He then anxiously returned the glass to his eye, wary of what might be joining them in this mystifying world. If a new enemy arrived, it had picked the perfect time to attack. Whatever was about to happen, *Righteous* was the only ship with all its officers aboard. It fell to Wyckham and *Righteous* to protect the whole squadron. But from what?

Something was coming through! All he could make out was a small glowing light, then another, followed by a growing cluster of the very bright lights. They kept floating as they came through, not crashing into the sea below as the squadron had but milling about in the air like confused pigeons. Then damned if they didn't suddenly start moving right toward *Righteous!* And now there were over a dozen of them, with more still dropping through the square gates. *Christ Almighty, first an attack from underwater, now one from the air!* There wasn't even time to sit down to a proper meal in this place.

The ship hadn't even cleared for action yet, and now the entire crew had stopped, mouths agape and staring bug-eyed at the approaching airborne lights. Well, at least these things weren't monstrously large like the goddamn pigs; actually, they appeared quite small, only two feet or so in diameter. Maybe his marines could hold them off long enough for the crew to get to quarters.

"Captain Donnelson, please assemble your ranks on the quarterdeck, ready for volley fire, marksmen to the tops." To the crew he yelled out even louder. "The rest of you lads, belay the great guns, prepare to repel boarders! Get your muskets loaded quick and make sure all the pikes are handed out."

The gun crews stopped unbowsing their pieces and headed to the arms locker as marines raced past—some still struggling into their red coats—to assemble in four ranks on the quarterdeck. Crewmen emerged from the arms locker, priming muskets and taking up firing positions. Dozens of hands ran to the gunwales with the eight-foot pikes, ready to impale intruders coming over the sides. With two hundred armed men on the deck, they should be able to fight off a bunch of flying lights. But Wyckham had a nagging fear that mortal arms might not work on these little flying suns.

But he sure would give it a go. "Mr. Donnelson, you may fire when ready. Please keep these things from approaching the ship any closer."

Donnelson nodded, turned to his marines, and barked out, "First rank, present! Aim! Fire!" A crisp volley of musketry banged from the front row of ten marines. Wyckham strained to see the attackers through the smoke as a second, a third, and finally a fourth volley crashed out in succession.

The breeze blew the gunpowder smoke away as Donnelson's first rank made ready to fire again.

And once again, in this incomprehensible world, Wyckham was confounded by what he saw. Emerging unharmed from the powder smoke were not shapeless lights, but women! All were young, for the most part completely stunning...and naked as Renaissance paintings! They were smiling with their hands out in supplication as they descended toward the ship. And damned if the leading goddess wasn't Wyckham's old flame, the Lady Tracy Brashton herself!

4

THE LADY TRACY BRASHTON

"Front rank, ready…" It was Donnelson about to order another volley. But then his eyes opened wide as he fixed his gaze on a red-haired beauty, (*Jesus, isn't that his wife?*), drifting down to him, which rendered him completely incapable of issuing any further orders to his men.

"Ah, belay that order, Mr. Donnelson! Belay all fighting," Wyckham shouted. "Your best efforts seem ineffective." He almost added, *Thank God*, because he was overwhelmed by the desire to talk to this girl he had grown up with and had hoped to marry. Here she was, flying down to him right now like a heavenly bird! Forget more shooting! He didn't care if it was the sirens of Homer's *Odyssey* luring him to destruction. Hell, he was most likely to die in this crazed place anyway, might as well pass over in the arms of the Lady Tracy Brashton.

Like the fresco on the ceiling of St. Peter's, the air was filled with a score of absolute angels. Lady Brashton gently settled on the deck before him, wearing a beatific smile and nothing else. God, she was beautiful! Wyckham had been crushed years ago when she had rebuffed his courtship and married Sir Edward Kemp, an older, landed baron with longer family reach than his own. Wyckham had never even kissed her, and here she was beckoning to him with open arms and the undraped perfect body he had dreamed about for years! Wyckham was frozen, motionless, completely in shock. There was probably something in the navy Articles about what he should do next, but he didn't care. At the moment, he had completely forgotten that he was a ship's captain.

His ever-watchful steward, Larkin, had not, however, and spoke brusquely to Miss Brashton. "Mum, this 'ere's the quarterdeck. No one allowed 'ere without the captain's say-so, mum." Here they were, God knows where, with beautiful naked women descending on the ship like angels, yet his loyal valet could still enforce rules concerning the captain's status.

Wyckham couldn't do anything; he was still speechless. But the vision of Lady Brashton spoke. "Greetings! May we thank you all for your wonderful assistance in our struggle." By God, it was her wonderful singsong voice, just as he remembered it. "We are massless beings from another universe. We wish to assure you of our friendship. We realize you must be very confused by—and suspicious of—what has been happening to you. We have adopted these female forms that you are comfortable with to assure you of our good intentions. May we couple with you? We understand that it is very pleasing to your species. Let us all have sexual congress now to seal our friendship."

Couple with us? Unbelievable! As she spoke, the rest of the ladies floated down to the deck, pairing off with crewmen as if it were the ladies' choice dance at a royal ball. And with that, Lady Brashton reached out to him, took his hand, and started to pull it toward her naked body.

That snapped Wyckham back to reality. British gentlemen simply did not put a leg over a woman on the quarterdeck of a frigate right in front of a whole ship's company! Finally, his noble upbringing had come to the fore and pushed him back to his duty. Beings from another universe? *For God's sake, man, ask this vision some questions!* She seemed knowledgeable and mayhap could explain this daft place they had dropped into.

"Tracy…aah, Madam, at present we are under Royal Navy ship's discipline; I must decline your proposal on behalf of the entire ship.

I have no idea who you are or how much you know about us, but this is not the place for that…ah…degree of fraternization. However, we would certainly like to hear all you know about our present situation." Proper formality took over. "Let me welcome you and your party aboard HMS *Righteous*. May I present myself, Captain Rodney Wyckham, and this is my first lieutenant, Pierce Rawlins." He made his best leg and a proper bow. "At your service."

Unsurprisingly, the entire crew seemed to disagree with Wyckham's declining the lady's offer and objected in a steady uproar. Pleas like "Oh, Cap'm, please, declare th' ship out o' discipline!" and "Please, sor! It's me wife, Betsy, come all th' way t' see me!" and "Oh, please, Cap'm! Ain't never 'ad a doxy like 'iss 'un, sor!"

He'd better act fast or for sure this ship would mutiny in less time than old Lord George could last in a French brothel. "Madam, I must insist that you go below. Your presence here is…ah…very disruptive to navy routine. Officers, please get these ladies below. Take them to the wardroom." He motioned for Rawlins to come close so he could speak in his ear. "And for Christ's sake, find them some clothing!"

He removed his coat and draped it over the gorgeous form in front of him. To his amazement, it dropped from her body to the deck, yet an exact copy appeared precisely where he had placed it upon her shoulders! And Lady Brashton just stood there smiling at him! *Christ almighty, what next in this crazy world?* Baffled as to how he should react to what had just happened with the crew watching, he simply pretended not to have noticed anything unusual. *Look like you're in control, man!*

"May I ask you to join me in my quarters below? I would be most obliged if we could discuss our present situation, about which you may be able to enlighten us. Do you have any…ah…officers…or mayhap, counselors, whose presence could be helpful during our discussion?"

"Yes, I do travel with the inner council. The six of them will follow." As if by silent command, six of the women behind her stepped up. "Please lead us to your council chamber, Captain Wyckham."

"Mr. Rawlins, will you please join us?" He trusted his first lieutenant and would probably need some additional counsel himself in this meeting. "Mr. Clifton, you have the ship." He gave out additional orders to the mates and other warrants for standing the ship down from quarters and serving the hands a meal. Better get the ship back into routine; he'd just denied the crew a sex orgy beyond their most fantastic dreams. He watched as his other lieutenants and warrant officers removed their own coats and placed them somewhat reluctantly over the visitors' shoulders, the clothes dropping, and then reappearing just as with Lady Brashton.

Shaking his head at the repeat of the bizarre occurrence, Wyckham headed the party toward the stern gangway, but was interrupted by Midshipman Moore. "S...sir, s...signal from *Zeus,* our n...number. I buh...believe the s...signal is 'C...Captain Repair on B...Board' an... and 'Disembark V...Visitors.'"

Bloody hell, it was Jarvis signaling. O'Neal's gig was still in the water on the way back to *Zeus.* The musketry aboard *Righteous* had finally brought Jarvis up on *Zeus's* deck and he had seen everything. Disembark visitors? Just as he was about to get some answers, Jarvis would have to get involved and make a hash of things! But maybe he could delay Jarvis's involvement just long enough to learn whatever his visitors knew about their present situation.

"You *believe* that is the signal, Mr. Moore? Surely the fine glass the navy has provided you with can read a signal at two cables' distance?"

"S...sir, with *Zeus* st...still heeled and their t...topmasts down, they're running s...signals up to the crosstrees, buh...but the flags are s...somewhat wr...wrinkled and hard to...to m...make out."

Perfect! "Mr. Moore, please run up 'Signal Unreadable.'" He turned back to the diplomacy at hand. "Please, everyone, continue below. Mr. Larkin, I will be engaged for a while; no interruptions."

The entire group descended the quarterdeck gallery and entered his cabin, dominated by the large cherry table used for entertaining officers and visitors.

"Please seat yourselves. May my steward bring you some hot coffee or tea? You must be...ah...quite chilled." Jesus, Lady Brashton certainly was! Wyckham's coat was still hanging open on her and damned if the nipple of her left breast wasn't at full attention!

"Yes, we would all love coffee and tea! We wish to sample all the physical sensations of your universe."

Sample our *physical sensations*? Wyckham shifted uncomfortably in his chair with a surging tumescence in his breeches. *Good Lord! Thank God I'm seated at table!* Larkin left to fetch the tea and coffee.

"Ladies, apparently you have some understanding of where we are and what is happening here. Please explain all that you may. We are quite puzzled by everything that has happened to us. In particular, share with us any knowledge you have about how we arrived here and how we may return to English waters."

The lady nodded in understanding. "Yes, it must be quite a shock to be suddenly taken from your home world, dropped in here, and then be immediately attacked by giant beasts. There is so much you are unaware of. It will be difficult for me to explain—we have many hours of discussion ahead of us. Let me start with a description of the cosmos of which your planet—Earth—is only a tiny part. Your world is part of a physical universe, whereas most other universes are mainly pure energy; they have no physical mass. We come from such a place. We have no mass—what you see sitting in front of you is an image formed by electrically based energy. This universe you have been thrust into is another one of the few mass-based systems. This world we are on is very like your own, with a similar gas atmosphere. It is the home planet for a species of very dangerous and very evil physical beings: the Draesh. Another mass-based system they attacked gave them that moniker. It means *bog creatures,* named after Draez, that system's name for this swampy planet of theirs. The Draesh have been devouring entire universes, and they have stolen weapons technology that even energy-based worlds have difficulty countering. Their fuel is the life force that they take from other civilizations by devouring their inhabitants. Your species is apparently unaware of the power of the basic life entity that lies within you; it is an immense power. The Draesh harness it, converting each life force, or soul as you would call it, into both physical and electrical power, and they use it to project their reach into all universes."

Wyckham shifted uneasily in his chair. Good Lord, there were many more worlds out there than the telescopes on Earth had viewed, and he was on one? And beings made of energy that can appear as people you know?

He had a hundred questions to ask, but he started with the most important.

"So, Madam, how did we get here, and how can we get back to Earth?" he asked. Were they stuck here forever, away from the navy, England, everything they had ever known? Were there a route home?

"Your arrival here may be an event of great importance to all other civilized worlds. This home world of the Draesh has been kept in its original state from the time before they started stealing weapons technology and conquering other systems. They keep it primitive, free of any weapons or technology of any sort. Otherwise, political squabbles among the Draesh here could escalate into a civil war. They know when they come here they can safely relax and rejuvenate."

She paused briefly and continued. "The only technology here is the transit device that brought you to this world; they use it to bring in life forms to devour at their leisure. This device is programmed to avoid bringing weapons into this undefended world. But apparently, your crude vehicles give off no recognizable weapon signatures—no signs of any energy, nothing electrical, chemical, kinetic, nuclear— nothing. So it must have brought you here in error. Please tell us all the details of what has happened here since your arrival? We became aware of a sudden crisis among the Draesh. They have stopped their attacks in several galaxies and have been returning here in great numbers. We took advantage of an unguarded portal and came here ourselves to assess the situation. We see several dead Draesh floating about your vehicles; we must congratulate you on striking such a blow against those who threaten the cosmos. Do you plan on continuing the fight? Please tell us more of your capabilities."

Wyckham gave his first lieutenant a questioning look. Should they trust these beings with military information? Were they really allies? Rawlins shrugged but then nodded. Wyckham agreed. They might as well open up to these ladies. Besides, it was hard to resist any creature that looked like Lady Brashton.

"Well, apparently we were drawn from the world we call Earth and arrived just in time for these bog monsters' breakfast. The 'crude vehicles' you refer to are ships of the British Royal Navy. With all their *crudeness*, it seems they were quite capable of disturbing these giant pigs' meal plans and sending a fair number of them to hell, where I hope they are currently burning painfully."

"Yes," added Rawlins. "We changed their breakfast menu, and it seems they found the 'whiff of grape' we served them somewhat distasteful."

Lady Brashton's brows knit in puzzlement. "The smell of fruit was used to vanquish them? I do not understand how this would change them into the shattered corpses we see floating about."

Wyckham shook his head. He'd explain naval slang and their weapons later. He wanted to steer the conversation back to the issue that their lives depended on.

"But please, ladies, may I ask again if you know how we may return to our home on Earth?"

"For that, you will have to take possession of one of the facilities that operates portals," Lady Brashton replied. "While we are only images and cannot move anything physical, we can certainly direct you in operating a portal if you were to gain control of one. It would take some time to locate your planet on their controls, but with our assistance, you should be able to return within a few of your days of cosmic searching. But these portal facilities are also habitations for many Draesh and their minions—you will have to fight and expel them for some time."

Christ, this is getting complicated. Wyckham mulled over this new information. *Now we've got another fight on our hands. We must attack and hold some strongly guarded position to get home?* Well, at least he was getting some answers. Might as well see what else these ladies knew that could assist in the upcoming expedition. As Wyckham's mind was reeling with the military questions he needed answered, Larkin thankfully arrived with the coffee and tea.

"Ladies, may I suggest you first try our coffee? There is sugar, but regretfully, there is no milk; we ran out two weeks ago." Wyckham watched them accept cups with puzzled but excited looks. Then, they suddenly seemed to realize what they should do with the beverages and sipped hesitantly but with proper etiquette.

Lady Brashton positively beamed at him. "How interesting! An extract of plant offspring, served at an elevated temperature. With many free ions! Very unique."

Unique? Well, if you've never had coffee, I guess it is. Wyckham suspected they'd never drunk anything at all before this. "Try putting some sugar in it, ma'am." He could just imagine the rhapsody they would be in with their first taste of sugar.

Larkin stirred in some sugar. "Ah, so this is sweetness." Lady Brashton didn't seem as excited. "But no extract of offspring, just body parts that have been processed and refined."

No offspring? Again, Wyckham shook his head in bewilderment. Who were these *ladies* anyway?

"Please do tell us more of yourselves. You say when we see you now, we are just looking at images? In truth, what do you really look like?"

Lady Brashton nodded. "Yes, we should discuss the nature of our being. As I have mentioned, we are pure electrical energy, as is our entire home universe. We have no physical appearance that you could ever see. You are familiar with the concept of electricity?"

Both he and Rawlins nodded. "Yes, we are aware of studies in the field by both Galvani and the Yankee scientist Franklin. Galvani has even demonstrated on animal specimens that it can cause muscles to function, though I'm not sure I believe his assertions that humans are chock full of it."

"He is correct," she replied. "Your muscles actually do function because of electrical messages. We may discuss that another time; you will find it a complicated topic. Our race is a species composed completely of electrically based energy, and we can control every aspect of it, both within ourselves and close about us when in a mass-based universe. For instance, you probably wonder how our appearance now reminds you of people you have known? This knowledge in your memories is electrically based. We can scan your minds and understand many facts stored there. When we arrived, we wished to appear as friends, so we scanned your memories, found strong memories of certain humans, and sent electrical impulses of their images to your ocular nerves."

Well, the image she was sending him was certainly a strong one. The continuing discomfort in his breeches confirmed that, especially with her breast still occasionally peeking out of that coat he'd given her!

"And when you handed us coverings, we realized you wished us to change our appearances, so we simply sent a new signal to your image receptors, one of clothed people," Lady Brashton continued. "The actual clothing you gave us had nothing physical to cling to and fell to the floor."

Wyckham still had trouble accepting that Lady Brashton wasn't right there before him. "If you are not really flesh and blood, how is it that I could feel your hand when you reached for me earlier?" The touch of her hand up on the deck had definitely been real; he knew a woman's inviting caress when he felt it.

"I simply sent an electrical message to the nerves in your hand confirming the perceived contact, again to put you at ease in this unusual situation. There is nothing before you to touch," she explained. "Let me also apologize for attempting activities which apparently were not acceptable."

Did he detect a note of disappointment in her voice? He shuffled in his chair again to ease his continuing discomfort "below decks."

"Sah!" His marine sentry's musket crashed to the floor outside his cabin's door. "Mr. Clifton, sah!"

Shite, can't ignore the officer in command.

"Yes, yes, enter."

Clifton entered and spoke softly to Wyckham. "Sir, boat approaching from *Zeus*. The party aboard appears to include the admiral and the flag captain."

Damn, here comes Jarvis. God knows what nonsense he'll decide to order—probably a court-martial. Ah, hell, might as well go above and face the coming broadside. We'll have to postpone figuring a way out of here for now.

"Ladies, I must end our discussion for the time being and go on deck to greet my superior officer."

Everyone went back on deck just as Jarvis was piped aboard with O'Neal and *Zeus*'s fleet captain of marines, Warren, along with the sniveling chaplain, DeGeorges, and someone Wyckham didn't recognize.

Jarvis looked around, sighted Wyckham, and came up to him in a fury.

"God will damn you, sir! So Lucifer has sent you your pay, has he? Naked women to fornicate with you and your crew? Has this whole ship signed a pact with the devil? And you ignore a signal from your flagship? Couldn't leave the orgy with Lucifer's whores to obey an order from your superior? Well, sir, divine justice is at hand for you! Captain Warren, place this man under arrest!"

But Captain O'Neal stepped between them. "Gentlemen, first things first. Admiral Jarvis, should we not hear what Captain Wyckham may have learned of our present situation? Let us start with proper navy routine; we must introduce all in our party coming aboard. Allow me to present Captain Warren, and especially our surgeon, Mr. Burgess."

Especially the surgeon? Why have they brought him anyway? Wyckham's eyes widened as he quickly realized what O'Neal was up to. *Well, O'Neal has gumption after all. All right, we'll give it a go.*

Without a change of countenance, he welcomed them aboard, taking the surgeon's hand in a warm greeting. "Your servant, sir." He peered into the man's eyes but read nothing. Well, might as well get the battle started. He addressed Jarvis but his speech was really for the surgeon's ears.

"Admiral, these ladies are beings from another world. They are at war with the devils that have brought us here and attacked us. They are very knowledgeable about this world and its inhabitants. We have been discussing how we may return to British waters, and they have told us that the solution is to take control of the transportation facility that brought us here, which will involve a land attack. Now, please understand that upon their arrival, these beings mistakenly took the shape of women dear to us, believing it would put us at our ease. As you apparently witnessed, I insisted upon clothing them immediately. There have been no improper activities. We have only been discussing our way out of here, which I believe is of paramount importance to the entire squadron. You should join us all in this deliberation and hear what they have to say—it is most illuminating. There is a way out of here, but it will involve the entire squadron."

Jarvis moved up into Wyckham's face, still raging. "Your involvement with the squadron's activities is over, Captain Wyckham! You will be court-martialed! I should take council with these hell-whores? I will commit no such abomination!"

Jarvis turned to the fleet marine captain. "Mr. Warren, you will place all these wanton women in a barge and set them adrift. They can go back to wherever in this hell they came from. We take no council with women of their sort. With the power of prayer and by the grace of God, I will be the one to lead this squadron back home."

Now came the challenge. Damned if Wyckham wasn't looking forward to this. He spoke loudly so all could hear.

"Admiral, God helps those who help themselves. So far, I have prevailed on this world by placing faith in my crew and a lot of grapeshot. I suggest we continue the fight. Let's follow the direction of our new allies, blow the hell out of any monsters in the way, and take control of this transportation facility so we can get home."

Jarvis's fury knew no bounds in the face of Wyckham's disagreement. Veins jutted out on his forehead and spittle sprayed all over the deck. "Your ungodly advice is no longer of any interest to the squadron, Wyckham! I will command, and you will enjoy the luxury of *Zeus's* brig! Put him in chains, Captain Warren!"

But Wyckham couldn't care beans about Jarvis's bluster. He was watching the surgeon, Burgess. And he could see doubt and confusion! You could always depend on Jarvis to make a fool of himself in public. Hopefully, this time, he had demonstrated enough incompetence for the squadron to be rid of him. How could the navy have such an idiot admiral when there were hundreds of qualified junior officers to promote? Well, there's going to be one less idiot admiral for this squadron to deal with. This was no time for Jarvis's nonsense, and Wyckham believed he could get the surgeon to agree.

Time to put his belief to the test. Wyckham approached Burgess.

"Sir, under Royal Navy Articles, Section Fourteen, I request the fleet surgeon to declare Admiral Jarvis unfit for duty. Understandably, the fall into this world and his near death at the hands of a filthy monster has rendered him nonsensical, turning him solely to religion and ignoring his duties of command. We must prepare for and execute an attack on a shore facility if we want to get home, not just sit around and pray. I believe Flag Captain O'Neal is in agreement?"

O'Neal jumped at his cue and approached the surgeon. "Certainly, we all have the highest regard for Admiral Jarvis and will write thusly in all ships' logs. But his encounter with that creature was enough to unsettle any officer. Clearly he is not coping with our dangerous situation here. His present health is not at the level necessary to command this squadron. I too recommend that he be relieved of duty."

Jarvis exploded in absolute rage. "You, too, Mr. O'Neal? As I've always suspected! My own captain, a common mutineer! Unfortunately for you both, our surgeon knows that those of quality must be protected from the manipulations of aggressive lower sorts who are obsessed with personal advancement! Britain is not revolutionary France! The order of rank must always be maintained, especially in the Royal Navy. Isn't that right, Mr. Burgess?"

The moment of decision had arrived. If the surgeon refused to rule Jarvis unfit for duty, both Wyckham and O'Neal would face an Admiralty board, ending their careers and possibly their lives. Everyone on deck turned to the surgeon.

Burgess anxiously looked about from Jarvis to Wyckham, clearly troubled by the pressure of making such a difficult decision. Finally he shook his head slightly and spoke up. "To relieve a ranking officer from duty, especially an admiral of noble blood, there must be absolute evidence of a serious medical condition. In my medical opinion, I do not see that Admiral Jarvis has such a serious medical impairment that he cannot perform his duties as the squadron's commander."

That was it. The surgeon didn't have the steel to rule against his betters. Wyckham and O'Neal would now be thrown in the brig to await a court-martial. But now that really didn't matter. With Jarvis in command the squadron would never be returning to England anyway. Not only had Wyckham's failed attempt to remove Jarvis sealed his own fate, but it had also sealed the fates of over a thousand seamen who would now most likely perish in this dangerous world they had been thrust into.

Jarvis burst out with a laugh. "Challenge your superior officer? How dare you, you mutinous, immoral, two-shilling popinjay! Relieve me from duty? Better you should prepare to be relieved of your life!" And damned if the little coward didn't draw his sword and point it at Wyckham. "The chains now, Mr. Warren!"

Before Wyckham had a chance to laugh out loud, a young boy jumped right in front of the point of Jarvis's sword! Where did he come from? It wasn't one of *Righteous*'s loblolly boys. This boy was dressed in country finery with blue satin breeches, a beige silk shirt, and a tight white neckstock. He couldn't be more than twelve years old. Wyckham suddenly realized Lady Brashton was no longer at his side. Jesus Christ, was this she?

Now this child addressed Jarvis. "Sir, listen to me, please. Captain Wyckham is correct. If you wish to survive and return to your old world, you will have to fight and beat this world's rulers, the creatures Wyckham has successfully fought already. Apparently, you disapprove of Captain Wyckham, but trust me, you must listen to him. You have always been my loving guide through life, but let me lead you with the truth now. Would the boy who has spent so much time in your bed, exploring your body as you have mine, be capable of lying to you? Listen to Captain Wyckham. He knows what must be done here."

Good Christ! Explored each other's body? Jarvis had repeatedly violated some young boy whose image Lady Brashton had now taken!

Jarvis had frozen stiff. He lowered his sword's point along with his lower jaw as his mouth opened in amazement, unable to take his eyes off the boy in front of him. "William…my William…How came you here? By God, you must be saved! Where is my steward? We must get William to my cabin where he will be safe. Yes, safe. I will protect you. You must feel chilled. But I will warm you. Yes, to my cabin please, William."

Wyckham watched as Jarvis dropped his weapon and approached the boy with his arms spread wide in welcome. *Jesus be damned—he is a pederast!* A quick glance around showed disgust on the faces of all present, especially on the surgeon's face!

Transformed, Burgess now spoke out angrily. "Admiral Jarvis, unnatural acts with children are forbidden by the Articles of the Royal Navy, and by our Lord God! You are hereby judged to be unfit for duty as shown by your own actions, sir! Such despicable acts as you have apparently committed have no place among the English nobility or the officer corps of the British navy!"

O'Neal was ready again. "Yes, Mr. Burgess, I have here a statement declaring Admiral Jarvis unfit for duty. Please sign it, and I will take command of the squadron as set down in Section Fourteen."

Burgess quickly scanned the page and scribbled his signature in disgust. O'Neal swiftly issued orders to have Jarvis, still staring at the young boy, returned to his cabin.

"This you cannot do!" It was Jarvis's chaplain. "God has blessed Admiral Jarvis with this command! It is not for you to rule against God's decision!" The officers around him stood silent, so DeGeorges turned to the crew. "Stout oaks of England—do not stand for this blasphemy! Throw these officers overboard! Save your admiral and stand with God!"

With that, Sean O'Neal's Irish temper erupted. "How dare you, sir! No one will encourage my sailors to mutiny! You may not impose yourself on the command structure of the Royal Navy, Mr. DeGeorges! Captain Warren, please put this man in the brig to await trial!"

"With pleasure, Admiral O'Neal." The captain of marines grinned and shoved DeGeorges to the starboard entryway. Both DeGeorges and a spluttering Jarvis were unceremoniously placed in a gig and rowed back to *Zeus*. Finally, they were rid of the crazy fool. Wyckham turned to see Lady Brashton magically reappear where the boy had been standing.

The skillful maneuver she had just pulled off left Wyckham shaking his head in admiration. She'd probably picket up Tracy Brashton's parlor politics from his own reminiscences. While he had always been besotted with Tracy Brashton, he was also aware of how socially manipulative she could be. Memories of her gamesmanship must be in his mind for this ball of electricity to read. But perhaps this being was already experienced in political maneuvering?

O'Neal approached him with his own satisfied grin. "Rod, my boy, apparently you've conscripted some helpful sorceresses here. So onward to solving our present predicament. I believe you've learned some important facts from the...ah...visitors? May I suggest we go below to your cabin, so that I may learn from my new, better-informed, Flag Captain? It seems that my cabin is currently occupied by a criminal against nature. And may I suggest you bring these fetching lasses with us? We certainly owe this lady our gratitude, and perchance they can all be of further assistance?"

Wyckham had smiled at hearing his new rank. And he could hardly believe that Jarvis was gone. Well, one problem solved. Now onto the next step down the path of returning the squadron home. Apparently, that would require a full amphibious assault supported by the entire squadron.

"My new admiral, might I also suggest the attendance of Captain Warren and the other three captains? I believe we will soon be in need of all the squadron's guns and especially all our marines."

5

PLANNING AN ATTACK IN HELL

S ignals were sent aloft, calling for the captains of *Vesuvius, Hedgehog, Scamp,* and *Zeus*'s new captain, Terhughes, to repair back on board *Righteous.* When they arrived they joined Wyckham, his lieutenants, O'Neal, Warren, and the group of "fetching lasses," who made their way below and got settled in the captain's cabin.

Before any discussion began, Wyckham called for his steward. "Ladies and gentlemen, forgive me for a moment while I get some dinner underway? I expect none of us have eaten since the morning's activities began several hours ago, and I believe our visitors and new allies would enjoy sampling our food. Do I presume too much? No? Then Mr. Larkin, please ask the cook to whip up a meal for twelve— the cod and those oysters we purchased yesterday from those French fishing boats off Ushant?" *Christ, was that only yesterday?*

"Cook's right here, sir," said Larkin. The short and sweaty Stuart knuckled his forehead and approached Wyckham.

"Gots th' ersters f'um th' firs' Frenchie, sor, but th' second bastard cheated us, sold us rotten fish. But we gots some fresh pork, real tasty."

"That will do nicely, Mister Stuart," Wyckham replied, a bit surprised since he thought for sure that *Righteous* had cleaned out her livestock pen weeks ago. Stuart scuttled below as Larkin stepped forward with an open bottle of claret.

"Might I offer your guests some wine, captain?"

"I don't know about our guests, but after the day's events, I am definitely in need of something stronger. Please pour me a glass of that American whiskey, but none of that for our new admiral; we all know the Irish do not hold with strong spirits," he japed with a straight face.

"Faith and begorrah, I will make an exception today due to our unusual circumstances!" O'Neal grinned in reply. "A full glass if you would, steward."

Larkin offered the officers whiskey and poured wine for the ladies, who were quite interested in everything and quickly sipped their drinks.

"Decayed plant offspring in liquid form!" Lady Brashton remarked. "With such a stimulating taste! And am I to understand this beverage is consumed for its euphoric effects?"

"Yes, and I am quite in need of a bit of euphoria right now," Wyckham said as he took a gulp. "But I must say you have gladdened all our hearts with your actions on deck just now."

O'Neal also addressed Lady Brashton. "Yes, indeed. Could you explain exactly what happened up there? Of course, we are all very grateful for your help, but I sit here in complete confusion as to what I have just witnessed, as well as being baffled by everything about us here. Might you enlighten me about our circumstances? Possibly you could start by explaining yourself? Exactly who are you?"

Lady Brashton gave the attentive group a lengthy explanation, similar to that which she had given Wyckham earlier. She explained her electrical nature and her ability to probe the memories of any humans in proximity and to project any image she wished.

"I had only hoped to put your Admiral Jarvis at ease by taking the image of the most beloved being I found in his mind. Someone he would listen to. I hope I haven't revealed something that was inappropriate—I only wished to calm him so that we could all work together as allies."

"No apologies necessary, Madam. Your performance saved the day," Wyckham stated. "With this last impediment to alliance removed, we look forward to aligning ourselves with you in common offense against the denizens of this world. But before we discuss those plans, please continue and explain to all present what you have told me about the nature of worlds and the struggle you are in against this world."

The lady continued for ten minutes or so, explaining as well as she could the nature of the cosmos, mass-based versus energy-based life, and the evil that the universe faced in combating the Draesh. Then she went further.

"I realize that your main concern is returning home, not joining our fight. But you should know that the Draesh threaten your world as well. In the mind of that gray-haired man on deck you call your Sailing Master, I recognize your galaxy from the stars he navigates by. The Draesh have already entered your system; they have actually advanced quite close to your planet. Probably within two of your years they will arrive on Earth, devouring your peoples and transporting others here to be tortured and devoured piecemeal in depraved Draesh revelry. Within another five years your world will be completely lifeless, like the many other worlds they have taken."

Well, that was certainly a sobering bit of information. Wyckham grimly looked about as he and the other officers silently absorbed this shocking news. Their entire Earth threatened? This changed everything. No sense in returning home just to die along with the rest of their world.

"But your arrival here has given hope to all peaceful systems everywhere. Right now our forces are gathering to come here and destroy this, the base of all Draesh activity. But we cannot do this without a portal to transit through, and the only way to open one in the correct place is for someone here to control a portal device and direct it at our forces.

"So I propose an alliance," she continued. "If you can get control of a transporter, our forces can arrive to conquer the planet, and then we will return you to your own planet, with its safe future ensured."

A delicious aroma filled Wyckham's nostrils as Larkin pushed through the door followed by some of the cook's helpers. "Oyster stew with bread fresh from the oven, sir."

"Ah, the food arrives!" Wyckham said with relish. "Ladies, may I ask that our discussion continue upon the completion of dinner? Only merchants and tradesmen do business with a mouth full of food."

Larkin and his helpers placed a large tureen on the table and began ladling out the steaming stew. The smell was heaven to Wyckham, a reminder of life on Earth. Would he ever return? Maybe not, but for now at least, it was eat, drink, and be merry, for tomorrow they might get eaten by giant pigs.

All ate eagerly, the ladies again commenting on the quaintness of consuming dead animals.

"Ladies, if I may inquire, you seem amazed that we eat dead plants and animals. Is that uncommon in your knowledge of the cosmos?"

"Yes, we have never seen this before in physical worlds. Generally mass-based species consume raw elements, or more often, other living beings. But not for physical fuel. They want the special energy of the basic life force you call *soul*," Lady Brashton explained. "The Draesh in particular consume living beings to harness this powerful force for their continuing conquests."

"Well, dash it, they're not going to consume any more British sailors if I can help it," O'Neal commented. "Watching that on my own ship is not something I'd care to repeat." That beast on his deck had devoured three men before Crawford blew its jaw off.

The group was silent as all the officers remembered that unpleasant scene. Rawlins took it upon himself to cheer things up.

"Well, let's strike that image from our minds with a toast," he proposed. "Although it's Friday, I think 'Sea Room and a Willing Foe' is not very meaningful in our present circumstances. May I propose 'Confusion to the Draesh?" asked Rawlins as he raised his glass in a toast. All the officers responded, "Confusion to the Draesh!" and raised their glasses as Rawlins explained toasting to the ladies.

The second course, the roast pork with a wine reduction and boiled potatoes, arrived and was dished out. "So, most beings in the cosmos eat live food?" commented second Lieutenant Clifton. "Can't say I mind eating live oysters, but I draw the line at eating live pigs."

"To dead pigs!" proposed Rawlins again, now well into his cups and reveling in the Royal Navy tradition of toasting and a good meal the night before a battle. Wyckham, feeling better himself, thought the meal was superb and called for the cook to come back to take a bow.

Stuart returned looking a bit nervous which surprised Wyckham. Any crewman singled out for compliment was usually overjoyed. Must be intimidated by all the strange ladies present.

"Applause for the cook," announced Wyckham, tapping his glass with a fork. The group joined in on their glasses is well, even the ladies getting the idea and delicately ringing their glasses with the silver. "My good man, but that pork loin was superb. An excellent sauce. And where did you get the pig?"

"Ah yassor, we…ahhh…found it down in the hold. She'd 'scaped outer the pen, she did, an' were livin off a barrel o' 'ardtack she broke open."

"Well, a toast to the smart hog as well, and for you discovering her at just the right time to entertain such important visitors," Wyckham said as he raised his glass around the table. When he turned back to give Stuart his final thanks, he was puzzled to see the cook had left. Ah well, poor fellow must be overwhelmed after first watching giant pigs attack the ship and then serving dinner to flying women.

After the pork came cheese and sweet biscuits, followed by glasses of port. Finally all the dishes were whisked away, and the group got back to the business at hand.

O'Neal addressed the group. "So we must execute a landing and take control of one of these transporting stations. First of all, we must locate one. Can any of you ladies guide us to one of these things?"

Lady Brashton looked at another of the ladies, seemingly in communication, though neither spoke, and then addressed the group. "Yes, we were able to access the memories of some wounded Draesh before you ended them. There is one inside a mountain, twenty-two point four of your miles away, on the other side of the island you see in the distance," she explained.

"Can you inform us about the nature of the coast at this location, such as how deep the water is near the shore and the location of any headlands?" asked the new admiral.

They could not. The information concerning the shoreline that the ladies had obtained from the wounded demons was spotty, and it certainly didn't include all the knowledge a naval squadron would need to land troops. They would need to scout the area if they were to plan a landing in force.

"Commander Hamilton, may I ask that you leave us now, return to your brig, and make sail in *Scamp* to investigate the station and find a good place to land troops? Take soundings, note prevailing winds and currents, all what's necessary for a landing in force. Return by first bell of the morning watch," requested O'Neal.

He turned to the ladies. "Madams, may I ask that one of your party that can guide Commander Hamilton to this place join him now in his brig?"

Again there was wordless communication among the foreign visitors. A stunning, raven-haired beauty got up and left with Commander Hamilton. Wyckham noticed Rawlins paying special attention to the woman who left: actually he seemed quite agitated. Could she possibly be some acquaintance from his past? Wyckham thought she looked familiar.

O'Neal turned back to Lady Brashton. "And now may I ask you to tell us of the forces and defenses we must overcome at this station? How many of these monstrous pigs will we face, and what weapons might they use against us?"

Again all the ladies went silent. Evidently, they communicated without speech.

Finally, Lady Brashton replied, "The Draesh you repelled represent most of those within over one hundred miles of here. Not more than a dozen would be at this station. The Draesh keep dispersed when they return to their home world here, much like a relaxing holiday you would take with family and friends. However, the station is staffed with their minions, the Krag, crab-like creatures with which they are allied, brought here from their own world as servants. It will mainly be these Krag that will be used in the station's defense. You should expect to encounter hundreds of them, and they will fight ferociously, as directed by their Draesh masters."

Jesus, a regiment of ferocious crabmen? Good God, what next? Wyckham suspected there would be more similar surprises for them on this world.

"And what sort of weapons will they employ against us?" O'Neal asked her.

"There are no weapons or martial technology allowed on this planet. You should attack quickly before they can alter their portal settings to bring any in. But even without weapons, the Krag should not be dismissed lightly. They are about four feet tall, their bodies encased in a soft pliable shell. They have a large, pointed claw that they stab with, and a shorter, thicker claw that can crush flesh and bone. They are quite fast, darting about to stab their enemies with their long claws until they can get in close with the crushing claw. They will be particularly difficult to fight in the approaches to the portal controls, which are tunnels dug into the mountain. They will dart out from hiding, attack quickly, and retreat back into hiding to attack again."

"Grenadoes." Everyone turned to Marine Fleet Captain Warren. "We employed them quite successfully in the forest approaches to Washington. Native savages allied with the Jonathans had laid ambushes for us on the forest trails. After we lost several men in the first one, we started throwing grenadoes ahead of us any time we saw a good place for an ambush. Killed a few and scared the rest back into the city."

O'Neal thought over Warren's comments for a bit, then spoke up. "Sounds like a good idea. I expect we'll need quite a few if we have to root out hundreds of these crabs inside tunnels. Captains Grimwald and Randolph, since your ships will not be involved in this action, set your crews to making up grenadoes—lots of them. What say you all? Two per man and a reserve for each marine company—maybe fifteen hundred in total?" All nodded agreement.

The meeting lasted another hour. It was decided that eight hundred seamen would accompany the squadron's four hundred marines.

All boats used in the landing would mount bow guns. If *Scamp* found a beach with a deep-water approach, *Righteous* would anchor close enough to cover the beach landing. *Zeus* would distribute its 180 marines to other ships as it continued repairs. Captain Terhughes was given the task of organizing boats from all the ships for picket duty around their current anchorage tonight. He didn't seem pleased with his assignment; most likely he was still angry at Wyckham for getting the promotion to Fleet Captain.

"So, all can be in readiness by dawn tomorrow?" O'Neal asked, getting nods from the assembled captains.

He turned back to their alien advisor. "Madam, after all this we do not even know your real names, or even what you call yourselves. Since we are now allies in an extremely important fight, we should probably have a way to address you. What may we call you?"

Lady Brashton smiled and addressed the group. "My name and the name for my civilization cannot be translated into noises physically made in this planet's atmosphere of oxygen and nitrogen. If I may, I suggest you refer to us as what we are—your allies, allies in the most important fight in the universal history of life."

"Then allies you shall be," said O'Neal with a businesslike nod. "We are blessed to have your assistance." Everyone rose to leave, but Lady Brashton stopped and turned back to the new admiral.

"By the way, if you only wait until dawn to begin, it will be starting quite soon. This planet has two suns orbiting it. Darkness tonight will occur only briefly, not for the several hours you are used to. After the burning star now nearing the horizon leaves your sight, the second one will reappear within three to four hours on the opposite horizon. We recommend you use them for navigation. You have probably noticed that your magnetic direction finders are not functioning, as this world has no magnetic field. Why this is true, we do not know."

The other captains nodded while Wyckham hid his embarrassment. He'd just thought the damn compass was broken! Well, he'd been busier than the others; he'd been shooting giant demons and could be forgiven for not investigating the compass's failure. But maybe an entry in the ship's log should state that he, too, had earlier noticed the failure of all the ship's compasses? Let the Admiralty read that Wyckham hadn't missed anything.

"Two suns!" O'Neal shook his head at this latest wonder of the new world. "Well, make it four bells of the morning watch. Our compasses may be useless, but navy hourglasses can always be depended upon. Any further questions? Then let's be about our business. Ladies, might you remain a bit? And Captain Wyckham as well?"

Once the rest of the party left, O'Neal addressed Lady Brashton. "Madam, we are short on accommodations. The flagship is under repair and not capable of taking visitors. Plus, I must state that your presence here is…ah…discomfiting to ship's discipline. Our superstitious crewmen generally consider women aboard ship bad luck. I must say I am in a quandary about where to berth you until tomorrow's action."

"Please do not concern yourself with us; we have no physical needs. My party and I can simply transform ourselves back into light and leave your ship. But I suggest that we, too, patrol the waters here—more Draesh could be about."

"An excellent use of your compatriots, though may I ask that you and a few others remain with us? I have a host of questions for you. Any additional understanding you may impart to me could be quite beneficial to success in our continuing activities. But for now, might I ask you to remain here with Captain Wyckham? I must return to my ship briefly to supervise repairs. Unfortunately, two guns went loose and damaged the hull, so we'll have to beach her. I will return aboard *Righteous* for further discussions with you as soon as I am able."

Lady Brashton nodded. Suddenly, the other women once again became simple balls of light, about two feet in diameter. They drifted to the door where they waited patiently until Larkin opened the door for them to drift out. Wyckham suspected they didn't need to wait for open doors and could pass wherever they pleased, but doing so was their nod to the laws of physical activity that governed humans. O'Neal then left and was piped over the side to his gig to return to *Zeus*. Lady Brashton turned and smiled at Wyckham.

"Might we have some more extensive discussions, you and I? There is some further explanation I owe you. Should we return to your cabin?

I believe the topic to be discussed is not one for your crew's ears." *And damned if she didn't wink and suggestively raise an eyebrow! A ball of energy from another world was flirting with him?*

Wyckham nervously replied with some sort of affirmative response and motioned her back toward his cabin. His senses were on full alert as they took their seats. He'd better steer their discussion to proper inquiries.

"Madam, I must confess you have the advantage of me. Apparently I still do not understand the true nature of your being and how I can feel the touch of an image. And how is it you seem so familiar with our culture and customs? You speak the King's English and even exhibit proper table manners." Not to mention that she seemed quite familiar with how to provoke a man to sweating!

"These matters are all simply explained. As for your physical sensations, we can release directed electrons that will stimulate your nerves to send a message to your brain. That message could be touch, heat, cold—any sensation your nerves normally record. Our knowledge of your cultural habits comes from examining your memories. Your minds are like electrical books, with all the facts you know recorded in its pages. We can access those memories quickly and place them in our own storage. Your knowledge of English, your experience in social matters—these are there for us to see and absorb. As was the image in your mind of the woman I appear to be, so I adopted it."

"So you can read our minds and know what we are thinking at all times?" Christ, did she know what he was thinking now as he recalled her naked body descending to the ship earlier? He had to discreetly wipe his brow with his handkerchief as his sweating increased.

"No, we cannot understand your thoughts or beliefs, only your stored experiences, facts that are important enough for you to remember. We cannot read your current thoughts. They are sudden electrical pulses, modified by your individual soul, your character. They move too quickly for reading, though sometimes we can deduce what feelings you have about a subject based on previous experiences. But no, we cannot tell what you are thinking." *Thank God for that!*

"Well, I am no electrical scientist and cannot claim full understanding of the topic, but I now have a rudimentary understanding of your nature and abilities, for which I thank you. But you stated there was another matter for discussion?" Wyckham had no idea how he would deal with whatever was coming. He was fearful, yet excited beyond description. He didn't trust himself to stay in proper control, but after sitting for fifteen minutes staring at the love of his life, he was at the point where he didn't care. A large drop of sweat fell from the tip of his nose to splatter audibly on the tabletop.

The lady remained silent and appeared deep in thought, undecided. Finally she spoke. "Again, I thank you for taking up our cause against the enemy on this world. Certainly the coming fight will not be easy. Hopefully, few of your sailors will perish. But besides the weapons you possess on your ships, there is another powerful contribution you can make to help stamp out the universal threat of the Draesh forever. It involves something that you have strong feelings about. I am not sure how to approach the subject."

Shite, she was only concerned with conquering her enemies. Apparently she did not realize the message her coquettish look implied. Wyckham felt foolish for reading something else into the lady's mannerisms. "Please, Madam, we are allies now in an important war. There is nothing you might say that would offend me. Ask for whatever would help our war effort, and I will do my best to act upon it immediately."

Lady Brashton smiled delightedly and appeared very relieved. "I am most grateful to hear you say that I may state my request without upsetting you. What I ask is that you give me your seed, as much as possible."

Wyckham froze, gasped, his heart raced, and his eyes went as wide as a three-pounder's muzzle. He couldn't believe what he had just heard! All he managed to reply was some stuttering babble as an excited Lady Brashton continued.

"Let me explain. Your species is unique in the entire universe in that your males carry immense quantities of life force within you, in the form of spermatozoa cells—many millions of them. My race, like the Draesh, can absorb this life force. It increases our own powers in all sorts of ways. Of course, we would use this power to defeat the Draesh and protect all worlds from them, including your own. It seems rational that you should share your seed with me, as it will help defeat our mutual enemies. I know your seed means nothing to you, since you mostly just leave it on your bed linens after emission." *Jesus, she knows that about me as well!* "It makes common sense to donate it to me. But how wonderful that you will grant my request immediately!"

And just like that her coat was gone, this time revealing her body clothed in nothing but stockings!

"I understand there are rituals to be performed before you emit seed, and part of that is the correct clothing for the female. Hopefully, these stockings are proper. Your memories of coupling with women wearing them seem quite positive. I've also enlarged my breasts, which you have also seemed to enjoy in past couplings."

She certainly had enlarged her breasts! *Jesus, they were big as breadfruit, and bobbing like harbor buoys in a tidal current!* He'd never seen the real Lady Brashton's breasts, but they couldn't have been what he saw before him now. They certainly wouldn't have fit into that white gown she wore at the officer's ball last year!

She noticed him staring at them. "I must say I wasn't sure how much larger to make them, so I copied the popular iron balls I see about your ship."

My God, she saw the shot racks, thought they were decorations, and made herself a chest patterned after eighteen-pound shot!

"And should I come to you as an angel would? I have seen the reverence that all of you hold for angels."

Wyckham watched in further astonishment as she actually floated up into the air, slowly progressing toward him, spreading her legs wide open! And damned if the lips of her quim weren't spreading wide open in greeting, as if they had a mind of their own!

By God, he didn't care about proper behaviour for a Royal Navy captain anymore! He was going to fulfill a lifelong dream and make love to the Lady Tracy Brashton! Reaching down, he unbuttoned his breeches and pulled out his surging manhood. Lady Brashton's smile brightened further at the sight of his engorged penis. Wyckham closed his eyes in anticipation as she descended toward his lap.

"Sah!" There was a crash as his marine sentry banged his musket on the floor outside his cabin door. "Lieutenant Rawlins, sah!"

"No! No! Hold!" But it was too late. Lieutenant Rawlins was already through the door, long accustomed to having open access to his friend's cabin.

"Signal from O'Neal. He's..." Rawlins stopped short, eyes and mouth wide open, almost falling over in astonishment as he saw the naked lady floating down onto Wyckham's distended member.

Wyckham stood up, tucking himself back into his breeches. "Damn it, Pierce. I said no! You can't just barge into a captain's cabin like this!" He turned to Lady Brashton. "Madam, our...ah...discussion is over. I must return to ship's business."

Rawlins stood up straight in his best impersonation of a guard at Westminster Palace. "Sir, my sincerest apologies. Allow me to leave," he said as he turned toward the door.

"Lieutenant, you will stay!" snarled Wyckham. He collected himself and turned back to Lady Aston. "Madam, thank you for your facts and advice. We will take your suggestions under consideration."

Lady Brashton, suddenly flat-chested and attired in a simple but well-made dress, said "Goodbye, Captain. I look forward to further... discourse." Then she smiled, looked him straight in the eye, again cocked that eyebrow with its suggestive insinuation, and headed out the door, leaving Wyckham's emotions reeling.

"Good lord, Rod, how can I apologize enough?" said Rawlins. "I had no idea that..."

"It's all right, Pierce. I let matters get too far anyway; it's probably better that you came barging in when you did," replied Wyckham. "Jesus, I almost had sexual relations with a being who's actually a ball of light! Next thing you know, I'll be topping farm animals. By God, she's hard for me to resist."

He fell back into his chair, drained and dejected. "You remember how smitten I was for years, and how crushed I was when she married Baron Edward Fucking Kemp. I'd finally gotten over her, and now she's re-entered my life, absolutely begging to jump into bed with me!"

Wyckham noticed the puzzled look on Rawlins's face. An explanation was in order. "Why would our new allies desire sexual congress, you're thinking? Let me tell you. Are you ready for another jolting bit of information?"

He explained the whole encounter as best he could, especially her race's apparent desire to obtain and absorb sperm cells.

Rawlins stood speechless for the first time Wyckham could remember. Then he shook his head while staring off into the distance and spoke slowly. "So they actually want our seed?" Wyckham couldn't tell if his friend was overwhelmed with amazement or planning his first otherworldly conquest.

"Well, Pierce, I think we both need a drink," Wyckham said and poured two brandies from the cabin's crystal decanter.

"I'm all in agreement with you there, Captain," stated Rawlins as he stepped up to the sideboard. "But we better just have a quick one and get above. I came to tell you that our new admiral is returning. He's probably climbing aboard right now."

O'Neal was piped aboard with all proper ceremony. He went below to the gunroom with several of their female allies, ostensibly to learn from them all about the world they were on and whatever might help in planning the morrow's attack. Wyckham begged off, claiming ship's business. He needed to avoid Tracy Brashton's presence right now; he wasn't sure he had himself back under control yet. He wondered just how much the ladies were telling O'Neal about their needs for battling the bog beasts. *Christ, knowing O'Neal's randiness, they were probably doing more than talking right now!*

But he really did need to prepare the crew for a land action. Boats had to be assigned coxswains and have bow guns mounted; sailors had to be assigned to their boats; and small arms needed to be distributed, along with the grenadoes sent over from the bomb ketches. Finally, he went to his cabin and fell into his cot, exhausted after the most incredible day of his life.

But sleep evaded him. The day's events kept his mind churning with visions of *Zeus* broaching, his own ship falling through the air, giant monsters devouring sailors, shattered seamen's bodies on the main deck.

But mostly he thought of Lady Tracy Brashton. There she had been, right on his quarterdeck, her smiling face just as he remembered her from their childhood together. The same curly blonde hair, the sparkling blue eyes, the long, lissome body. After sharing her friendship all through childhood, he had been shattered when she ended up marrying the local baron.

Of course, in hindsight he had been a fool to believe she would ever be his. The Brashtons were one of the oldest families in Cornwall, and Tracy was always considered the most desirable match in a county filled with young men set to inherit large, landed estates. Once she reached proper age, an endless stream of suitors with far better prospects than his were constantly calling at the Brashton estate. At the same time, Rodney's own father had made it clear that his second son would receive little inheritance from the Wyckham estate. All of his father's efforts were instead focused on his firstborn son, Chauncey. It was Chauncey who got the Oxford education, the personal introductions at all the London clubs, and the resulting attention from all the highborn girls. At age thirteen, Rodney was simply sent off as a midshipman for a life in the Royal Navy. Now, even with a successful naval career, his post captain's pay was nowhere near enough to provide for Lady Tracy Brashton in the way she was used to. Rodney Wyckham had never been in consideration for her hand.

But today, a naked Lady Brashton had been hovering in the air about to settle onto his lap, virtually begging for sexual congress. While he had dreamed of making love to her a hundred times, what almost happened today put all those dreams to shame. Sound sleep was not to be his this night; he just couldn't get that vision out of his mind.

6

LAND ACTION

Wyckham awoke with the first bell of the morning watch. All seemed peaceful as he stared at the familiar beams above his bed. Maybe all yesterday's incredible happenings were just the nonsense of a dream? He feared not.

"Sah!" Crash. "Mr. Moore, sah!"

"Yes, yes, enter." What was the latest news from this wildly unpredictable world?

Midshipman Moore entered. "S…s…signal from th…the flag, sir, 'All Ca…Captains Repair on Board.'"

Moore's continued stuttering reminded Wyckham that the young gentlemen aboard *Righteous* were probably having a very tough go of it here on this new, very frightening world. But he was too busy to be a nursemaid for them. "Has *Scamp* returned?" Wyckham simply asked the teenage boy as he rolled out of his cot and called for his man, Larkin.

"Y…yes, s…sir, anchored s…starboard of *Zeus*, s…sir."

Hopefully, *Scamp* had found this magical portal station and a suitable beach nearby to land over one thousand seamen and marines.

Zeus must be all pumped dry now and sitting level enough for O'Neal to assemble all his captains and first officers aboard to go over the attack plan. With a bit of luck, they would also get a good feed. Jarvis had always kept *Zeus* well stocked with fresh provisions for his wardroom.

Larkin, always one step ahead of things, not only had Wyckham's day uniform out but also had Rawlins and Donnelson ready and his gig in the water—and most important: a steaming pewter mug of coffee waiting for him. The three of them were rowed over to *Zeus* and piped aboard.

Going below, Wyckham caught the tantalizing smell of bacon. Thank God for that at least; you could always depend on the British navy to fill your stomach before a fight.

O'Neal greeted them. "Joy of the day, gentlemen. A bit of breakfast before we finalize the day's activities?"

They sat down at Jarvis's crudely repaired table, along with the squadron's other captains and first officers, and were served poached eggs, bacon, and fried potatoes. Lady Brashton and the lass who had gone off aboard *Scamp* also joined them. Again, the ladies seemed to delight in the taste of physical food.

"And now to the business at hand," said O'Neal as the plates were cleared away. "Commander Hamilton, with the help of our allies," he nodded to the raven-haired beauty, "has located the entrances to the portal station we seek, along with an excellent beach nearby. Here is a sketch of the area Hamilton has drawn for us."

Everyone bent over a crude drawing of a deep cove with depths marked throughout and four locations on shore about half a mile away, each one marked "Entrance."

Hamilton stepped up to the table and explained his drawing. "The cove is about a mile deep, the wind abeam for entering ships. Soundings showed at least five fathoms to within one hundred yards of the shore." That was excellent. It would allow *Righteous* to get close enough to support the landing with her great guns.

"We were unable to land anyone to look around further," Hamilton continued. "There were groups of the crab-like creatures demonstrating at us along the shoreline—rather nasty-looking beasts and decidedly unfriendly, clacking their claws at us like Brighton crabs not wanting to get et, haw haw! But the cove should be ideal for a landing in force."

Wyckham rolled his eyes, trying not to shake his head at the young commander. This young lieutenant thought all too much of himself and his weak humor.

"And I would like to thank our ally, who has appeared to us as Miss Catherine Burford, for her guidance and knowledge of the area," Hamilton continued, absolutely aglow as he smiled at the woman.

Wyckham could just imagine what sort of "guidance" she had given him. Hamilton was enough of a rakehell with human women; God knows it must have been quite the romp in *Scamp*'s cabin last night with one of these very forward allies. Christ, she'd probably been flying around the place, landing on him like a duck in a pond!

Then Wyckham noticed Rawlins scowling. Shite, wasn't Catherine Burford that woman his lieutenant had been engaged to back in London? Christ, it was! Goddamn if he wasn't seething with jealousy now, staring angrily at Hamilton. Wonderful—another development they didn't need right now.

Wyckham had to focus back on the battle planning. It was being arranged for the marines to get rowed in first. Hopefully, they could surprise their enemy before it concentrated its forces and establish a protected beachhead for the rest of the force to land on safely. They would use a total of sixteen boats taken from all the squadron's ships; it would take three or four trips by each boat to get everyone ashore. *Righteous* would serve as flagship, and *Zeus* would get towed in after the battle and careened on the beach for repairs.

"So that's it," concluded O'Neal. "Let's hope their sentries are sleeping, and we don't have to fight our way ashore. Too bad we don't have any scouts or skirmishers to go ashore early to check out the area and deal with their sentries."

Too bad wasn't the half of it. God only knows what they might blunder into here. Intelligence was the key for success in any raid. Usually, when the British navy landed a force in France, it had good maps, knowledge of the defenses, and even direct assistance from royalist sympathizers. When those elements were lacking, chances were good for a complete cock-up. He had heard of several land assaults that had gone terribly wrong when the navy landed forces right in the midst of French regulars, or the landing force got lost and was eventually taken.

An idea crossed his brow, and he turned to Lady Brashton. "Is it possible for some of our new allies to fly over there and scout out our target?"

"That would not work out very well," said Lady Brashton. "The Draesh know us too well—we have fought them for millennia. They would sense our presence well before our arrival, and they know how to capture us in a physical world like this. Our fate from then on would be singularly unpleasant. I am currently quite concerned that one of our party patrolling about the ships last night has not returned. If she was taken by the Draesh, she will be most viciously interrogated about our plans, and your military capabilities."

Well then, they certainly couldn't ask her to send a scout. But the lady continued. "You say you need the cove scouted out? I have seen the word *scout* in the memories of several men aboard Captain Wyckham's ship. I believe they have actually served as these scouts you are seeking."

"Really!" said Wyckham, leaning forward. "Which of my men have performed as scouts?" This would be a stroke of good luck they could use, though for the life of him he had no idea which of his crewmen had ever been scouts.

"It was those men who stay below in the room with bars across the door," responded the lady. "Are they special that they do not have to sail the ship or fight its battles?"

They were special, all right. She was referring to the imprisoned Yankee captain and his crew. But it certainly made sense that these men had scouting abilities—they had all lived in the Virginia wilderness before their current war. All of them were probably experienced hunters and excellent marksmen.

"She speaks of our Jonathan captain and his mates," said Wyckham to the group. "Let me speak to this Yankee officer on the matter."

"You would trust this pirate to go off scouting on his own?" blurted Hamilton. "Don't be daft! He'll just run off rather than face returning to England for his date with the noose." Hamilton arrogantly nodded to everyone in the room, basking in his brilliant observation.

Wyckham bridled at the language and disdainful tone from the brash young captain but stayed calm. This was not the time for dissension among the squadron's officers.

"Let me meet with the man and bring him up to snuff on the current situation. At this moment, he has no idea what has transpired over the previous day. Hopefully, he has the intelligence to realize that joining our effort would be his best course of action."

Then he turned specifically to Hamilton. "And we, too, should act intelligently and recognize that everything has changed for us as well; we need to forget the man's past transgressions as we will ask him to forget what he believes to be ours."

Hamilton took offense and objected strenuously, but O'Neal quickly hushed his bluster with a stern look and a muttered remark about "youthful blarney."

"An excellent thought, Captain Wyckham," said O'Neal as he turned back to address Wyckham. "Might I suggest you depart for your ship and see if we can enlist our past enemies' Crawfordation for today's action? Everyone else, please remain to work out some final details."

Wyckham nodded and headed off to climb down to his gig for a quick row back to *Righteous*. After being piped aboard, he went straight below to the brig where the Americans and their captain were being held.

As he approached the brig, the marine on guard stamped to attention. But even over this racket he could hear a piercing voice. "You will all be damned if you don't! God has selected one of noble blood to command here, and he will note who stands with this man of righteousness! Any who do not do their best to break out of here and restore Admiral William Jarvis to his command will spend millennia in hell itself!"

It was that bloody priest, DeGeorges, still agitating for mutiny. Well, thought Wyckham, even though the priest had previously said enough to enjoy the Crown's hospitality on a Thames prison hulk for quite a spell, Wyckham would make sure DeGeorges got an additional charge of incitement to mutiny for what he was yelling now.

But as it turned out, Wyckham would owe the man a debt of gratitude.

There was James Harrison, in the same cell as DeGeorges, sitting on a stool with his hands over his ears, shaking his head, and moaning as if in pain. He was about thirty-five years of age and as lean as a sapling. He wore his long brown hair in a *queue de cheval,* and he had a burnt craggy face from a life outdoors. Over DeGeorges's continuous bellowing, Wyckham had Harrison removed to a nearby storeroom where they seated themselves on water casks. He dismissed the sentry, who left with a raised eyebrow, concerned for Wyckham's safety.

"So the British still have some brave ones left," said Harrison. "Sitting here alone with an American pirate? Aren't you afraid I'll overpower you, break my lads out, and follow that priest's God-given orders and restore your friend Jarvis to his rightful place?" he asked with his palms turned upward.

"Actually, I'm not sure just what you'll do," said Wyckham, "but if you Yankees have any brains at all, you'll listen to me and help us all survive and get the hell out of here. First let me attempt to tell you of all that has happened."

He then recounted the recent events, from their entry through the portals, the battle with the Draesh, and an uncomfortable description of the ladies' arrival. He made sure to mention that Earth was soon to be threatened by this planet's vicious residents. Harrison was very attentive but not amazed; though imprisoned below decks, he must have heard and seen enough to realize that strange things had been going on. But to his credit he remained under control and thoughtful, trying to fathom what he was hearing.

Finally, Wyckham got to the reason for his visit. "Today, we will attempt to take one of their transit portals. A full assault of over one thousand marines and sailors will land and attack the enemy's forces guarding a nearby portal station. Once taken, it will be used to bring in our allies' reinforcements; after that, we can use it to get back to Earth.

For our attack on the portal to be successful, we'll need some scouts—men we can put ashore who can find their way about without being seen, report back on the disposition of enemy forces and the facility's gates, and take out any pickets so we can achieve surprise. In short, we need you and your men. Are you and your lads up to the task?"

Harrison waved a dismissive hand. "Sneak about in the bushes and slit some throats? All my boys are fine hunters. Most learned how to sneak up on a kill from our Shawnee neighbors—no better teachers than Shawnee on stayin' low and blendin' in with the forest. Some of my men even served as scouts for the Virginia militia before the war. But do you actually expect me to help this fleet get back to England so we can all be strung up in Tyburn Square for the amusement of your stinkin' nobility? Nope, not for me and not for my boys. We're better off anywhere than in London. We'll take our chances here."

Wyckham was prepared for this. "I'll not lie to you and guarantee you'll get a pardon if we return to England. American letters of marque have been ruled illegal by the high court; you'll all be treated as pirates and hung. You in particular are infamous in England due to the number of British ships you have taken, and there is great public pressure for your execution. Plus, who knows what anyone will make of the entire squadron, returning with a story of magical planets and monstrous creatures. Admiralty might just hang us all for desertion as well."

He was trying to show the Yankee he was being forthright. Now came his offer.

"But you could stay here and be a colonist all over again. I'll provide all you need from our stores to get started, including plenty of powder and shot. When we get back to England, we'll just declare you were all killed in action, and the issue will be settled."

Wyckham leaned over and looked him straight in the eye. He needed to tickle his interest. "You know, this should be a grand place to live. Vast lands for the taking, lots of sunlight, and plenty of strange new animals for you Yanks to hunt. Think of it—a whole world to explore."

Harrison raised his eyebrows in thought but stayed noncommittal. Wyckham continued. "Why don't I let you out of here so you can come up on deck and survey this place for yourself? It really is a pretty world. But if you prefer, you can stay here and listen to DeGeorges's sermons while better men fight to save the Earth from a future of the foulest depredations."

That got him moving. "Christ, get me out of here! That infernal priest has me ready to jump overboard. Anything to get me away from him!"

So the Reverend DeGeorges had his uses after all. As they stood and passed him on the way out, Wyckham addressed DeGeorges with a grin. "My thanks for your efforts on my behalf," he said sarcastically with a deep bow. "Thanks to you, I have a new ally." Wyckham and Harrison left a suddenly quiet DeGeorges looking quite puzzled.

As they headed up the stern gangway, Harrison stepped up nose to nose with Wyckham and looked him angrily in the eye. "But one more crack about *better men*, and I'll be calling you out. Do you understand, sir?"

Great, thought Wyckham. *Just what we need right now: a duel between a British and Yankee captain. That would just get their new alliance off to a perfect start.* But he actually respected the man for standing up to him. And truth be told, his comment had been a little strong. He did owe the man an apology.

"My apologies, Captain Harrison. All England knows you are a courageous officer. I beg your forgiveness for my brash words. The unbelievable occurrences of the past day have obviously taken a toll on my manners." Harrison's head bobbed in acknowledgement. Maybe even a look of respect in his glance as well? Wyckham escorted Harrison on deck thinking that this officer just might be a real leader. He and his crew could be an important addition for the coming battle.

Once on deck, Wyckham handed Harrison his telescope to look about. Not only did Harrison survey the shore, he also spent a lot of time checking out all the ships of the anchored squadron. *There's a military man reviewing the forces*, thought Wyckham. This Yankee knew his business. Maybe it was time to win the man over with a little professional courtesy due a fellow officer?

"How about a decent meal in my cabin?" Wyckham offered. "Although I'm sure my cook can't match the delightful meals of dried beef and hardtack you've been enjoying in our brig, he should have some superb roast pork loin, along with a glass of French red from Burgundy."

It would be the first decent meal for him in weeks. Harrison's eyes opened wide in anticipation; he was almost drooling. *This contract is sealed*, thought Wyckham.

7

HELP FROM THE YANKS

The cove reminded Wyckham of lush Caribbean islands. But the trees were more densely packed and taller, and there was less ground cover. Above the cove was a valley extending miles back, flanked by mountains with several tall waterfalls. The beach was bleached-white sand, about three cables deep. It really was a beautiful, quiet scene… maybe too quiet? There had been no sign of either crabmen or the giant bog creatures.

Yesterday, after a hearty meal and not a few glasses, Harrison had agreed to join the squadron as captain of a light company of skirmishers. His American crew had been quickly persuaded to join up as well, but it had taken a while to get them fed and prepared, and the attack had been postponed a day. Today, they had been equipped with rifles and a few telescopes and had their precious tomahawks returned to them. Then, three hours ago, they were set ashore to reconnoiter in two groups. As the Americans disembarked, they had impressed Wyckham as prepared and competent scouts.

Righteous's cutter now appeared a mile off to larboard, tacking around the cove's point and returning with the scouting company.

Soon Harrison and three of his men were below in Wyckham's cabin. O'Neal was there along with the squadron's captains, first lieutenants, and Lady Brashton, all eager to hear what the American had to say.

Harrison started sketching a crude map on the back of a chart. "We could see several trails which lead from the beach through the trees to caves about a half mile back." Lady Brashton indicated to everyone that those caves would be entrances to the transportation station.

Harrison continued. "But surprising them is not to be. Above the trails, on the valley walls are huge numbers of these ugly, crab-like beasts hiding in the trees, clearly waiting in ambush." Harrison looked up at them grimly. "I would estimate their numbers at three to four thousand." Three to four thousand! Their enemy had been busy.

Apparently, the Draesh were quick learners and had wisely chosen not to have their forces dispute the beach landing in the face of *Righteous*'s great guns. Instead, they had assembled a huge army of their lackeys to fight from hiding. Wyckham felt drained. Had everything come to naught? There was no way they could fight such a large force in unknown terrain. Again, despair washed over Wyckham. The prospects for returning to England looked dim.

"So here's what I would suggest, if yer interested in advice from a pirate," Harrison continued. "They're packed heads-to-backsides in there. A target begging for the attention of those giant mortars you have on those two ketches. Let me and my boys have three hours to get to the hilltops on each side of the valley. We'll fell some trees and set up signal stations with a line of sight to your ships. With some of your midshipmen and signal flags, we'll direct a hellstorm of exploding shells right onto this army. Be like pissin' on an anthill—sudden death from above. They'll run like hell."

For a privateer captain, this Yankee certainly had some ideas on land battle. Would this work? Would these crabs run, or would they stand under a brutal bombardment of thirteen-inch exploding mortar bombs?

Wyckham addressed Lady Brashton. "Madam, what kinds of fighters are these Krag? If we drop fiery explosions into their midst, will they run or will they stand and wait to counterattack when we land?"

Everyone turned to the woman. "The Krag have been brought here from their own planet to serve the Draesh. The ones on this planet have never been in combat; they mostly perform menial tasks and personal service. While they can fight viciously, they are not very intelligent and react in fear to the unknown. From the memories I can see in the minds of officers here who have witnessed these mortars in action, I would not expect the Krag to endure such an attack for long. And if only a few start running, the rest would take flight in a complete panic."

Several of the men present shuffled uneasily at realizing that their minds had just been invaded, wondering what other embarrassing facts the lady had seen. If they only knew that there was nothing to be embarrassed about with this lady!

"Capital!" exclaimed O'Neal. "Captain Harrison, we'll also give you two squads of marines to set up a defense about your hilltop stations. Captains Grimwald and Randolf, it turns out you are in this fight after all. Go move your ships to the cove's center, springs mounted and ready for action. Captain Warren will be overall commander of the landing force, assisted by Captain Donnelson for the marines and Lieutenant Rawlins for the sailors. Let's get our sailors and marines on the beach under *Righteous*'s guns to await my signal for the bombardment to begin. Captain Harrison will observe the bombardment from his hilltop and declare when the enemy is in sufficient confusion for us to advance from the beach. Once the enemy is routed, Captain Wyckham will go ashore with Madam Brashton and her group to immediately begin operating the transport station. Are we all in agreement?"

Those assembled, including Lady Brashton, nodded assent and left for their assignments. Wyckham would not be allowed ashore until the issue was settled. Navy tradition stipulated that captains stay aboard ships during land actions; first lieutenants generally led sailors fighting ashore. For Rawlins's sake, he hoped these Krag were as spineless as Lady Brashton had indicated. If they dug in and endured the bombardment like the Americans did at Baltimore's Fort Henry last year, the landing force would be overwhelmed in a massive counterattack.

Within an hour, things were well under way. Boats were ferrying sailors and marines to the beach unopposed. On both sides of the valley, Harrison's men were seen felling trees and erecting signaling poles on two nearby hilltops. *Vesuvius* and *Hedgehog* had been moved into positions at the center of the cove. They had dropped anchors fore and aft and had placed rope springs on their anchor cables for turning the ships so they could aim their giant mortars.

With no immediate duties, Wyckham called for his gig and went aboard Captain Grimwald's *Hedgehog* to witness the coming bombardment. He had never seen a bomb ketch in action and was curious to watch the huge guns being worked.

Grimwald was known as an expert with these mortars. He'd participated in many attacks and sieges, including the recent bombardments at Baltimore and Copenhagen. When Wyckham arrived, he was supervising the loading of his two guns. The squat mortars were each about six feet long and four feet in diameter, sitting in cradles on the main deck. To Wyckham, they looked like the giant pots used by savage cannibals in Africa for cooking visiting missionaries. The mortars had a thirteen-inch bore and fired an exploding shell packed with gunpowder. Both sat at forty-five-degree angles to maximize range; distance was controlled by the amount of the gunpowder charge.

Grimwald himself was weighing out the powder charge on a balance scale for the first shot, as gunners' clerks kept a log. With the gun charged, he used a ruler to cut a fuse about eight inches long and inserted it into the fuse hole of a thirteen-inch shell. Two gunners lifted it up in a cradle and dropped it into one mortar's muzzle.

Anchor springs had been turned to rotate the ship, aiming the first shot according to the direction of one of Harrison's men. The scout had come aboard and pointed out the enemies' location he had seen from the left hilltop observation post.

When Grimwald was satisfied, he signaled a midshipman to hoist a ready signal. Similar signals were being raised on *Righteous*'s mainmast, the two hilltops ashore, and the landing force that had now formed up on the beach. With all in readiness, flags went up on *Righteous* with *Vesuvius*'s and *Hedgehog*'s numbers, followed by "Open Fire."

Looking at his watch, Grimwald first bellowed, "Light fuse!" waited a few more seconds, then shouted, "Fire!"

The gun's eruption shook the whole ship and blew Wyckham's hair back. The rigging was still shaking from the blast as he watched the smoking trail of the shell streak skyward, level off, and finally drop down toward the left side of the valley about a quarter of a mile away. Then came the flash of its star-shaped burst about two hundred feet in the air, followed momentarily by the thud of the distant explosion. Trees below it shook from the shock of the detonation. Even from this far away, the shellburst was quite impressive.

Signals immediately went up the left hilltop's flagpole. A midshipman next to Wyckham snapped his glass out, then quickly read aloud: "In two hundred, left three hundred, lower two hundred." Not bad for the first shot. Grimwald shouted out orders to crewmen on the springs to spin the ship a little to larboard. He then measured out a smaller powder charge on his scale and cut another fuse, this one a little longer.

A mortar aboard nearby *Vesuvius* crashed out. Wyckham watched as its shell descended on the right side of the valley and exploded somewhat lower. Flags appeared on the right hilltop to be met with cheers from *Vesuvius*.

"Right tower signals 'On Target,'" said *Hedgehog*'s midshipman slowly, angrily snapping his glass closed.

"Young fool got lucky," muttered Grimwald, watching as his second gun was readied. Apparently, he had a low opinion of Captain Randolf on *Vesuvius*.

The second shell's fuse was lit, the gun fired with another tremendous blast, and everyone aboard watched for the shell burst. This time it was lower, closer and a little to the left of the first shot. The middy reading the signals snappily yelled out, "Lower one hundred."

It was almost a direct hit, just exploding one hundred feet too high. That might not be so bad, thought Wyckham. Even if fewer Krag were killed by the high explosion, the airburst would be seen by many and might induce more panic. The idea wasn't to kill them all—no gun could do that. If they could just get a few to run, panic might take over, and the enemy force would dissolve into flight.

Both mortars fired aboard *Vesuvius*. With their first shot on target, *Vesuvius* had the right combination of powder charge, fuse length, and ship angle to fire away. Then both mortars aboard *Hedgehog* fired in succession as well.

Pretty soon the firing was almost continuous. It seemed to Wyckham that there was always a shell on the way or exploding in the valley. He didn't know how the crabmen were managing, but he knew that if he was underneath this bombardment, he'd be thinking about getting somewhere else and damn quick, too. He'd better return to his ship. Very soon fleeing crabmen might be dashing onto the beach where *Righteous*'s guns could get at them.

Wyckham returned in his gig to *Righteous*, finding the ship cleared for action under Second Lieutenant Clifton. Larkin was there to help him buckle on his pistols and sword. He and O'Neal continued to watch the bombardment.

Suddenly both hilltop signals were the same. "Enemy F...Flying!" read Midshipman Moore, victory in his voice.

Well, that didn't take long, thought Wyckham. Now it was up to the landing force. O'Neal had Moore signal Warren ashore to commence the attack up into the valley.

But Warren's marines didn't move. He kept them fanned out on each side of a stream where the valley met the beach.

Then Wyckham not only saw but also heard the reason for Warren's hesitation. At least some of the panicked Krag were heading toward the beach. Running down the valley's sides and onto the beach, like a child's worst nightmare, were hundreds of these strange crabmen. They made quite a racket as they ran, the beach thrumming from their legs hitting the sand, making a thunder like a cavalry charge. Each Krag was four to five feet tall, enclosed in a mottled yellow and gray shell, with a wide flat head that resembled a normal crab's body and eyes bouncing around on foot-long stalks. Like land crabs, they had mismatched claws, a pointed one about two feet long, needle sharp and thin, the other short and squat. They ran along on four legs with pointed feet. The air was filled with the strange clicking sounds they were making.

Warren had kept his men back so *Righteous* could fire directly up the valley. With the ship moored less than a cable from the shore, *Righteous* would fire canister, tin cans filled with musket balls. Each eighteen-pounder on the main deck was double loaded and would fire almost two thousand balls with each shot. Canister was used to decimate packed troops; it was the most feared weapon on the nineteenth-century battlefield. And the furiously charging crabmen were about to learn why.

Wyckham spoke calmly. "You may fire as your guns bear, Mr. Clifton. Get some balls above the beach up into the valley, I suspect there are many more of them up there that we cannot yet see."

Clifton nodded acceptance and turned to the battery. "Larboard battery…ready…fire!" The giant crash of sixteen guns heeled the ship over as O'Neal and Wyckham strained to see the beach through the smoke. But even before it cleared, fountains of crab parts spurted up through the smoke, spinning and flying every which way. A moment later the moderate breeze blew the smoke away, revealing a scene of wriggling claws and dismembered bodies. Dead and wounded Krag were spread over the entire valley floor. The ground was yellow-gray, covered with shards from shattered crab shells. Creatures with missing legs were still trying to run over the heap of corpses and onto the beach, emitting high-pitched screeches of pain. And apparently these crabs had blood similar to humans, because blood was everywhere, splashed over piled corpses and running in rivulets down the beach.

"Warm work, that," said O'Neal to Clifton, nodding as he surveyed the scene with hands clasped behind his back. "Tell your gunners 'Good shooting' from me."

"The admiral says 'Well done, *Righteous*!'" yelled Clifton to the larboard battery. "Get the guns back out, and let's earn his praise again!"

But that was not to be. On the beach, the marines were up and moving forward into the field of fire. Apparently Warren could see more crabs about to break onto the beach before *Righteous* would be able get its portside guns reloaded, and had ordered an attack. Sergeants were shouting orders and red-coated men with fixed bayonets ran to the valley opening. They quickly formed up behind the still wriggling mound of Krag, bayoneting any nearby wounded. *I guess we're not taking prisoners today*, mused Wyckham. A sudden volley of musketry from the marines filled the end of the valley with more smoke. When it cleared, scores more dead and wounded Krag could be seen strung out along the valley floor.

But the issue was certainly still in doubt. Unhurt Krag were spilling over the heap of corpses and launching themselves at the marines; there were hundreds of them running onto the beach. Men fired pistols and sergeants yelled as they swung their hangers and cutlasses at the charging foes. The crabmen used their vicious claws, stabbing chests and crushing limbs.

Wyckham's watched a marine thrust his bayonet at a particularly large Krag, which danced sideways and parried the bayonet with its short claw. Wyckham's gut wrenched as the creature then lunged and ran his rapier-like long claw right through the marine's throat. Immediately it attacked another, hooking his coat and pulling him close with its long claw, then crushing his neck in the short one. But not a man hesitated at the sight; marines were trained to just keep fighting no matter what. A stocky corporal clubbed the big crab right in the head with his musket butt, knocking the creature to its knees. His sergeant then swung at it with a heavy cutlass and cracked its head wide open. As its shattered pieces fell to the ground, Wyckham was reminded of diners pounding crab shells at a Brighton tavern.

Scores more of the creatures were leaping over the marines, apparently trying to get to the waterline. But hundreds of sailors were drawn up there in a defensive line, crouched behind beached boats, whose bow guns began firing their own deadly canister rounds. Krag spun as they were hit or just exploded into disjointed parts. Sailors with eight-foot pikes were keeping the foe at bay while their mates fired muskets and pistols point-blank into the massed creatures. The boat guns on the flanks switched to solid shot, sending two-pound balls down the line of foes stalled in front of the sailors. Like a game of ten pins but using crustaceans, as each ball cut a gash along the front line of charging Krag. The entire beach was a cauldron of flame, smoke, shouting, and the tumbling bodies of crabmen.

Suddenly all went quiet, except for the continuous screeching of wounded foes. Clearly, the enemy charge onto the beach had been broken and the foes had retreated back into the valley. Several companies of marines rose from their position, formed up, and headed off the beach, presumably toward the transporter's cave. Wyckham waited for sounds of their fighting, but everything remained quiet.

"S...Signal from larboard h...hilltop," said Midshipman Moore with his glass to his eye. "'En...enemy F...flying Inland,'" he read aloud.

O'Neal and Wyckham surveyed the valley through their own telescopes. There was some sporadic musketry below the two signaling stations, where marines assigned to protect them were probably keeping any wandering Krag away from the hilltops. The mortars aboard *Vesuvius* and *Hedgehog* continued firing, still directed by Harrison's signals, following the fleeing enemy deeper inland. Other than that, they saw no signs of enemy action.

Lady Brashton was standing nearby and had witnessed the entire battle. She walked up showing astonishment. "Well fought, gentlemen! I am amazed at what your simple weapons have accomplished. Now, get us into that transport station, and the universe will have a chance to remove the scourge of the Draesh forever. May I ask that you bring along some capable assistants, people you believe can follow instructions to work the transporter? There are days of work ahead of us, first to bring our own forces here and then to get all of you home."

O'Neal was bridling at her denigrating assessment of their weaponry. Yes, Madam, now that our 'simple weapons' have put complete flight to the enemy, let us assist you in doing your part. Captain, would you be so kind as to take our new allies ashore and get them inside that mountain?"

Wyckham nodded and headed for a barge with Midshipman Moore, whom he took along in case they needed to signal the ship, and his steward, Larkin, who would never leave the captain's side in a war zone. The landing party also included *Righteous*'s carpenter, Jones, and a few others that the carpenter had selected to operate the transport device. Wyckham was surprised to see Seaman Crawford among those the carpenter had picked. They all climbed down as Lady Brashton simply floated into the small boat. Soon they were being rowed to the beach, followed by a group of her compatriots, balls of light floating along behind them. Many of the sailors and marines from the other ships were gawking in amazement at the little parade. Wyckham calmly accepted the spectacle—it made him realize how he was getting quite used to the astonishing things that occurred on this planet.

Righteous's Marine Captain Donnelson met them on the beach. "We found three tunnels that enter the mountain. Lots of crabs have retreated into them, and our company is currently clearing them out with cold steel and the grenadoes." A marine corporal, whom Wyckham recognized from his ship, approached and saluted Donnelson smartly.

"Beg tah repaht, sah! Sergeant O'Malley sends 'iz respects an' states that the cave system is now safe tah entah!"

Donnelson thanked the man, turned back to Wyckham, bowed slightly and extended his arm towards the cave. "Shall we?" he said, like a duke inviting his guests into the ballroom.

"Most kind of you, your grace," Wyckham japed as he put out his arm for the Lady Brashton. "Madam, the dance awaits us."

She took his arm with a puzzled look as they followed the corporal toward a tunnel, preceded by a squad of marines. Behind them came more marines, followed by the rest of the allies floating along a few feet in the air. Wyckham could just imagine this procession entering the annual officer's ball at Westminster Palace. He could picture the grand old dams of London society, fluttering behind their fans. "Isn't that Baron Sir Rodney Wyckham and the woman from the moon that saved us all from being devoured?"

But now his only admirers were battle-weary sailors and marines, who momentarily stopped whatever they were doing to watch them go by. Surely some were having their own fantasies about the stunning woman on his arm. Many of them had seen her arrive naked, and the rest had certainly heard all the details from the marines and sailors from *Righteous*. Wyckham hoped they'd never find out what these ladies really wanted from human beings!

But it was a day to be proud of British arms. For all he knew, the day's efforts were the first step in preventing the destruction of all life on Earth, though probably no one back in England would ever realize it. While all England had gone wild over Nelson's victories, which hadn't even won the war against revolutionary France, Wyckham would probably get court-martialed for mutiny if he ever got back to England. Here they had just saved the whole universe and no one would ever know what they had accomplished, much less laud Wyckham and the squadron for their victory today.

His reveries ceased as they came upon the scene of the heaviest fighting. While the ground was mostly covered with dead foes, there were plenty of dead sailors and marines strewn all around. The Krag had ripped some men completely apart, and human limbs were scattered all over the beach. Surgeons were examining the wounded, signaling to waiting sailors which ones should be moved back aboard ship. Groups of the less wounded were limping back toward the boats on their own.

Wyckham had been in plenty of fights and seen similar scenes before, but the aftermath of a battle always shocked him. One moment, he was proud of his victory, and the next moment he was humbled by the men who had died under his direction. And in this case, they died horribly and far from home. No family or friends would ever be able to pay their respects and grieve at their gravesites.

Snap out of it, Rodney! You've still got work to do; better get the allies into the station to begin whatever the hell it is they need to do.

Accompanied by a score of marines with bayonets on their muskets, the group walked along a dirt trail through a cluster of trees toward a cave opening above them in some rocks. The ground about them was swampy and covered in ferns and other strange plants. A few of them had open-maw-like buds on the ends of their stalks. Clearly, they were some kind of predator plants. *No way I'm sticking a finger in there*, thought Wyckham. On the ground, lizard-like creatures went scurrying out of their way as they walked along. One made the mistake of getting too close to one of the open plant buds. The plant snapped closed on it and then rose up and swallowed it like a pelican would a fish. *Christ, I hope this place doesn't have larger versions of that goddamn plant*, Wyckham thought with a shudder.

After a few minutes of walking, they climbed about thirty feet to a large cave opening in some boulders. Wyckham tensed with a wave of cold dread as he realized this entrance was made for the giant bog monsters' use. He hoped he'd never meet up with any of those horrible creatures again. Let the forces soon to arrive from other worlds deal with the big ogres.

They were greeted at the entrance by a marine sergeant holding an impressive hanger in presentation.

"Cap'n, sah! Sergeant O'Malley, third companah!" He saluted with the sword. "Allow me tah escort yah through this 'ere cave. Ahll be safe inside thanks t' third companah Royal Marines. Thar be a right strange room at th' end I believe is yor goal, Cap'n, sah."

Wyckham nodded his thanks to the Irishman with a "Carry on, Sergeant," and walked through the cave opening. Escorting marines lit oil lamps as the party entered. The walls of the passage had been carved from rock; there were large boulders and crevices along both sides. Dozens of dead and wounded Krag littered the floor, those still alive squeaking in anguish. It was clear they had attacked from hiding, fighting the advancing marines at every step. After two hundred feet or so, the cave expanded into a large cavern over two hundred feet across and fifty feet high, with large boulders all along the walls. Mounted on these rocks were dozens of metal boxes with glass dials lit up from within. Some boxes had tree branches mounted in slots. Large woven tree roots and rock shelving supported the boxes. Other devices were connected to tree limbs coming directly out of the ground. Several marines were lounging about, drinking water or tending to their weapons.

"Yes, this would be it," said Lady Brashton, as her comrades started flitting about in the air above the boxes. "And now I see where it gets its power. The device is tied into the life forces of this entire planet. These tree roots you see are part of the device and connect it to the rest of this world."

She approached the largest box, examining the dials and touching some of the protruding wooden shafts.

Suddenly, the room was filled with loud grinding noises. Was the device starting up? But a marine's shout from behind Wyckham showed the real source of the racket.

Several of the large boulders against the wall were pivoting inward and from behind them came waves of more Krag. These were yellow-orange in color, larger than those on the beach and festooned with flowers and vines about their heads and chests. *Great, a fanatical palace guard making a last stand,* thought Wyckham as he drew his pistols and cocked back rtheir hammers.

And they fought like palace guards, too. Unlike the Krag on the beach, these didn't rush pell-mell onto the marines' bayonets, but danced about like fencers, dodging musket fire, then lunging in close to stab with their long sharp claws. Damn things had learned quickly about British fighting tactics, Wyckham grimly realized. Several marines fell while trying to aim their big unwieldy Brown Bess muskets in the close quarters. Wyckham aimed his first pistol and fired at a crabman running right at him, but it danced to one side and lunged at him with his long pointed claw extended like a fencing foil. Instinctively, Wyckham ducked so the claw went *passé* above him, then shouldered his attacker in the chest as it passed, knocking the creature to the ground. Wyckham rolled on top of it, put his other pistol to its head, and fired. Its head shell split wide open and the beast went limp.

But more screams and shouting filled the cave as Krag kept pouring into the room from behind the boulders. The room was total chaos, packed with yellow-orange Krag dancing and stabbing and red-coated marines swinging and thrusting their bayoneted muskets. Sporadic musketry filled the room with smoke, making it hard to see how the fight was going. But the increasing screams and moans of wounded marines told Wyckham that it wasn't going well. This chaotic mêlée simply favoured the agile Krag; they were just too damned fast in this frantic, close-quarters fight. And the damned things now had tactics—they approached hidden in the gunsmoke, then darted out to stab marines when they reloaded.

Like any British troops, marines needed to form up to be effective; they weren't trained for individual combat against wild animals.

Someone needed to get the marines formed up. Where was Donnelson? There was no sign of *Righteous*'s marine captain. Hopefully, he hadn't fallen. Maybe that sergeant could get his men organized into a line or defensive square? But was he down as well?

Wyckham's question was answered as he heard the sergeant's booming voice from across the room. "Now, me boys! Throw em now!"

Sparks flew through the air as concealed marines threw lit grenadoes into the tunnels behind the boulders from which the Krag were emerging. The rolling explosions threw Krag all over the room. More grenadoes were thrown as the first batch exploded, keeping more Krag reinforcements from joining the fight. But marine reinforcements were arriving, led by Captain Donnelson, who had wisely run from the cave to bring in an organized marine company from the beach. He formed them up at the room's entrance.

"Second company, form line on me! Present! Aim!"

They were about to fire a volley, but the Krag were jumping about too erratically to be hit, and the large cloud of smoke would allow the Krag to move in even closer and skewer more men.

"No! Belay that order!" Wyckham shouted at the last second. "Captain Donnelson, have the men advance in line with bayonets! Each man to fire only when there's a bugger right on his point!"

"Marines, fix bayonets!" Donnelson yelled, following the order. "Ready, ad...vance!"

About forty red-coated marines started to advance in lockstep, the agitated Krag jockeying about in front of them, looking for a place to break the line. Whenever they collided or bunched up, muskets exploded, and Krag started to drop. Others got unexpectedly stabbed from the side; all British line troops were trained to thrust their bayonets sideways into unwary foes. Grenadoes continued to explode behind the boulders. On Wyckham's side of the room, small groups and individuals were furiously fighting hand-to-hand. No tactics here – just a very desparate, ugly brawl.

Wyckham drew his sword and looked for an enemy to engage, hopefully from behind. To hell with fair fights in this furball. His eyes came to rest on Midshipman Moore, armed with a sword, right in the center of the room, facing off with a particularly large Krag. Squirming at his feet were three other badly wounded Krag, twitching in spasms of pain. The shy young Moore had put them all down?

While all the other sailors were hacking left and right with their naval cutlasses, Moore had a hanger, which he held *en garde* like an experienced fencer – point high in *quarte*, palm up, rear arm back and high for balance. But while his body was turned sideways like any fencer's should be, his *en garde* position was an extremely low crouch, unlike any fencer Wyckham had ever seen. And he was bouncing on his toes, moving more like a pugilist than a proper fencer. The active stance apparently worked, because as another Krag approached him, Moore extended his point and lunged off his deeply cocked back leg, flying at least ten feet though the air, thrusting his blade right through the crab's chest before the creature even realized it was in range of the spry young midshipman. The impaled crabman immediately dropped to the floor to writhe along with the others.

Another foe ran at Moore, repeatedly stabbing with its long claw, but the young middy deftly retreated one step each time, sweeping his blade across his chest in *quarte* and *sixte* parries. Each parry crossed the crab's long claw at its very tip and deflected it to the side. Frustrated, the creature gathered itself and leapt at Moore with all its strength, its long claw fully extended. This time Moore turned his body slightly, closed the outside line with his blade in a high *sixte* parry, and held his blade there for a split second to guide the Krag's claw well past him. Then he crisply dropped his point and made a snap *riposte* through his foe's armpit, skewering the creature like it was ready for cooking. Its falling body pulled Moore's hanger from his hand as it landed on its side, the point of the sword sticking a handswidth out of its back.

As the midshipman bent down and pulled his blade free of the downed foe, another Krag with an intricate headband made of woven vines (an officer?) danced up to engage the midshipman, its four legs beating out a tattoo. Moore also advanced to fighting distance, then suddenly dropped his point in an invitation to attack. The agile Krag took it, lunging at the opening with blinding speed, thrusting his long pointed claw in *sixte* toward Moore's chest. But Moore retreated just as quickly, leaping backward with his knees deeply bent, landing like a cat ready to spring and parrying the claw high inside in *quarte*. There followed a flurry of flashing blade and whipping claw that Wyckham's eyes could barely keep up with. First Moore feinted a low-line attack in *octave* towards the groin. The crabman swept his claw across trying to parry Moore's blade, but the young midshipman dropped his point in a classic *disengage,* let the claw pass, then raised his point back up in *quarte* to threaten the Krag's chest. As his opponent lifted its claw to parry high, Moore pulled his blade back to let the claw go past one more time, then lunged and with a lightning *coupé* flicked his point behind the long claw and thrust it high in *tierce* right through his opponent's hose-like throat. Moore yanked his blade free just as the creature dropped to its knees and fell forward with blood pumping out its neck.

Moore's performance had Wyckham standing open-mouthed in amazement. Where did that young man learn to fence like that? Midshipmen weren't even allowed to carry swords. And the shy, stuttering Moore, of all people!

But it wasn't Moore's dueling clinic that would win the day. More marines had entered the room and formed a second line to begin a flanking advance. Slowly the two lines herded the crabman in the room into a corner. Other marines had taken up positions behind the boulders, firing muskets and throwing grenadoes at the Krag jammed in entrance tunnels trying to get into the fight.

Just as it appeared the fight was won, a huge crash filled the room as an enormous boulder fell from the roof, crushing marines and Krag alike. Fighting slowed as dust filled the room. *Goddamn bloody hell, now what?*

Wyckham watched in horror as the now familiar head of a huge Draesh emerged above the dust. With a roar, it lashed out with a ten-foot-long arm, sweeping marines against a wall, their shattered bodies bouncing to the floor. Muskets boomed out but seemed to have no effect on the huge creature. Towering over them this close, the evil monster was like a wasp among ants. What could they do? They had no weapons here that would hurt the damn thing!

Wyckham slumped in despair. This monster was going to kill them all in a matter of a few moments. It jumped forward, cocking its arm to lash out again, when it looked at Wyckham and stopped in mid-swing.

Suddenly, Wyckham heard the most frightening sounds of his life. "You! The Captain Wyckham!" the beast actually bellowed out in proper English! Its voice was so loud that the cavern walls vibrated, the words repeated several times over by the echoes inside the stone room. *Christ, it could speak English! And it knows me!* And it clearly wanted him dead.

Larkin, his side bleeding from a claw thrust, stepped forward and fired a pistol at the giant, to no effect. The demon responded by visciously backhanding Larkin against the cave's wall, where the man dropped to the floor, a mangled heap of shattered bones. Then with a leap the Draesh was upon Wyckham, picking him up in his huge hand and bringing him right up to its face. The captain had a closeup view of bloodshot eyes, huge flaring nostrils, and vicious, foot-long teeth.

"What have you got for me, Wyckham?" it said in a frighteningly soft, determined voice. Then with what Wyckham swore was a smile, it opened its giant jaws. Wyckham was staring down into its drooling, foul-smelling mouth. Good Lord, the demon was going to eat him!

"Cap'n! Use this!" It was Sergeant O'Malley, throwing him a lit grenadoe. Wyckham dropped his sword and caught the little bomb, burning his hand on the fuse but holding on. With a flick of his wrist, he dropped it down into the monster's open mouth. The creature had seen nothing of this, its wide-open jaws momentarily blocking Wyckham from its view. Now it lifted Wyckham above its gaping mouth, about to throw him down its throat right behind the sizzling grenadoe. Well, at least he'd die from an explosion instead of being most roughly chewed to bits.

Suddenly, the huge Draesh tensed, roared out in anguish, and opened its hand, dropping Wyckham to the floor. With both hands it reached down to its groin area, emitting another roar of pain. Then the grenadoe exploded inside the beast with a muffled thud, sending flesh and grenade fragments flying across the room from a hole in its stomach. With its eyes bulging out and tongue hanging out, it dropped sideways to the ground, slowly moving its arms and moaning.

Wyckham slowly staggered to his feet, his right ankle in pain from the fall. *What the hell had happened?* He searched about for whatever had caused the demon enough discomfort to suddenly drop him.

And there was Crawford, standing near the creature's legs, with Wyckham's sword in one hand and a bundle of some hairy flesh in the other.

"Chopped 'iz bollocks off, oy did, sor. Figgered twood get 'iz attention fer a bit." He held up his left hand, and sure enough he was holding the cursed animal's bloody scrotum! "Didn't hold with em mistreatin' 'r cap'm. And 'iss devil didn' need 'iz balls anyway. Ugly a bastard as ee were, 'm sure no lady devil wooda giv' em even th' time o' day." With a heave, Crawford nonchalantly tossed the mangled mess to land with a splatter on the creature's head, which was still rolling back and forth in agony.

No wonder the filthy monster had tensed up and dropped him! Crawford had picked up Wyckham's dropped sword and slashed the animal's testicles right off! Wyckham shuffled his own legs, imagining the feeling of a sword slicing into his own groin. But once again he owed his life to the old salt Peter Crawford.

The fighting in the room was just about done. More and more marines continued to flood into the room from the beach. A few Krag had managed to escape through the entrance opened by the Draesh's arrival. All the others were pinned up against the wall by a ring of bayonets where the two lines of marines had met. Marines were nonchalantly shooting them as they reloaded their muskets while keeping the vicious little buggers at bay with their bayonets.

It had been one hell of a fight. Wyckham was actually encouraged that their enemy had fought so desperately for this place. It showed the transporter was as important as Lady Brashton had indicated.

"Please! Spare us some! Don't kill them all!" It was Lady Brashton, appearing out of nowhere. "Especially the Draesh! Let us have time with them to scan what they know. It will be as helpful to us as it has been for them. They may have a wealth of knowledge about this world. The distribution of Draesh, the location of other transport stations, even their plans for the coming battle between us, any of this could be listed in their living memories. Leave some alive!"

Wyckham saw great concern on her face. Apparently, her species showed their true feelings in the images they projected. And his ally knew some things he didn't. Time to find out what the hell was going on.

"Madam, this fight is over. So why are you so concerned? We have gained access to the transport device as you requested. Now, did I hear you state something about our foes possessing certain helpful facts? Would that have anything to do with that big pig knowing my name? Why, here I am meeting the gentleman for the first time, and he has the advantage of me! I didn't even know his name when I blew him to hell! And what was that the old boy said about 'getting something from me?' Hmm?"

The lady looked directly into Wyckham's eyes. "One of our party never returned from patrolling last night. It is now clear that she was taken and used as a source of information about all of us. Do you see those bright globes inside this Draesh?"

Wyckham looked into the hole in the creature's stomach. Inside he saw globes similar to the ones he had seen inside the Draesh corpse the previous day aboard *Righteous.*

"Over the millennia, the Draesh have added devices to their own bodies, part biological and part electrical. These allow them to copy our ability to gain powers from other beings' life forces and to read their memories as we do. The missing member of our group was consumed, and all she knew about you and our plans is now common knowledge among all the local Draesh."

So that's it. No wonder their Krag minions knew to keep inland at the start of the day's battle, away from *Righteous*'s guns. Too bad they panicked and ran onto them anyway.

Lady Brashton continued. "And they clearly know of you and believe you to be a formidable warrior, one that would be very beneficial for any Draesh to devour."

Wonderful news. I am the prime target of an entire population of giant flesh-eating demons, Wyckham thought with a shake of his head. *They're probably all sitting down having a glass and bragging about who'll eat me.* "Arrgh, ahm gonna fillet the bastard an' pud em in a roll wif some kippers, I will!" *Well, forget about it, Wyckham. It won't be the first time someone's after your hide.* The day was won and the field was theirs. Time to get to work on the controls of the transport station.

"Madam, my condolences on your loss this day; we all have lost comrades in today's fight. Sadly, I have lost my steward, a man who has been in my employ for years. But he and the rest of the fallen would want us to push on to success. Allow us to clean the room here so you may begin your work with these devices. Let me reassemble the crew members we had assigned to help you."

At first the lady didn't respond; she was standing over the moaning Draesh, apparently scanning its memories. Then she looked up at Wyckham.

"Wait, there is something else you should know. That Draesh you shot the jaw off yesterday with the green band about its head? It was their ordained leader, what you would call a king. He has put out a call for your capture. He plans a long, torturous death for you, conducted over many days in front of an audience of Draesh in one of their public gathering places."

Oh, just wonderful, even better. Now, by comparison, a quick death from consumption by one of the big devils was looking pretty good. Why couldn't he have just mangled the face of some lowly Draesh commoner? No, it had to be their goddamned king, and now there's a royal warrant out for him. His motivation to avoid capture took a substantially higher leap in intensity. From now on he'd better walk around with grenadoes in his pockets.

Wyckham saw his carpenter, Jones, approaching with a bloody shoulder. *Forget about avoiding capture and get to work, Wyckham!*

Jones spoke in a weak voice. "Ready to begin work 'ere, Captain. Jes lemme get a rag on 'is pinprick, and I'll 'ave a go at this thing, with the ladies' guidance." He nodded expectantly at Lady Brashton.

Wyckham lifted the carpenter's torn shirt away from the wounded shoulder. The wound was a deep puncture from a Krag claw. He could see the colors of threads from the shirt pressed deep into the carpenter's flesh.

"I appreciate your eagerness to do your duty." He glanced sideways at Lady Brashton. "But this wound needs to be cleaned out without delay before it festers. We'll get all the help we need to get started from the men you've brought. It will probably take the ladies a while to sort things out anyway. Just get back to us when you're able."

"Aye, sir," Jones said as he walked off, a bit dejected. Now Wyckham needed to appoint a replacement leader for the work crew and right away. For all they knew, the Draesh were already landing forces someplace on this world for a counterattack.

And there was Crawford, the only man he recognized on the work detail.

"Seaman Crawford!" Wyckham walked over to him in a show of respect. "My deepest thanks. Once again you've made a very timely effort on my behalf. I owe you much, but right now, I must ask you to take over this work detail. Mr. Jones is headed to the orlop and will not return for a while. Do you think you can follow the instructions these ladies will give you in operating this device? Our returning home depends upon it."

The floating balls of light were turning back into female human forms, presumably to communicate more easily with the crewmen. At least they had clothes on. Crawford's eyes lit up as he watched stunning women float down to the ground about him.

"Aye, sor, you ken count on me t' work…ah…closely…wit 'r lady friends 'ere." He was barely able to talk as the pulchritude surrounded him. The sight was almost too much for the weathered seaman, who hadn't been ashore for months. Clearly, Crawford was recalling how they looked naked; he had been there when they first arrived. *What the hell*, Wyckham thought. *Let the man ogle the image of my first love.* After today, he certainly deserved what for him was probably the best work detail in naval history.

The room needed to be cleaned up so work could begin. "Sergeant O'Malley! Let's get your men to work here removing prisoners and corpses. Where's Sergeant O'Malley?"

The corporal who had escorted them in walked over and saluted, knuckle to his forehead. "Fallen, sah! Stabbed from behind by a crab right after ee threw yah th' grenadoe, sah!"

Wyckham went silent upon hearing the sobering news. He never even had the chance to thank the man for saving his life. But he brightened up when he saw Midshipman Moore, who had put on that sterling display of sword-fighting skill. He still had that sword and was supervising some sailors who were trying to tie up the wounded Krag for Lady Brashton to interrogate. The first one they approached had a crushed leg, but it still lashed out with its long claw at anyone who came close. Moore shook his head and moved up close in that dancing *en garde* of his until the thrashing creature glanced at another sailor for a moment. With a sudden jump-lunge, Moore closed the distance and bashed the crabman on the head with the flat of his blade.

"Did you enjoy that? Want to get knighted again, you foolish little crustacean?" he quipped, waving his weapon in front of the stunned Krag's face. Clearly having no interest in becoming a peer of the realm, the creature put up no further resistance and was promptly tied up. The rest of the watching Krag quickly decided that they, too, were not interested in knighthoods and submitted meekly.

Wyckham walked up to the young officer as he sheathed the sword. "Mr. Moore, congratulations on some brilliant fighting. Where could you possibly have learned to handle a sword like that?"

"My older brother attended Haversham, sir, same as you," he replied. "He was on their fencing team. When he came home, he taught me all he knew. Taught me too much, I'm afraid. I developed a bouncing stance, was faster than him, too, and ended up beating him every time. So when that marine corporal fell, I grabbed his sword and jumped into the fight."

Wyckham couldn't help but notice that the boy had suddenly lost his stutter. A courageous fight often turned a boy into a man; clearly, this young man had earned a lot more self-confidence today. He'd probably matured ten years over the last fifteen minutes.

Captain Donnelson walked up and addressed Wyckham. "No need for you here, sir. We've got four hundred marines already deployed in makeshift fortifications around this cave, and the ladies are safely at work on the portal device. My compliments to Admiral O'Neal, and I'll report back aboard in another hour or so."

Wyckham did need to report back to his commanding officer. "Well, I must go. But I was quite impressed, Mr. Moore. Our admiral will hear of your bravery and skill. Depend on it!"

As he left, he saw Larkin's gruesome body on the floor. It was too horrible for Wyckham to examine any closer. The man had been at his side for years and had died trying to protect his captain. Wyckham turned away before tears filled his eyes in front of the men.

Donnelson was arranging parties to get the wounded out to the beach and clear the room of enemy corpses. Wyckham left to emerge onto the victorious scene on the beach. Once outside, he felt better, his head clearing in the bright sun, and his nostrils breathing clean air instead of the rotten stink of those crabmen in close quarters.

The beach was a beehive of activity. Marines were digging redoubts and felling trees to construct a perimeter wall. Sailors were moving supplies ashore and heaping Krag corpses onto a pile for burning. Ship's barges had already started moving some of *Zeus's* guns ashore for mounting in the redoubts. In a few hours, the area would be a fairly defensible base.

The captain's gig was on the beach, ready for a quick row out to the anchored *Righteous*. As they approached, his boat was hailed to establish how big a side party to line up. Just because there'd just been a battle with monsters on another planet didn't mean the Royal Navy would forget its manners. The coxswain raised four fingers indicating a post captain was in the boat. Wyckham was quickly piped aboard by a line of officers and crewmen and then greeted by an excited O'Neal.

"By God, man, what happened in that cave? Clearly there was a hot fight in there. I'd thought everything looked done; everyone on the beach was standing down. Then all of a sudden, I hear some shooting, and I see half the marines on the beach running into that cave, loading muskets and fixing bayonets as they ran. Now I hear you were in there and have quite a story to tell! Let's hear it, man!"

Wyckham smiled at his old mentor. "My admiral, of course I will recount every detail. But has your recent promotion caused you to forget the good manners expected of a Royal Navy officer? Shouldn't such a report be done in your cabin? Maybe over a glass?"

O'Neal smiled and motioned toward his cabin. "My God, of course, what was I thinking? What's happened to me? Apparently the promotion to admiral has turned me into a gossip-mongerer, just like the lowest scullery maid. Please accept my deepest apologies. But I suppose character flaws and rudeness come with the job; mayhap soon I'll be another Jarvis?"

Grinning, they went below to sip brandy poured by O'Neal's steward. Wyckham went over everything that had happened in the cave, going into particular detail when he described looking down into the Draesh's gaping mouth—not a vision he was likely to ever forget. O'Neal tensed with concern when he heard the Draesh could speak English and had gotten other significant intelligence from a missing allied energy being.

Lieutenant Rawlins and the other three ship captains came in and reported, each with their own butcher's bill provided by dispatches from shore. Altogether, the squadron had suffered only seventeen dead sailors and thirty-two wounded. Many of the dead and wounded came from the fight in the cave.

They all sat down and made plans for the base. Through the stern windows, Wyckham saw a jury-rigged *Zeus* with a temporary foremast getting warped into the cove. She would be careened on the beach to repair the holes in the hull that loose cannons had made when the ship breached. All her heavy thirty-two-pounder long guns would be offloaded and placed in the fortifications being built on shore. Following traditional navy doctrine for protecting beached ships, O'Neal also ordered several guns to be hoisted up to the tops of the nearby hills and mounted in additional redoubts.

Captain Harrison arrived to the acclamation of all present. O'Neal's steward poured him a glass as O'Neal proposed a toast to "Our new American ally." Everyone pressed him for a description of the battle he had just witnessed from his hilltop perch.

"Those mortars did right pretty work. There was a bunch of crabs right in the center makin' a big ruckus—musta been their officer core. Damned if the first shot from *Vesuvius* didn't blow up right above em, turned em all into crab stew."

Young Randolf beamed, as Grimwald scowled and shot him a nasty glance. "A minute later a shot from *Hedgehog* hit the ground right in the middle of em, and the stampede began. They started inland, but another round from *Vesuvius* landed right in the far end of the valley where they were headed. Its fuse musta been long 'cause it didn't explode right away; it started rollin' back down the trail toward the whole lot of em. You shoulda seen those buggers all turn around right quick and run like hell back toward the beach! Then after you gave em a right good thrashing there, they finally turned back up the valley again and headed inland. Thankfully, only a few came up the hill for us to deal with. And as much as I've always hated your goddamn marines, they sure stood fast up there and kept my boys safe. I think you lost three of em with a couple more wounded. They were brave men."

Finally Marine Fleet Captain Warren arrived and was also toasted. Despite losing twenty-two men with twenty-seven wounded, he was rightfully proud of his marines. They had maintained their tradition of fighting discipline, even in the face of a new and savage foe.

O'Neal finally put an end to the impromptu celebration and issued additional orders for settling into their new base. All the captains retired to various duties ashore or back on their ships.

As O'Neal was headed ashore to survey the field and manage the building of the fortifications, he gave everyone a final word. "If Captain Wyckham will grant me the use of his cabin tonight, I invite you all to dine aboard *Righteous* at eight bells. Don't worry about the fare, Rod. I'll break into the food locker on *Zeus* and bring my own cook over. But might I ask you to invite your Lady Brashton and those of her party she seems fit to bring along as well? As our allies, they must be offered... ah...every courtesy."

Wyckham nodded with a smirk and headed up on deck to return to the beach. As his gig scraped the sand, he saw Lady Brashton heading toward him while several of her fellow beings emerged from the cave. The others were still in light form and floated up and out to sea.

As he watched, he saw that another line of square portals had appeared two cables or so above the water about five miles off. Then the air erupted with a giant boom and a huge silver shape came flying through at incredible speed. It quickly slowed down so that Wyckham could make out details. It looked like a sterling plate that had been stretched, amorphous in shape, all edges rounded, like a blob of molten silver. A huge orange flame was roaring out of the stern. There were blinking red lights on its edges and oval details on its sides.

As Wyckham watched in growing alarm, those ovals turned dark. Then strange-looking glowing rods emerged and pointed right at him. Wyckham gasped in alarm. He had faced gunports opening on all types of foreign ships; there was no need to guess what this was. The whole squadron was about to get blasted by this unknown foe! Christ, the Draesh have beaten our allies here and gotten a gunship in. God knew what its weapons were capable of. Confirming his worst fears, beams of intense blue light issued from the thing, hitting the water surface, which violently erupted in steam. The beams quickly started moving toward the beachhead and the assembled sailors and marines. They would sweep the beach in just a few moments. Clearly, they produced intense heat and were about to vaporize everyone ashore instantly.

Then, just as the light beam got within a half mile of the beach, it disappeared! The ship stopped about a quarter mile from one of the ladies, who were still in light form floating in the air. Did their female-form allies have the power to stop such a craft?

Lady Brashton walked up, beaming. "Wonderful news! We were lucky enough to encounter an alliance scout vehicle with the first portal we opened. It is manned by physical beings that you would see as wolflike, but we know them as fellow warriors dedicated to eliminating the universal threat of the Draesh. After we explain our plans to them, hopefully we can quickly transport them to the League headquarters so the forces we will need for the final battle with the Draesh can be assembled for transport here."

"They're our allies?" Wyckham asked. "It looked to me like they were going to roast us all with that hellish heat weapon!"

"Yes, there was a moment of confusion when they first arrived. They realized they had been transported to the Draesh home world and came in 'with guns blazing,' as you would say. But we quickly contacted them through their ships' electrical communication devices. They recognized us, and we quickly convinced them that those they saw here were allies. Hopefully you will be able to meet them before they leave."

Of course they had to meet. "Well, I would hope so. We all have to coordinate our plans for continuing the fight," Wyckham stated bluntly.

Lady Brashton hesitated before responding. "Captain, we are all so thankful for what you have done for us here. But now it is time for our Allied League of Planets to carry the fight to the enemy. Please understand that the coming battle will be different from anything you have ever imagined. The display of weaponry from the ship that has just arrived is nothing compared to what will be loosed during the actual fight. Huge fighting ships will be arriving that dwarf the scout ship that is here now. The battle will be fought by forces at great distances from each other, far out of the range of your human vision, not to mention your weapons. And the weapons about to be used by both sides have incredible destructive power. They can vaporize an entire mountain in a single moment."

She moved closer and put a hand on his arm. "The intergalactic forces of goodness and decency are deeply indebted to you for what you have done so far. But now is the time for more advanced civilizations to take over the fight if we are to end the Draesh scourge. You can contribute more to the effort, but not by further fighting with your ships." As she said this, she looked him straight in the eye and smiled brightly.

Before he had a chance to inquire what she meant by this, one of her fellow glowing balls floated up and apparently communicated with her. Lady Brashton then explained she had to leave him to go aboard the recently arrived ship to meet with the newcomers. Wyckham quickly invited her to the dinner that night, to which she beamed an acceptance as she, too, turned into a ball of light and floated off.

The following hours kept Wyckham busy back aboard *Righteous* with the usual tasks to be attended to after a battle. The wounded had to be visited, promotions had to be made to replace casualties among the warrants, and ammunition stocks needed review. As he was assessing the dwindling food stocks with Rames, the ship's purser, a bewitching scent of cooking food wafted into his cabin.

"What's that wonderful aroma I smell?" Wyckham asked aloud. "Has O'Neal's cook arrived already? Damn, I haven't even told our cook to be prepared for tonight."

"No sir, he's not arrived yet," said the purser. "What you're smelling is actually our lads cooking up a crab feast on the beach. Turns out our dead foes make for an excellent meal. I plan to cook up a bunch of them and put them in *Righteous*'s food locker. I'll save you some claws, sir— they're quite meaty."

Wyckham's brows went high, not knowing what to make of this latest assault on decency. *Jesus, now my men are eating our foes?* Well, you could always expect British tars to do anything for a fresh meal after weeks of bully beef and hardtack. One daring soul must have tried cooking Krag, and that was all it took. Hopefully they weren't all going to be sick in a few hours. He made a mental note to have the surgeon check on the crew's health tonight.

But he had to see what was going on. Stepping up on deck, he could see cooking fires all over the beach. Work had halted for the day. Several groups danced around men playing flutes or sat, singing bawdy seamen's songs. God bless them—it was a party they deserved. They'd just won a fight in a strange world against a foe unlike anything they had never faced before. Not only had ordinary men like these carved out a huge empire for England, here they had possibly just saved the entire planet Earth from destruction.

He turned back to the purser. "Mr. Rames, let's get a double grog ration on the beach in time for the crew's dinner. God knows they've earned it."

Rames left as seven bells chimed out from the binnacle. Time to get back below and get cleaned up for dinner. Wyckham suddenly realized he needed to appoint a new steward if he wanted a proper toilet and help getting dressed. It was hard to accept, but after years of devoted service, his steward Larkin was gone. But then the perfect choice to replace him just happened to walk by.

It was Obujimi, the freed African slave who spoke English like a royal secretary. The man certainly had lots of experience in service, he'd probably arranged many formal balls at the Virginia mansion he'd managed. He'd make the perfect valet.

"Landsman Obujimi—a word if you will." The man had been aboard less than a year and still held the rank of landsman, the lowest rank for enlisted men. He stopped his task of returning weapons to the arms locker and walked up to the captain, crisply knuckling his forehead. Wyckham got to the point. "Sadly, my steward did not survive the day, and I am in need of a new man. Would you be interested in accepting the position? While I'm sure being close to me will be quite unpleasant, as my steward you will have first crack at leftovers from the captain's table, not to mention access to soap and all my toiletries, and some clean and proper uniforms. What say you?"

Obujimi's face lit up like a chandelier. It was as if a disinherited noble had been invited back into his family. After months of chewing tough dried beef and banging hardtack rolls on the table to get the weevils out, the thought of decent food must be overwhelming for one who once took his meals in a mansion's kitchen. Plus, if the man really had been a prince of his tribe, he would have been regularly bathed in scented waters and dressed in ornate finery, routines he must miss.

He bowed eagerly, making a formal leg. "I accept your most gracious offer and will work extremely hard to be an excellent valet for you. Frankly, sir, I've noticed your raiment to be a bit lacking for a man of your position. Though the task of making you presentable may seem a Herculean task, rest assured, I will bring you up to snuff."

Why the gall of the man! Damn cheeky already! Well, he'd been a majordomo in Virginia plantation society,that would infuse arrogance in any man. And Wyckham needed help right now, clearly Obujimi was the man for the position. This was certainly no time to be training some deckhand in the use of toiletries and maintaining his captain's uniforms.

"All right then, let's put your plans to the test, "he managed with a smile." I've a dinner to prepare for, and I don't believe a uniform covered in alien blood will be very appropriate. Let's get below and see what miracles you can work."

They went below to his newly improvised cabin. O'Neal had moved into the *Righteous*'s great cabin, but a decent one had been partitioned off from the officers' quarters for Wyckham. Obujimi surveyed Wyckham's toiletries with a sneer but soon brought him a basin of hot water for a thorough scrub and a skillful shave. He then efficiently got Wyckham dressed in his formal uniform: tan breeches, white stockings, a silvered waistcoat, white silk shirt and stock, and a white lace cravat. Lastly, he helped Wyckham into his freshly brushed formal blue coat with the two epaulets signifying post captain.

Finally, Obujimi strapped on his sword and handed him his bicorn hat, which he put on his head "fore and aft" in the new style instead of the traditional sideways placement. Wyckham believed that British naval officers were changing the way they wore their hats because portraits of Napoleon had been circulated with the French Emperor wearing his ridiculously ornate hat sideways. No British officer wanted to look remotely like the "Little Corsican Ogre."

Before eight bells, he was on deck to greet the arriving dinner party. O'Neal joined him to do the same, something Jarvis had never done on the rare occasions he entertained aboard ship. Thank God, they had a decent, reasonable leader during these unbelievable events. They'd all be dead by now if Jarvis were still in command.

One by one, gigs were hailed, and their officers piped aboard in order of seniority. The last boat was a barge with several of the ladies on board. Everyone stared in rapt attention as they were brought aboard one by one in the bosun's chair. Wyckham had advised them to appear in human form and had them brought on deck in the chairs according to standard navy practice for bringing women aboard ship. It just wouldn't do to have a bunch of glowing blobs flying onto a Royal Navy ship for dinner.

But he hadn't advised them to dress the way they did. Obviously, they had probed some officer's mind (maybe his?) and seen how royalty dressed for a palace ball. There were eight of them, all attired in magnificent white gowns of taffeta and silk. Their hair was piled high upon their heads with beribboned curls dangling about their ears. And all wore jewelry of varied styles, from strings of pearls to magnificent diamonds.

But jewelry wasn't what the officers present were staring at. Each of the ladies sported an incredible display of *décolletage*. Every one of them had breasts bulging up nigh to her chin, pushed up by magical contraptions made of stays and wires. Wyckham wondered if their leader, his Lady Brashton, wasn't behind all this display.

But Wyckham himself had to try hard not to stare—couldn't have the crew see their captain wide-eyed like a young midshipman at his first ball. Members of the better classes at a dinner party just didn't ogle women's breasts with their mouths agape. *Get it together, man! Remind yourself that nothing you are seeing is real; it's just another crazy vision in this strange adventure you're on.*

But his heart beat faster as a smiling Lady Brashton walked up to him and took his arm to head below. Real or not, she was ravishing. Her blonde hair was held in place with a ruby-studded gold band, her face powdered, her cheeks rouged, and an adorable beauty mark had been painted to the starboard side of her mouth. Dangling about her magnificent breasts was a string of diamonds that put the crown jewels to shame.

Wyckham also noted that the other ladies had walked directly up to various officers as if they knew each other. Then he realized that they did. These officers greeted their partners by name, though some had trouble speaking because they were so astonished.

O'Neal greeted a stunning redhead. "By God! Cathleen! You're here! And look at you!" He should have said, "And look at these teats!" because that's what he was staring at directly, his eyes almost out of their sockets.

As Wyckham reached the gangway, a commotion broke out behind him. He turned to see Lieutenant Rawlins and Commander Hamilton of *Scamp* nose to nose as the raven-haired Catherine Burford stood to one side. Shite, they were arguing over her companionship for the evening! He'd seen this coming. Catherine Burford was Rawlins's fiancée back on Earth, but she had accompanied Hamilton in *Scamp* on its scouting mission. A furious glance from O'Neal stopped the bickering. Commander Hamilton extended his arm to the lady, looked at Rawlins, and sneered, "Excuse me, *Lieutenant*," and walked below with the lady. Rawlins turned his back and stormed off, hopefully to get himself settled down.

Now Lady Brashton stopped, her head tilted like a dog listening to its master. "Captain, your earlier wish can be accommodated. One of our new allies who came in on that scout ship will be left here as a liaison and would like to meet the commanders of your force. May I invite him to join us now? He can be here momentarily."

Wyckham cleared it with O'Neal. The lady sent out some sort of magical message, and everyone turned toward shore to search for a boat. Instead, they saw and heard a small silver vehicle emerge from the hovering scout craft and fly through the air toward them. Sailors nearby were grabbing some pikes, which were still on deck, getting ready to repel boarders.

Wyckham quickly yelled out, "*Righteous,* belay that. This is a new ally coming aboard. Put those pikes back!"

Lieutenant Clifton, in command of the deck, looked quizzically at Wyckham. "Ah, sir, do we pipe him aboard? And with how large a side party?"

Good question. What was the accepted side party to greet a wolf coming on board? To be smart it should be two men with cocked pistols. *Now, Wyckham, be civil with foreign officers.* "I don't know. Ah, call him an ambassador–four men should do," he told Clifton. "Give him a show."

Clifton turned to the bosun on watch. "You heard the captain, Mr. Greaves. Hail the…uh…boat?"

But before the bosun could get out a word, the small flying craft was above them, slowly setting down toward the deck, a soft humming sound filling the air about them. Only about fifteen feet long, it, too, was silver and seamless, though there was clearly a glass viewport on its bow. When it was about ten feet above the deck, a rectangular panel on the bottom opened up, a mechanical stairway unfolded, and out walked their latest ally in this crazy, unpredictable world.

This creature did look like a wolf in some respects. It had a canine jaw, and its face was covered in gray-brown fur. But it had a human physique—it was dressed head-to-toe in a shiny metallic suit, it had hands, and it walked upright. There was some strange stringed device strapped to its head, and other small devices were mounted on its belt. And it was big, probably six feet tall and ten stone in weight.

The flying gig retracted its magical stairway and flew off on its own as the thing walked up to Wyckham. There was a moment of embarrassing silence. What the hell was he supposed to do now—throw it a bone? But damned if it didn't start talking in English!

"Greetings to the humans from Earth." Its voice was raspy and sounded like it was coming from a cave. "We welcome you to our alliance. Together may we tear the accursed Draesh to bits and dine on their livers. You are Wyckham. Which of you is the commander O'Neal? My name is…*Rahrrr.*"

Up until the last word, the fellow's mouth hadn't opened; all the speech was coming from the device on its head. But it spoke its name through its own mouth, though it just sounded like a goddamn growl to Wyckham.

Lady Brashton, in her formal gown with its surging bustline, approached Mr. Growl. Wyckham suspected that underneath the silver suit, the wolf's tail was wagging. After some kind of silent communication with the canine ambassador, she turned to Wyckham. "As you see, he can communicate in English using the translating device on his head. All the mass-based civilizations fighting the Draesh with us use these to communicate with each other. My own race helped with the electrical programming in these translators."

An electrically powered program could translate the wolf's language into English? Wyckham had no idea what kind of program she was talking about. Were they all actors in some otherworldly theater, and she wrote its program? Anyway, the wolfman could understand him. Better be polite. He bowed.

"Welcome aboard His Majesty's frigate *Righteous.* I am Rodney Wyckham, its captain. Allow me to introduce the squadron's commanding officer, Admiral Sean O'Neal."

O'Neal walked up, made a leg, and welcomed the new ally. Mr. Growl just stood there in silence. Well, at least he didn't walk around behind the admiral and sniff his arse. Finally, it spoke in that the raspy voice through the translating device.

"Forgive me. I was receiving background information from the energy being you call Lady Brashton. I congratulate you on your recent courageous victory and thank you for the invitation to join your dinner celebration. You have opened the door for the Allied League of Planets to invade this world and given my race the chance of final victory over the depravations of the Draesh. I feel honored to be here with you and your brave men."

"You are more than welcome, sir," O'Neal replied. "We hope you find the evening enjoyable. I'm sure it will be informative for both of us. After dinner, I would be happy to give you a tour of this ship. But might I ask what we should call you? I'm afraid we would do a rather poor job of attempting to pronounce your name in your own language. Is there an appellation in English you would feel comfortable with?"

"Please feel free to call me whatever makes sense to you," the wolf-man replied.

"Just call him 'Vulfe.'" Heads turned to see where that suggestion had come from. It was Shroeder, the Prussian surgeon. Like all other officers and warrants, he was permitted on deck during state formalities, just restricted to the forecastle.

"Das ist un namen uff honor in my country," he said. "Many nobles unt varriors mit dis namen haf bin great Prussian leaders. Ve all velcome Vulfe," he finished with a snap to attention and a click of his heels together. Cheers of "We all welcome Wolfe!" went up from all the men assembled forward.

"Yes, I understand." Their visitor nodded and actually seemed to smile at the cheering crew. "Wulfe is the right name for me in your language. Wulfe it shall be." And damned if the creature didn't bow and extend a leg as well as any baron attending court at Westminster! Lady Brashton had prepared him well.

"Then Wulfe it is," beamed O'Neal. "Now let's all proceed below— I believe dinner is served."

As guest of honor, the wolf walked below with O'Neal and headed toward *Righteous*'s great cabin. Wyckham just hoped the goodam thing was housetrained.

8

A MOST UNUSUAL DINNER PARTY

Righteous's stern cabin had been opened up to accommodate the large group. Her two nine-pound stern chasers had been removed and some dividing partitions knocked down. White linen tablecloths, fine china, and elaborate silver candelabras from Jarvis's locker aboard *Zeus* had been placed over some crude table extensions that the carpenter Jones had quickly made up. O'Neal's new steward had even potted some large arrangements of the local flora to decorate the table. Hopefully the damn things wouldn't snap at them during dinner.

Wulfe and the being in the image of O'Neal's Cathleen sat on the admiral's left and right. The admiral immediately became engrossed in conversation with them about Wulfe's flying ship. Wyckham sat to the lady's left, with Lady Brashton to his right, followed by the other captains and commanders in order of seniority, the ladies interspersed between them. Marine officers and navy lieutenants with their own female companions sat on the opposite side. Some sat alone, including Lieutenant Rawlins, who was giving Hamilton a murderous look as he sat next to Catherine Burford.

When the steward had finished pouring everyone a glass of a sweet western French white wine (borrowed from Jarvis's locker), O'Neal rose to propose the first toast.

"Ladies and gentlemen, lift your glasses to yourselves. Today, a great victory, in which you all participated, has not only protected our entire planet Earth, I understand, but the worlds of many other good peoples. To our further success! Confusion to the Draesh!"

All the officers echoed "Confusion to the Draesh!" and emptied their glasses, including Wulfe, who seemed familiar with spirits. The ladies sipped demurely at their drinks and again appeared quite delighted with the experience. The assembled officers kept the stewards busy pouring refills.

Soon the first course arrived: steamed local clams which the surgeon Shroeder had declared wholesome to consume (after demanding a few from the cook's pots for himself). Sailors on the beach had been harvesting them and eating them along with Krag parts. Of course, there would be no crabman parts on the table tonight. British officers simply did not eat their vanquished foes.

A plate of clams was placed in front of Donnelson, *Righteous*'s marine captain, who was seated directly across from Wyckham. Then, as he reached for his first clam, so did a tall purple flower in the vase on the table! It bent over, closing its flower petals on the meat in the open clamshell, and then it straightened up and swallowed the clam's meat like a feeding shore bird! Wyckham could see the bulge in its stem where the clam was lodged.

After a stunned moment, the assembled officers exploded in laughter. "I say, Captain, you defeated giant demons today, but you cannot defend your dinner from a poaching posy?" bellowed Fleet Captain Warren on Donnelson's right, almost falling from his chair with laughter. More chuckling and japes at Donnelson's expense filled the room.

But the flower must have enjoyed that clam, because damn if it wasn't reaching for another! Cries of "Defend your feed!" and "An affront from a common flora! Call him out, Donnelson!" erupted from the room. Donnelson got into the spirit and pointed his fork at the descending flower. "*En garde*, you thieving cutpurse!" he yelled with excessive martial emphasis. "No posy can steal dinner from a royal marine without a fight!"

To the delight of the party, the flower didn't give up. Delicately steamed clams in wine sauce must be worth fighting for; the plant had probably never had such a treat. It feinted left, then lunged around the fork's right for a quick stab at another clam. But Donnelson was there with the parry, swatting the flower's open jaws aside with the *forte* of his utensil, then riposted toward the plant's stem with a loud "*Et là!*" But the posy had quickly spun behind a docile daisy, resulting in the poor thing being skewered by Donnelson's *riposte*, despite not having committed any offense at all. Roars of disapproval erupted from the watching officers. "Oh, foul play, posy, most foully done! Hiding behind your own second!" Others were apparently concerned for the daisy's survival. "Summon the surgeon!"

That put an end to the posy's offensive. Having seen the unfortunate daisy bent in half, with fork holes in its stem, the posy wisely retreated deep into the vase, hiding in the maze of stems and leaves. But most of the officers, well into their cups, went wild. "*Bon touché,* Donnelson!" his fellow marines shouted. But the navy officers yelled out, "Not fair! Get the worthy opponent a blade!" and started throwing forks to the unarmed posy, several hitting the vase with a ringing clank. *Better watch it,* thought Wyckham. *I'll wager some of those forks just fell into that vase, and at any moment a whole bunch of well-armed flowers might leap out onto the table, form up, and make off with the whole next course!*

Lady Brashton leaned over and spoke, her voice a warning. "Captain, I suggest you and your colleagues take care around those purple blooms. Contact with their petals will give you an extremely painful rash of large red pustules that ooze for days. I certainly wouldn't want you feeling ill on this, your night for…celebration." And with that, Wyckham felt her ankle suggestively brush his calf! Just the kind of parlor game the real Lady Brashton had often played when toying with him years ago.

O'Neal was unaware of the shenanigans under the table, but he had overheard the lady's warning. He addressed all his officers.

"Gentlemen, enough! We best let our noble adversary be. The lady here says these blooms are quite poxy. Let's get the bloody things away from our dinner. Sentry!"

Jovialities ceased as smiles turned to expressions of alarm, and the nearby officers rapidly pushed their chairs back from the now-threatening flowers. The cabin door banged open, and a red-coated marine sentry took one step into the room, stamping to attention.

"Sah!" A resounding crash followed as his musket butt hit the floor.

"Sentry, be so kind as to escort this rowdy visitor from the room," said O'Neal as he shoved the vase forward. But the bewildered marine was looking about the room, assuming he was to remove some drunken human reveler. O'Neal shook his head, grinning at the absurdity of it all. "Private, this is the offender right here in this vase, the purple one. I suggest you hold him at a distance. He's fast, and if he touches you he'll give you a nasty pox." As if it heard its name, the purple bloom slowly rose up and peeked out from the middle of the arrangement.

For the first time in his life, Wyckham saw real fear in the face of a British marine. Fear of the unfamiliar, fear of the black magic on this world, but mostly fear of failing at a task he wasn't trained for: conquering a poxy flower that had been attacking officers. What did his admiral want him to do with the thing? He stood motionless, overwhelmed with indecision.

O'Neal prodded him to action. "Private, for God's sake, just dump it over the side." The rest of the room disagreed loudly. "Don't let the posy off so easily, Captain Donnelson! Demand satisfaction! Pistols on the gun deck at dawn! That red petunia can be his second!"

Shouldering his musket, the marine slowly lifted the vase from the table, held it at arm's length, and headed toward the door, eyes wide in fear. Several young marine lieutenants were in a dress line, knuckles to their foreheads. "You who are about to die, we salute you!" they all shouted in unison, then snapped their arms crisply back to their sides. The laughter slowly subsided as the ill-mannered flower headed for a swim.

A marine lieutenant stepped up with glass held high. "A toast to our captain! What a brilliant display of fencing technique, sir! Your handwork was blindingly fast, yet always controlled. No wonder that vicious brute ran off and hid."

Other marines voiced their approval of their commander's incredible fencing abilities. "Hear, hear!" They emptied their glasses, then immediately searched for a steward with a full bottle.

Donnelson waved to his worshippers and nodded in gracious humility as the praise was poured on. "Aye, he was a dangerous opponent. But now he knows not to cross blades with a Donnelson!"

Then he looked at Wyckham. "But I've heard there is one aboard *Righteous* that I really wouldn't want to cross blades with. Captain Wyckham, I understand you had a midshipman named Moore putting on quite a show in that cave? Some marines who watched him fight inside the cave have told me he was like an artist with a blade, just too fast and smooth for those buggers. Dropped several attackers and then dueled with their officer, finally thrusting his point right through the neck joint in the crabman's shell."

"Yes, he surprised the hell out of me, too," acknowledged Wyckham. "I must say I've never seen anyone fence like that. He was light on his feet like a dancer, constantly moving, keeping his knees bent at all times so he could spring forward or backward. When he lunged, he must have traveled ten feet—his back leg just shot him forward. He said his brother was in the fencing club at Haversham and taught him how to fence on holidays. Said he ended up consistently beating his brother with his speed and constant movement."

Donnelson smacked the table. "I knew he had to be related! His brother, Brent Moore, was the best fencer Haversham ever had—graceful, smart, and very fast. I saw him in competition several times. He was superb. And this younger brother was better? I'm amazed."

"I was amazed as well," said Wyckham. "His footwork was lightning quick; he just danced around the enemy." Certainly Moore had shown himself to be a real asset in a fight. Wyckham made a mental note to keep close to Moore in any future scrap in this wild hell they were in.

Calm had returned to the table as the second course arrived: freshly killed mutton in mint sauce with roast potatoes. How sad that

Jarvis's livestock pen on *Zeus* had to be cleaned out when the ship was careened.

Wyckham motioned for another refill. He had to admit that naval camaraderie like this had become special to him. While he had joined the navy to impress his family by achieving fame and recognition, he now took pride in being a part of the Royal Navy, with its traditions and fellowship. Here they were, thrown into conflict in a distant, magical world, fighting to save everything in God's creation, and they were winning, thanks to good old British discipline, tactics, and the stout hearts of oak that crewed the British navy. A warm feeling pervaded his soul, assisted by his fourth glass of wine.

A steady stream of officers took their turns standing up and proposing toasts. Warren, Donnelson, Harrison, and Wyckham himself were toasted for various acts of valor during the day's conflict. Notably absent were toasts to "King and Country." No one here was fighting for King George anymore. All the officers realized that if they did make it back to England, the royal court would never believe what they'd done. They might even put everyone in front of an Admiralty board for mutiny; Jarvis would do his best to see that happen.

Toasting ended for the moment as O'Neal became absorbed in a discussion with Wulfe about flying a ship through the heavens. Wyckham relaxed and sat back, reaching contentedly for his glass. But a suggestive touch to his calf by Lady Brashton put him on full alert. He'd better start some conversation to avoid a public lapse of control.

"So, tell me, Madam, how is it you knew that flower was dangerous? Can you read the minds of plants as well?"

"Yes, I can, though there would be nothing there to read about rashes since these plants have no awareness of what their touch can do. The nature of that plant's toxin came from the minds of the Draesh and Krag that I have surveyed. They had very clear memories of the rash that the flowers cause."

Wyckham shifted uncomfortably in his chair, again made aware that this woman here could look into minds. Hopefully, she wasn't seeing his carnal thoughts concerning her that the wine had brought on. *Better change his thoughts!*

"So, are you enjoying the wine? I'm curious. Does the wine affect your mind and give you the same feelings of gaiety that we experience?"

"Well, of course not," said the lady. "The human brain's interaction with alcohol does not occur with us. But we are an inquisitive people, and we learn much from having experiences in physical worlds. By creating certain pulses of energy to our own minds, we mimic the same feelings in ourselves as you get from drinking wine."

The way she was looking invitingly at Wyckham also confirmed she was having the same thoughts as human women often did when drinking wine. Similar thoughts had been storming through Wyckham's mind for a while. Better think of another engaging topic for discussion to get himself under proper control. Maybe he should enter a deep discussion about cricket?

But the lady was one step ahead of him. "Captain, isn't it customary for men and women to couple together after drinking alcohol at a party like this? Excuse me for my ignorance of your customs, but have we drunk enough now to engage in intercourse?"

Old Grimwald on his right immediately gagged and sprayed a mouthful of wine across the table. *Christ, he'd heard the lady's bold invitation!* Wyckham was frozen in his chair. He had no idea how he should respond—though he damn sure knew how he wanted to respond!

"Yes," said a fetching blonde from across the table. "I was wondering when the sexual coupling would start. We know that you have certain customs to be followed, which are difficult for us to understand, and we do not wish to do anything improper. But will we have sex with you tonight? We've all been looking forward to it so much. It will be very helpful to our cause, and we would all enjoy the new experience immensely."

"What do you mean, 'helpful to the cause'?" said a shocked Grimwald. "What balderdash! I've never heard of such a lascivious proposition draped in patriotism! How will promiscuous behaviour help the cause? I suppose rutting like deckhands in port will spur the troops on to victory?"

"Please let me explain to you all," said Lady Brashton, standing and addressing the entire group. "The Draesh are not the only beings who gain power by consuming the electrical force of a physical life. We can do the same. Of course, we do not destroy entire civilizations for our own benefit as the Draesh do. But the life force of physical beings is very useful to us. And the amount of physical life you discharge during your orgasms is astonishing—what is it?—thirty million living cells each time? That is often more than the Draesh get by devouring entire worlds. It would provide us with great resources for our conflict. And if that many life cells were given to us, we would certainly find some unique beings with new types of energy which could be invaluable to us in the coming battle. Why not give these life cells to us? Typically, you just leave them all on your bed linens to die anyway, as you do almost every night, Captain Grimwald."

Wyckham forced himself not to laugh aloud as Grimwald sat stunned that his nocturnal masturbation habits had just been revealed to all at a formal dinner party. Several younger officers were snorting and coughing, hiding their own laughter. But the senior officers were all still stunned and speechless by what they'd just heard from their ally. None dared even move, but they all were trying to sneak glances sideways at their superiors. In all their excited glances, Wyckham could read their desperate plea: *For God's sake, let us accommodate the ladies!*

The silence seemed to exasperate Lady Brashton further. "I must say I don't understand your hesitation. We see very clearly in your memories that instances of coupling with women have been among the highlights of your entire lives. And your sperm contributions would be of great benefit to defeating the Draesh. I am aware that there are certain rituals to be followed in coupling, but I must say they baffle me. Can someone here give me guidance as to what would be the correct thing for us to do next?"

Plenty of officers knew exactly what they wanted next. They wanted to have an orgy right now! But none had the courage to say it. Everyone was looking at O'Neal. Commanding officers had to lead. Everyone wondered what he was thinking.

O'Neal sat there, quite muddled by drink, stroking his chin, occasionally glancing at Cathleen to his right. He wasn't capable right now of giving his opinion on anything, much less his blessing to start the most improper and outrageous event in the history of the British navy. Well, it was probably better that way. British officers just didn't have dinner orgies along with their admiral while on duty aboard ship.

Finally O'Neal's flag captain, Terhughes, who did not imbibe, stood up. "Ladies, you do not understand the character and discretion of British sea officers. What you are requesting would be acceptable only to the lowest sorts; we are members of a better class of people. I suggest we end the evening now and keep our contacts in the future focused on doing what we must do to get this squadron home."

The hair on Wyckham's neck bristled. He was too drunk to endure this shite from some high and mighty squire's son. *Christ, a captain for one day and he's in charge of everyone's morality?* Even if it was the proper course to take, he resented some young upstart lecturing them all on the proper way for the better classes to behave. Enough of the Jarvises in the British navy!

And besides that, he realized, he wanted to put a leg over this gorgeous image in front of him right now! To hell with what his family and everyone else back in England would think. He was in a dangerous foreign world, fighting for the salvation of all mankind, and now it was time to be rewarded for his efforts!

He turned to Lady Brashton. "Madam, sometimes it is up to the lady to take the first step to begin the mating ritual. Why don't you ladies all just get things started? I suggest you and I take up exactly where we were in my cabin last night when matters were interrupted."

"Wonderful!" she replied. As everyone watched in amazement, Lady Brashton floated up into the air and turned to face him. Her dress magically disappeared, and there she was, attired in only a white corset and silk stockings, descending onto his lap.

The other ladies all gleefully followed their leader's move. The air was filled with floating, near-naked women descending onto officers' laps. O'Neal seemed delighted, not too drunk to mutter, "Oh, come aboard, Cathleen. Come aboard!"

Terhughes flew into a rage. "Good God, Admiral, stop this immediately! Think what they will say in London! The newspapers will make it a bigger story than Napoleon's mistress! Admiralty will put us all ashore on half pay forever!"

But O'Neal's attention was completely absorbed by his onetime paramour Cathleen as she settled onto his lap wearing naught but corset and stockings. "By God, lass! I dreamed of this moment many a time! How could you spurn me for that fop Lewis, dressed in that ridiculous macaroni style all the time?"

"I cannot speak for any woman back on Earth," she replied, "but let me make up for whatever neglect she showed you." And with that she grasped her rather spectacular breasts and lifted them onto his face. O'Neal closed his eyes in ecstasy and started making grunting noises like a hungry baby.

With that, Terhughes exploded in disgust and headed for the door, chased out by parting calls from the lieutenants to "Join the party, Captain! Davis here needs a partner!" and "At least leave your spunk here for the ladies! No need to soil your bed linens again!"

Thanks to the scene about him and the wine he'd consumed, Wyckham was more than ready to finish what they'd started last night. His breeches had a tent in them like Wellington's field pavilion! Lady Brashton noticed.

"I'm pleased to see you are interested in helping the cause," she smiled coquettishly. And then, still floating in the air above him, she spread her legs straight out, grasped her ankles, and started slowly spinning as she descended down to him! It reminded him of a ballerina at the Bolshoi in St. Petersburg. Unbelievable!

Well, Wyckham wasn't going to miss out on this! If he had an audience, who cared? He opened his breeches and pulled himself out, just as the lady landed and took him inside her. Wyckham was in heaven.

Lady Brashton smiled contentedly. "Well, this is pleasant. I now understand why this is such a popular pastime on Earth. Should I try to increase your enjoyment? If you like, I can send you some electrical impulses to enhance your physical pleasure. Let me show you." Suddenly a wave of warmth and sensual excitement washed over his groin. It was like his first sexual experience, only ten times more stimulating.

"Also, I believe I should now be clenching my internal muscles as quickly as possible?" With that, her groin started buzzing like a loud bumblebee! Wyckham not only felt it but he also heard it! The sensation on his member trumped all; it overwhelmed him and sent him into gibbering ecstasy. Orgasm was imminent. Lady Brashton seemed aware of that.

"And for your climax, I believe I should rapidly bounce up and down?" And Jesus, she certainly did! She started moving up and down so fast she was just a vibrating blur, just like a hummingbird! It was impossible to see that there was a woman there, just a streak of light making a rapid slapping on his thighs.

Wyckham's body exploded in a wracking orgasm. All the pent-up frustration and anxiety of the past two days were cast away as his body wrenched back and forth. He banged his knees hard on the underside of the table but scarcely noticed. After some final twitches, he collapsed in complete exhaustion.

Suddenly, Lady Brashton seemed withdrawn, tilting her head in some kind of analysis. Then a smile of amazement broke out across her features. "Fifty-eight million, six hundred twenty-two thousand, one hundred and thirteen! Amazing! Thank you so much. Be assured your living cells will be put to good use. Oh my, there's more."

With that she slid off him, started picking up the errant seed from his lap and licking it off her fingers while she continued to smile at him! Wyckham was too exhausted to be amazed. The fact was, he was getting used to the unbelievable—nothing here surprised him anymore.

He looked about the room to see that the party had turned into the Roman orgy of every sailor's dream. Two marine lieutenants sat facing each other about ten feet apart, thrusting their loins out in unison to propel two beautiful women back and forth through the air between them. Each time the two women flew by each other, they extended a hand to make a single handclap, then somersaulted a full turn in midair like acrobats in a traveling circus, finally landing and spearing themselves on the other marine's manhood when they landed!

Admiral O'Neal himself had his head tipped back with his eyes closed as Cathleen did handstands on his lap with his member in her mouth, her toes pointed like an upside-down ballerina.

Two other women standing in a group of navy lieutenants were lapping semen from their lips and comparing their experiences. "My word, I received over thirty-eight million from each of those two officers!" That resulted in many congratulatory backslaps for two lieutenants standing in the center. "Thank you, thank you," they responded to the assemblage. "As officers and gentlemen, we could do naught but give as much as possible for such a noble cause."

Every single lady in the place was conjugating in some amazing position with an officer, while the single officers were politely watching, obviously hoping for a chance to join the orgy. Even old Grimwald had been persuaded to join the festivities, standing up with his breeches about his ankles as he ferociously rodgered a young lass over the table. She was vibrating so much the table she grasped was humming loudly, its glasses bouncing and spilling. However, the wolfman alone seemed to want no part in it all. Downing his final drink, he stood up and walked somewhat unsteadily from the room.

There was no sign of Rawlins. Wyckham did see Commander Hamilton slouched down in his chair with a drink as the image of Catherine Burford rolled her loins back and forth across his lap as she bent backward over the table.

"Tally ho, wondrous maiden! You've got the fox now! Ready, here's the final jump!" Hamilton thrust himself upward as Catherine flew five feet into the air with her legs spread wide, whinnied like a jumping filly, and landed with precision right back in the saddle.

Wyckham felt badly for his old friend Pierce Rawlins. All the others were having the time of their lives, but Rawlins had left rebuffed and humiliated. Trouble was brewing here. Jesus, he hoped Rawlins had left earlier and hadn't seen his fiancée performing this equine fantasy with Hamilton.

He couldn't sit there and witness Hamilton's drunken debauch any longer, knowing how much it hurt his oldest friend. It was time for him and his lady to leave this noisy party. "My dear lady, might we leave the dinner table for a little…ah…dessert in my room?"

Nodding agreement, she arose, took his proffered arm, and accompanied him down the hall, still naked as a French courtesan.

Wyckham himself had his breeches wide open. They passed several stewards who nodded, "G'nite, sir," as he staggered down the hallway with his member swaying about. Wyckham was too drunk to care. No sneering superiors were here to judge him. On this world, all the old rules governing proper behaviour for an English gentleman no longer applied. Wyckham would do whatever felt good for Wyckham. He nodded courteously in reply to some hands as he opened the door to his temporary cabin and retired for a night of bliss with his childhood sweetheart.

But there was his new steward, Obujimi, clearly not pleased with the condition and dishabille of his captain. With a raised eyebrow, he asked, "Sir, will that be all for the evening, or perhaps in your present condition you would like me to remain and assist your aim?"

Wyckham was well past comprehending any sarcasm. Why, his new servant was concerned with his well-being after all! "Thank you for your offer of assistance, my good man, but I will be just fine." Obujimi stormed off shaking his head, as his captain produced a parting belch.

9

A FOE'S FINAL TRIP TO THE NECESSARY

Wyckham awoke with his head in turmoil. He finally managed to sit up, but the room was spinning like there was a full gale blowing. Lady Brashton's soft "Good morning" landed like a broadside on his ears. He moaned and lowered his head into his hands.

"You are in pain from last night's drinking?" she asked. "Let me rearrange the electrical pulses in your pain receptors." Wyckham's head cleared immediately. He sat upright, perky as a babe after napping. This ally was very handy to have around.

"Joy of the day to you as well, and thank you for your magical administrations. You are truly a wonderful ally, not to mention an absolutely superb…ah…dinner partner," he said as he looked over her naked form once more.

He reached for her and drew the lady close. "I hope last evening was enjoyable to you as well? I'm curious—how does copulation with a physical creature like me feel to a being such as yourself?"

"Oh, it was most fulfilling. Our kind learns much from physical species—we especially enjoy simulating their important feelings. And the millions of living cells you have donated to us will increase our scanning abilities. Our goal is to develop the power to project sensations into our enemies' nervous systems, and, with your donations, we are getting closer to gaining that ability."

Project sensations into an enemy? Like pain? That would be rather effective against any foe. But he still couldn't really understand how having sex with her was contributing to the war effort.

Wyckham sat up and looked at the lady. "Could you explain further to me how our intercourse gives you strength and additional fighting abilities? Please understand that where I come from, fighting ability depends on matters such as training and weight of shot, not on how much…ah…quim you've explored." Crude slang no longer seemed improper in discussion with elegant women.

Lady Brashton nodded. "Certainly, this is a concept very difficult for any being on a mass-based world to comprehend. Let me explain as best I can. There is a certain force in any individual life that is unique. Every single being is somewhat different from any other. Taking that difference and infusing it into collective beings such as ourselves fills in the gaps connecting us to the universe about us. We are constantly looking for life energy that has certain, very rare features, elements that fill in important missing pieces in the puzzle that would create an all-powerful being. While that is far off, finding a being with certain rare features would be a great addition to any race's well-being. As certain remarkable humans have contributed greatly to your history and advanced your race, so would ones with special electrical markers advance our race. And, of course, we must keep the rare finds away from the Draesh."

Wyckham wasn't sure he was any wiser on the subject. It all sounded like a blend of religion and advanced physics, two subjects he didn't understand or really care about. He expressed that to the lady.

"I do not pretend to grasp the concept here, but please be assured that I understand its importance, and I will be happy to…ah…*contribute* as frequently as possible to your search. British officers will always 'rise up' for a just cause!"

Not even a smile. This energy being in front of him may have had the knowledge of a hundred Socrates, but it didn't seem she had much of a sense of humor. Nor did she have any comprehension of the excessive sexual appetites of sailors.

She grasped his hands and pumped them thankfully. "How wonderful that you will continue to supply me with your seed," she said. "I know it is very exhausting for you, and I cannot thank you enough for what you must be going through to do this for me."

Ah, the duties of a Royal Navy officer. "Madam, I assure you, it is no trouble at all—far from it, actually. The time I spent with you last night was extremely gratifying; the physical sensations I experienced were simply incredible. I hope to spend lots of time with you...uh...shall we say...experimenting?"

"Oh, thank you, thank you! I do know that different sexual maneuvers can increase seed production. We will go on a journey searching for high seed production. And I will do my best to keep your physical exertions to a minimum."

Jesus, thought Wyckham. *Does a situation get any better than this? Time to get out of bed, or I might never leave.* "Madam, I must now attend to ship's duties. Might I ask you to leave...ah...surreptitiously? It will be better for ship's discipline if the crew is unaware of our intimate... work...together last night."

She smiled in acceptance. "I will do so, although I do not understand why allies working together must keep their efforts hidden. Hopefully, I can eventually learn all the proper customs surrounding human relations." With that, she absolutely disappeared. Maybe she was now a fly or a roach on the floor? Better be careful where he stepped.

Wyckham called for his new steward who arrived with a basin of hot water and a faceful of cold disapproval. *Christ, my steward treats me like an errant schollboy.* After a quick toilet, Wyckham put on his dress uniform and hat from the previous evening, still in a celebratory mood despite Obujimi's obvious disgust. He made his way up on deck with a spring in his step and content in his soul.

The ship was in its usual perfect order, every rope coiled, every gun spotless. The crew was employed at the standard morning work detail, scrubbing the deck. Rows of sailors on their knees were scraping the deck with holystones, the only thing that would remove the dirt and smell from unpainted oak decking. Wyckham failed to notice their sidelong glances at him and the muffled laughter.

It was a spectacular morning. Both of Draez's suns were up, a few puffy clouds dotted the skies, and moderate winds blew across the deck. Squalls in the distance were bringing rain to the interior. Squadrons of bright red gulls worked the shallow coastal waters. It was a perfect sailor's day.

Strolling across the deck with his hands clasped behind his back, he came up unnoticed behind one of *Righteous*'s marines talking with two from *Zeus*.

"Ey say twere unbelievable, th' goins on. Wimmin were flyin' 'bout like bees gatherin' pollen." All three guffawed. "Movin' from one off'ser t' th' next. They even kept a count o' which off'ser give em the mos' jiz! An' twere ar own cap'm, Dick'em Wyck'em, [more laughter] what started th' whole thing!"

Christ, the whole ship had found out about what happened last night! Servants and cooks had probably watched the whole thing from the gallery. Sounded like they knew every damn detail, too, right down to his leading role! And "Dick'em Wyck'em"? That was his new nickname? *Bloody...fucking...hell!*

Wyckham's exuberant morning had blown away like a cloud of cannon smoke on a broad reach. He looked about the deck to see sailors grinning at him and talking under their breath. What's next? "Over fifty million! Good shootin', Cap'm!" or maybe "Three cheers for our captain, the navy's best cocksman?" He was filled with an urgent need to get off the ship and away from the pointing and muttered jokes.

Suddenly Terhughes exploded angrily up the gangway, walking briskly forward to the forecastle. Wyckham greeted him with a nod and "A good morning to you, Captain." But apparently there was to be no conversation. Terhughes stopped, gave him a stare that would have sunk a French liner, snorted in absolute disgust, and continued on his previous course. Wyckham felt chastised and guilty. Terhughes had every right to be enraged by the drunken improprieties Wyckham and the others had committed last night.

O'Neal followed Terhughes up from below, eyes ablaze. Wyckham walked over to make a second attempt at a morning greeting, but O'Neal flew into his own rage before he could say a thing.

"Damn that man's eyes! Threaten to take me before the Admiralty for behaviour unbecoming an officer, will he? The cheek of the man! I should throw *him* in the brig for disrespecting a superior! Lock his skinny arse up right next to his good friend Jarvis! Let him piss and shit in a bucket for a few weeks!"

"Ah, I don't think you should do that, Sean," Wyckham counseled as he pulled the admiral away from some watching crew. "We did put on quite a show last night, you know. Jarvis will certainly find out and add a detailed description of last night's events to his list of accusations against us when he meets with Admiralty. Putting Terhughes in irons to boot would be just the thing to guarantee we get fully cashiered."

But O'Neal wasn't listening. He was looking about at all the crewmen who were speaking in hushed tones and pointing at the two officers with wide grins on their faces.

"Damn it all. They know about last night, don't they," he realized aloud, his voice betraying his shock.

"Without a doubt," responded Wyckham. "We're now the leading topic of discussion among the fleet's foremost philosophers, from every fo'c's'le to every wardroom. Sean, don't we have some duties ashore? I've a sudden desire to get off this ship."

"Yaasss…a cracking idea. I must check out the progress on *Zeus* anyway. Let's get the hell away from here right now; we can have breakfast ashore."

Wyckham called to Obujimi for his sword and pistols, just in case there was still a crabman hiding in the bushes around *Zeus*, then climbed over the side along with O'Neal for a quick row to the beach.

Minutes later they were walking along surveying *Zeus*'s hull. O'Neal's steward had brought a tray with fresh bread, the last of the oranges, and coffee for them to down while they examined the progress on *Zeus*'s hull. Declining cooked Krag parts from several sailors sitting about a fire, they walked the full length of the flagship's exposed hull. The patching was almost complete; next, she would be righted. Crewmen were fixing blocks and cables to her masts to haul her upright, and then they would roll her on logs down to the water and warp her into the cove. Following that, her great guns would be put back aboard, and she would be fully shipshape.

With his fast broken, O'Neal sat down with his carpenter and purser to go over the ship's stores. Before they began, he addressed his friend. "Captain Wyckham, I need to remain here for a while. I'd be obliged if you were to ascend the heights here and inspect the batteries above us. Let them know we should be bringing down their guns tomorrow but make sure they remain vigilant today. Corporal Kenyon here will escort you."

Wyckham nodded and headed with the marine corporal over to the foot of the larboard cliff, atop which *Zeus* had placed several guns. Following a trail made by some kind of animal, it took them about twenty minutes to climb to the summit. They emerged under a dense canopy of gnarled trees about twenty feet high. Arranged in a circle under the trees were seven of the massive thirty-two-pounders. A crane had been rigged on the hilltop with dozens of blocks, cables had been run back to the anchor capstan on *Zeus*, and the guns had been hoisted up fairly easily. In front of the guns was a wall of thorny branches which the sailors had removed from the surrounding ground to make a free field of fire. Four of the guns were sited to cover the beach where *Zeus* lay on its side; the other three were pointing inland into the valley. Some fifty sailors manned the guns with a squad of marines in support. The Yankee Harrison was also there, using it as a base for his scouts patrolling into the surrounding plateau. And to Wyckham's surprise, his saviour Seaman Crawford was there as well.

Wyckham hailed him. "Crawford, the man to whom I am forever indebted! Our paths cross again. What brings you up here from the cave where you were assigned?"

138

Crawford walked over, beaming with pride to be so respectfully addressed by the captain in front of dozens of his mates.

"Seems oy were jes' too pop'lar wif th' ladies, sor. Loo'tenant Drummon' from *Hedgehog* sent me up here, said oy were too distractin', keepin' th' ladies' f'm doon their work."

After last night, Wyckham had a pretty good idea what kind of distractions Crawford was referring to, but the voyeur in him had to discover what kind of sexual activities the common sailors in the cave had been involved in. Rather depraved ones, he found himself hoping. What an unbecoming thought for an officer! But damn if the strange goings-on in this world hadn't turned from deadly to rather interesting, especially for a red-blooded man like himself!

"Crawford, I must say I have no idea what you could have done to distract everyone from their work. It must have been quite serious for the officer in command to dismiss you. Could you enlighten me as to exactly what you did to merit such a disciplinary action?"

"Warn't me fault, sor. One o' th' ladies, sor, we was takin' a rest from pushin' on knobs an' such. She asked me wud I like er t' be me fav'rit woman, th' one she saw 'n me mind? Why not, sez oy? And then like magic, there were Queen Car'lyn 'erself, standin' before me naked 'n' all, tellin' me t' put a leg over right then 'n' there! Wot cu'd I do, sor? Say no to roy'lty?"

Good Lord! Crawford and the image of the Queen of England rutting on the floor of a cave? Right in front of dozens of sailors? What a scene that must have made!

Queen Caroline was a corpulent, promiscuous woman very popular with commoners, known for her sexual appetites and poor hygiene. The thought of Crawford and the queen rolling about the dirt floor was just too shocking for Wyckham. He could just imagine the queen's flabby breasts flapping around as a bunch of sailors yelled out "Giv' et t'er, Pete, give et t'er!" A long silence occurred as Wyckham, dumbfounded again by this crazy world, had no idea what to say.

Thankfully, just then Harrison walked up to greet him. He needed to get his mind off this shocking image and back to his duty.

"Captain Wyckham!" the lanky American said. "A very good morning to you. What brings you to our mountain paradise today?"

"And joy of the day to you as well, Captain Harrison. Just checking on our sailors here for the admiral. Where's our Lieutenant Clifton?"

"He's taken charge over to the other hilltop. The officer there had to go see your surgeon down on the beach, had a wound from yesterday that was festerin' a bit. Left me in charge. Nothin' like a Jonathon rebel to keep British sailors in line," he said with a broad smile.

Wyckham smiled back. He liked this American, a man that could take charge and achieve success. "So all looks correct, the redoubt looks stout and the guns well sited. Any enemy activity in the area?"

"Not really," Harrison answered. "Occasionally we get some crab-men doin' a little scoutin' on their own, prob'ly tryin' to tell their masters what we got up here. But I got my men in a perimeter about three hundred yards out, all with tomahawks. Any crab wanders close, my boys take him out real quiet-like. And if there're crabs down in the valley, they're too far away to see anythin'. With this tree cover, I don't think they got any idea we're up here with a battery of artillery."

"Yes, these trees hide this fortification quite well. I doubt the birds flying by even know we're here," Wyckham commented as he looked about. Daylight was barely penetrating the dense canopy of branches above them. Whatever type of trees they were, their foliage was very thick and their thorny branches very entangled. No enemy on another hilltop would notice anything amiss if it looked down on the redoubt. The fortification was extremely well concealed.

"So we've got very little to do up here," said the American, starting to grin. "Fortunately, your seaman Crawford arrived to regale us with tales of his relations at court! Ain't nothing like a common man's version of an experience with your good Queen Caroline. Must have been quite a party down there, what with all those other common sailors watching and all."

Blast the man now! "Humph!" was all Wyckham could manage. All Harrison's Yankees up here were clearly going to have a grand time spreading this tale of British royal humiliation to the whole squadron. Harrison was keeping his lips tightly pursed to avoid exploding in laughter.

"And have I told you that I am a fair hand at writin'?" Harrison finally managed to continue. "Maybe I will go back to London and pen the whole story, send it off to the *Times*? Make sure to interview every sailor that was there in that cave watchin'; should make for quite a story, don't you think? Doubtless all the royals will be so proud that the common people have such a regard for the queen."

Terrific, thought Wyckham. Another thing to look forward to when they returned to England. Even if Harrison stayed on this world, certainly the word would get out about what happened between Crawford and their allies' version of the queen. So much for their heroes' welcome.

Wyckham's previous appreciation of Harrison had quickly dissipaited. Wyckham really wasn't sure what he was going to say as he opened his mouth, but no damn Jonathon was going to slur the Crown in the presence of a Royal Navy officer and go unchallenged. He was angry enough to consider calling the man out right now.

But suddenly both he and Harrison had something else to think about as the air was filled with a strange humming sound, growing louder by the second. Large branches above them started cracking off the tree trunks and falling from above, landing all over the redoubt. Men were running and dodging, some cursing as the falling limbs hit them. The noise of shattering branches increased, then doubled in intensity as entire trees started falling over, their roots heaving the ground upward. Wyckham, Crawford, and Harrison all lost their footing and slipped as the tree next to them bent over in a splintering crash. The canopy of branches above was being steadily pushed down, pinning the men all the way to the ground until most of them couldn't even crawl. Then some rising roots from a falling tree pushed the gun next to them upright against the tree's trunk. Three tons of cast iron were about to crush them if it came off its carriage and fell. But thankfully it came to rest against a fallen tree as all the branches stopped moving and everything suddenly went quiet.

Then new sounds came from above: a softer humming sound and some metallic clanking. Pushed to the ground, Wyckham managed to look up and make out the edge of a huge shiny surface covering most of the redoubt. It was another flying craft like the one Wulfe had arrived in, just much larger. But no wolf emerged from this one.

Through a gap in the leaves above, damned if he didn't make out the hairy leg of another giant Draesh! Thumping sounds followed as their enemy apparently walked across the surface of the flying craft.

Now he could hear sounds of the beast crouching down and crawling to the far edge of its ship. It must be peering down at the beached *Zeus*. He was clearly a scout sent to gather intelligence on the forces below on the beach. At least the thing was apparently unaware that it had landed right on top of dozens of its enemies. Hopefully it would remain ignorant of that fact. There was no way they could defend themselves against it here on this hilltop. Christ, they could barely move a finger.

Damn if someone didn't start moaning just then! The captain turned to see a sailor bleeding from a gash caused by a felled tree branch.

Wyckham spoke in a whisper to another sailor next to him. "Quiet that man down! There's one of the damn monsters right above us!" The sailor cupped his hand over the wounded man's mouth as Wyckham motioned to the rest of the men for silence.

Everyone was cautiously looking up, hoping that the evil thing would finish its business and fly away. They could hear steps as it came back to the spot directly above them where it had emerged from its ship. But new sounds came to them: strange clinking and shuffling sounds they couldn't recognize, followed by some low grunting. *What the hell was going on?*

More branches cracked as something slowly descended right above Wyckham. Entangled in thorny branches, he couldn't move, and now the beast was aiming a weapon right at him! Whatever it was, it had gotten stuck in the crushed foliage above him. He had a chance to get away! Wyckham struggled to release himself from the vines and branches that had him pinned, but to no avail. With a crash the weapon fell free and hit him right on his head. Its weight pushed his face into the soft ground.

In the split second before it detonated, Wyckham resigned himself to death once again. This time there was no last minute help coming. Even his previous rescuer Crawford was pinned down by crushed branches as well. Hopefully, the damn thing on his head would just explode and kill him quickly. Who knows what kind of slow, painful death some Draesh weapons are capable of?

Seconds ticked by. Nothing happened. Whatever was on his head was quite warm and soft. Then his eyes started to burn. Had he been infected by a laboratory culture, filled with some horrible alien pox? He tried to lift his head a little to view the substance. Puddling beneath him was a lumpy brown ooze.

A familiar foul odor, unbelievably strong, filled his nose with recognition at the same instant as Crawford yelled out. "G'ddam filthy rotten bugger! He jes' took a shite on th' cap'm's 'ed!"

The Draesh had stuck its arse over the side of his ship and dropped its foul waste right on Wyckham's head! The captain's mind filled with mixed feelings—glad he wasn't about to die, but absolutely revolted to have a three-foot turd sitting on his best uniform hat. An unbelievably horrifying situation for a gentleman to find himself in!

Apparently, the enemy above them still didn't know they were here, and Wyckham intended to keep it that way. "Crawford, keep quiet, for Christ's sake!" he whispered. "Don't let the goddamn thing know we're here, or we're all done for!"

Crawford quieted dowm but managed to get himself freed from the crushing branches. He crawled over to the dismounted gun standing upright next to them. "Think th' cap'm's 'ed's a latrine, do ye?" he mumbled as he worked. "Well, I got a presen' fer ye, too!"

Damned if he wasn't trying to aim the gun up at the Draesh! The surging grounds had left the big cannon almost vertical, and with a shattered tree limb as a spike, Crawford was trying to quietly lever the gun's muzzle over a bit to point directly up at the creature. With a final shove, the gun shifted a foot to the left so it was bearing straight up. Crawford immediately cocked the hammer, grabbed the lanyard and yanked. The flintlock hammer released and struck the pan.

Nothing. *Damn it all!* Wyckham strained to move his head to see what the matter was with the firing lock. The answer was clear. When the gun had been moved by the falling tree, some branches had hit the lock's hammer and bent it sideways, so the hammer missed the frizzen and created no sparks. While misfiring locks were easily dealt with onboard ship by firing the guns off with burning slow matches, they had no such alternative to turn to here.

Wait! Maybe they did! Wyckham struggled frantically to free a hand near one of his pistols. He was close enough to the cannon to use the pistol's discharge to light it off. But a large branch had his arms pinned to his sides.

"Cap'm, sor," whispered Crawford, "I sees wuts yer tryin' t' do, but ye' better be quick about it, yer 'bout t' git anudder turd on yer 'ed, An' it looks like a great big 'un, too!"

Wyckham looked up to see an immense brown mass slowly descending through the foliage. *Christ, this one is enormous! The filthy demon is about to shite a cow right on my head!*

What a way to go. He could just imagine officers in the sitting room at London's Admiralty, discussing his death while they awaited their postings. "Yes, got his head knocked off by an enemy turd in the battle for Earth, poor Wyckham did. Shitty way to go, that, har har!"

That enraging image gave him extra strength. In a fury, he finally wrenched his right arm free and was able to grab a pistol. Holding its firelock right next to the thirty-two-pounder's touchhole, he pulled the trigger just as the huge turd came free and fell down toward him. Then all was obscured by flame and smoke as the thirty two pounder fired off with a thundering crash. The blast, deafening so close, blew Wyckham's hair back as the gun broke free of its carriage to fall toward Crawford. The seaman quickly rolled to his left, just avoiding the ten-foot gun barrel as it crashed to the ground, only missing his head by inches.

All was silent. Trying to view the outcome, Wyckham wiped debris from his eyes. *Christ, it was the monster's shite!* Fecal matter was absolutely everywhere. The melon-sized ball had fired right up through the giant turd and into the creature's innards, scattering feces over the whole redoubt, but especially on Wyckham.

"Well doon, Cap'm!" cried Crawford as he crawled over to free Wyckham. "Put that ball right up 'iz arse where ee d'surved it!"

Pulling out his seaman's dirk, he started cutting away the greenery holding his captain down. After a minute of Crawford sawing away, Wyckham was finally able to crawl out from beneath the flying ship and stand upright to peer through holes in the branch canopy above them. The Draesh's corpse had crashed to the ground a few feet away. The thirty-two-pound ball had gone up through its entire body, blowing the top of its head off as it exited. There were no sounds or signs of any other Draesh. Apparently, the craft was a single-occupant scout ship.

Harrison had also gotten free and stood up next to him, barely holding his laughter at bay. "Nice shooting, Captain. Too bad that fancy officer's uniform of yers got a mite soiled. But I'm sure you'll be all clean and pretty soon. Can't be an officer in the British navy unless you can strut like a peacock! Just put your steward to work, that servant aboard your ship whose sole duty is to keep you feeling you're better than everyone else in the world. And I suggest you get him right to work because you are in quite a state! You know it's just not very British for a nobleman like yourself to smell like a refuse pit."

That was it! Here he was, covered in foul-smelling shite from killing an enemy, and this Yankee upstart thought he had the right to humiliate him and the entire British navy! Self-control left him as he backhanded Harrison across the face. The American's face spun sideways from the blow.

"Sir, such untimely comments are beyond decency!" Wyckham snarled. "Disparaging a comrade in arms and the Royal Navy is bad enough in private, but not what a gentleman does on the field! If you disagree, we can find a time and place to settle this matter."

Harrison slowly turned back to face him, staring hard into Wyckham's eyes. Slowly he reached up to wipe his face, which now had a streak of alien feces from Wyckham's hand smeared across it. Wyckham awaited the inevitable acceptance to a duel, which always came when a gentleman was struck in public. Or maybe this crude Yankee would just pull out one of those big American hunting knives right now! Wyckham inched his hand toward the grip on his sword.

But surprisingly, a smile crossed Harrison's face. He wiped his face and looked at his filthy hand. "I reckon I deserved that. Well struck! Now I'm shit-covered just like you!" He extended his hand. "My apologies, Captain. God knows your quick action probably saved us all. My comments were out of line." He extended his hand in apology, cooling

Wyckham's anger. The British captain accepted Harrison's hand, and they both gave a firm squeeze. Draesh feces oozed out between their fingers, the disgusting feeling giving them both a moment's pause. Then the two burst out laughing. Here they were, two officers lost on a distant world battling giant devils, standing and shaking each other's shite-covered hand. It couldn't get any more daft.

"But I do have to say, you look a sight!" said Harrison, shaking his head as he looked Wyckham over. He was absolutely covered in filth—the damn creature's second turd had been a monster. When it was struck by the big roundshot, it had splattered violently over Wyckham's best uniform. In addition, there were other indescribable things from inside the creature's guts flung all over him.

"Captain, why don't you head down the trail and get yourself cleaned up?" said Harrison. "Please," he added, waving his hand in front of his nose. "I can manage things here. My respects to the admiral, and might I request he get some swivel guns up here in case we get more visitors? And I recommend he instruct the sailors on the other hilltop to construct a well-concealed observation platform above the forest's crown; we'll be doing the same here."

So Captain Rodney Wyckham, escorted again by Corporal Kenyon, left to begin the most embarrassing walk of his life. Of course, there didn't happen to be a stream along the return path where he could get himself cleaned up. He emerged from the trail right in the midst of hundreds of sailors and marines, covered head-to-toe in alien feces. Christ, he should have borrowed some clothes from someone up on the hilltop. *Well, nothing for it now. Jesus, now I have to walk through the entire squadron looking and smelling like a latrine shoveler.*

He stepped out onto the beach and headed for the waterline. Just to make things perfect, someone must have rung the dinner bell in the insect world, because an immediate cloud of sandflies suddenly appeared and started swarming around Wyckham. And these were no mere English sandflies but big green things the size of crickets, making loud smacking sounds as they feasted on Draesh fecal matter, apparently a delicacy in the insect world. Everyone on the beach turned to look at Wyckham, seeking out the source of the strange sounds.

Three hands moving a log nearby snapped to attention, knuckled their foreheads in salute, but then started coughing violently, their eyes watering. Following behind him, Marine Corporal Kenyon was also coughing and holding his nose from the unbelievable stench, the noise drawing more attention to the pair as they walked down the beach.

With head held high and hands clasped behind his back in a proper captain's posture, Wyckham passed through the entire force deployed on the beach. All work on the beach stopped as everyone stared at him in silence.

But sailors close enough soon erupted in coughing and mutterings like "Bloody 'ell, Tom, Cap'm smells even worse 'n you!" Quiet reigned as everyone ashore watched the captain's progress. It was like a leper walking through a nervous crowd in a public square.

Just as Wyckham got halfway to the water, the silence was broken by a resounding *plop* as a large ball of fecal matter, warmed up in the sun, dropped off Wyckham's shoulder to hit the beach. *Christ, just what I needed to draw further attention to myself,* thought Wyckham. The sight caused the nearest hands to step back further in fear of getting hit by something deadly.

Finally Wyckham reached the water where he quickly and unceremoniously jumped in and tried to remove as much of the fecal matter as he could. But the damned filth had stained his skin and dried on his uniform; it didn't wash off so easily. Walking back onto the sand, he encountered a stunned Obujimi.

"For a group known for its propriety, British officers never cease to amaze me," the servant stated with a shake of his head. "Bathing in defecation is now all the latest?"

Reaching his boiling point, Wyckham snapped at his steward, "Sir Thomas, instead of another display of arrogance, possibly you could assist me here? For a start, maybe you could summon my gig to return to *Righteous* for a bit of a bath and some fresh clothes?"

The African shook himself from his astonishment and hurried off to assemble the gig's crew. Rawlins and his officers started to approach, then stopped in their tracks once they saw Wyckham's ferocious glare.

But after a brief consultation, Lieutenant Gregory seemed to get an assignment, broke away from the others, and walked up to Wyckham.

"Sir, the admiral sends his regards and asks you to repair immediately aboard *Righteous*."

"Exactly what emergency requires my presence right now?" snarled Wyckham, not in a mood to talk to anyone.

"The French are here."

10

CONFUSION TO THE FRENCH

Capitaine Jean Badoin paced the quarterdeck of *Leviathan,* eighty guns, furious that they had not seen the English brig for over three hours now. He thought he'd had the small ship trapped on a lee shore, but it had apparently found an island to hide behind while *Leviathan* passed. Every passing hour decreased the chance of getting back in the chase. *Zut!* The filthy *Anglais* were probably well on their way home now, drunk and celebrating their escape. His lookout in the crosstrees, who had lost sight of the British ship, was going to wish he had fallen overboard in the earlier gale when Badoin was done with him.

Badoin had a score to settle with the English for what they had done to his father. His entire family had been leaders in the revolution from the beginning, especially his father, Louis Badoin. He had been a tailor in Paris, barely eking out a living for his family by making ornate formal dress for the nobility. When the first protests had broken out, Louis Badoin was at the front of the mobs storming the Bastille, shouting *liberté* and *egalité* with all his might. Luckily, he sided with the ultimately successful Jacobin faction, rising to a prominent position in the Paris committee. When war broke out, he got himself posted as a capitaine in the revolutionary navy—first with a sloop-of-war, but rising quickly to command the seventy-four-gun *Fougueux*. His son, Jean, was commissioned a lieutenant and began his own naval career.

But at the Battle of Trafalgar, the incompetent and cowardly royalists in command of the combined French and Spanish fleet were outfought by the filthy *Anglais*. His father was made prisoner when his ship was sunk by HMS *Royal Sovereign*, 100 guns.

After he was paroled, the upstart Napoleon had used Louis Badoin as a scapegoat and cashiered him and his son out of the navy, shaming the family name. His father died two years later, impoverished and humiliated. But politics in Paris were fickle, and the Badoin family still had friends in powerful committees. After simmering in anger on the beach for years, Jean managed to get himself command of *Leviathan*, eighty guns, newly commissioned and specially armed to deal with English convoys.

On this, its first cruise, they had encountered a wild storm, which had blown them far from the Northern (he refused to call it English) Channel into a group of seemingly uncharted islands. The fact that his old charts failed to show these islands confirmed his low opinion of the noblemen who had run the French navy when these charts were made.

The gale that brought them here had been a strange one. One wave during the night must have had a twenty-meter trough. It had awakened Badoin, something that never happened at sea to the experienced captain. The foolish lieutenant on watch had insisted the ship had fallen off the edge of the world or something! But it had been too stormy for the man to really see anything. Badoin had lectured the officer on the prevalence of giant waves in a gale—clearly that was all it had been. But the idiot insisted that a flying window in the air had swallowed up the ship! Capitaine Badoin had immediately demoted the man from second to fifth lieutenant for his irrational explanation of events. The revolution didn't tolerate the fantasies of the church, and it certainly wouldn't tolerate the childish ravings of a disrespectful lieutenant.

Nonetheless, the weather certainly had been strange since that wave. It had continued to rain after the wave hit, but the wind had fallen off immediately, and the temperature had increased. Now it seemed that the day was running long—had they been blown far to the south? Both compasses on the ship had been broken during the gale, and Badoin had no idea where *Leviathan* was heading. At least the skies were finally clearing. Soon they would get a bearing on the sun—and then the English shipping in the area would learn to fear him, *L'Aigle de Mer*, the Sea Eagle.

Since the French navy was blockaded in port, all sorts of artillery had been available for *Leviathan*. With the choice of whatever he wanted, Badoin had completely equipped both main batteries with carronades—big ones shooting thirty-kilogram balls. *Leviathan's* total broadside weight would be at least twice that of any other ship on the ocean. Faster than English ships of the line, she would use her superior speed to sail up close to an opponent and quickly pound it to bits. He had slipped out of Brest on a foggy night and would now wreak havoc with any anglais merchant convoys he encountered.

Ah, the sun was coming out. Soon they would know where they were and head for the nearest English sea-lanes. His sailing master came up on deck with the ship's log and a sextant to get a reading on the sun.

The clouds broke and the master hoisted his sextant to look at the sun, but then dropped it on the deck in astonishment and stared at Badoin. Because above them, one a bright orange, the other a darker red, were two suns.

11

ALIEN DIPLOMACY

As he climbed aboard *Righteous,* Wyckham sighted the missing brig, *Gnat,* with a jury-rigged top foremast anchored further out in the cove. So when he went below, he wasn't surprised to see her commander, Robert Wallingford, seated at the table in the captain's cabin with O'Neal.

Wyckham was quite excited to see the young lieutenant in good health after his ship had been missing for almost two days. Wallingford had served under him as a midshipman back in the sloop *Harrier,* and Wyckham knew him as a smart and resourceful young man. Without realizing what he was doing, he gave Wallingford a hearty welcome with a vigorous clap on the back.

"By God, it's good to…" Wyckham cut his greeting short as chunks of wet alien feces broke off his coat sleeve and flew about the room. *Oh, Christ—this is bad.* Some shite berries had landed right on O'Neal's face.

The admiral started to boil as he gave Wyckham a silent going-over. Panicking, Wyckham tried to repair matters. He pulled out his handkerchief and moved over to wipe the admiral's face.

"Oh God, Sean, I'm sorry, let me get that off of you!" But all his wet handkerchief did was smear the filth across O'Neal's cheeks. Fortunately, before he could look in a mirror, O'Neal's steward came to the rescue with a wet towel and got the admiral cleaned up and cooled down.

O'Neal finally spoke in a steady tone. "Damn it all, Wyckham, I've dueled men for less." But his anger cooled to sympathy as he surveyed the disheveled captain in front of him. "However, looking at you, whatever happened to me looks a lark. Clearly, you've had the rougher go of it." He waved his hand in front of his face. "Phew! Good Lord, man, exactly what have you been up to? You look and smell like you've been locked in a cow barn for months!" To complete the admiral's indignation, a large sandfly left Wyckham's shoulder to land right on O'Neal's nose, getting immediately shooed away by O'Neal's attentive steward.

Wyckham was too tired for explanations right then. "Just another unbelievable episode in this unbelievable place. With the admiral's permission, might I tell you the tale in a bit after I get cleaned up?"

"Sorry, no time for that," said O'Neal. "You're to set sail in *Righteous* right away. I'll be leaving as soon as we're done here."

O'Neal had to stop and move to an open window, coughing along the way. "Ah, Jesus save us, I'll just stay upwind of you for the next few minutes. Commander Wallingford here can bring you up to date on the recent developments." As he spoke, O'Neal pulled out his own handkerchief to wipe his eyes. "But first, I heard a gun go off up there. What the hell happened?"

A resigned Wyckham slumped down into a chair and described the whole hilltop Draesh encounter, not mentioning his stroll through most of the squadron covered in the goddamn thing's shite. He did mention Harrison's request for some swivel guns and the Yankee's suggestion about building observation decks on the hilltops.

"And I'm sure our female allies would like to look at that flying ship; maybe they could learn something from it or tell us how to put it to use."

O'Neal nodded, called his coxswain, and started writing quick notes for delivery ashore. He motioned for Commander Wallingford to begin speaking.

"Aye, Admiral." The young commander turned to Wyckham, waving his hand back and forth across his nose. "As you know, *Gnat* fell into this world first. We were about three miles ahead of the rest of the squadron in the Channel when *Gnat* dropped through the first hole. The torrent of water from the flying gates pushed us right into a cove, where we went aground and lost the main topmast and the rudder. It took us a day to get under way again. Making a new rudder took some eight hours alone. Finally we set out in a squall. Then, about an hour later, when the weather cleared, we blundered into a French eighty."

Startled, Wyckham's eyebrows popped upward, pulling his eyes wide open. A French ship-of-the-line here? Now? *What could possibly happen next? Maybe Napoleon himself and the whole goddamn Imperial Guard dropping in for tea?*

Wallingford continued. "It saw us and chased us toward a lee shore. Luckily, with our shallow draft, we were able to get into a delta and hide in a forested cove. Couldn't get out for another day as the damned frog kept patrolling the coast. Finally, it left for good, and we tried to find the squadron, a difficult task with our compass broken. Then, yesterday, we heard the bomb ketches firing and sailed to the sound of the guns."

O'Neal took over. "Thank you, Commander." He turned back to Wyckham. "So I need you to screen this frog liner and let us know what he's up to. To continue the war back on Earth here is beyond reason. Although being reasonable has never been a strong point with the crapauds, especially since their damn revolution. Just keep your distance from him, and don't let him get you downwind on a lee shore. Try to keep him away from here for at least two days when Zeus should beback in the water and fully armed. We don't need some hot-blooded frog in an eighty coming into this cove blazing away with *Zeus* still on the beach."

Wyckham was deep in thought. Hadn't he heard something from the French fishermen they'd dealt with about a new eighty-gun liner, *Leviathan*, being readied at Brest? It was supposed to be completely armed with sixty-five-pound carronades and captained by some fanatical revolutionary who named himself the "Sea Eagle." Just what they needed now, some lunatic frog in a ship-of-the-line with *Zeus* still careened and no allied forces yet arrived.

Diplomacy was the answer. Maybe they could explain the impotance of the battle being fought here and persuade this fellow earthman to join them. The squadron could certainly use another ship-of-the-line in the next confrontation with the Draesh. They just needed to talk this French captain into forgetting the war back home and fighting alongside his English archenemy here—that was all.

But then an idea struck him. It would involve his dear Lady Brashton. Mayhap she could come up with another creative masquerade to save the day, like she did with Jarvis?

O'Neal and Wallingford stood up to leave. "I'll be staying here; must get *Zeus* back in the water," explained O'Neal. "You should be able to weigh anchor as soon as Captain Wallingford and I get off. I've had Lieutenant Rawlins ready the ship."

O'Neal had to stop for a retching cough, then pulled out his handkerchief again and waved it in front of his face. "And for God's sake, leave Rawlins in command for a bit longer. Let him warp her out, because you, sir, need to spend some time with your toilette right now. Remain below and get cleaned up." He paused to put the handkerchief over his nose. "No need to show us out. We're quite able to find the gig ourselves."

With another cough and a muttered "Holy Jesus!" O'Neal led Wallingford above. Wyckham called for his man, Obujimi, who immediately appeared with a steaming basin, soap, towels, a fresh uniform, and musket cartridges stuffed in his nostrils. Above him, he heard the crew being called to stations for setting sail.

After a thorough scrub down, a fresh uniform, and some pea soup, the captain climbed to the quarterdeck to watch Rawlins bring the ship about one last time and weather the cove's larboard point. Spotting

Wyckham, the lieutenant walked up to deliver the ship back to him. But Wyckham had other priorities. Rawlins would stay in command for now.

"Well handled, Lieutenant, not a hint of a luff," said Wyckham approvingly. "Please continue and get the ship on the south-southeast course." The squadron was using the point of the first sun rising as east and navigating accordingly. "*Gnat* encountered the Frenchman somewhere in that direction. The frog captain must have heard the mortars firing yesterday and is probably laboring his way here right now."

Now came the time to find out what he really needed to know. "Lieutenant, have you seen our Lady Brashton recently? We may need her help on this cruise."

The Lady Brashton appeared immediately. That was a short search. Was she always nearby? She'd probably assumed the image of a halyard or something and had been hanging about him ever since he'd returned to *Righteous*. Fortunately, she appeared fully dressed, wearing a simple country frock.

"What, no puff of smoke as the magic fairy returns to us mortals?" Wyckham quipped.

The lady furrowed her brows in consideration. "I suppose I could do that. I could mimic one of your big cannons going off every time I arrive. Should I do that?"

"Ah…no, actually, that would not be a good idea. Might make some hands a bit jumpy to have explosions going off on deck. My apologies. The comment was just a joke." *Gads, better be careful kidding around with these alien beings. Joking around might end up anthing but humorous.* "But I'm glad to see you, for I wish to ask for your assistance. An enemy warship from Earth has arrived here and could cause us all serious problems. I believe this is an occasion where your unique abilities could again work diplomatic miracles. Is it possible that you and a few of your compatriots could join *Righteous* on a short cruise?" Wyckham believed she'd prove to be a secret weapon that the French would be absolutely powerless to deal with.

Lady Brashton appeared deep in thought for a moment. Then she awoke as if she'd been in a daze and replied, "I can certainly join you, and three more allies are now on their way here. The rest must

157

continue their work in resetting the transporter. They are very near the point where we can start transporting allied fleets to this planet."

Soon, three glowing balls of light appeared flying above the trees and headed to *Righteous*. Once aboard, they again transformed into images of human women and sat down with Wyckham as he laid out his plans for them.

Skies were clear, and by early evening, they had sighted the French ship. She was on a direct course for them, making all possible speed with even her studding sails set. Thankfully, they had intercepted her before she'd gotten to the cove and realized that she was currently the most powerful weapon on this world. Now the first order of business was to see if they could meet and talk some sense into this frog fanatic.

But the ship needed to be prepared for any outcome. Drums beat the crew to quarters as *Righteous* cleared for action. Loblolly boys, none over fourteen, scurried up from the magazine with powder and shot, dodging marines with their muskets heading up into the crosstrees. Guns were loaded but not run out. Wyckham wanted to appear peaceful. When they got within two miles, *Righteous* raised signal flags to spell out *P-A-R-L-E-Z*.

The Frenchman's response was to open her gunports and run out her guns. Apparently, he wasn't interested in diplomacy just yet. Staring through his telescope, Wyckham shuddered as he recognized the giant muzzles of sixty-five-pound carronades bristling from the sides of the big two-decker. With thirty-six of the large guns per side, the French ship's weight of shot was eight times larger than that of *Righteous*. In just one broadside, the Frenchman could reduce *Righteous* to kindling.

Thankfully, the range on those guns was very short. And with her superior speed, *Righteous* could keep her distance and peck away with her long guns, though her gunnery would be poor at long distance and probably not inflict much damage on the massive French liner. But if the French captain wouldn't talk, Wyckham needed to play a cat and mouse game and lure him away from the squadron's base. If *Leviathan* got into that cove, it could destroy the entire squadron at its leisure.

Righteous came about to a leeward reach, keeping out of range of the Frenchman's carronades. Frigates like *Righteous* were the fastest and handiest ships afloat. No big liner like *Leviathan* had any hope of catching her if she were well handled. Once on the new course, Wyckham called out to Midshipman Moore. "Mr. Moore, let's try another tack with the signal flags. Spell out in French, 'French Refugees On Board,' if you please." Like most young gentlemen serving as midshipmen in the British navy, Moore spoke French fluently.

"And let's get our bait in plain sight. Ladies, could you gather here by the starboard railing, if you please?" His four allies moved next to him, appearing in long coats with hoods hiding their faces. Turning to Rawlins, he said, "Now let's see if we've piqued this crapaud's curiosity enough to accept our proffered olive branch."

Through his Leica telescope, Wyckham watched the French officers on their quarterdeck studying *Righteous* and the four ladies with their own glasses. *Leviathan* finally returned the signal for a parley, hove to, and ran her guns back in.

Wyckham addressed his first lieutenant. "Mr. Rawlins, the ship is yours. I will be going aboard this Frenchie with the ladies and Captain Donnelson. Please be so good as to put the ship in irons two cables downwind of her. Stay prepared to drop away quick. For all we know, this wild revolutionary has no honor and is just trying to get us close. If he runs his guns out again, drop off and get out of range. Don't worry about me. With our lady and her squadron here boarding his vessel…" He paused to smile at Lady Brashton and her group. "That Frenchman doesn't stand a chance."

Along with Marine Captain Donnelson (nothing like a bright red uniform to impress the frogs), the party climbed down into his gig and was rowed over to the imposing French ship. With the ladies keeping their heads bowed, the party climbed aboard without fanfare, just surly French curses from ragged crewmen with leveled pistols. Rather than greeting them on the waist, the French captain and his officers rudely made Wyckham's party walk up to them as they waited on the quarterdeck. Just what Wyckham was hoping for: a few more seconds for the ladies to be close enough to the French captain and his lieutenants to figure matters out and get themselves ready.

He leaned over to Lady Brashton and spoke softly out of the side of his mouth. "See anything of use yet?" he inquired.

Lady Brashton didn't answer. Still searching their opponent's mind, no doubt. She finally spoke. "Hmm…no family or children held dear; he hates all his previous lovers…Ah! There's what we need!" She turned to her comrades. "Everyone else set?" They nodded agreement and the group headed over to the quarterdeck, getting occasional shoves from their escort.

Reaching the quarterdeck stairs, Wyckham asked, *"Permission pour la platine arrière?"*

"Oui, eef you Engleesh are sobaire eenoff today to climb a stair," the captain sneered. "And speak Engleesh! You deesgrace a beeootifool langouage with your horriblay aytempt to speak eet."

What a surprise—an arrogant Frenchman. Still wants to kill the English, hasn't yet realized that maybe things change when you drop into a world where giant ogres are trying to eat you. Obviously hasn't been attacked by the local demons yet. Too bad, nothing like watching some of your crew get devoured by a slobbering demonic pig to make one a little more open-minded about allying with an old enemy. *Well, let's try explaining to this frog exactly what kind of hell he has fallen into.*

Maybe honesty and rationality would carry the day, although something told him that these concepts might not have much appeal to this Frenchman. "Certainly, I must apologize for my poor French," he began. "Please accept my compliments on your excellent English. Allow me to introduce myself: I am Post Captain Rodney Wyckham and this is my Captain of Marines, Malcolm Donnelson. Earlier today, I was informed of your ship's presence on this world. We welcome your arrival with such an impressive ship. Is it possible for us to sit down for a while? There is a war going on here against an enemy that gravely threatens our own world and all that we know. I would like to explain the situation in the hope that for the good of both England and France, you can forget we are at war back on Earth and join forces with us here."

The French captain said nothing, just stared at them in obvious disgust. This was one haughty frog. Finally he replied, "I am Jean Badoin, known and feared bah you Anglais as zee *Sea Eagle.* You come to my sheep and theenk I will forget everything you stinking goddamns have done, because we 'af been t'rust into zees strange place? Now should we go beelow to my cabeen and dreenk togethaire like old friends? Maybe you 'af depleted your rum sooplie and are desperate for some good French wine, *non*? You may speak to me here. Who are zees passengaires? And where are we?"

So much for diplomatic effort—it was time for a little magic.

"Certainly. Allow me to introduce our passengers, who can explain matters further. This is…" Shite, he hadn't asked Lady Brashton her new name!

"*La Comptesse de Pittard*," Lady Brashton said as she stepped forward and pushed her hood back from her face. "*Enchantée, Monsieur le Capitaine.*"

No longer was she Lady Brashton, but a beautiful French noblewoman, rouged and attired for the royal palace at Versailles. She had black hair piled up on her head in a bun, held in place with bejeweled brooches. Her long white gown was embroidered with pearls, and her bodice so low and tight that a moderate cough would create quite a memorable moment. She even had one of those ridiculous black birthmarks the French were so fond of drawn on her cheek.

One glance at Badoin showed that Lady Brashton had chosen her new identity well. His eyes and mouth were wide open like a country bumpkin in his first brothel. Since he was completely unable to respond, Lady Brashton made his own introduction for him.

"So you are Jean Badoin, zee Sea Eagle we 'af 'aired so much aybout?" she said with admiration as she stepped forward and took his arm. "Ooh la, such a strong arm! Since you 'af such egsellant anglaise, may we speak in eet so my Anglais friends 'ere may ondairstand?"

With her touch, his jaw dropped further, if that was possible, and he let out a soft gasp. So this dedicated revolutionary was actually besotted with a noblewoman! Would wonders never cease! Shaking his head and smirking, Wyckham tried not to laugh out loud and spoil everything.

With Badoin still astonished and speechless, Lady Brashton continued the formalities. "Eef you please, let us name oware friends to you. Zis eez Madame Muriel Devillier, and 'ere we 'af Mademoiselle Amelie Bouchet, and zis eez Mademoiselle Fannie Farnsworth."

As they were introduced, each one of the three other ladies stepped up to a French officer and removed her hood to show her face. The first lieutenant, approached by a beautiful Mademoiselle Devillier, dropped to his knees and kissed her hand. He rattled away in French, something to the effect that he was so glad she had apparently left her wealthy husband and searched him out, true love had triumphed over money, God had brought them together here, and so on. Amelie Bouchet, who couldn't have been over fourteen years of age, produced absolute euphoria in the rather elderly sailing master when she walked up and excitedly kissed him, white hair and all. But Badoin's marine captain was obviously embarrassed when the corpulent Mademoiselle Fannie Farnsworth walked up, slapped him hard on his backside, and with a mouth that was missing some teeth yelled out, "Ef et ain't th' French cap'm agin! Oi mus' say, ya gimme the longest ride o' me life thet nite en Calay! Gots anudder un in ya, luv?"

Well, the ladies got three out of four right. But it didn't matter because Jean Badoin was oblivious to everything about him except the Comptesse de Pittard. For an alien being with no experience in European social maneuvering, this ally and lover, now in French form, had apparently read enough in English minds over the last few days to know just how to wrap any human around her little finger.

"Ooh, what a wonderful sheep you 'af! You must gif me a tour of zees magnificent vessel. But first we are ayefrade we most ask for your help; my friends and I are all een terreeblay dangere from which may-bee zee famous Sea Eagle can save us? Possiblee we go below to your cabeen, just you and I, zo I may egsplane our situashon?"

"*Oui, certainement, certainement!*" Badoin exclaimed in wild affirmation as the countess gripped his arm to guide him below.

The other three officers headed off in different directions, excitedly babbling away in French about how wonderful it was to be reunited with the loves of their lives, leaving Wyckham and Donnelson on the deck to wonder what the hell to do while the ladies won the French over to the cause.

"What now, Captain?" said Donnelson. "Hell, why not just signal a few of my lads to come over, and we'll make this ship ours? I'll warrant

162

this frog crew is mightily confused on this world and would follow anyone who could explain things."

"Aye, a tempting thought, that," responded Wyckham. "But this ship might be in action soon—a change in command would hash things up for weeks. We want their officers to run their ship but follow our orders. Which I expect will not be a problem once our allies get done with them. I suggest we just return to *Righteous* and pass the time with a glass. The ladies will contact us somehow when their job is done here."

He certainly could use a drink, because there was one matter barging into his thoughts that had his dander up. Now that their diplomatic effort was on its way to success, his Lady Brashton would soon be in that ridiculous Frenchman's bed.

For God's sake, forget it! Wyckham thought. She's just a moving painting. She's not real. She's not Lady Brashton! She's just a ball of electricity with excellent diplomatic skills, that's all—and some unbelievable other skills he couldn't forget either.

12

THE FORCES ASSEMBLE
FOR BATTLE

After three hours on the return voyage, Wyckham and *Righteous*'s entire crew had assembled on the main deck in awe of the scene in the sky above them. A glance behind at *Leviathan,* now part of the squadron, showed her French crew gaping up as well. As far as the eye could see, the air was filled with an array of gigantic flying craft.

The Frenchman Badoin had turned out to have more flexibility and common sense than Wyckham had expected. He'd quickly grasped that victory over the Draesh here was far more important than the latest war between England and France back on Earth. Of course, how could he not understand when the issues were so clearly explained to him by the Comptesse de Pittard? So the diplomatic mission had been a success, marred only by the unfortunate sudden death of *Leviathan*'s elderly sailing master, who sadly had not been up to the physical demands of making love for hours with an energetic fourteen-year-old girl. But he passed over *un amoureux*—the way a true Frenchman would want to go.

Lady Brashton, who had returned from *Leviathan* a while ago and was standing beside Wyckham, had assured him that every ship they were now seeing was carrying new allies transported here to fight the Draesh. Apparently, once they had gotten rid of Crawford, the work in the cave had progressed rapidly.

As everyone watched, another immense craft emerged from one of the square openings in the sky, roaring and emitting flames from its stern. It must have been five cables long and a cable wide, with all sorts of protuberances that Wyckham believed had to be weapons. As a naval officer, he had to wonder about the workings of such a massive ship. How big was the crew? *Zeus* carried six hundred and fifty crewmembers—this thing must have thousands aboard, but thousands of what…insects? Who knows what types of creatures were manning these ships? He would be fighting as part of the strangest armada ever assembled—that much was certain.

As they got closer to the British squadron's base, Wyckham could see dozens of other craft hovering in the air or floating in the waters outside of the cove, apparently too large to enter it. While some of them were clearly anchored, others were moving about slowly, water bubbling up from their sterns and sides suggesting some sort of propulsion devices below the waterline. Certainly, none of them used the wind for power.

As he watched, a long, gleaming vehicle dropped from the air onto the water, then rapidly accelerated toward the cove, its wake a hundred-foot-high torrent of water. *Christ, it must be doing fifty knots*, thought Wyckham. This flotilla was truly astonishing. Compared to them, a frigate like *Righteous,* pride of the world-leading British navy, was a silly antique. Lady Brashton had said that these ships held weapons with range farther than the eye could see. Maybe she was correct when she told him that the British squadron would not have a place in the coming battle.

The closer they sailed to the squadron's cove, the more amazing sights they saw. All sorts of small airships were buzzing about. (Shuttling officers back and forth?) Many of them had landed on the beach, which was already covered with various kinds of strange-looking contraptions and many containers of all shapes and sizes. These did not appear to be weapons—more likely stores and shelters.

But there did seem to be a channel open through all the moored craft. Wyckham had Rawlins reduce sail to working jibs only, and *Righteous* slowly crept into the cove's mouth.

Now they had closeup views of the crews at work in the cove. If their ships were amazing, the occupants were even more so. Closest to them was some kind of metal barge covered with ants. *Jesus, some of our allies actually are insects!* And the ants were as big as large dogs. They were working at a frantic pace, unloading rounded metal containers onto the barge from a ship made of three large, black spheres that must have each been two hundred feet in diameter. Next to them was what looked to be a huge floating tree trunk, wrapped in giant vines that were actually moving about, performing unknown tasks.

Scanning across the anchorage, Wyckham saw ten-foot-tall lizards walking upright on gleaming metal ships, groups of living metallic poles flying about on flat disks, and jellyfish-like blobs crawling around on the flat decks of a floating stone hemisphere. Each ship had groups of Lady Brashton's energy beings floating about them, doing God knew what, but apparently they were an important part of the fleet's activity.

Wyckham felt completely lost. He could see no sign of any British ships because of all the water traffic in the roads. But someone else saw them.

Midshipman Moore called down from the main crosstrees. "Deck there, signal on the left hilltop redoubt." Moore adjusted his telescope and resumed reading. "Relayed from the flag…our number… 'Anchor South of Flagship One Mile Southwest'."

"Thank you. Acknowledge, please," said Wyckham to a midshipman handling signal flags on the main deck. "And signal to *Leviathan* 'Follow,' then our number. Helm, southwest if you please. Keep an eye out for *Zeus*. She's here somewhere." He'd never have thought a ship-of-the-line like *Zeus* would be so dwarfed by other ships in a port that it would be hard to find.

Righteous dropped off two points and headed between two glossy, bulbous crafts that looked like they were made of porcelain. They were attended by the strangest beings Wyckham had seen yet. They were over seven feet tall, with gangly arms and white, glossy skin. Their heads were round and bulbous, tapering to a pointed chin. Their hairless faces were almost devoid of features—just two vertical eyes and a slit for a mouth. Wyckham noted with astonishment that they had an additional pair of arms, shorter ones attached to their rib cages. They were dressed in various kinds of tight suits with lots of pockets and small devices dangling from their belts. Translating devices similar to Wulfe's were strapped to their heads, but none of them hailed *Righteous* as she slowly passed by. There was not even a wave or any acknowledgement at all.

Well, he would show these newcomers the proper manners for entering port. British ships had always saluted each other and allied ships when joining a fleet, and that was not going to change just because they were on another world. "Mr. Rawlins, ready fourteen starboard guns for the admiral, if you would."

They rounded the last of the port traffic and there was *Zeus*, back afloat and anchored in the cove's southern corner. Wyckham smiled to see its gunports opening, too. He and O'Neal were about to give this menagerie quite a show.

Righteous's first gun crashed out as she turned toward the anchorage behind the flagship. Her guns continued firing the saluting charges as *Zeus*'s first gun fired in return. Then damn if *Leviathan* didn't also begin its own fourteen-gun salute! Lady Brashton must have really Badoin in the palm of her hand to get him to salute an English ship.

The other four ships in the British squadron also started firing salutes for *Righteous* using their smaller six- and nine-pounders, the retorts echoing back and forth across the cove. The gun flashes became eerie blurs in all the smoke, which mostly remained in the cove due to the light winds. After a few minutes, the thunderous ritual came to a close and the smoke started to dissipate.

Wyckham then heard all sorts of strange noises. Among others there was loud clicking, some banging, moaning, squeaks, buzzing sounds, and staccato slapping, all filling the air. As the last of the smoke finally blew away, he could see all the various beings present looking at the sailing ships and producing the strange sounds. *Hmph. They're cheering!* So even with all their advanced ships and weapons, they could appreciate what the squadron had done here against the Draesh with only "crude" weapons and a lot of courage. *I guess we actually are respected comrades-in-arms here.*

Wyckham smiled at all the beings facing him, giving bows and mimicking their salutes as best he could. He tried to keep smiling back, but the applause continued on endlessly and it got harder to keep up the façade...because each ship they encountered seemed to have an even more repugnant crew to gaze upon than the previous one. And, of course, the last one was the worst, covered with amorphous piles of mud. They applauded *Righteous* with a medley of sounds that could only be belching or flatulence. *Yes, thank you. I'm sure that especially unpleasant fart was saved just for me. Sorry if it wet your breeches, thank you so much.*

Finally the otherworldly hurrahs subsided as *Righteous* made its way to the end of the cove. She swung to anchor just alee of the flagship, with *Leviathan* anchoring a cable further off. After acknowledging *Zeus*'s signal, "Captains Repair on Board," Wyckham and Lady Brashton joined the procession of gigs from all the other six ships rowing their captains over to board the repaired flagship. After everyone, including their new ally, Badoin, was properly piped aboard, O'Neal invited them into *Zeus*'s expansive great cabin below.

Representatives of the other races were already there aboard *Zeus*, wearing those translating devices. There were also several of Lady Brashton's attendants present, appearing as the same women they had been at the wild dinner party. Wyckham tried to flush the images of that night from his mind and settle down to business.

"First of all, some introductions are in order," said O'Neal, looking at Wyckham to continue.

"Yes, certainly. May I introduce to you all Capitaine Jean Badoin, known as the Sea Eagle, of the French ship-of-the-line *Leviathan*, eighty guns?" Wyckham's stomach was turning as he said that, but he knew it paid to toady up to frogs.

"Most welcome, sir," said O'Neal. "You are to be commended for putting aside our differences and joining this noble cause." Badoin acknowledged the compliment with a deep bow and one of those silly angled tilts of the head that the French favoured.

Then O'Neal gestured to one of the beings with four arms and glossy skin, saying, "And this is the leader of the fleet assembled here from the League of Planets, who goes by the name of Twenty-Two, which he assures me is a very high rank on his world." Wyckham noted the sarcasm in O'Neal's voice. *We don't even rate an officer above a ten?*

"We thank you for opening the door to this world," the creature spoke through its translating device. "Due to your taking of this area with its transporter, we have been able to get our forces here before the Draesh could reprogram the other transporters on this planet and bring in their own forces. We will now kill every Draesh. Their continuing devastation of other worlds will end."

In turn, O'Neal introduced them to the others including one of the ants, some kind of bush with one big eye, a mud ball, and a hairy, ape-like creature with empty holes in its face where its eyes should have been. They all sat down and O'Neal addressed Mr. Number Twenty-Two. "So now, I have gathered my captains here for a council of war with you, our new allies. Just tell us how we may assist you in the coming fight."

"Go away." Number Twenty-Two's blunt response stung the assembled human captains. Eyebrows went up all around amid angry glances. O'Neal tensed his lips, probably trying to keep from exploding in the arrogant alien's face.

We've been here fighting your fight, and you can't manage a little courtesy? Wyckham thought. Well, what could one expect from a being with no face. Probably didn't have a goddamn heart either.

Lady Brashton at least realized the snub and tried to smooth matters over with everyone. "All the civilizations here cannot thank you and your forces enough, Admiral. Your heroic actions have allowed the League to get here and put an end to the Draesh. The combined forces of the multiple worlds that are now here should easily win the coming battle. The hard part was getting here first and forcing the gate open, which your forces did so valiantly."

"This battle will have a level of violence inconceivable to you," she continued, "one for which you are neither prepared nor equipped. Both sides have hand-held weapons with which a single adversarie can destroy your entire squadron in moments. Let the League of Planets fight the rest of this battle. You have done your part. When it is over you can return home to a galaxy freed from the threat of the Draesh, thanks mostly to you."

The alien representatives got up and left without a further word. Apparently they had met here just to see one of the quaint ships from Earth. O'Neal was left drumming his fingers on the table, clearly at a loss for words. A glance around the table showed the other captains disgruntled as well. Badoin looked ready to call Number Twenty-Two out. Again Lady Brashton jumped in.

"While you await your return home, we have constructed facilities ashore to help you pass the time. One of those square constructions on the beach is for feeding and entertaining you. We have brought in food supplies you should find quite pleasing. Though we could not get the same plants and animals you are used to eating, we have tried to duplicate the flavors of your favourite dishes. And we have even fermented plants to make those intoxicating beverages you are so fond of. Hopefully, this establishment will meet with your approval in every way. We have copied elements from all the places we saw in your minds that were your favourites. I believe you sailors refer to them as 'taverns'?"

That shook Wyckham from his sulk—a tavern out here? That would definitely improve the wait to return home. It'll certainly help morale around here, too. He noticed eyebrows perking up and captains sitting upright to hear more. He was curious himself.

"That is extremely thoughtful of you, Madam," said Wyckham, his voice dripping in thanks. "I expect you have done your usual excellent job of reading our minds and have built a place all of us will find more than acceptable."

"We hope so," continued the lady. "And I must confess that many members of my race hope to gain from attending this establishment as well."

Alarms went off in Wyckham's brain. Oh God, he could guess what was coming next.

"I know we have much to learn, but my race wants to provide you with the usual services that we understand these seaport taverns provide to sailors on Earth. Of course, we will benefit greatly from such interactions with you, but please remember, it can help both the cause and benefit our entire race. Hopefully, you can forgive the initial errors we are sure to make as tavern workers. I promise you, we will try hard to constantly improve our services."

Good Lord, I'm sure they will achieve the "hard" part quite easily, thought Wyckham. His mind started imagining the royal beauties he would have them conjure up for him to choose from. It would make Sultan Mahmud's harem in Constantinople pale by comparison.

But O'Neal wasn't so sure about the idea. "Ah, Lady Brashton..." said O'Neal with some regret. "What you describe certainly sounds excellent, but it would be extremely divisive to the squadron. It's true that we officers would love to have a broth...ahh...an accommodating tavern nearby, but all the common seamen would hear of this place and cause riots trying to enter. It just wouldn't do."

"Oh, I'm sorry. Apparently, I was not clear," apologized the lady. "We plan to accommodate all your ships' crews, officers and seamen alike. The building is quite large; it will hold thousands of beings. It is fully stocked with excellent foodstuffs and enough of your beer, wine, and rum to provide each of your men with two of your gallons per day. We can increase that amount if more is needed. My only concern is the large number of my race who have heard of the plans for this establishment and have arrived here in the hope of receiving your human life force. Several hundred have traveled here already after learning about the empowering abilities of coupling with your race. But we will strictly allocate visits by our people. We will make sure that there are never more than three of us present in the tavern for each sailor."

Sweat rose to Wyckham's brow. *Three women per man?* Absolute heaven for any sailor in the British navy. He looked over at the admiral. *Christ, Sean, why not? Say yes, for God's sake!*

Wyckham gave him a look that made it clear how he felt about the matter. O'Neal raised his palms to Wyckham in frustrated inquiry.

"Sweet Jesus, Rodney, you expect me, now an Admiral of the Red, to approve the running of the largest whorehouse in history? 'Admiral O'Neal, as his first official act, constructed an enormous brothel to make sure his entire squadron was rodgered daily.' Christ, this place would be so large, it would need advertisement. Can't you just imagine? Bills being distributed, 'Sleep with Cathleen, the admiral's favourite! A special bargain tonight: Cathleen and a grog ration for just two orgasms!' Oh, I can just envision returning to Earth and facing Admiralty on this. They'd forget about trying me for mutiny. Christ, that's nothing compared with running history's largest whorehouse, catering to officers and common seamen alike! Admiralty would just love to have an entire squadron carousing together without respect to rank!" He turned back to Lady Brashton. "Madam, I'm afraid I must declare this facility of yours off limits."

But by no means would Wyckham allow the squadron to miss out on the lady's offer if he could possibly help it. After what they'd been through, the squadron deserved this tavern! He got up and sat next to O'Neal.

He spoke softly. It was a private conversation between two officers and old friends. "Sean, think realistically about our future. Forget about Admiralty; who knows if we'll ever get back to England anyway? That largely depends on our friend Number Twenty-Two here, and we've both seen overconfident admirals like him get their arses kicked and lots of their men killed. My bet is the Draesh will fight like hell for their homeland. I'll warrant they have a few surprises in store for this league of worlds or planets or whatever. I believe their record fighting the Draesh so far hasn't been very sterling."

"Now if this allied force loses the coming battle," he continued, "we won't be going home for a while. The squadron will need to run off and hide, gathering intelligence and fighting a hit-and-run war, waiting for the League to regroup. With no chance to get home soon, squadron morale will drop like a seaman's turd off the bow. We have to give our lads some reason to fight for this world. So let's give them the absolute time of their lives here in this tavern! It'll be every sailor's fondest dream! Once they try the place, they'll do anything at the chance for more; they'll follow us anywhere. And even if this base falls and their precious tavern gets taken, they'll fight so furiously to get it back, God help the poor Draesh."

O'Neal stroked his chin in consideration. "Humph! And if we do get back to England, Jarvis's cronies in Parliament and Admiralty will have my bollocks in a sling anyway. In truth, sanctioning a brothel is actually nothing compared to the mutiny he'll pin on us."

He's almost aboard! Now for the final shove. Wyckham leaned even closer and spoke right into the admiral's ear. "And don't tell me you don't want to sit around for a few days drinking with hordes of beautiful women begging you to put a leg over em. Think about how fantastic it will be with hundreds of these ladies begging for your attention! Dammit, it's our turn to take a break, and let someone else do the fighting around here for a change!"

"Bloody hell, you're right. Let's go check the place out now!" said O'Neal as he stood up. "Must make sure our seamen will be getting their 'semen's' worth, ha hah!"

Wyckham had persuaded him to do it! But why? While Wyckham really did believe it would be good for morale, he didn't kid himself that it was the main reason he wanted the tavern to open. During the last few days, he'd been in three close-run fights, barely survived another scrape by blowing the bowels out of a carnivorous monster, been covered in bushels of the universe's foulest feces, and had to kiss the arse of a fanatical frog captain while staring into the muzzles of his sixty-five-pounders. Goddamn it, after all that, any sailor in a foreign port sure as hell deserved a spell in a good tavern. And this port was extremely foreign. No one back home would ever know about whatever depravities he might descend into here!

"Let's away!"

13

A QUIET DAY AT THE RUPTURED KRAG

Wyckham pushed back from the table and sighed, stretching out on the stark but very comfortable chair. Whichever of the odd beings now around here had built these things, you had to respect the creatures. The chair frames were fashioned from that lightweight ceramic some of the foreign ships were made of, and the cushions were stuffed with plush material. And best of all, these furnishings could change shape. The chair back hinged to let him recline, and the seat magically pushed up to support his thighs as he moved.

Across the table, Wulfe tipped back the large metal stein apparently preferred by alien wolfmen, finishing a pint of the beer-like beverage one of his ships had provided. He motioned to one of the scantily clad women waiting eagerly behind them. "Just another drink, thank you."

The disappointment on the lady's face was quite evident. She understood him since English was the common language in the Ruptured Krag Tavern. So Wulfe was done with women for the day. Whoever thought a canine would ever need a break from humping?

Actually, Wyckham could understand not being interested in more sexual activity right now. After some six hours of copulating with almost every female who had ever fueled his teenage fantasies (including three of his nannies, several of his schoolmates' sisters, and the daughter of his local vicar), Wyckham needed a break, too.

Wulfe spoke up. "So how do you like these seats?" he asked Wyckham.

"Remarkable," he replied. "Most impressive how these things change their shape—always comfortable. How do they do it?"

"They have electrical power units built right into them," Wulfe explained. "They sense movement and adjust themselves to support whatever's in them. Must feel good on your weak, human buttocks. All our fleet uses them. Everyone's body needs support when flying our ships, which, unlike your wooden scows here in the cove, are capable of some acceleration," he quipped in a jab at the British squadron.

Well into his cups, Wyckham couldn't understand these alien space voyagers. How could you run a ship while seated? Any decent officer should be walking about his ship, making sure it was properly handled. And these chairs have electrical power? He wondered what might happen if the bloody things broke. Maybe shoot a lightning bolt up some poor sod's arse? He shifted nervously in his seat.

He then surprised himself with a loud belch. What a meal! Whatever bird that was, whatever fruit was in the sauce, they'd both been quite superb. Food, drink, and female companionship—this establishment certainly had everything a traveling gentleman needed.

He looked around the officer's room. It was a pretty quiet day at the Ruptured Krag. Thank God there was no band playing. For the first two days after the Krag had opened, various members of the League had brought their bands in to impress everyone with their species' music. But no matter which of them were playing, it seemed all their music was just an unbearable racket. The singing was worst of all. You couldn't even consider your feed, no matter how enticing it appeared, until the alien caterwauling had been over for at least fifteen minutes.

The only other occupants of the room were two bashful midshipmen tucked into a dark corner with a handful of the ladies fussing over them. For the first time, the officer's room at the Krag was almost empty. Could the squadron's officers actually have grown bored with this tavern already? More likely they were just hung over and too exhausted from time already spent in the place.

Three days had passed since O'Neal had given his blessing to open the tavern. It was a large structure, made of the same rippled, lightweight metal sheets as the other buildings that had been quickly erected on the beach. Although its outside was plain, Lady Brashton's cadre had done their best to make the interior pleasing and comfortable. There were varnished wooden bars and stone fireplaces in both the seamen's and the officers' rooms, just like a good public house back in England.

The walls were covered with local vines and flowers, which provided hours of amusement for the hands. They threw little bits of food to stick on the walls, making wagers as to which flower or vine would snatch them up, either with superior speed or brute force. Dead plants from the continuous combat were constantly being replaced, like the gladiators of ancient Rome. But as entertaining as the planet's plant life was, drinking and debauching with Lady Brashton's race was the main reason to visit. During the first two days the place had seen orgies that would have made Nero blush.

O'Neal had encouraged all his captains to give shore leave to as many of the hands as possible; over a thousand men had been in the place over the first two days. Thankfully, Lady Brashton had provided a separate room for officers, since the common room was usually packed.

Despite the size of the place, the new tavern was running like a Swiss watch. Amazingly, the Ruptured Krag had been able to keep food and especially drink in ample supply. Several of the species here to fight the Draesh had brought their own types of spirits in as well. And, surprisingly, there had been very few fights. The provosts O'Neal had appointed only had to break up a dozen or so brawls.

How wondrous the calming influence of naked women and endless sex can be, thought Wyckham.

But there had been one major altercation in the officer's room that had caused quite a stir. On the very first day, Lieutenant Rawlins had walked in to see his betrothed, the naked Catherine Burford, upside down on Commander Hamilton's lap with her legs wrapped around his head. Rawlins immediately challenged Hamilton to a duel, but when the lady stood up with semen on her chin and he saw Hamilton's erect member protruding from his breeches, Rawlins went into an animal rage. Grabbing a metal cup from the table, he jammed it into Hamilton's face, breaking his nose. But that didn't suffice for Rawlins, who kept pummeling Hamilton even as he slumped to the floor. Worst of all, a crowd of seamen had witnessed it from the doorway, and the altercation was now common knowledge on the lower decks. O'Neal had been furious over the whole matter and almost threw Rawlins through *Zeus*'s stern window when he summoned them both aboard for a dressing down.

Lady Brashton had solved the whole problem by simply having another lady approach Rawlins in the image of Catherine Burford, assuring him that she had decided on him over Hamilton. The two Catherine Burfords made sure that they never got near each other. Both officers were now content, each believing they had won the lady's affection, of course due to their superior manly attributes. And to prevent more serious problems in the future, the tavern had banned the carrying of weapons, with exceptions for the swords Wyckham and O'Neal were permitted to wear.

Any physical being who could pay in "life force" was welcome at the Krag, as the tavern had come to be known. Hundreds of aliens of all descriptions were working daily, ferrying materials to the beach and erecting structures for God knows what purpose. Apparently they, too, had something Lady Brashton's species wanted; all sorts of fantastic beings patronized the Krag in their spare time. Wulfe was a frequent visitor. He and Wyckham had even become drinking buddies. The canine alien had even introduced Wyckham to the fiery berry drink from his world that translated in English to "Den Drippings."

So it was a nice, peaceful day to spend settled in at the Krag. No orders to give, no bickering lieutenants to referee, no entries to make in the ship's log, no frightening monsters to fight. *God knows I deserve a quiet day in this superb tavern,* he thought as he finished off another glass.

But then a figure entered the room with the ability to change the mood right quick. It was one of the creatures Wyckham had named Highwaysnakes, seven-foot-tall serpents that slithered about upright on their tails and reminded Wyckham of the highwaymen who cruised the taverns back in Portsmouth. Although they were singularly unpleasant and untrustworthy beings, they were tolerated by the League of Planets because they smuggled chemicals from their conquered world, chemicals that were necessary to fuel propulsion of the League's ships.

And this one was a particularly nasty character whose name translated to "Lightning Fangs." Many of the Slicks believed him to be not just a smuggler but some kind of intergalactic pirate. The rumor was that he was responsible for the mysterious disappearance of some League ships and was possibly even colluding with the Draesh, despite the fact that they had brutally conquered his home planet.

The vile-looking creature looked about, saw Wyckham, snarled its lips back to reveal its four-inch fangs, and started slithering over. *So much for a peaceful day.*

They had met before and it had not ended amicably. It had been two nights ago, on the Ruptured Krag's opening night. Mr. Fangs, having tipped one too many, had seated himself uninvited at Wyckham's table and taken offense that Wyckham was allowed to wear a sword in the tavern. Probably the snakeman was upset that for once he couldn't bully the other patrons at a tavern, having been forced to surrender a host of personal weapons to get through the transporter. The dispute was promptly settled when, apparently at Lady Brashton's bidding, one of the mud-creatures rolled over, absorbed the obnoxious snake until only its tail was visible, and then rolled out the door with him inside. Later Wyckham had heard that the mud-creature had dropped the angrily hissing snakeman into the common refuse pit. Which, in a port with hundreds of sailors defecating ashore, not to mention all sorts of aliens excreting God knows what disgusting fluids, was certainly a rather unpleasant place to end your night.

With its long, forked tongue flicking, and its sunken, red eyes glowing menacingly, it clearly hadn't forgotten the matter and was looking for a fight. As it got closer, Wyckham could see all its familiar ugly features, from its scaly face to its surprising beard. But now it was dressed differently, in a shiny silver waistcoat, a single red silk breech, and a black stocking. Christ, somehow it had found out what a corsair back on Earth looked like and had taken up pirate's attire! Already the humans had become famous throughout the galaxy, and some aliens had started dressing and acting like them. To Wyckham, the creature looked absurd in the gaudy waistcoat with empty holes where its arms should be.

Shaking his head in disbelief at the latest incomprehensible sight on this crazed world, Wyckham leaned forward and prepared to defend himself. While he would be perfectly justified in standing up and drawing his sword, gentlemen did not start fights in taverns. But under the table he did pull his fine Moroccan blade from its scabbard and placed it in position for a low thrust.

Just get close, you rotten sod, and I'll stick three inches of steel right in your jewels, thought Wyckham. But snakes had no crotch—where the hell was its groin? He'd just have to guess and extended his point under the table to point at the middle of Mr. Fang's single breech. Wulfe was settled back in an alcoholic stupor and didn't seem to be aware of the impending scrap. No help there. Wyckham leaned forward to get the maximum distance with his sword's thrust.

But the damn serpent stopped just outside the range of Wyckham's blade!

"Foolish, sweating mammal!" it hissed through its translator. "You think to best me because you service those who run this place, and they let you have that puny weapon you've prepared under the table? My tongue smelt that trick from across the room! Now witness your death strike—real warriors don't need a weapon!"

It leaned back and coiled its tail to strike, its jaws spreading to reveal two long, deadly fangs dripping a purple venom. Wyckham started to pull his weapon back to defend himself, but it momentarily snagged unbder the table. He was just getting the blade free when his foe lunged. He was done for.

With blinding speed, the snake's head shot at Wyckham, propelled by its coiled tail. But with an even faster move, Wulfe exploded out of his seat with an ear-piercing snarl, spinning his body to ferociously backhand the creature's jaw with his heavy drinking stein, shattering the serpent's right fang. The blow turned its head sideways and the big snake shot over Wyckham's right shoulder. Before Wyckham realized what he was doing, he'd reacted and his point was under the snakeman's exposed jaw and thrusting upward. The Damascus-steel blade effortlessly passed through the creature's skull, coming out the top of its head as its momentum wrenched the sword from Wyckham's hand, and the creature fell to the floor in a heap.

Wyckham looked at Wulfe, astonished at the speed and skill just exhibited by his quite inebriated friend. "So the day isn't such a quiet one after all," was all Wulfe said as he signaled to a server. "Slimy little reptile made me spill a fresh drink."

Still speechless and shaking from having a poisonous fang miss his neck by inches, Wyckham watched as Wulfe then bent over the dead snakeman, put a foot on its bloody head and pulled Wyckham's sword free. Then damned if he didn't put the blade to his lips and give it a long lick! He quickly wrinkled his nose, turned his head, and spit loudly to his side. "Aach! Never could stomach snakeman. Despite what they say, snakemen don't taste like chicken." With a shake of his large canine head, Wulfe leaned back over the corpse and wiped the blade clean on the snake's fine livery, offered the blade to Wyckham, then turned to face the room. "Anyone going to clean up this mess?"

Another mud being waddled over, absorbed the lifeless snakeman, and rolled out the door, undoubtedly taking the snake for its second and final visit to the port's refuse pit.

"So it's a very interesting establishment your allies have built here," mused the wolfman as if nothing had happened. "While I'm welcome here, it's you humans they really want to 'tap.' It's known throughout the fleet that they want you to stay here with them if the Draesh are defeated. They sure like what you've got." He grinned with a mouthful of shiny canine teeth.

Jesus, we just fought a giant snake to the death, and all he's thinking about is drink and women! Well, he probably has been in fights with all sorts of strange aliens, so compose yourself, Wyckham, and show that Royal Navy officers take such events in stride as well. Wulfe had just brought up the subject of the allies. Here was a chance to learn things; Wulfe must know a lot about them.

"My friend, could you enlighten me concerning this race that we are now so…ah…involved with?" Wyckham asked, his voice still a little shaky. "Your world seems to have known them for years. Just what is their goal here? Who are they? What do you even call them anyway? We only know them as *allies*. I know they have no spoken name for themselves, but you must have a name for them?"

"When they first came to us eons ago, our ancestors called them *Fireflies*, and the name persists," responded Wulfe. "They have been very helpful to the wolf worlds in our wars with the Draesh, supplying technology and intelligence. They'd like our seed also, but they do not get much from us. We do not spray it all about as you humans do. It is a resource we husband carefully, far too important to be thrown away for an evening's entertainment. But the Fireflies still help us any-way. They appreciate all forms of life and have dedicated themselves to ending the Draesh devastation. Nowadays, they are especially helpful to us with espionage and League diplomacy."

So the ladies were decent folk after all and apparently quite compe-tent intelligence agents. Wyckham was glad to hear it. Though he was starting to believe these light beings were a lot more powerful beings than their frail feminine images projected. Had they just coincidentally been able to provide all the intelligence needed for the attack on the transporter? Or had they been manipulating matters right from their arrival to get control of the station for themselves? Well, they hadn't shown any signs of betrayal so far. Hopefully things stayed that way.

But he couldn't believe that Wulfe's race hadn't been enamored enough with the first arriving Fireflies to give them the same thing they wanted here in the tavern. "Come now, Wulfe. How were you able to resist these beings when they arrived in beautiful female form?"

"Oh, they didn't arrive in female form," responded Wulfe. "They knew that wasn't the way to win over our race. They arrived as male wolf warriors, completely unclothed of course, to show off their manly attributes. You should've seen the cock on your lady friend. Must have been as big as a Krag claw."

That image shocked Wyckham's still-shaken mind into sudden focus. *Lady Brashton travels around the cosmos with a giant phallus? Good God!*

"The…ah…Firefly who currently appears as Lady Brashton came to you endowed with…ah…male genitalia?" Wyckham asked, not wanting to believe what he'd just heard.

"Oh yes," replied Wulfe. "Humped me with the damn thing, too, trying to show me she was an alpha male. And she was quite excited doing it—as we say on our world, that red rocket was out!"

Wyckham's mouth gaped open in shock. The vision of his lifelong love a humping canine and enjoying it? She had a penis as big and red as a rocket? The only rockets Wyckham knew of were the Congreve rockets the navy had bombarded Baltimore's Fort McHenry with a few months ago. Was it that big? Did it too explode at the end in a red glare? The vision of his lifelong desire with an exploding penis filled his mind. Good Lord, how could he ever look at her again, much less continue their amorous liaisons?

Loud cheering from the common room thankfully drew his attention away from the horrible image raging through his thoughts. While festivities in the officer's room had slowed down, as most officer's were sleeping off the effects of attending the tavern for two whole days after it opened, apparently something was still going on in the common sailors' room next door.

Why not join my men? Damned if my mind doesn't need a distraction right now! Wyckham hadn't yet been in the common room. Now was his chance—there were no officers about to voice their disapproval, and he was especially curious to see what the average sailor did at this tavern. What kind of woman did a typical seaman have stored in his mind for the ladies to mimic?

"Wulfe, old boy," he said as he stood up, wobbling slightly from both drink and his brush with death. "Might I suggest we enter the common room and see what the ruckus is all about? Seems the lads are having a good time over there without us. This room's dead as old King George's member." A few days on this new world had greatly lessened Wyckham's respect for the order of things back home, especially the Crown.

The two officers entered the large common room and looked around. It was mostly empty except for a group of about a hundred seamen standing about a small stage, shouting their lungs out. As they crossed the room, they passed a few aliens enjoying whatever each species desired here at the Krag. There was one of those bizarre tube-like beings grasping a small, lit box on his table that was buzzing and shaking. The alien twitched and barked with each light and movement of the device. *Seems he's having a jolly time.* Next to him were two of the slick, four-arm beings from Number Twenty-Two's fleet, drinking some foul looking green brew and ignoring everyone else. Twenty feet away, several of the mud people were just sitting at a big table drinking glasses of water through long tubes, sitting motionless and doing nothing. Of course, as far as Wyckham could tell, besides occasionally establishing order in the Krag, they always seemed to be doing nothing. Christ, what could mud do anyway? He could just imagine one on his ship, trying to up-anchor or haul sheets.

But as he got closer he realized something actually was going on around their big table. Some of the mudmen were bubbling and shaking—and didn't they appear larger than usual? *Ah, Christ, are these mud-man copulating?* His belief was confirmed when one of the mud balls at the table moved over to be absorbed by another, and the resulting, larger, ball started shaking and bubbling as well. Then the enlarged mass produced a sound of flatulence so loud it hurt the ears. What a perfect ending for the act of lovemaking.

Suddenly Wyckham realized that he had probably just witnessed a Firefly, very like his own Lady Brashton, in the image of a mud being, mating with a real ball of mud! Not something he needed to consider a moment longer. He turned away and approached the stage. On it

184

were five men seated in a row, being attended to by three women each. Naturally, the women were completely naked. About ten feet across the stage were five more naked women kneeling in a line facing the men, calling out encouragement. "C'mon, Will! A big one for your girl, Flora!" and "Forty-two million this time, Andy, forty-two!" Wyckham noticed that each man had his manhood out, their attending ladies feverishly working each one. What the bloody hell kind of game was this?

Looking around for an idle hand to explain what was going on, he noticed—who else—Seaman Crawford, who was standing on a table, of all things taking wagers on the action. His hands were full of some small white tubes. "Two-t'-one odds on Tiny Tommy 'ere! Hey, ye *Scamps* there! Bet fer yer mate 'n' git a big payout besides!"

Wyckham shouldn't have been surprised at the bizarre goings-on. Sailors always seemed able to find the strangest things to gamble on. But betting on a competition in some sort of public, circle-jerk orgy? Good Lord, were there no limits to how low human behaviour would descend on this world? And what the hell were they using for money to bet with? They'd been at the end of a six-month cruise when the ships were diverted here. No seaman had any coin left.

"Forty-two million! No wonder the Fireflies love you humans," said Wulfe with a chuckle. "Your fellows are more productive than the race of bulls they usually play this game with."

The shouting reached a crescendo, and Wyckham turned his attention back to the stage. If any event could be described as coming to a climax, this was it. One after another, men onstage erupted in sudden yelps, sending their seed flying across the stage. Damned if it wasn't flying over ten feet through the air to the other women; apparently these sailors were incredible cocksmen! The kneeling women cheered, doing their best to catch every drop their partners had shot. With mouths open and palms up, they caught every drop and quickly swallowed them. They froze for a moment, deep in thought, then yelled out numbers.

"Thirty-eight million, six hundred and fifty-eight thousand, one hundred forty-one, Barrows!" yelled a plump young Scandinavian woman.

"Beat yah, Gretchen!" a dark-haired Welsh woman countered. "My Tom gimme thirty-eight, eight hunnerd sixty-four 'n' seventy-three!"

Unbelievable! They were betting on which hand gave his girl the most semen to devour! Apparently, none of the other women had gotten a sperm count greater than the Welsh lass who declared her man the winner. But Crawford objected and jumped down from the table.

"'Old on 'ere, 'old on!" he shouted angrily. "Tom, yer gal sucked up yer short rounds! I saw 'er—she somehow pick't up th' seed fum the floor what didn't make it t' 'er! Rules are rules. Ye gots ta shoot all th' way fer it t' count! Barrows's th' winner!"

"Sez you!" shouted the fellow apparently referred to earlier as "Tiny Tom," jumping down from the stage with his penis flapping about. "Bollocks, sez oy! You'll pay up now, Crawford!" He turned to his shipmates. "*Scamps,* this bugger thinks ee c'n cheat us! Thinks ee's better'n us cuz ee's on Dick'em Wyck'em's frigate! Grab em! Don' led em git away wif 'ar cartr'ges!"

Cartridges? They were betting musket rounds? No, clearly the small tubes in Crawford's hands weren't musket cartridges, but they were the currency of choice. What in the hell were they?

Several hands from *Righteous* rushed to Crawford's side, and the fight was on. Fists filled the air along with the Krag's metal cups and not a few chairs. The air was hard to see through from all the drinks being thrown. Most of the women changed back into energy balls and backed away. Provosts appeared from nowhere with billy clubs and rope starters shouting "B'lay now! Get back!" and separating the two factions. The provosts had been selected from the bosuns in the squadron, and every hand knew better than to cross one. Matters settled down rather quickly, thankfully before the mud beings needed to intervene.

Greaves, *Righteous*'s own bosun, called all the competitors over and soon had the truth of it. The neutral ladies all agreed that Gretchen's competitor had scooped up some semen from the floor faster than the eye could see by using some kind of electrical polarization. None of the men understood the scientific details, but everyone accepted the ladies' explanation. Crawford doled out handfuls of the white tubes to winners; the balls of light magically turned back into women bringing drinks; hands from the two ships sat down to drink with each other, naked ladies on their laps, and the Ruptured Krag was at peace again.

Finally Crawford was alone, and Wyckham used the chance to get some questions answered. He strolled over to the table where the Cockney seaman sat counting out his profits.

"Greetings, Seaman Crawford," he said with a courteous nod. "Might I share a drink with you? I must say I'm puzzled by this game you're engaged in. Maybe you could explain the intricacies of this sport I just witnessed?"

Crawford looked up in surprise at seeing his captain in the common seamen's room. He moved to jump up and knuckle his forehead in salute, but Wyckham waved his hand to stay seated.

"Please, my gallant saviour, no need to stand or salute. You are on leave here. Besides, I should be saluting you, much as I owe to you. May I sit down?"

"Aye, sor, sit ye'self down. Fergit me manners, oy did, sor, bit startled t' see you, sor," said the topman quickly as he swept aside empty cups and betting chits on the table in front of Wyckham.

"A drink, sor? Lemme git me gurl t' bring us sump'n." Crawford waved to a rather large woman at the bar who smiled broadly and started right over. *For the love of God, tell me it is not she!* thought Wyckham. But it was. It had to be. Even at a distance Wyckham recognized what had to be the Tippoo Sultan's jewels pinned on the lady's dress and about her neck. Brought back from India to England by the British army, the biggest rubies and emeralds in the world had been taken to the Tower of London and added to the crown jewels.

And the only person who could wear them was Duchess Caroline of Brunswick-Wolfenbuttel, the Queen of England, who was walking over now to serve them a drink in the flesh—a lot of flesh. As rumored, she was fat and slovenly, her dress pulled down to reveal her large, flabby breasts. But all the lower classes in England loved her for her fights with Parliament to increase commoners' rights. Sailors were especially fond of her because of her extramarital affairs with servants and the stories of her appearing at social functions with her breasts exposed.

He could just imagine facing an Admiralty board back home when this got out. Admirals Cochrane and Philip would be glaring at him across the big mahogany table. "So you gave the hands a tavern so that a deckhand could have sex with an effigy of the queen? While the whole squadron cheered him on? Do you know Caroline is actually delighted with the whole story and wants King George himself to knight your sailor? Maybe 'Sir Semen, Spare Cock to the Queen'? The king is so furious he's asked Parliament to dismiss the Admiralty itself and hand the entire navy over to Wellington and the army! He'll have us all kowtowing to a bunch of bellowing sergeants, if we're not thrown into the Tower, thanks to you!"

Queen Caroline approached the table and curtsied. Wonderful, the queen bowing to a commoner after he'd ravaged her in public. The royal family would gag on their morning brandies when they read that in the newspapers. Wyckham couldn't bear to be near her.

"Thank you for your courtesy but nothing to drink right now, I think," said Wyckham, trying to avoid even looking at the woman.

"Caroline, me luv', jes' one more o' them drinks th' ants brung en, wif sum yeller fruit juice," Crawford said to his paramour with a slap on her buttocks. "An' then later ye'll git wots ya' really want, me li'l queeny."

The corpulent royal giggled and headed off to fetch his drink like a common tavern wench. *Christ, I'm sure the hands can't wait to tell everyone back home how Crawford talks to the queen.* Wyckham shuddered. But at least the drink order got her to leave for a bit.

Back to his query. "So I'm curious about this game you're running here at the Krag, Crawford," said Wyckham. "I'd especially like to know what those things are you're wagering with."

Crawford finally got down to explaining everything that had just gone on. "We jes' bets on who kin shoot the mos' inter 'iz gurl's gob. Them cartr'ges we bet wif cum fum sum world full 'o men look like rabbits, they say; them mud peoples gots em. Swaller one 'n ye ken fook fer 'owers! An' when ye fyne'ly gits off, iz like a thirty-two-pounder firin' away! Ya gots some o' these, makes th' doxies go wile' fer ye."

So that's why those seamen on stage could range so far with their "great guns." Crawford had gone into business supplying the hands with some sort of alien aphrodisiac! Christ, the hands would probably all hump themselves to death. Well, he couldn't blame them if they did. What sailor wouldn't want to pass over "in the saddle"? Certainly beat the normal death a sailor in the navy could expect, either wasting away from disease or a slow death from an infected wound.

Yet the contraband didn't seem to be affecting discipline. While they were talking, several sailors had walked by, knuckling their fore-heads to the captain with a "Thankee, sor, thankee, 'iss 'ere's a wun-nerful tavern," or "'Avin th' time o' me life 'ere, thanks t' ye, sor. 'Opes we gets annudder crack at them pigs, sor—we'll show em wot th' navy kin do." Wyckham's plan to let the hands raise hell in the tavern actu-ally did seem to be good for morale.

And then events took a turn that would severely test the squadron's morale, for Lady Brashton suddenly appeared in a panic, speaking of what he hoped wouldn't occur but had fully expected.

"Captain, please come to the League's flagship immediately! Our forces have been routed. But there is a plan for your ships to bring us victory."

14

DUTY CALLS

So much for a quiet day at the Krag. Midshipmen from every ship were coming into the room, calling their crews back aboard. "*Hedgehog*s over here!" "*Zeuse*s to me!" Wulfe made a quick exit through the kitchen on his own, while all the navy crewmen were quickly rallying around their bosuns and getting fired up. "Them pigs thinkin' t' take the port wif' 'r tavern? Well, 'ey gots annudder thing comin'!" That comment was met with many hands nodding "Aye t' that!" Wyckham had never seen sailors so eager for a fight.

Wyckham and Lady Brashton left through the main door, passing under the swinging wooden sign hanging out front. Some artistic sailor had made the sign and painted it with the image of an unhappy Krag, skewered on a bayonet right through its groin, with "The Ruptured Krag" painted above in bright red letters.

As they walked, Lady Brashton was feverishly explaining the military situation. Try as he might, Wyckham couldn't help but wonder if the lady bore a red rocket under her clothing today. *Forget it, Wyckham. There are more important issues at hand!*

"The Draesh did have weapons here after all," she said in haste. "There is a fortress inside a mountain about 120 miles from here, shielded by power tapped from this planet's core. They had stored everything inside it: armed flying ships, long-range artillery shooting highly explosive missiles, even devices to emit deadly beams. We attacked and our forces were devastated. Fourteen major ships were destroyed while we could do no damage to the protected fortress. But we have an idea for a successful attack using your squadron. Admiral O'Neal and all your captains have assembled on the League's flagship to hear our proposal."

Wyckham had not heard her last words—he was staring up in open-mouthed wonder at a ship larger than the Great Pyramids or any construction on Earth. It must have been—what?—over three hundred yards long? It was oval shaped, had a rounded bow and stern, with many towers and other protrusions of unknown purpose mounted along its sides. The ship floated over the cove like a giant soap bubble, keeping the entire British squadron below in shadow. Directly beneath it, a much smaller ship with a stretched bulbous shape floated ten feet above the beach. As they approached, another mechanical stairway miraculously unfolded from the smaller ship and extended down to them.

Lady Brashton motioned for him to climb aboard. "This shuttle will take us up to the League's flagship. Admiral O'Neal and the other captains are already awaiting you there. I'm sure you will enjoy the brief flight."

Wyckham wasn't so sure about that. *Christ, I'm going flying?* But then he reassured himself. *Steel yourself, Wyckham. If O'Neal got up there this way, so can you.*

They climbed aboard and seated themselves on benches along the sides in an otherwise barren interior, facing bare metal walls. The stairway magically pulled itself up, the door closed itself, and away they went. The upward acceleration was like rising up on a big wave, reminding Wyckham of being in a small boat during a storm.

The craft had oval portholes, and Wyckham was glued to his. As the craft heeled and then leveled, Wyckham looked down at the cove and imagined himself a soaring bird, looking down on the greenery ashore, the white beach, and the dozens of alien ships taking flight.

Were they getting into the fight or running? The appearance of a line of portals in the north of the cove answered that question, as all the ships below suddenly made bee lines towards the gates.

Amazingly, the shuttle craft had no crew. It slowed and guided itself toward the giant flagship, which opened a door in its side to receive it. The ferry flew inside and glided softly to a stop, its door reopened, and Lady Brashton motioned for him to exit.

Well, this time the Slicks weren't completely rude—there actually was a side party to greet them. Five of Number Twenty-Two's people, wearing leather-like clothing and devices which were clearly side arms, were standing in a line.

A sixth Slick, clearly a warrant or bosun, with a larger side arm and a translation device on his head, stepped forward. "Welcome aboard the League of Planets' ship...ah...*Fatso*?" He paused a moment, looking confused. "Translator having difficulty. Name means large ship."

Wyckham made a leg in return, briefly puzzling the greeters. Then they led him away through a vast empty space, down a long hall to a meeting room filled with the British captains, Capitaine Badoin, the Yankee Harrison, and a circus menagerie of members from the League.

O'Neal motioned for him to join the group of humans standing together. While smiling and nodding at various alien officers, he spoke to Wyckham from the side of his mouth in a low tone. "What a surprise! It seems the enemy is not quite vanquished despite Number Twenty-Two's plans to the contrary. Seems they want us to rejoin the fight after all. Apparently they already have a plan for us to save the day."

Mister Twenty-Two, the League's leader, called out, first in English and then in other strange tongues, for all to be seated at the large meeting table. "Ahah! I suspect we're about to hear exactly what they've come up with," O'Neal said, and all sat down.

"In order to defeat the Draesh, we must destroy their fortified power source," the featureless Slick said in English through his voice device. Several other alien officers nodded, the devices on their heads translating the message for them. "It is inside a mountain, shielded by power tapped from the magnetic core of this planet. As you all know, our frontal assaults have failed."

He turned to face the British contingent. "But there is a way for the humans' ships to enter the stronghold from below. Inside the facility is a churning lake, bubbling with energy released from their magnetic mining operation at the planet's core. Naturally, there is a gap in their shield to allow mined magnetic core into the station for conversion to energy. While our ships would be identified by the enemy's sensors and the shields closed well before we could approach, your small ships of wood and iron, with no energy signatures, would appear on their sensors as simply more mining byproducts. Your ships could achieve complete surprise, coming up from below right inside the fortress."

What unbelievable nonsense! thought Wyckham. *Do they think our ships can just swim into the place like fish?*

O'Neal gave voice to the obvious problem with the plan. "Sirs, it would be an excellent plan, if my ships could proceed *under* the surface. But my ships can only move *on* the surface. They would immediately sink if they got beneath the surface, and there is the additional minor problem that all my crews would quickly perish with no air to breathe." The Slick seemed to take no offense at O'Neal's condescension. *Probably has no understanding of the concept*, thought Wyckham.

The alien admiral responded. "Your ships will be enclosed in a barrier formed by the living energy beings you call Fireflies, a feat now possible for them due to your donations of so much life energy. We will transport your squadron inside this cargo ship to a surface location near the mining shaft. Your friends will enclose your squadron in a protective film and then submerge you down to the gap in their shielding. You will rise alongside the mined metals and decayed plant life in the shaft, surfacing in the lake right behind the station's command and control area. The energy field will collapse, and you can open fire with your weapons."

Jesus Christ, are they serious? They think this could actually work?

Lady Brashton saw the disbelief on the British captains' faces. This this was a pretty dodgy proposition. She tried to reassure them all.

"I know you find this astounding, but if the League can just get us near the shaft, yhen safely submerging you and bringing you inside the fortress will be relatively easy. The difficult part of the operation will begin once you get inside the fortress. You will have to combat the entire Draesh leadership assembled there."

"Yes, your friend is correct," continued the League's leader. "While there are no heavy weapons inside the fortress, both the Draesh and their Krag allies will have many hand-held beam weapons that can slice through your ships in an instant."

He stopped and glanced around at each of the squadron's officers. "The Fireflies will bring you up so your starboard batteries are bearing on the Draesh base. Use your opening salvo well—it should cause mass confusion. Try to kill as many as you can right away. Bring the walls down on them. But expect that some will survive long enough to counterattack."

He stopped again. His head started nodding slightly as he kept his eyes on O'Neal. Maybe this was a fellow sailor who actually cared about other seamen.

"Unfortunately, we cannot take part in this attack. They would detect our ships and weapons miles from their base and close this gap in their protective shield. We do have liaisons to go along with you on each of your ships. They will at least be helpful in identifying targets. As soon as you destroy the enemy's shield controls and their power supply station, our forces will come to your rescue and quickly kill all enemy forces in the fortress."

Well, he might care about his fellow sailors, but he was still an arrogant arse. Were admirals the same everywhere in the universe? Still, Wyckham had to ask the obvious question, though he knew he would not get a satisfactory answer from Number Twenty-Two.

"Might I inquire as to how long it will take you to accomplish this coming to our rescue and killing all the enemy?" he said, sarcasm dripping off his lips.

"Possibly minutes, possibly hours," was the flat response. "We attack as soon as their shields drop. The Draesh do have dozens of capable ships we will have to fight past. How long that will take, I do not know. The length of a battle is always difficult to predict."

Well, he's got that right, thought Wyckham. Could they hold out long enough? This would be a tough decision for Admiral O'Neal.

After a brief pause, O'Neal responded to the alien. "And I suppose that if we refuse this fight, you have nothing else in mind. The Draesh will take us all."

"That is correct. Their forces are advancing as we speak. If we remain here, we will all be devoured within hours. We must leave now to get your ships to the shaft safely."

Wyckham saw O'Neal deep in thought, weighing the decision whether to fight or not. But really, they had no choice. O'Neal looked around and surveyed his five captains. "So do we fight?" he asked. Wyckham nodded along with the others. Even Badoin managed a *oui*.

"Well then, let's be quick about it. Mr. Twenty-Two, get our ships aboard. Captains, get to your ships to monitor the loading, then get to my cabin aboard *Zeus* to plan the battle." O'Neal rose up from his seat. Soon all the officers were headed back to shuttlecraft for the return flights to their respective ships.

Woven metal ropes descended from the huge flagship and hauled the British ships one by one directly underneath its immense cargo hatch. Giant slings were lowered, the ships were miraculously hoisted up through the air by large electrical cranes and placed on improvised metal cradles in the cargo bay. All of the squadron's officers, including five from *Leviathan*, then assembled in O'Neal's cabin. They were barely settled when they felt the motion of the big cargo ship moving up and away. Shortly thereafter, they were joined by some thirty aliens of all types, the promised liaisons.

Lady Brashton was also present. "If I may, Admiral, let me show you a view of the battlefield. This image was taken from the wounded Draesh in the transporter cave."

Suddenly, she was gone, and in her place was a five-foot floating image of a giant cavern. Dozens of Draesh and hundreds of Krag were sitting or walking along its sides, clearly attending large electrical devices built into the walls. In the foreground was a lake bubbling with colored pools of sediment, rocks, and trees.

The lady was gone but her voice could still be heard. "Note this room here. It contains the power distribution device for the Draesh's most powerful weapons."

As she spoke, the cave's image enlarged and focused on a large cave midway up the right side. Then the image shifted to the left. "Over here is a station for operating the fortress's shield."

Again the scene grew, showing a boxlike metal structure tucked into the wall. "These are your two main targets. Disable them, and the League can quickly come to your assistance."

The cave image disappeared and was replaced by the image of a Krag holding a black metal device with an oval pack on its back. "This is a Krag equipped with a beam weapon. They will be deadly to your ships. Here is a memory I scanned from a wounded Krag in the transporter cave. It shows their beam weapons in use in a previous attack on a wolf world."

A new image appeared in which several Krag on a field fired beam weapons at a tall structure of some sort. White beams shot from the guns' muzzles and sliced through the base of the building, collapsing it in mere seconds. Dozens of wolfmen could be seen falling to their deaths or being instanly burnt to dust by the hot beams.

The aliens that were present looked bored. They'd seen it all before. But the squadron's officers were astonished and silent; their faces extremely grim.

Lady Brashton suddenly reappeared as all the images faded. "You can expect there will be fifty or so Krag guards patrolling the cave with these weapons. While the Draesh usually let the Krag do the shooting, you can expect them as well to pick up these weapons and use them in this battle. If they do grab one of these from a fallen Krag, you have about two minutes to disable him before he gets it powered up and starts shooting."

O'Neal was again drumming his fingers on the table, deep in thought. "Well, nothing else for it. We'll come in with guns blazing. We just have to hold them off until help arrives. Let's make that room such a continuous bloody hell-storm that no chancer will dare stick his head up. I suggest we form line: *Zeus* in the van, followed by *Leviathan*, then *Righteous; Vesuvius* and *Hedgehog* behind in a second line; *Gnat* and *Scamp* on the wings a bit back. For the crucial opening broadside, *Zeus* and *Righteous* will load with round shot, aiming for the two targets and the walls above them. *Leviathan* will fire grape. With her carronades, she should continually blanket the field of fire and keep the enemies' heads down. The two bomb ketches will try for airbursts, targeting any place the enemy takes shelter. With less gunsmoke out on the wings, *Gnat* and *Scamp* will have a better view of the battle. They're to look for individuals popping up with these beam shooters. After the first broadside, *Zeus* and *Righteous* will also switch to grapeshot. Your thoughts, gentlemen?"

"*Monsieur Admiral,* you say zees Droosh monstairs are ten metairs high?" the Frenchman Badoin asked, clearly alarmed. "Weel grapeshot harm such large demohns?"

The fiery revolutionary had a fear of demons? Apparently, he still believed that he might be in hell, as many of the British still did as well. But Badoin had a good reason to be afraid of meeting the devil's minions. After what his Jacobite committees had done to the church in France, God would certainly not be on his side in any fight with real demons. This man needed reassurance. They desperately needed him to confidently captain his ship in the coming battle.

O'Neal realized this. "Yes, have no worries on that score," replied O'Neal. "Grape works quite well for these demons. They're just flesh and blood. One ball of grapeshot, and they bleed copiously, like any stuck pig. *Righteous* blew a bunch of them into hash with just her eighteens."

Hopefully, that put him at ease. But Wyckham thought the overall plan had lots of problems. "Admiral, with no wind to steady us, this bubbling lake will toss the whole line into a complete cock-up. We'll more likely be facing each other instead of the enemy. And our gunnery will stink with the ships being continually tossed about in this boiling lake."

Lady Brashton broke in. "But there *is* wind in the cave. It has giant fans that keep…" She paused for a moment. "…eight point three five knots of wind blowing to remove the noxious gases coming up from the mining operation. It blows from right to left…ah, starboard to port, as you face the control stations."

"Eight knots!" said Wyckham. "With no anchorage or room to maneuver, that'll dash us on the rocky shore within minutes." Silence spread over the group as everyone considered this latest problem.

Lieutenant Rawlins spoke up. "Let's tie up the entire line to the shore. Before we arrive, we'll run cables connecting all ships in their line order. Then, to anchor the ends of our two lines ashore, we get boats over the sides of *Righteous* and *Hedgehog* bearing cables from their two sterns, crews ready. Once the squadron gets in the water, we lower these boats to wait until we surface. After the first broadside, they row ashore and anchor these cables in the rocks, and the entire line will be stationary."

"Capital idea!" exclaimed O'Neal. "And all ships to run fore and aft springs. We'll be able to traverse onto any target we see in there."

"Put plenty of marines on those boats," commented Warren. "Even after the entire squadron's point-blank broadside, some buggers are bound to survive and try to untie the shore lines."

The British officers were all nodding and discussing details with each other. Wyckham saw the Frenchman nodding; even Badoin was on board. But there was one objector.

"Oh, capital, capital! We'll just get ourselves all killed within ten minutes, that's all." It was the American captain Harrison, sprawled back in his chair, shaking his head. "You regular British navy men think your glorious artillery is all you need to win any fight. Maybe some fights, but not this one. Does anyone here really believe we can kill every single foe in there with a bombardment? Never happened yet, not even in Copenhagen, which you boys shelled for days. And if just even one single enemy survives here, he'll pick up a beam weapon and broil this whole fleet. And it won't take long, neither."

The sobering argument struck home with the group. No one voiced disagreement.

"So how would our outspoken American approach the matter?" asked O'Neal bluntly.

"In order to win a fight on land, you need to land your own trrops, no way around it," offered Harrison. "Feint a marine landing in the center, but have my boys actually go ashore on the flanks. That way, the enemy will have three threats to keep them busy—artillery from above, marines in the center, and sharpshooters on their flanks. We'll do most of the fighting in the beginning. Give us rifles and grenades. We'll stay on the flanks in skirmish order. The rocky cover I saw in the lady's presentation will suit my boys just fine. If any bastard stands up with one o' these beam things, we'll shoot him right quick. If the battle progresses well, the marine commander in the center can decide if and when he should actually row ashore and join the fight."

Once again, Wyckham couldn't argue with Harrison's reasoning. *Hell, if we've got a land fighting force, might as well use it. Get the Yanks and the marines into this battle; use everything we've got. We'll all probably die today anyway, but it's better than surviving just to get eaten by some monstrous pigs.*

O'Neal seemed to agree as well. He solicited the opinions of the three marine captains: Warren's, Donnelson's, and that of *Leviathan's* French marine captain. They all approved of the plan.

"Now give us cover when we set off," Harrison continued. "Keep your guns firing even if you can't see anything to shoot at. The gun smoke will hide us until we get ashore. Then stop firing for a minute and let the smoke clear. You'll probably want to do that anyway to see if your opening salvo destroyed the two control areas. When the smoke clears, disembark your marines right in the center where every foe can see them. Then resume the artillery. Hopefully, the boats full of marines get concealed in the smoke again. The stupid critters spend the whole battle running around in the smoke looking for redcoats on the beach, while we stay concealed high on the flanks shooting anything what grabs a gun."

It actually sounded like a damn good plan. Harrison must have learned a lot from fighting Indians. *Christ, it just might work!*

The meeting broke up into small groups to arrange details. After an hour, their alien hosts advised them that it was time to get aboard their ships. They were nearing the place for their ships to be lowered into the sea. The time to start the attack had arrived.

15

A UNIVERSAL FIGHT

Wyckham, Rawlins, and Lady Brashton mounted a rolling stairway next to his ship and climbed aboard *Righteous* to the pipes of the greeting party.

"Thank you, Mr. Clifton. Be so good as to beat the ship to quarters," Wyckham said. "We will run a cable across the room from our bow to the Frenchman's stern. Once in the water, we'll haul up within pistol shot and mount a spring. We will also ready boats for twelve seamen and twenty marines to go ashore off our stern and tie us up to the land as soon as we surface. Once we are cleared for action, I will address the ship. Everyone needs to hear the plan for this fight."

Plus a little rousing speech from the captain was in order to instill courage in the crew. This fight would be a very hot one.

"Aye sir," Mr. Clifton responded, and soon drums were beating aboard *Righteous* as well as on all the other ships stored in the vast cargo hold. The sound grew to a roar as the echoes of the drumming bounced back to them off the giant room's walls. It seemed like the whole alien craft was throbbing—a big noisy beginning to what was sure to get much noisier. An action with the fate of the entire universe hanging in the balance.

Once *Righteous* was readied for battle, the crew assembled in the waist. Wyckham addressed the men from the quarterdeck rail.

"Lads, it's been a strange cruise so far, and today will not be any different. The entire squadron is about to be transported to the inside of the lair from which our monstrous friends run this world. Our task is simply to keep blasting the hell out of the place for as long as it takes for alien reinforcements to arrive."

He called attention to the alien liaisons. "About you are officers from our allies that are more familiar with the foe. They will assist us by pointing out two targets in the foe's cavern that we must quickly destroy."

"To get inside the enemy stronghold," he continued, "our lady friends here will transform themselves into a big bubble that will enclose the entire squadron. It will protect us as we actually go underwater and then surface inside the monsters' fort."

The eyes of seamen and officers alike went wide as that information sank in. "I know it sounds daft, but we've seen a lot of crazy doings in this place so far, haven't we? Our ladies assure me that we will arrive without difficulty."

He raised his voice for the rousing climax. "This is a day for us to show the entire universe what British ships, and the stout hearts of oak who man them, can do. You all know what will happen if we lose this fight. The Draesh will get to our Earth and destroy everything and consume everyone—your families, your friends, everyone. But just keep the guns firing, follow orders, and we can all get back home to England!"

After he had finished, there was just silence, no cheers. *Christ, what was the matter? That was a hell of a speech, if I do say so myself!*

Then a voice bellowed out. "Not oy! Oy'l be stayin' 'ere, runnin' me game 'n th' Ruptured Krag!" Naturally, it was Crawford. The hands wildly cheered him. If beating the Draesh meant they had to go back to England, they'd rather lose. Go back and leave the Ruptured Krag, the best tavern in the universe, just to return to the tedious life of a common seaman? They wanted to stay here.

202

That's when it finally hit him. He didn't want to leave, either. So let them all know it! "Then stay if you like!" bellowed Wyckham to the cheering crew. "I'll be staying—join me!" For God's sake, why not? Why go back to his disapproving father, incompetent superiors, a snobbish and self-centered ruling class, and a mad king? He preferred this world too.

The men were shouting in approval. There was just the minor detail of defeating an incredibly powerful enemy. He waited a moment for them to quiet down. "*Righteous*, we need to win this day to make it safe to stay here. Lose it and you know what our foul foes here will do to the Ruptured Krag and the ladies in it. But if you save the ladies from destruction, I think I can definitely promise you that they will be extremely grateful to every one of you." He turned to Lady Brashton. "Am I correct, Madam?" *Why do I bother to ask?* Knowing the carnal interests of the Fireflies, Wyckham wouild have bet his inheritance that his promise to the men would be accepted.

Lady Brashton nodded. "Of course we would be forever obliged to you wonderful seamen. There is absolutely nothing we would not do for those who provided us salvation."

Wild cheering again, even louder. "Hurrah for th' cap'm! Three cheers fer th' ladies! God bless Dick'em Wyck'em!" *If we win this day, it's due to that tavern*, thought Wyckham. *Forget king and country. If you want British tars to fight, make the battle about drink and women.*

Changing sounds from the giant carrier craft signaled that they were approaching their destination. The battle for the world was about to begin.

Bright lights flashed and loud horns blew as the carrier ship settled down on the surface, and water began to flood the immense hold. The ladies took on their Firefly images, balls of light floating above the ships. Soon *Righteous* began to bob as the rising water lifted the 200 foot long ship off its cradle. A minute later the giant hatch below them opened and the carrier craft slowly began to rise up, leaving the squadron rolling in a choppy sea. The balls of light above them started to stretch into a luminous film, reaching out both above and below the ships until the Fireflies had all blended together. Immediately the sea calmed—the squadron was now fully enclosed in the bubble. Wyckham watched in amazement as the water level outside the bubble's barrier wall steadily moved up its sides. They were sinking! In another few moments they would be completely underwater.

The carrier ship above them slowly closed its cargo hatch and lifted rapidly into the air. Just as it started to speed away, Wyckham noticed a red light growing rapidly in the sky to his left. The carrier above him spun in the air, changing course in a sudden burst of speed. An evasive maneuver? But it was to no avail. The ball of red light hit it at extreme speed, slicing clear through it. The carrier bent in the middle and spun violently, crashing into the sea in a fountain of spray and fiery explosions.

Normally he would have the ship heave to and rescue survivors. But they were inside a giant bubble which was now taking them down; none of the ships could control their course. Water covered the bubble almost completely.

Wyckham was in shock. He had just witnessed the deaths of hundreds of beings, possibly including the League's admiral himself. *Good Lord, soon we'll have to face weapons like this—some kind of hot missle that can strike from over the horizon?* Hopefully, the squadron's *crude vehicles*, as Lady Brashton had put it, were still invisible to the enemy and wouldn't draw any fire.

Apparently, only a few officers had seen and understood what had happened above them. All of the crew were working feverishly to prepare the ships for the coming battle. Thank God for that. Half the crew might just give up if they knew how powerful their enemy was.

Tow cables connecting the ships were hauled in until the squadron was in two tight lines. Springs were mounted and boats put over the sides. Marines, sailors, and the American skirmishers scrambled to climb down into them with all their weapons and equipment. Wyckham could see similar activity aboard the other ships.

"We will surface inside the Draesh station in eight minutes." It was Lady Brashton. Whatever she was now, she could still speak. She said nothing of the carrier ship's demise. Had all its crew in this drop-off operation known of the danger? Wyckham changed his opinion of

Number Twenty-Two, who had gone bravely into range of the enemy's weapons and given up his life for this cause. Wyckham clenched his teeth. He would not let the death of the alien flagship's crew be in vain. Strange as they were, they were all in this together.

Large rocks and decayed trees were visible outside the bubble. They must now be in the water column surging upward in the mining operation. The water outside was getting brighter; he could see light above.

Suddenly, the bubble was filled with light as the ships emerged above the surface. The water level inside the bubble rose a few feet above the water level outside, then settled back down until the inside water level was even with the outside. Then the bubble disappeared, showering the deck with a light spray.

Wyckham faced a rock wall in an immense cavern, near a quarter mile in diameter and several hundred feet high. Along the wall to starboard was a small city of walkways and platforms that had been carved out of the rock. They were covered with scores of busy crabmen, all facing lighted glass panels on the walls and fiddling with all sorts of devices in front of them. And there were also dozens of the giant Draesh. Wyckham's anger boiled up as he stared at the vicious, evil creatures. *Retribution is at hand, you sodding swine.*

All work in the cave stopped as its inhabitants became aware that seven enemy ships had just appeared fewer than a hundred yards away, right inside their supposedly impregnable fortress. The Krags' faces were too small to read, but Wyckham smiled at what was clearly terrified astonishment on the faces of the Draesh.

"All ships—run out!" It was O'Neal's clear Irish voice, addressing them all through a speaking trumpet.

Along the line of ships gunports banged open, sounding to Wyckham like a firing squad stamping to attention. An ominous rumble began as ninety-one large-caliber cannons were rolled up snug to their gunwales, coming to rest with a final thud. The halt of the drumroll right before the execution.

"Guns ready!" The alien liaisons aboard *Righteous* pointed out the two control stations they were to target along the wall. Gunners all along the line peered down their barrels and handspiked guns onto their targets with a final shove. Wyckham saw a flurry of activity ashore as many Draesh dashed frantically for cover. But they were too late. In just a moment there would be no safe place in this entire grotto.

"Fire!" The three batteries of heavy guns along the line's starboard side exploded as one. The blast inside the cavern was the loudest noise Wyckham had ever heard. A stab of pain shot into his right ear just from the echo off the walls. *God help any ears on the muzzle end of such a deafening blast.* Being in the midst of a storm cloud when it erupted in thunder could not have been any louder.He saw dust and small rocks fly off the rock walls just from the sound, even before the balls hit.

But hit they did. Besides the big solid shot from the British guns throwing rock shards everywhere, *Leviathan*'s broadside delivered over four thousand rounds of egg-size grapeshot. It was as if gravity inside the room had turned sideways, because every single thing and being that Wyckham could see got slammed up against the wall. But it was a much rougher form of gravity; both furniture and foe were already in pieces when they hit the cavern's sides. All the blood splashed on the wall looked to Wyckham like the first crush in a new wine press.

Then a new noise, the ominous boom of fissuring rock strata, filled the cavern, followed by a growing rumble. With one final ear-shattering crack, a wall the size of a cathedral tower split from the wall, dislodged by the enormous weight of shot hitting it, and slowly crashed down into the chaos on the ground. When it hit the floor, boulders large as haystacks broke free and went hurtling through the exposed creatures scattered about. Wounded Draesh and Krag had a moment to stare up at the flying debris before their cries were suddenly silenced. Wyckham saw one large rock roll to a stop with several flattened Krag stuck to it like bugs squashed on the sole of a boot.

A thick pall of gun smoke rolled across the shoreline, obscuring everything. For a moment it made Wyckham think of a thick fog in Portsmouth harbor, until the squealing and screeching from wounded Draesh and Krag started to fill the air.

Some of the smoke cleared, and Wyckham saw the devastated control stations, the rocks and walls splattered with blood, dozens of wounded foes wailing and wriggling on the ground, and scores of dead foes doing nothing.

He turned to Rawlins. "Some warm work to start, 'ey?"

Most crewmen had stopped serving the guns, still shocked from the ear-shattering sound, or staring awestruck at the devastation they had caused.

Captain, you'd better keep this ship fighting. Wyckham turned to the starboard battery. "Well done, lads, looks like a bad day at a solicitor's office!" The rows of creatures working at the control stations had reminded Wyckham of the clerks in his advocate's office back in London, where his attorney and his brother had plotted to steal his inheritance. "Now a bit of double grape, and we'll completely end their workaday!"

Wyckham turned to the frantic activity along the stern gunwales. "Boats away, right quick now." He wanted no time wasted in getting the battle line anchored; he could feel the ship drifting forward in the steady breeze even with no sail set.

The cutter and a barge set out from the stern carrying sailors and marines to attach hawsers to the shore. Along the starboard side, the rest of the ship's marines made a show of descending into a barge with great fanfare, hopefully right where the enemy could see.

On the port side, Harrison's men, with some supporting marines, set out in barges and headed into the smoke toward the right side of the cavern. Wyckham could see more barges launching from *Zeus* and *Leviathan.*

The cutter astern scraped up on the rocky shore and sailors jumped out with the six-inch cables, looking for a big rock to wind them around, the squad of marines from the barge fanning out in a defensive line to protect the effort. The group of sailors found a good rock, quickly wrapped several coils around it, and signaled *Righteous* to haul the line in. Twenty hands on the stern capstan put their shoulders to it; within seconds the cable tightened up, and Wyckham felt the ship straightening out. Other sailors from *Vesuvius* had taken a line ashore and tied up the bomb ketches as well. First task accomplished.

The smoke was dissipating. Wyckham looked over at the boats full of Harrison's Yankees. They were getting too visible. Rawlins, overseeing the starboard battery, was already instructing some guns to fire above the two cutters. Guns started firing in a rolling barrage, keeping the smokescreen up and, hopefully, the enemies' heads down.

With the three ships in the first line firing away, guns were going off every couple of seconds. Wyckham could hear the staccato clacking of grapeshot bouncing around the rocks ashore. The eerie screeching moans of wounded aliens grew in intensity, audible between gun bursts.

Then the two bomb ketches behind *Righteous* opened up with their thirteen-inch mortars, their duller thuds reflecting the reduced powder charges they were using since they were only two hundred yards from the enemy. Some shells went too far and hit the back wall, dropping down onto the workstations before exploding. *Had they cut their fuses too long?*

Wyckham saw both Krag and Draesh blown into the air after hiding behind a ridge. *Hmph. Actually, that's good shooting. Now they have to worry about death rolling up from behind them as well.*

Above the smoke to his left and right, Wyckham saw that Harrison's men had made it ashore and were climbing into sharpshooting positions high up on the rock walls. He called out to Rawlins that he could now lower the guns' elevations.

A sudden rattle of musketry turned his attention to his sailors and marines ashore around the anchoring ropes. He saw some dead and wounded Krag a few yards away from them, the nearby marines reloading muskets as the sailors continued to work at securing the lines more permanently. He'd better make sure they held. If the enemy were able to untie the lines to shore, all the ships would be swept onto the rocks and accurate gunnery would be impossible.

"Mr. Clifton, be so good as to have the stern chasers cover our lads ashore." The two brass nines didn't fire a big charge, but they were very accurate. "I'll thank you to splatter canister about those rocks whenever you see the enemy moving up." Lieutenant Clifton climbed up onto the poop deck toward the two gun crews manning the stern chasers.

Then, what they all feared occurred. A white-hot beam lanced out of the smoke into the water in front of *Righteous*, turning the water it hit into a steaming cauldron. It started to move toward the ship as the invisible shooter lifted his aim. Just as Wyckham took a deep breath and braced himself to be incinerated, four rifle shots popped, two from each side of the cavern. The beam shot skyward and then disappeared, the enemy apparently dropped by Harrison's sharpshooters. The Yanks must have found positions over the smoke with a clear view of the field. Wyckham exhaled with relief. *One down, but how many more still to go?*

Rawlins smartly directed fire onto the area the beam had shot out from, trying to disable the weapon or make the area too hot for any foe trying to pick up the thing. Every few seconds one of his great guns blasted dozens of grapeshot to ricochet around the rocks near the shooter. No second beam would be coming from that foe.

But another beam shot out to his left, aimed high at *Leviathan*. It sliced through her fore topmast, which caught fire as it dropped to the deck. But more American rifles fired, and the beam shut off like a shrouded candle. French crewmen threw water buckets on the burning mast, others hauled full buckets up to men in the tops and the flames there were quenched as well.

Two more beams lit up the cloud of gun smoke, but Wyckham couldn't see where they landed. What were they shooting at? Maybe searching for the marines they feared were in the water? Wyckham heard more reassuring pops of rifle fire along both sides of the carved out mountain. The light from the beams in the smoke disappeared as rifles kept firing.

The American marksmen had sight of those with beam weapons and were keeping them under fire. They were now picking them off before they could even get off a shot. Cannon fire continued to ripple up and down the line of ships, a steady thunder in Wyckham's ears. Every minute or so, one of the four big mortars lobbed another shell against the far wall to drop into the huddled enemies and burst in a tremendous explosion. Behind him, *Righteous*'s stern chasers were occasionally firing canister to support the sailors and marines, who were keeping the ship tied up ashore.

The fleet had settled down into a steady routine, one it was capable of continuing for many hours. Guns crashed and leapt back into their rope restraints, muzzles briefly bouncing up when the cannons hit the end of their tethers. Gun crews jumped to swab them out and worm them clean. The bundles of grapeshot were rammed down the guns' muzzles, locks were primed, and the crews hauled them back up to the gunwales for firing. Powder monkeys ran back and forth across the deck with fresh powder charges. A Royal Navy ship in action always reminded Wyckham of the precisely staged Russian ballet he had seen in St. Petersburg—except that the firing of Royal Navy guns had been rehearsed even more.

He looked toward the cave wall to try and see how the enemy was faring in all this. It had to be complete chaos over there; the creatures had to be totally disoriented. They probably couldn't see five feet in front of them from all the smoke. There was grapeshot continually in the air and ricocheting all about. Shattered rocks were flying everywhere. The Yankee riflemen were shooting at the creatures if they moved, and every now and then, for extra measure, a thirteen-inch bomb would roll up from behind and explode. The enemy must have lost all its fight by now. Maybe the day was won, and they could hold out until the League arrived after all?

Alarmed cries from the tops dashed Wyckham's hopeful thoughts. Apparently, the lookouts could see through holes in the smoke as they looked down.

"Ahoy the deck! Crabmen 'r 'n th' water! Lots uv em, swimmin' fast, right to'rds th' ship!"

Wyckham jumped to the taffrail, and there, under the smoke, were Krag by the dozen, propelling themselves toward the ship with jerky strokes of their legs, their claws clacking menacingly in the air. Gunners rushed to pound their quoins in to fire their loads of grapeshot down into the water.

"Quick, lads, quick! Those buggers are swimming fast!" As the first gun fired right into them, Wyckham saw bloody shell parts spurting upward in fountains of red water. Other guns got their muzzles down, fired, and the Krag disappeared into the guns' smoke. Despite all the wounded Krag in the water screeching in pain, Wyckham knew that some would reach the ship.

"Idle hands, repel boarders!" he yelled out unnecessarily, as sailors with muskets and pistols had already jumped to the starboard gunwales to shoot down the ship's side.

Donnelson's marines, still in their boats alongside, added their musket fire to the storm of balls hitting the water. But through a gap in the smoke, Wyckham saw hundreds more crabmen swimming toward them. Christ, where were they coming from? Must be tunnels through the rocks to some sort of living quarters. There were just too many, and they were swimming fast. *Righteous* was about to be overrun by a huge horde of the buggers, and the marines in their boats would be swamped by the damn things. They needed to move now.

"Donnelson, get your marines back now! There's too many!" The marines cast off from the ship and began to row around behind *Righteous*. It appeared they would not be making a landing in this fight.

Wyckham yelled over to his gunners, "Starboard battery, double canister!" Loblolly boys ran to the guns with the tin cans of musket balls. While not as accurate or as hard-hitting as grapeshot, it was better for taking out charging foes at close range. With double canister charges, *Righteous* could fire thirty-five thousand balls in one broadside.

But there was no way *Righteous*'s gunners would be reloaded in time. The damn Krag were swimming too fast; they'd be climbing up the side in a few moments.

"Pikes to the side!" he shouted. Sailors swinging the long pikes would be more effective than those with swords or firearms at keeping the vicious little crabmen from climbing over the gunwales. Wyckham pulled out both his pistols and checked their priming; he'd take down at least two of the buggers before they ripped him apart.

The cannon fire in the cavern had suddenly quieted down a bit. When Wyckham looked over at the silent *Leviathan*, he was elated to see that it had hauled in its spring and angled itself to aim right at the crabmen about to swarm *Righteous*!

Say what you wanted about this French captain—he was battle-hardened and no fool. Badoin had realized that if *Righteous* was lost, the anchoring bowsers ashore would be cast off and the whole squadron would drift into chaos. The French ship was getting set to fire into the water in front of *Righteous*.

"*Prêt!*" It was Capitaine Badoin yelling out the French word for *ready* through a speaking trumpet. "*Tirez!*"

The big two-decker's side erupted in orange flame, and the water below absolutely disappeared in a geyser a cable wide. Badoin had even loaded his guns with canister while his ship was being turned! Each of his big sixty-five-pound carronades fired almost eight thousand balls with a double load. Over a quarter of a million rounds hit the water in front of *Righteous*.

When the spraying water settled back to the surface, Wyckham saw the extent of the devastation. Many dozens of Krag bodies and parts were bobbing in the water—some were floating three high on top of each other. But the ones in the back now had a solid surface to run across, and hundreds more crabmen appeared out of the gun smoke, rapidly heading toward *Righteous*.

Christ, how many of these things are there?

Righteous's guns had been reloaded with their own canister rounds and opened up a rolling volley, but the Krag kept coming. *Damn things may be stupid but they do have spine*, he had to grudgingly acknowledge. These things were going to make it aboard, no doubt about it. Panic welled up in his gut.

Settle down, Wyckham. British officers must at least appear calm and unperturbed in the face of danger. Take a deep breath. Be calm, carry on.

He yelled reassuringly. "Get ready, lads! Just stand firm, and it's plenty of fresh crab for supper tonight!" He leaned over the side to see the first Krag reach the ship and climb up the side, only to be swept away by seamen swinging their eight-foot pikes. Marines in the tops were also firing down with their muskets, and a rotating line of crewmen came up to the gunwales, fired pistols over the side, and then stepped back to reload, like the rotation of pistol firing horsemen in a Spanish *caracole*.

Smoke from the great guns firing down close to the ship made it hard to see the course of the battle. But suddenly the number of Krag reaching the ship multiplied—there were just too many. By sheer numbers they started to overwhelm the men manning the gunwhales. First one, then another seaman was grabbed by long claws and dragged over the side.

Time to pull the men back. "Mr. Donnelson, form your men in a line here!" Wyckham pointed out a spot twenty feet back from the starboard side.

Donnelson bellowed orders and his marines rushed to the place with fixed bayonets. "Mr. Rawlins, pull the men back and reinforce the marine line! Pikemen to the flanks!"

The first row of furious Krag boiled over the side, swivel guns barked fore and aft, and the entire bunch was knocked back into the lake. The next group arrived just in time for the formed line of marines to deliver a volley of musketry, and most of them went back over the side as well. But more kept coming, and soon the deck was full of crabmen dancing about, trying to get past the extended points of bayonets and pikes protecting the crew, even as swivel guns and muskets took a steady toll among them.

Finally, their numbers started to tell. More and more Krag were getting past the crew and onto the open deck. Some crabmen had scampered up the ratlines and over the boarding nets despite the marines in the crosstrees firing down at them. They got past the marines' line, and then dropped back down to the deck. Seeing the success of their mates, others quickly climbed up and over, and the ship's organized defense broke down into a complete mêlée. The agile Krag were dashing left and right, stabbing at sailors and marines, then jumping back to avoid slashing cutlasses and thrusting bayonets. A sergeant's call of "Form square!" got some marines in a defensible box, but many sailors and other marines were spread out in fighting all across the ship's waist.

Stymied by the marines' square, four Krag noticed Wyckham and made right for him, their long claws up and snapping. Wyckham lifted a cocked pistol, fired, and the first one's head cracked open as it dropped like a stone. Wyckham fired at the second, but it jigged sideways and the shot went wide. Cursing, he dropped the pistols, drew his sword, extended the point in defense, and looked for a corner to back into.

He faced three foes, who were certainly more skillful at using their claws than Wyckham was at using his sword. Fencing had never been his strong point at school nor in the navy. For scrapes on a pitching deck, he'd always put more faith in his Nock rifled pistols. Maybe now he'd pay for that choice.

The three crabmen spread out to threaten both his flanks as they backed him into the corner at the base of the quarterdeck, their long claws snapping, clicking sounds coming from their bubbling mouths. Their eyes bobbed on their long stalks as they looked for a way past Wyckham's extended point.

Christ, what truly unpleasant creatures. The one on the right stamped his foot in a feint, but Wyckham kept his point out waiting for the real attack. The foe on the left lunged first. Wyckham batted his claw aside with an outside parry in *sixte* and then made a riposte in *quinte*, catching the Krag's shoulder. He pulled his blade back just in time to parry an attack in *quarte* from the one on the right. Though he diverted its claw, the creature's momentum brought it crashing into Wyckham's body *corps à corps;* he couldn't get his point inside for a reply. The Krag, however, had that vicious short claw which was perfect for mauling an opponent in close, and it was trying to gore Wyckham's side with it. Wyckham had to keep flapping his elbow sideways to keep the small claw away, while still holding the large claw with his blade in a binding *quarte* parry.

But suddenly it didn't matter, for the third Krag in the center now had a stationary target to run its long pointed claw right through. It cocked its arm for the killing blow. Wyckham was about to be a dead captain.

Then a blade flashed behind the Krag and its cocked arm went flying sideways, severed at the elbow. It spun around to face its new foe, but too late. A point burst through its back, and it fell to the deck, revealing a grinning Midshipman Moore who had come up behind it. The Krag leaning on Wyckham didn't seen the newly arrived midshipman either, and with a horizontal cut Moore severed its head, sending it flying to land right next to the first Krag's severed claw. Moore then turned to the one Wyckham had wounded, but it wisely decided to back out of the fight and ran back into the general mêlée.

"What's the matter, crabby?" he taunted after it. "No taste for a fair, one-on-one fight?"

But the issue was far from settled. More Krag had dropped to the deck and were headed straight for Wyckham.

Christ, is this entire species on a mission to kill me?

Moore jumped in front of him, slashing his blade back and forth to keep them at bay. The agile creatures gathered around the two of them, bobbing and foot-feinting, waiting for an opening to lunge behind Moore's blade after it passed by. It was only a matter of moments before one of them would get through, and then Moore would be quickly overwhelmed.

But suddenly the mass of Krag stepped back, and a taller one with a very long claw stepped through and stopped to stare at Moore. It seemed there *was* a Krag who wanted a fair fight, and it was clearly inviting Moore to a duel. This one was more reddish than the others and had an exceptionally long primary claw. His short claw looked thicker as well. It also wore a necklace of what appeared to be teeth from Krag claws—probably trophies from power struggles within the Krag hierarchy. Its long claw snapped loudly and its mouth bubbled and clicked at Moore, clearly calling for a duel between champions.

So these animals actually had their own code of chivalry! Moore acknowledged the challenge with a kiss to his sword's guard and a sweeping salute. He grabbed the tip of his blade with his off hand and flexed it back and forth as he eyed his opponent. The warmer a well-tempered blade, the more it could be whipped like a fishing pole around a parry. The big Krag facing him was dancing in place, snapping its head left and right and shaking its arms out, warming himself up as he politely waited for Moore. Finally the young midshipman settled into his low, crouching, *en garde* position, knees coiled, ready to spring.

The Krag wasted no time and attacked with a jumping lunge, leaping and extending its long, pointed claw over ten feet in a split second, a straight attack in *quarte*. Moore leapt back staying over his feet, parried high outside in *sixte*, extended a feint back in *quarte*, then finally disengaged under his foe's claw and extended his point low in *septime*.

But his opponent had read the feint and did not react. It, too, stepped back, then closed the line with his claw in *septime*. Both combatants started circling: Moore bouncing on his toes, the Krag constantly rattling its four legs on the deck. They both feinted in different lines to test the opponent's reactions. Moore then made two feints, whipping his blade wide left at the Krag's *quarte*, then over to the right at his *sixte*, looking like a flyfisher casting in a Scottish stream. With his second feint he advanced, pulled his point back and cocked his elbow for a strong final thrust in *quarte*. *Al final* he extended his arm and launched himself at the Krag with one of his long explosive lunges, his point traveling too fast to see.

But this crabman knew a threat when it saw one, and it was fast—very fast. It had retreated a step with each of Moore's advances, covering the line with his long claw, warily eying the midshipman's cocked arm. With Moore's final lunge, the creature took a long leap back and the midshipman's final attack touched naught but air.

Now the young middy started tapping the point of his weapon on the deck, clearly showing the crabman an opening, the irritating rapping sound emphasizing the untaken invitation. Finally, the Krag feigned a lunge high in *quarte*, recovering forward to close in on Moore, landing with a clean stamp of its rear legs to complete a fine *balestra*. Now back *en garde*, it immediately disengaged to lunge low outside in *prime*. Moore's parry was barely in time and the foe's claw nicked his flank. "*Bon touché*, my worthy opponent," he spoke out with a grin. "Very pretty! Learned that in the *Académie d'Escrime de Paris*, I'll warrant?"

The big Krag then made two mistakes. It thought Moore was vulnerable because he was talking (just as Moore had planned), and it thought the same move would work better if it just did it faster. As it made a bigger feint, Moore stepped inside past the Krag's extended point to get *corps à corps* with his opponent, clearing his weapon by lifting his arm high over his head while aiming his point straight down. As his blade went by the Krag's head on the way up, Moore deftly flicked it right and left like a lady waving her fan upside-down, and damned if he didn't neatly sever the crabman's two eyes right off their stalks! The big Krag froze motionless, puzzled as to why it suddenly couldn't see, as Moore stood on his toes and arched his back to make a little space, looking like some Don performing one of those flamenco dances. Still in the fight, the crabman pulled both its claws back and opened them wide, about to lash out and gore anything in front of him. But before the Krag attacked, in an astonishing move *à la fin*, Moore whipped his blade over and behind his head, his point coming down to thrust three inches of his blade into the Krag's neck right at its jugular vein. Blood spurted along his blade's grooved fuller as the creature went limp and crumpled to the deck.

Meanwhile, many of the Krag aboard had foolishly stopped fighting to watch their champion's duel with Moore. Apparently, the Krag code of chivalry said that combat should cease while champions duel. But British sailors weren't taught such nonsense, and crewmen had worked their way behind them to hack away with their cutlasses and stab with their dirks. It now appeared that the deck struggle had changed in *Righteous*'s favour. Some Krag were still coming aboard, but their numbers were dwindling from throwing themselves at the marine's square. Gunfire from *Leviathan* was still blasting away at Krag in the water, and apparently the reinforcements ashore had finally run out.

Relief and a desire to just relax for a moment washed over Wyckham's body like a welcome wave. The fight on *Righteous*'s deck was won. But Wyckham recalled having this dangerous feeling in previous fights, relaxing for a spell while the enemy was pressing his advantage on a flank or in some other aspect of the battle. *Bloody hell, the shore party!* Was this whole surge of crabmen just a diversion while the shore party was attacked and the lines anchoring the ships cast off? Wyckham dashed to the rear taffrail to make sure the ship was still securely tied up. While matters there seemed momentarily quiet, he saw that the surge in enemy numbers had happened along the rocky beach as well, and the fighting had been fierce. There were dismembered corpses of several marines and sailors strewn about in front of the improvised redoubt that had been established around the tied-up hawsers.

And Wyckham could make out claws and crabheads popping up over rocks on the other side of the redoubt—lots of them. It looked like the Krag were planning a final rush to overwhelm the remaining crew and marines astern. Smartly, they were approaching the shore party from the side opposite from *Righteous,* where her stern chasers wouldn't fire for fear of hitting her own shore party. They were assembling to attack in a final rush, staying low among the rocks as they worked forward like sappers conducting a siege.

The little whoresons had certainly figured out some infantry tactics quite quickly. Then the explanation for everything hit him. They couldn't have planned this attack without help from their Draesh masters. And those big pigs had already shown themselves capable of surprise. It explained the entire course of the fight so far, and the final blow that was yet to come. *Christ, how did I miss it?*

Before he could do anything about it, the action ashore froze his attention as the Krag rose up and attacked. There must have been a hundred of them, rising up from behind rocks and rushing toward the tied-up hawsers. Muskets banged but there were too few left around the position. The defenders were about to be wiped out and the shore cable untied, releasing the squadron to be pushed sideways by the wind from the ventilator device and grounded.

A barking broadside of six-pounders announced that salvation might be at hand. It was *Scamp,* emerging close-hauled from behind *Righteous* at an angle to safely cover the defenders ashore. With her triangular sails, she could hold tight to the wind in the cavern and had sailed past the redoubt to fire grapeshot in enfilade along the rows of charging Krag. Her shallow draft had allowed her to get within a hundred feet from shore, a range at which every ball struck home or sent deadly rock chips flying into the foes. After the broadside from her great guns, her crew fired their swivel guns and muskets at the remaining gun-shocked Krag, who immediately ran back into the rocks seeking cover. For a time at least, the line was still secured.

Thank God for Hamilton and his little ship. Wyckham saw the brig's commander looking back at *Righteous*. Wyckham wanted to shout out a "Well done, Commander!" but could only wave to him over the din of battle.

Surprisingly, Hamilton was grimly looking back toward *Righteous*. What was he looking at so angrily?

Wyckham glanced to his right and there was Lieutenant Pierce Rawlins standing at a swivel gun, the lanyard in his hand, ready to fire. *Good Lord, he was aiming right at Hamilton!* Rawlins was going to eliminate his rival in love by killing Hamilton right in the middle of a battle, where he could get away with an act of cold-blooded murder! Wyckham had heard of this happening on battlefields but never actually been a witness to it. He shouted out to Rawlins to desist, but his warning went unheard, drowned out by the continual discharge of artillery.

As *Righteous*'s captain, Wyckham could not abide murder by an officer, no matter if it was about to be committed by a lifelong friend. At his feet was a cocked musket; the fallen sailor nearby no longer needed it. Wyckham picked it up and sited it on Rawlins's chest. Emotion welled up in his own chest. *Damnation, this trigger is hard to pull.* Yet he had to do it. Slowly he pressed the trigger. But just as he fired, the port stern chaser fired and crashed back into its restraining ropes, shaking the deck enough to spoil his aim, and the shot went wide. It struck Rawlins's swivel gun with a clang, and he snapped his head around, looking through the smoke for whatever foolish crewman was shooting at him. Then he looked back at Hamilton, dropped the muzzle on the swivel gun, and fired.

The water below *Scamp* exploded into the air and some Krag there were hit, their mates turning around and swimming away. For a moment, Rawlins and Hamilton stared at each other. Then Hamilton nodded and turned back to commanding his ship.

Had Rawlins changed the gun's aim when he realized that his captain was the one shooting at him? Or was he about to fire at the Krag in the water anyway? Or perhaps Pierce's British decency and self-control had simply overcome his revenge and animal passion and he had changed his mind on his own?

No time for this, thought Wyckham. He had to return to the immediate demands of running his own ship. He needed to ready *Righteous* for the attack he had only just realized was coming. Did he have enough time?

Wyckham surveyed the battlefield. *Zeus* was still banging away at the shore, but *Leviathan* was silent. There were no more Krag in the water for her to shoot at. His own deck was quiet. The Krag aboard had run out of either numbers or courage; the last few survivors on deck were leaping over the side to safety in the water. Or maybe they too knew something was coming.

"Swivels!" Wyckham yelled at the top of his lungs. "Hold your fire! Load with grape if you can! Prepare for the big buggers coming aboard!" He turned to the starboard battery. "Mr. Rawlins, hold fire! Wait for them coming up the starboard side!"

He yelled to the lieutenant on the forecastle manning the two twenty-four-pound carronades. "Mr. Clifton! Swivel your carronades inboard to bear on the starboard gun'nels! Draesh are about to board us!"

Wyckham had realized that all the Krag were just a distraction. The Draesh were repeating the same trick that had worked when one came aboard *Zeus* the very first day the ships had arrived. They'd simply swim up underwater while the ship was focused elsewhere. And they wanted his ship. First the crabs, and now the big devils would attack only *Righteous.* If they got control, they could cast off the entire squadron's rear anchor line and the ships would be quickly swept away, unable to fight. If more than a couple of them got on deck, the ship was theirs. He had to attack them climbing up the side.

Wyckham grabbed a speaking trumpet and called out to Badoin, who was standing on the big French two-decker's quarterdeck.

"Capitaine Badoin! Load your guns with grapeshot and prepare to fire on this ship! Draesh are swimming up to it under the water! Fire down our side!"

Leviathan was still angled toward *Righteous* and could fire her guns into the water and along her side. Hopefully, her grapeshot fired at an angle would ricochet off *Righteous*'s foot-thick oak scantlings without causing much damage to the ship, just to any Draesh climbing up the side.

He'd still better warn the gun crews manning the starboard battery to step back from the side, away from the Frenchman's muzzles. "Lads, get back from the gunports. We're about to get a social visit by the big ugly pigs themselves. Our French friends will greet them by sweeping the starboard side with grape. So take a step back, don't be greedy and take a ball meant for our callers."

Gun crews moved back with smirks on their faces but concentration in their eyes. They kept the long lanyards in their hands, ready to fire.

Wyckham cautiously walked over to the starboard rail and peered down into the water. The vast numbers of floating Krag corpses obscured any vision below the surface, and there was no sign of activity ashore.

Maybe after such horrendous losses the enemy had finally given up? Wyckham doubted that. Lady Brashton had told him that the Draesh could not lose this power center. That would result in catastrophic defeat from the League of Planets attacking them all over their home planet. They had to regain control here and repair their power source, or they would be viciously exterminated by an assembly of planets out for revenge.

The sudden appearance of a dozen long arms spurting from the water confirmed that, unfortunately, Wyckham's predictions had been correct. He watched in despair as emerging Draesh grasped the muzzles of *Righteous*'s guns, not only deflecting their aim, but also using them to haul themselves up out of the water!

Christ, another obvious tactic I should have seen and prepared for! I should have closed the gunports and had the gun crews fire right through them as the damn Draesh climbed up the side!

Just in time, Wyckham remembered what he did have planned, and he pulled back from the rail just as several guns aboard *Leviathan* went off and blasted a volley of grapeshot all along his ship's side. The firing continued in a long rolling barrage; Badoin was firing his guns one or two at a time as targets appeared. *Righteous* thrummed steadily with the glancing impact of thousands of the one-pound balls. But quite quickly that sound was overwhelmed by the screeching of dying Draesh.

Didn't plan for that, my ugly friends, did you? What was it the American Captain Jones had said during the first American war? *I have not yet begun to fight!*

He backed further away from the starboard rail as the storm of grapeshot scouring the ship's side intensified. He couldn't see what was happening down there, but he could see body parts and chunks of flesh flying above *Righteous*'s starboard gunwales. It was a churning malestrom of flame, smoke, splinters, and demons' limbs, all bathed in a sparkling shower of burning cotton gunwadding. Confirming the ferocity of the cannon fire, the huge head of a Draesh came spinning over the starboard gunwhales and landed on the deck with a splattering thud. *Jesus!*

It must be a scene of indescribable violence over the side. To be under fire from over thirty pieces of heavy artillery shooting down from just a pistol shot away was hard to imagine. If the grapeshot didn't directly strike a foe, it would bounce off the side for a second try, along with an absolute malestorm of splinters. Wykham couldn't think of more deserving recipients for such a whirlpool of death. *Think you're from hell? I'll show you hell.*

But he knew at least some would make it aboard. *Righteous* was ready. All the ship's swivel guns and its two twenty-four-pound carronades were aimed inward at the starboard gunwales, their gunners crouched and waiting with lanyards taut in their hands.

After about a minute *Leviathan*'s rolling barrage finally went silent. Was it all over?

"*Mon capitaine!*" It was Badoin yelling through his speaking trumpet. "I sink zey are all done! Zaire attack eez ovaire!"

A giant Draesh hand that was gripping the starboard rail fell onto the deck with a loud thud, no longer attached to an arm. Wyckham cautiously walked back up to the starboard rail and peered over. It was a strangely silent scene of dozens of dead Draesh. They had been ripped apart so badly by the Frenchman's big sixty-five-pounders that there wasn't even any of that annoying squealing of wounded demons—every Draesh in the water was quite dead. The barrage of the small balls had been so intense that half the thickness of the foot-thick oak planking along the ship's waterline had been blasted away. Many of the Draesh corpses floating about were embedded with splinters over three feet long, making them look like gigantic sea urchins.

They'd done it! *Zeus* was still firing to keep smoke in the air and heads down ashore. That and the sporadic rifle fire from Harrison's men showed that there were still enemies among the rocks, but the threat to the squadron was destroyed. They could wait forever, if need be, for reinforcements to arrive.

His crew knew the fight was over and was celebrating. "Three cheers fer th' French! Veeve la France!" Crew and officers alike were cheering "and waving to the Frenchmen on *Leviathan* who were also cheering 'ale Brittanniah!" and waving back. Wyckham never thought he would see such a scene of British and French sailors cheering each other.

Lieutenant Rawlins walked up and slapped his old friend on the back, leaving bloodstains on Wyckham's coat from an injured hand, but neither cared.

"A rather warm day, what?" he smiled, looking over the side at the hundreds of Krag and Draesh corpses bobbing in the bright red water.

"Certainly was! But a day to be proud you're in the British navy," replied Wyckham with a return slap on Rawlins's back. He opened his mouth to yell congratulations to the crew when he realized some of the yelling he was hearing was not celebratory.

Christ. It's not over.

"Ahoy th' deck! Ahoy th' deck!" It was the marines in the boats that had earlier pulled back around the ship's bow to avoid the Krag attack. "They're comin' up th' portside!"

Wyckham's stomach wrenched as he watched two long hairy arms reach over the port gunwales and slash through the boarding nets. With long swipes they threw aside two sailors manning swivel guns. More long arms came over the port bow and swatted the crew at the port carronade into the water.

Then, in a vision like the entrance to hell itself, five grinning Draesh heads appeared above the port rail, roaring like a full gale, their eyes filled with hatred for the annoying little humans who were causing them so much trouble on their home planet.

What an idiot I am! God, I don't even have the brains to deal with god-damn animals!

Of course, the aquatic monsters had simply swum under the ship and climbed up the idle port side. And they were going after the ship's only defenses against them: the swivel guns and carronades. A third swivel gunner was smashed into the deck like a swatted fly, his flesh splattering across the deck.

With the crew assembled on the starboard side, all of the starboard swivels were masked from firing to port. At least the two swivel guns that Wyckham had mounted up in the crosstrees started firing down on the boarders. The small cannons shot only a few balls with each discharge; it would take a lucky shot to take down a moving, thirty-foot Draesh. But the first three foes wavered as balls ripped into their arms and legs.

The starboard bow carronade's crew was pushing its gun around on its circular mounting to fire at the port side. All they needed was a few more seconds to get it around. But the monster on the bow recovered from the shock of taking a ball to the shoulder and finished climbing over the bow gunwales, heading for the twenty-four-pound gun being handled by its six-man crew. They would not get it around before the monster reached them and killed them all.

Then Wyckham noticed Crawford running up the bow gallery with a pike.

"C'mon, mates! Time fer a pig-stickin' party!" he yelled out to other pike men as he ran, prompting several more to follow him forward.

What the hell does Crawford think he can do with a pike against a giant monster with ten-foot-long arms slashing about?

Hooting and hollering, Crawford bounded up the forecastle stairs, drawing the beast's attention. As soon as he reached the top of the stairway, he planted his left foot, cocked his right arm, and threw the eight-foot pike right up at the creature's head. The Draesh ducked away and slashed out to obliterate Crawford. But the seaman slid sideways behind the base of the mizzenmast step, and the monster's claw smacked harmlessly into the thick mast.

Other sailors followed his example and threw their pikes. Damned if one of them wasn't Obujimi, his steward! Looking like Achilles himself, he planted his feet, cocked his arm, arched his back and threw, spinning his body for extra force as he did when hunting lions in Africa. His throw was true, and the barbed pole stuck right in the beast's neck. Now in a wild rage, the porcine demon slashed out and threw two nearby hands across the deck to smash into an eighteen-pounder.

That was the last British sailor it would ever throw around. Crawford and Obujimi had given the starboard-side carronade's crew enough time to get it turned around, and the gun now erupted with a thunderous crack in yellow flame and churning smoke. Almost one hundred balls of grapeshot hit the creature point-blank, grinding it up like sausage. One moment a giant dangerous demon, now it was a pile of wet gore spread over the deck. More swivel guns fired, and many more seamen started throwing their pikes, keeping the other Draesh busy.

And there was Crawford again, with several of his mates, pushing the port-side gun around to aim right down the line of Draesh along that side of the deck. The instant he got it around, Crawford grabbed the lanyard and fired.

The foes were all in a row along the port side, and the one hundred egg-size balls hit every Draesh on deck. The two closest to the gun were minced into hash; the other two went down squealing with broken limbs and gushing wounds. Pikemen moved in to dispatch the two wounded.

Both carronades reloaded, and everyone prepared for more of the big monsters coming over the port side. Wyckham watched anxiously from his quarterdeck. All was eerily quiet.

A loud rumbling sound on the deck behind him gave him a start. Turning astern, bile again rose in his throat as he saw the latest threat. A Draesh had snuck aboard during the deck fighting, sweeping the few hands astern over the sides, and was now uncoiling the mooring lines from the stern capstan that ran ashore to anchor the fleet. And the bastard that was doing it had some sort of bandage about its mouth where there should have been a jaw! *It was the goddamn Draesh leader himself!*

It threw the last of the lines overboard with one hand. Then its eyes opened wide as it saw Wyckham.

"Captain Wyckham!" it snarled in a low, guttural voice, sounding scratchy through its translator device. "It's over, you little fool! You just lost this battle!"

Before any guns could be brought to bear, it reached out, grabbed Wyckham, and leapt over the stern.

This time there would be no rescue from Crawford. Wyckham was doomed. As they hit the water, he saw the strong wind and current take the unsecured *Righteous* and bang it up against *Leviathan.*

"Such ridiculous, crude ships!" the beast sneered in Wyckham's face as it waved its free hand at the foundering squadron. "To depend on wind and water currents! Now your weapons can't even be aimed! And you thought you little beings had won, eh, Captain Wyckham? Watch the real attack begin!"

All along the shore, dozens of the massive Draesh were entering the water and swimming toward the ships. *Zeus* had to stop firing as *Leviathan's* bow pushed her stern sideways and her guns no longer bore on the shore. The three ships were now pressed together like the folds of an accordion, unable to sight their artillery. They were completely defenseless.

Jesus Christ, I failed again! The attack plan of the Draesh had been well thought out and had fooled him completely. All the action up to this point had just been feints to get the ships loosed into the lake current. It had worked perfectly.

The beast continued speaking in its terrifying guttural voice. "I have been dreaming of this moment, Captain Wyckham. I get to witness your horror as you watch your own men get devoured. When that is done, I will tear off your own limbs and have you watch me eat you, piece by piece!"

It didn't matter to Wyckham. He had resigned himself to death. But watching the entire squadron get destroyed and all the men devoured by foul demons right before his eyes was more than he could bear. Anger welled up inside him for what this filth was about to do to his squadron. And dammit, the hellish thing spoke the King's English, knowledge that it had picked out of a sailor's brain the fiend had consumed! Well, at least Wyckham would get in a final insult before what was sure to be his slow and painful death.

"My good man, may I suggest you get a teacher in public discourse? Your voice is unpleasantly scratchy. Oh, I see why! You silly bugger, you've misplaced your jaw! Might we postpone further conversation until you find it?"

Infuriated, the creature drew back his free arm to backhand Wyckham, a blow that would kill him instantly. But then it stopped. "Nice try, Captain Wyckham. But there will be no quick death for you. You would not want to miss the grand *pique-nique* we've invited your fellow humans to, would you?"

Wyckham watched, hoping for a miracle, but catastrophe struck quickly. With no artillery keeping heads down, and no smoke hiding the ships or Harrison's men, white beams flashed at both groups from the rocks ashore. First, he heard Harrison's men screaming as the rocks they were hiding among were vaporized. Then several beams hit *Zeus*, slicing through her and setting her afire.

Wyckham could make out O'Neal, standing by the starboard gunnels directing some sailors firing swivel guns. Leaving a fiery trail, one of the beams was walking across the deck towards him. O'Neal saw it approaching but didn't move. Royal Navy officers never flinched in the face of fire. *For what we are about to receive, may we be truly thankful.* The beam cut him in two like a sliced tomato, and the two halves fell to the deck. O'Neal was gone.

Then one of the beams hit the magazine and the ship erupted in a tremendous explosion. The ship heaved up out of the water and its sides bulged outwards. Debris flew everywhere, including the entire mainmast, which went flying through the air like a giant Celtic caber being tossed at a country fair.

There was no doubt that many of the crew had just perished. Yet it was probably better to go that way than what *Zeus*'s survivors now faced, a horribly painful death from fire or getting ripped apart and eaten by demons. Wyckham hung his head and closed his eyes.

"Ah, how convenient! We won't even have to cook that batch!" the demon roared in mirth at its own hellish joke. Draesh were climbing the sides of all three ships, eagerly reaching for sailors to devour. Hopefully, Wyckham wouldn't have to watch much longer, because now the demon pulled Wyckham close to start in on him, and he'd soon pass out from the pain.

But the huge beast knew how to make him suffer. "Look, Captain Wyckham! It's teatime on Draez!" It grabbed Wyckham's head and forced him to gaze out on the horrible scene.

Draesh were grabbing wounded seamen from the squadron's decks and tearing off their limbs. They laughed as they chewed on the men's arms and legs while they yelled to their comrades, clearly commenting on what parts were the tastiest. Wyckham closed his eyes in an attempt to shut out the scene, but with all gunfire stopped, Wyckham could hear every scream as each seaman was slowly devoured. The caverns walls twisted their pitiful cries and sent them echoing back in a surging wave of ghastly moaning. The horrible sounds struck panicked terror into the deepest parts of both Wyckham's brain and soul. Behind his closed eyes, his mind flashed to the vision of Hieronymus Bosch's painting of hell that he had seen in Spain years ago.

The Draesh king turned his head back with its maniacally grinning visage. "Now it's your turn to be invited to dinner! Let's see, maybe an arm to start? All white and tender!" The creature loosened his grip and reached to rip off Wyckham's left arm with his free hand.

Suddenly, the top of Wyckham's head was burning. The demon felt it also, for it stopped what it was doing and looked upward to see the source of the blistering heat. Above them, part of the cavern's roof was glowing with white-hot heat. As they watched, a fifty-foot section of roof exploded, dropping enormous rocks into the water and sending large waves crashing ashore. An alien craft emerged, flying through the gaping hole in the stone roof. It reminded Wyckham of the scout craft they had captured back on the hilltop redoubt.

The Draesh king was pleased. "Ah, one of ours! Now watch a real ship do battle!"

A volley of the white beams shot out from the craft as it came to a halt and hovered in the air. Wyckham could hardly bear to watch the additional destruction it would wreak on the squadron.

But the beams didn't hit the ships! Instead they raked the water, ripping through the swimming Draesh! The single ship increased its assault, with dozens of beams flying out in every direction. Some beams were thick and took out several Draesh at a time as they boiled through the water. Others were needle-like and cut down individual demons boarding the ships. More beams pinpointed targets ashore, and the enemy beams hitting the British ships immediately disappeared.

Additional flying craft burst through the hole in the roof. They looked different from the first ship, but they fired similarly lethal beams at the Draesh below. They were being sliced in half by the dozens, their spurting gushers of blood turning the very air a dark red.

The Draesh king holding him was silent, completely stunned by the turn of events, watching his forces being annihilated. Slowly, it turned to the one enemy it could still reach, its eyes widening in fury as it looked at Wyckham.

"You pitiful little pricks! Look what you've done! You've brought all my enemies to sacred Draez! Right to to my house!"

The creature's grasp tightened with incredible force about Wyckham as it reached for his head with its free hand. Stabs of intense pain shot through Wyckham's sides as his body was slowly crushed. The compression was causing Wyckham to black out. His head swam with visions of the battle. At least he was going to his death with the image of the defeated Draesh king accompanying him to his grave.

Suddenly, the creature froze as a tiny beam emerged from its right eye, narrowly missing Wyckham but leaving a smoking black hole in the monster's skull. The beam had entered at the back of its skull and must have hit a motor center in its brain, for it slowly dropped lower in the water. Bobbing in the bubbling current, it looked at Wyckham with bewilderment, trying to figure out why it could no longer move.

A wave of elation swept over Wyckham. *I'm saved!* But Wyckham's feelings of elation changed quickly into a vengeful fury. It was now his turn to give this filthy pig a violent death.

The hand holding him went limp, and Wyckham wiggled free. The creature bobbed in the water as Wyckham, anger mounting, climbed up on its shoulder, grabbing a motionless, two-foot fang to climb up, and drawing his fine Moroccan sword.

"Feeling a bit peckish? Hoped to eat me just now, did you? I thought you would have saved me for a royal buffet, seeing as how Captain Wyckham is so famous in your pissant society ever since I blew your jaw off! Well eat this, you filthy cannibal swine!" Wyckham ripped the bandage off its mouth and thrust his blade deep down the demon's throat. Masterfully crafted in Damascus steel with a needle-sharp point, it went though the monster's flesh like a hot knife though lard.

"Taste good? Oh, you're still hungry? Here's the second course!" He stabbed down again. Blood spurted up into his eyes, but he wiped it off and kept thrusting the weapon down the demon's throat.

"A little dessert? Nothing like a little dessert to complete a fine meal!" Finally there was no flesh left in the demon's throat to stab— it was all mutilated pulp. Wyckham pulled the sword out and began slashing at the creature's tree-trunk neck instead. Though the weapon had a razor-sharp edge, it was light and had trouble slicing through the Draesh's thick neck muscles. But Wyckham kept hacking away like a woodsman. Chunks of flesh went flying like wood chips. Blood cascaded down the monster's chest like Victoria Falls, turning the waters about them bright red.

"Oh, now it's time for the port! It's a fine red—very red! See?" Wyckham held his bloody blade in front of the beast's one wavering eye.

His assault on the demon's neck exhausted Wyckham before he was able to behead the giant, and he finally slumped down on the dead Draesh's shoulder. No more blood spurted from the beast's neck. It had finally moved on to hell along with the others.

Wyckham looked about the field. This time the battle was definitely done. *Zeus* had split into three separate burning sections, which were sinking into the lake. Boats from the other two ships were swarming about them, taking off survivors, and pulling men from the water.

Those of Harrison's men who had survived ashore stood up and leaned on their long rifle barrels, calling around for missing mates.

But despite the loss of so many fine seamen and officers, Wyckham was too experienced an officer to let grief ruin a victory, especially a victory that saved his entire country, his world, and the entire universe. As he gazed over the battlefield, he was filled with pride at his own role in that victory, and the roles played by his fellow seamen.

The number of dead foes was uncountable, and the mountain fortress was a complete wreck. Both the water and the shore were covered with the bodies of violently shattered foes. There was so much blood running down the rock walls that the sounds of the many falls were audible between the screeching and squealing of the wounded. Dismembered crabmen were trying to run but spun in circles as they bled to death, while the wounded Draesh ashore squealed in rage that none of their Krag minions were coming to their aid. It was well beyond reality. But it was very real, the fight that had truly saved their England and the entire plane Earth. *Victory is not a strong enough term for such a scene*, thought Wyckham.

The first flying craft had stopped firing and now slowly dropped down to hover right beside Wyckham and the dead Draesh, its propulsion system humming softly. A hatch banged open and damned if Wulfe didn't emerge onto its short deck! Wyckham now realized this craft was the same one that he had captured earlier back on the cove's hilltop, just with a few modifications. The League had certainly used it after all.

Wulfe saw that Wyckham was looking over the Draesh ship. "Of course, it's a scow compared to the scout craft on my world, though I did install a complete Lycan Deathdealer 2000 weapon system. But it fooled them long enough for me to get in here. After your ships took out the power supply for their sensors, they had to rely on visual identification for friend or foe. The stupid pigs let this ship go right past their defenses. Sorry that it took some time to get here; I had to blast open a path for the rest of these ships to get through. I'm sure you found plenty to keep you entertained while you were awaiting my arrival."

Wyckham grinned back at his lycanthropic saviour. "Yes, we've had quite a party here." Thank God for the Deathdealer 2000, whatever that was. He climbed up off the dead Draesh king's shoulder and next to Wulfe on the ship's small deck.

"Hopefully, that shot I put through your playmate's head here didn't damage your fine uniform," Wulfe continued. "Must look pretty for your lady friends back at the tavern!"

As if on cue in some fantastic theater, a string of glowing bulbs flew out to the ships from a cluster of rocks ashore, well above the lake. *The ladies must have all sail set,* thought Wyckham. He'd never seen them move so fast. One ball split off and headed directly for Wulfe's craft.

It changed into Lady Brashton as soon as it arrived. She floated right down to him, beaming from ear to ear. "Joy of the day! I believe for once public sex is in order?" With that she gave him a warm hug. But what had she been doing up there in the rocks?

"Yes, all thanks to Wulfe here," said Wyckham. "He managed to fight through the enemy defenses in time to save me from a singularly unpleasant end, and he prevented the complete destruction of our squadron. We are deeply in debt to this gentleman." Wyckham tipped his head to the wolfman.

"Couldn't have done it without these Fireflies here," said Wulfe. "They had the Draesh so confused we pretty much breezed in here."

"You had them *confused?*" puzzled Wyckham. "What exactly were you doing ashore?"

"We were feeding their forces all over this world erroneous information through their own system about all aspects of the fighting, both here and all along their defensive lines," she answered. "Once you took out their sensor controls here, and the operators fled, we simply sneaked in there and manipulated the electrical currents in their connections. The signals they received at the front indicated our forces were in a totally different area on this world, and that everything here was completely calm and normal. Otherwise, Draesh forces would have been here immediately after you surfaced."

So a bunch of ladies just waltzed into the middle of a ferocious battle and fooled the entire enemy force. Probably sneaked in as bugs or something. Besides getting the squadron in here, her group had played a major intelligence role in the battle. Wyckham shook his head in admiration at all she had accomplished.

But now it was time for all officers to deal with the grim aftermath of battle. The butcher's bill. Looking out over the squadron, he saw that the French ship was the center of the rescue effort.

"Wulfe, can you get me over to *Leviathan* on this 'scow'?" Wyckham asked. He needed to get there because, unfortunately, he was most likely now the squadron's commander.

16

RETURNING HOME

Even on his second day here, Wyckham was still marveling at the military base the Draesh had carved out in the cavern. Not only were there underground barracks for over three thousand Krag and hundreds of Draesh, there were enough storage bays for a complete flying navy.

There were caverns for scout ships, battleships, even mother ships carrying small attack craft. Most of the ships from the base had flown off and been destroyed in the battle, but there were examples of each type of ship still there. Wyckham would have to come back and examine every Draesh ship.

The butcher's bill was high, too big to total up in one day. Wyckham had spent the first hours of the previous day aboard *Leviathan* coordinating rescue efforts and transferring lightly wounded crewmen to *Righteous* and the other British ships using the Frenchman's boats.

In total, there were over three hundred wounded. Every ship in the squadron had its orlop full and its surgeon busy. It was impossible to get an estimate on the number of dead by counting bodies—most corpses had been devoured or ripped into pieces. They wouldn't know the exact counts until each ship got its crew back and was able to determine the missing. Most of the casualties would clearly be from *Zeus*.

But apparently their bill was nothing compared with the enemy's bill. Three major battles had been fought at distant locations axcross the planet, with the allies destroying over eighty ships and thousands of Draesh. It had been a relatively easy fight for the allies, with the Draesh power supply eliminated and the Fireflies corrupting their information like poison thrown down a well.

Zeus's captain, Terhughes, had surprisingly survived and was now the squadron's temporary commander, since Wyckham had some cracked ribs that needed to heal before he would be up to much activity. *Righteous's* own Captain Donnelson was now the fleet captain of marines, Captain Warren having been lost in *Zeus's* magazine explosion.

Unbelievably, Admiral Jarvis and his chaplain, DeGeorges, had also survived. A day earlier, O'Neal had thrown Jarvis in the brig as well after he too was discovered fomenting mutiny among *Zeus's* crew. After the battle a small part of the hull containing the ship's brig had been found intact, floating along with the two of them still in it, both of them screaming wildly to be rescued.

Most of *Zeus's* surviving crew had been rowed ashore and billeted in the Draesh barracks, which turned out to be quite well appointed. Each of their immense feather beds had enough sleeping room for fifteen seamen to recline like royalty. A galley had been set up in the kitchens they found, and soon the tantalizing smells of fresh crab and, yes, roast "pork" had persuaded even Wyckham that he was too famished to be squeamish about what he ate right then. *Why not eat a vanquished foe? Plenty of civilizations had done it over the centuries. Un-British? Poppycock.* The days of concern about proper British decorum seemed long gone.

Today found Wyckham, walking slowly with a cane, entering a large dining hall built for Krag. It was huge and filled with tables, far more than were necessary to seat all the squadron's officers. Terhughes had called an officers' meeting, including midshipmen and warrants, to gather there on the second day at two bells of the afternoon watch.

It had surprised Wyckham that Terhughes had been sensible enough to arrange this gathering. They'd been victorious in a special fight, and all the officers deserved accolades from their new commander, whether they wanted to go back to Earth or to stay on Draez. Lady Brashton had told him that the portal to Earth was already established just outside the mountain. As soon as an opening to the ocean could be made in the cave wall, any ship could sail out and be transported back home.

Wyckham, of course, planned to stay. There was no reason to go home to an unwelcoming family and an unknown future in the navy. Here he was going to have the cruise of a lifetime—a whole new world was waiting to be charted and explored. With the tavern as the central attraction, he was sure that enough of his hands would choose to stay. There would be no shortage of crew to man his ship here.

Wyckham entered the room and was a little puzzled at the sight of red-coated marines ringing the hall—probably just Terhughes with his affection for formality. The new admiral was seated at a table in the front of the room. Assuming it was the captains' table, Wyckham approached it to sit down. But Terhughes's steward shook his head and motioned for him to sit at a second table set off to the side.

What the hell? This was starting to look like a courtroom, and he was to be seated at the defendant's dock! His worst fears were confirmed when none other than Sir William Jarvis himself strolled in and sat down at the head of what was apparently the judges' table!

Always his lackey, Terhughes had relinquished command to Jarvis. Next to Jarvis was his sniveling chaplain DeGeorges, and of all people, Wyckham's own marine captain, Donnelson!

Terhughes stood and greeted Jarvis, then told everyone in no uncertain terms to be seated right quick. Jarvis sat and addressed the meeting.

"Order has been restored! God has smitten the mutineer O'Neal and placed me once again in command of this squadron, as He intended all along. We will all soon be leaving this filthy hell and returning to England. All of you, I say!"

Everyone stood up in shocked silence as he continued. "There has been talk by some of you mutinous scum of leaving the British navy and remaining here. But you signed the Royal Navy Articles when you joined and will be held accountable for fulfilling that pledge. Any man, officer or common seaman, who jumps ship will be hunted down and hanged! Then when we return to England, rest assured that all the mutineers among you will be put in front of a court-martial and made to pay for your crimes, hopefully with your lives! The example you officers set for this squadron's crews was the lowest...foulest..." He lost his way, overcome with anger, spittle flying from his mouth as he searched for the words to sufficiently condemn the officer core that had just won the most important battle in human history.

An angry buzz filled the room, and some enraged officers shouted their own condemnations back at Jarvis. He recoiled in surprise that anyone would dispute his obviously correct assessment of matters.

"Captain Donnelson, your marines!" he shouted out in fear, his bluster gone. Donnelson signaled, and the marines in the room leveled their bayonets and formed a line around the yelling officers.

Wyckham, too, was boiling inside over this turn of events. He had promised his brave crew that they could stay here on Draez if they wanted. After all, they had fought and risked death under his direction.

He really couldn't understand the betrayal by his own marine captain. Donnelson had been on board with everything they'd done, especially putting Jarvis away. He stared at the Scottsman, deeply angered. Donnelson looked back at him, quickly glanced sideways to see if anyone was looking, then smiled at him surreptitiously. He held up a finger, indicating he should wait. *What the hell was going on here?*

Now that a line of marines was protecting him, Jarvis got his confidence back.

"Comport yourselves like gentlemen officers, and I may see fit to treat you mercifully. But this man here..." He pointed at Wyckham. "This...scum, this...demon worshipper, this..."

Jesus Christ, after all Wyckham had done here, including saving the daft admiral's life, he was to be taken back to England and completely ostracized, held up to public abuse, and probably strung up to rot in Tyburn Square?

Wyckham slowly stood up and stared furiously at the madman. He had to restrain the urge to draw his sword and run the man through right then and there. *Calm yourself, Wyckham. Calm yourself. Words always work better than rash action.*

"Since I am apparently accused and on trial here, may I speak in my own defense?"

Jarvis nodded in gracious agreement, as if to show all he was fair with even the worst sinners.

"I simply want to say that these accusations should all be completely disregarded," he flatly stated, "since they come from an arrogant arse who is a complete idiot, a grossly corpulent glutton, a proven coward, so ugly that he is distressing to look upon, and above all, utterly and thoroughly loony! May I humbly state to the room, sir, that you are most certainly a mad little dog and a disgrace to everything the British navy stands for!"

The room roared in approval as Jarvis went into a wild fit, blustering and standing up to gesture madly, searching in vain for words to condemn Wyckham. But he did finally signal to Donnelson, who spoke out clearly. "Marines, take the captain under arrest!"

The marines started toward him, but damned if those of his fellow officers near him didn't rush forward with drawn swords to form a protective ring around him! Some of the marines surrounding them cocked their Brown Bess muskets.

This, Wyckham realized, could degenerate quickly into a violent mutiny, which no one wanted. Wyckham was first and always an honorable British officer and wouldn't allow it. He addressed the circle of officers about him. "Gentlemen, I thank you for your concern, but please stand down. We've lost enough of our fellows here. Let's not add to the bill. I'll go back to England and place my trust in the Admiralty." A bad place to put it, but as a gentleman and an officer he really had no choice.

The officers parted and two marines stepped forward to put him in shackles. But they stopped and turned their heads at a puzzling sound, the rustle of many feet and the mumble of many voices in the hallway outside. It increased in volume until the doors flew open and scores of seamen, all carrying cutlasses and pistols, burst into the meeting. At the van, Wyckham recognized several crewmen from *Righteous*, led, of course, by Seaman Peter Crawford.

"Avast, there, avast! Cap'm Wyck'm don' 'av t' go nowheres ee don' wish t' go!" Crawford warned the marines around Wyckham as he barged into their midst, briskly shoving them left and right.

Standing in front of his captain, Crawford glared at Jarvis. "Lis'n 'ere, Sir Stoopid Fookin' Wanker Willy!" That caused Jarvis's eyes to bulge out and his mouth to flop open. "Th' cap'm 'ere jes' saved th' whole world, while ye did'n' do shite! An' this be 'ow ye thank em? Put em in chains fer a courts-martial? Well now, that'll not be what 'appens 'ere."

Crawford settled down a bit as he turned to face the assembled officers. "Th' 'ands 'ere, fum ev'ry ship, we all voted as t' whether we wants t' stay 'ere or go back t' England. Mos 'r gonna stay, speshly us fum *Righteous*. We're goin' where th' cap'm goes, 'n we know ee's stayin' 'ere; ee's not goin' back jes' t' git imself hung. Ye officers best decide eff yer stayin' 'r not, 'n figger out which ships 'r goin' back so's the 'ands goin' home kin board them ships. Doan worry wots iss ol' sod 'ere sez," he stated bluntly, jerking his thumb at Jarvis. "Ee's daft an' doan matter shite no more."

With that Jarvis exploded. "By God, no common seaman will address me in such a manner and tell me what's to happen with my own squadron! You'll all be returning to England to stand trial! Any officer who sides with this mutiny will have his family destroyed and their lands taken back by the Crown. I swear it! I've friends in both Lords and Commons who will see justice done. Do not doubt it, sirs!"

That did it for Crawford. "Go after their fam'lies, will ye?" He pulled a dirk from under his shirt and started to lunge for Jarvis. Wyckham grabbed his collar from behind and yanked him back.

"Peter, no, that's not the way. If a common sailor kills him, every seaman returning will get blamed for it and strung up. Just let him go."

Copper looked over his shoulder at Wyckham and nodded an "Aye, sor," but Jarvis was by no means done.

"Damn straight, I'll hang your friends! Every one of this mutinous, godless, lower sort that ever even knew you! God and Admiralty will have an example set!"

DeGeorges behind him nodded in approval. "God is with you, Sir William. Amen."

That did it for Wyckham. *How dare this coward plan the deaths of dozens of true British heroes! And in the name of God!* Furious, he shoved Crawford and then two marines roughly aside, dropped his cane, drew his sword, and stomped right up to Jarvis.

"So you will work ceaselessly to harm these brave men when you get back?" He took a step closer to the admiral. "Then why don't you ask yourself why in God's name I should let you live any longer? You can go ahead and try to destroy my family back in England, I don't care, they never showed me any kindness. Though I doubt you can; the Wyckhams could always play politics as well as any. But you'll not live to harm the stout fellows I've fought with here on this world. Defend yourself," he snarled. "Now! Right here and now!"

Although Jarvis was wearing the fine sword given him by the House of Lords, he made no move to draw it. Fear gripped him as he saw his immediate death looming in Wyckham's eyes. Backing away in terror, he begged for his life. "No, Captain, stop! Please! I'll forget the whole matter! Just spare me! Let me return to my life, and I'll see all your sailors get feted by both the Crown and Admiralty!"

"Why don't I believe that?" Wyckham took another slow step forward with his point extended toward Jarvis's throat. He was calm yet at the same time angrier than he had ever been in his life. "Permit me to answer my own question." He took another step forward and backed Jarvis up against the wall. Some marines tried to intervene but Crawford's seamen restrained them.

Another step. His point was now circling menacingly, just inches away from Jarvis's pulsing neck veins.

"It's because you've gone way too daft to remember a promise for even a few minutes, much less by the time we return to London." Closer. Now his point dented the skin on Jarvis's chin.

"Not that I believe you've ever hesitated to break promises, even back when you used to be a little less crazy. Because you've always been one hell of a selfish bastard."

With the next step, his point penetrated through the lower jaw and entered Jarvis's mouth. Jarvis inhaled to beg further but gagged on the blood dripping back down his throat. One more step and the blade would poke up through Jarvis's skull like that snake's in the tavern.

"Please, enough, Captain Wyckham!" It was Donnelson, trying to prevent a cold-blooded murder. "Consider us surrendered officers, and follow the articles of war! No execution of prisoners! Officers do not murder fellow officers!"

He was right, of course. Wyckham cooled a bit, enough to withdraw his blade as Donnelson stood up and walked over to him. He put an arm around Wyckham's shoulder and walked him away to an isolated corner for a private talk.

"Let him go, Rodney," he spoke softly. "You have friends here with plans for him. Just watch." And he was chuckling softly under his breath.

Now what? There was another ruckus in the hall and in came a delegation of alien leaders, including a bunch of the familiar floating energy balls. There were stick beings, mud-creatures, Slicks, and lots of those big ants. Grouped together were Wulfe, Lady Brashton in human form, and the newly arrived Number Eighteen. (Number Twenty-Two had died in the carrier craft's demise—apparently the squadron now rated a higher-ranking delegate from the Slicks' world.)

Arrogant as his forerunner, Number Eighteen stepped forward and told everyone the League's decision about their fate.

"The League of Planets has made this world a monument to peace and recreation. Anyone here has sanctuary guaranteed by our alliance; no one can be forced to leave or to do anything not agreed upon. Anyone violating this principle will be forced to leave. Your Admiral Jarvis here has just qualified as the first to be exiled."

Clicking noises came from his translator, and several ants swarmed over the bleeding Jarvis, picked him up, and unceremoniously carried him toward the door.

Jarvis had been kept below decks from the day the squadron arrived and hadn't been exposed to the cornucopia of alien beings here. Apparently the shock of being taken away by a horde of these strange creatures was overwhelming; he started to jabber and drool like a village idiot. "Demons! I'm being carried off by demons!" Jarvis struggled futilely in abject terror, blood from the hole in his jaw spluttering all over his ruffled silk shirt. "They're taking me to hell! Chaplain DeGeorges, in the name of God, you must stop them!"

DeGeorges repeated his earlier mistake and tried to summon some hands to intervene. "Sailors of the British navy! For God's sake, rise up and save your admiral! Strike down these mutineers and their demonic compatriots!"

Number Eighteen spoke again. "The second one has now qualified." More clicking noises came from Number Eighteen's translator, and another bunch of ants hoisted DeGeorges up as well. The two exiles were carried out the door, screaming like terrified children, followed by a parade of cheering sailors.

Donnelson patted Wyckham on the back. "I would have loved to stay, Rodney. It's been the greatest adventure a Scotsman could ever dream of. But I'm done. I've a pretty wife and children that need me, so I'm going back. I'll try to keep Jarvis from causing our lads any harm in England, though if anyone listens to him anymore, I'd be surprised. I exoect that getting thrown off this planet by a bunch of giant ants has pushed his fragile brain into complete delirium. Even his friends in Lords won't listen to a raving lunatic."

By God, Donnelson had planned this whole thing! "This whole exercise was your doing, wasn't it?" exclaimed Wyckham.

"Yes, it was," Donnelson grinned. "Terhughes approached me with his dastardly plans. He needed my marines to control any opposition. I let him think I was with him, but I told everything to Crawford, and with my keys to the arms locker, we planned both the mutiny and the allied intervention together. Hopefully, I've made it look like I had to surrender, facing hopeless odds, saving Sir Willy's life and all. I need to look blameless when I go back home to Scotland. I want to be a free man and watch my three wee ones grow up."

Wyckham was about to shower Donnelson with thanks and praise when he too was hoisted up, this time by Peter Crawford and a group of cheering seamen. He was carried out to the rocky beach to see a screaming Jarvis and DeGeorges dumped rudely into the water to await a gig summoned from *Gnat*.

17

SHERIFF AND INNKEEPER

Wyckham drained his glass and signaled for another. *Damn, that was good!* Whatever fruit the mud people fermented to make this stuff, it was smoother than the finest French brandy. And the lightness in Wyckham's mood confirmed it was not short on alcohol either. Sitting across from him at their special table in the Ruptured Krag, Wulfe smacked his lips in agreement.

Two weeks after the Battle in the Mountain, the squadron's affairs had been settled. About a third of the men and most of the officers had elected to go home, among them Wyckham's own lieutenants Sorenson and Gregory. Three days after the cavern fight, *Gnat* and *Hedgehog* had sailed out through the completed opening in the mountain with some four hundred men aboard. With Crawford and the Fireflies at the controls of the transporter, a single square portal had appeared in the water, the two ships sailed in, and they were gone.

Two hundred and fifty-six British, one hundred twenty French, and seven Yankees were going nowhere. That was the final count of dead from the battle. About two hundred wounded had remained, making remarkable progress under the care of Slick surgeons, who used all sorts of remarkable lifesaving devices. Some of these wounded would undoubtedly be returning to Earth later once they were whole.

French Capitaine Jean Badoin had also elected to stay; no way was he going to leave his beloved Comptesse de Pittard. Most of his crew had left, however. Something about no substitute for real French food, probably wanted to get away from Badoin's tyrannical rule as well. However, Wyckham couldn't help but like the fanatical revolutionary; he'd sure saved *Righteous*'s crew from complete annihilation. Wyckham was even helping the Frenchman recruit alien replacements to man his ship.

Because they had a job to do. The League had declared the Draesh home world would henceforth be a world for peace, recreation, and commerce. All races were welcome to visit, but no weapons would be allowed. Enforcing this policy and keeping general order would be the newly appointed governor and guardian of this world, Captain Rodney Wyckham himself. Under him were the other three captains: Hamilton with the brig *Scamp*, Randolf with the bomb ketch *Vesuvius*, and, of course, Badoin with the big French two-decker *Leviathan*.

The Yankee, James Harrison, had also decided to stay, along with all of his men. They, too, were assigned a job. The League had asked him to explore and map the planet's interior, documenting all its unique flora and fauna. Hopefully, they'd survive contact with God knows what kind of unpleasant creatures the Draesh had bred on this world. The thrill of the unknown called and off they'd rowed, into the lush planet's interior using boats from the two departed ships. Wyckham looked forward to their return and hearing of their discoveries and adventures.

The League of Planets gave Wyckham one additional gift–the Ruptured Krag was his. With the Fireflies continuing their construction efforts and involvement, the Ruptured Krag was expected to be the main tourist attraction on this world, even more popular than the planet's many interesting natural wonders. And the cove where the tavern was situated was to be the only entry port to the planet.

So Wyckham could easily manage his inn and keep watch over new arrivals at the same time. Outside the Krag, structures were quickly going up as alien beings established concessions of all sorts to interest the planet's visitors. Already there were other inns, a zoo, tour operators, manufacturing, mining and farming operations, and real-estate ventures.

But those numbers of those enterprises pailed in comparison to the number of trading companies being established. With the portal's unique ability to bring in ships from parallel universes, the planet was becoming a crossroads for all sorts of different species with their various goods to trade. Previously, it had been extremely difficult for any beings to travel between parallel universes, though why that was true Wyckham couldn't grasp. If universes were lined up in parallel to each other, didn't that make it easier? Anyway, the portal's capability to cross these parallel boundaries was making this world a trading hub for all worlds.

Wyckham and his naval force would keep this business controlled, especially watching for weapons smuggling. As a tribute to Wyckham's contributions to the conquest of the planet, the League had named the mushrooming town Port Wyckham.

Yelling from the common room next door confirmed that Peter Crawford was at his post as official Gaming Manager at the Krag. Wyckham had given him this position along with that of Sailing Master aboard *Righteous*. God knows he owed the man his life several times over. Wyckham even looked the other way whenever he heard about Crawford's smuggling of the popular aphrodisiac sticks.

Lady Brashton approached the table. She was the Krag's manager, keeping it stocked with provisions and managing the other "services" the inn offered. With the mind-reading capabilities of its workers, every visiting species left the Krag raving about the experience. The Ruptured Krag was already the talk of the cosmos. Each day brought increasing numbers of strange new customers to the Krag. Looking about the room, Wyckham saw several species he'd never seen before, including some kind of turtle-like things, human forms with writhing hair like Medusa's serpents, and floating balls of bubbling oil complete with a few rather unbecoming hairs. Again he wondered about the escalating involvement of the Fireflies in the port. Did they have some nefarious objective? The fact that they too consumed human life energy made Wyckham wonder. While they had worked selflessly so far to protect the entire cosmos, Wyckham was always suspicious of free assistance, thanks to his experience with colonization and organized religion on Earth, two movements which actually believed they were helping people but in reality only visciously pursued their own goals. These energy beings must have some self-serving plans—were any dangerous?

His thoughts were interrupted by the attention of Lady Brashton, always hard to ignore with its constant concern for Wyckham's pleasure. "Are you sure you want another of those *mudslingers*?" she asked. "You want to make sure you have the energy for the afternoon's entertainment I have planned for you. You have no duties today. Why not spend the afternoon 'giving to the cause'?"

She smiled suggestively and motioned to the glowing balls floating above her, which immediately formed into a bevy of gorgeously dressed ladies whom Wyckham did not recognize.

"Since we've already been through every woman you have memories of, allow me to introduce to you the most famous crowned heads in the history of Europe? Maybe you'll enjoy some time with them? Most of their images are based on portraits and books you and your officers have seen. I believe they are reasonably accurate. First, Queen Isabel of Leon and Castile."

A young woman with blonde hair braided in medieval fashion walked up and nodded to Wyckham but said not a word. This was the woman that had first dispatched challengers to her throne and then helped kick the Moors out of Spain. She had a reputation for resisiting arranged relationships. Wyckham thought the Firefly playing this role was overdoing it a bit, this woman seemed like the type to climb into your bed just to stick a stilletto in your back. But then she smiled and curtsied; apparently this discerning royal had decided she approved of him.

"And this is Marie Antoinette, Queen of France." Confirming her reputation, this young woman was dressed in a most ornate silver gown, her breasts revealed by a low bodice, her hair actually dyed silver. She managed to curtsy to Wyckham carefully so the two-foot-long silver ship model in her hair didn't fall out.

"And finally, Catherine the Great, Tzarina of all the Russias." In her late thirties and stoutly built, the most powerful female in European history ostentatiously bowed to Wyckham.

"How exciting to meet the saviour of the universe!" she said, stepping closer to whisper in his ear. "Powerful people such as ourselves should keep very close company." And then damned if she didn't growl in his ear like a hound in heat!

That got an alarmed reaction from Wyckham. Well, he was certainly in for an interesting day. But before he became fully immersed in merriment, there was one discussion he needed to have with Lady Brashton. Because although he was still ignorant of the Fireflies' goals, he had realized that there was one fact they had hidden from him, and he wanted to hear Lady Aston's explanation.

"Lady Brashton, again my thanks for all you provide me with. It's more than any sailor ever dreamed of. But I do have one question that has been troubling me. How did you initially manage to aim the Draesh transporter at our squadron back in the English Channel and start this whole war?"

Lady Brashton nodded acceptance that her secret was out. "Yes, I knew you would figure out that the transporter scooping you up was no chance incident. My race had an agent hiding here in the Draesh homeworld who was able to access the transporter controls and find your squadron, a force that could fool the transporter's weapon filter and get through to Draez. While we initially gave you only a small chance for success, you surprised us and did what was necessary to end the universal Draesh menace. As far as not being forthcoming about the matter, we believed we needed to hide from you the fact that we could send you back to earth at any time. Should you have known that, you may not have stayed on to win us this planet and save the cosmos."

So just as he expected, the Fireflies had orchestrated events right from the beginning. And they had given him only a small chance for success but had brought in six ships and fourteen hundred men in to face almost certain death anyway? Yet he couldn't argue with those actions. With untold billions of beings threatened, including Earth's entire population, were he in her place he would have done the same thing. And it had all worked out, hadn't it? So far, anyway. Though he would certainly keep an eye on the Fireflies' activities in the future.

But he might as well enjoy the fruits of victory. Wyckham invited the four ladies to seat themselves on the plush couch built especially for his table. The three queens were new Firefly arrivals. As first-time visitors they were, of course, quite eager to sample real, physical food and drink, as well as other physical experiences. Wyckham looked about to order them some more of the roast fowl from that planet, whatever it was called, along with a container of the wolf world's reasonably decent attempt at Chardonnay.

Ever efficient, Obujimi popped out from wherever he'd been hiding. He was spectacularly dressed and coiffed, having gotten into Jarvis's sea chests for his uniform. Along with a white silk shirt and beige satin waistcoat, he wore a purple formal coat heavily embroidered in gold striping and floral details. Topping off the presentation, one of Jarvis's curled and powdered wigs sat perfectly on his head.

But despite all his new finery, he was clearly upset about something. "Would the captain and his new friends like some food and drink before beginning the usual depravities you regularly commit here in a public room? Or are you unable to wait another moment before rutting like animals in front of everyone?"

Wyckham supposed he should take offense at the steward's impertinence, but any sort of disputation was far from his mind right now. A musical trio of mud beings was singing and playing strange percussion instruments which Wyckham actually found himself enjoying. It had an interesting sound: very earthy, ha hah! His three newfound friends were bobbing in their seats with the music, looking at him fetchingly.

Wyckham sent the African off to fetch the food and drink. Ah, yes, this would be another most relaxing day at the Krag. Wyckham was going to enjoy himself today. *Why not? Christ, I've earned it!*

"Some assistance here, if you might?" he called out to a passing servant, a stately tall specimen passing herself off as an Egyptian goddess, dressed in only a few filmy ribbons. "Please be so good as to go to the common room for me, give my respects to Mr. Crawford, and could he give you a few of his wondersticks for me? Tell him I'll just add them to the substantial debts I already owe him."

Yes, today would be fun. He always loved welcoming new visitors to the Krag. The band broke out in a stirring rattle that sounded amazingly like a British army marching tattoo. But nothing here surprised him anymore. He was getting used to the place.

White Hot Grape
The sequel to *Grapeshot and Demons,*
coming Christmas 2013

ON THE WALLS OF PORT WYCKHAM

Post Captain Rodney Wyckham ascended the last set of stairs and emerged into the sunlight atop Port Wyckham's main city gate to see preparations well under way for the morning's planned exercises. Gun crews from HMS *Righteous* were preparing to fire the gate bastion's four thirty-two pounders, some of the sixty-three guns that had been salvaged from HMS *Zeus*, sunk during the final battle for the planet. Their allies, the League of Planets, had brought in a group of some strange octopus-like creatures, which had been able to swim down and attach lines to the guns submerged in Hollow Mountain's lake. Cranes aboard the frigate *Righteous*, thirty-eight guns, and the big French ship-of-the-line *Leviathan*, eighty guns, had raised the three-ton cannons and put them on barges. From there, they had been towed back to the city, raised up onto the city walls, and sited to cover the cove and beach about Port Wyckham.

Both ships were 150 feet below, along with the bomb ketch, HMS *Hedgehog*, tied up at one of the three wooden quays that had been constructed along the beach. The morning sun had lit up the three ships, their newly painted giltwork sparkling with fiery light. *If only they could see this back in Portsmouth*, Wyckham mused. It had turned out that gold was actually common on this planet, and the sailors had used it in paint for all the railings, scrollwork, bowsprits, the lines of gunports, and anything else they felt like. Naturally, the French ship's captain, Jean Badoin, had gone completely overboard with the gold paint on his *Leviathan*. Now the big warship brought to mind a canopy bed in Louis XIV's boudoir. The gilding on the quarterdeck made it look like an altar in a baroque cathedral. The British captain had once marveled at the Doge's royal barge in Venice, but it was a Thames barge hauling night soil in comparison to what Badoin had done with his ship.

From the wooden quays, a short beach lay in front of the stone walls that now surrounded the city. Along the waterfront, the walls of square-cut stones were over seventy feet high, a height the Fireflies had assured him the Draesh could not get over. The entire curtain wall had gone up in less than two months, thanks to the large alien ants, which could carry heavy stonework all day without fatigue. The bastion he was standing on, straddling the main city gate, was almost two hundred feet high, giving its four guns command of the entire cove. Though the fortifications had no ravelins, tenailles, or other modern constructions, its medieval layout was strong enough for defense against an enemy with no artillery. If any aliens ever did succeed in bringing their magical beam weapons or exploding rockets onto the planet, nothing Wyckham could build would stand up anyway, no matter how well designed.

Within the city walls was a hodgepodge of hastily erected commercial buildings, most of them constructed of rippled metal sheets, laid out along meandering stone streets. Dominating the city was his Governor's Palace, a large stone complex built on a rise in the city's center. It resembled a medieval castle's keep, with its own walls, defensive towers, and a surrounding dry moat. But unlike an old keep, it had two batteries of thirty-two pounders sited to cover the open area around it. Well, the city needed a fortified refuge of last resort, and as the manager of a whole planet, Wyckham needed a suitable residence to impress visitors, didn't he? Letting some merchant or mining interest build a bigger one just wouldn't do. Wyckham loved the way the massive structure's white stone columns and gilded dome glistened in the morning light. Hell, every British colony always had an imposing capital building to impress the locals. Why shouldn't he?

Above the three sailing ships tied to the quays were over a dozen alien spacecraft of different sizes and shapes, just floating in the air like those new hot air balloons over Paris. During the months since the victory over the Draesh, Port Wyckham had become a major trading and tourist center for aliens from many galaxies. All sorts of strange beings were coming to commercially exploit the newly freed planet. There were large mining and farming operations getting established all around the port, and all the workers and intergalactic tourists visited the fantastical taverns that the Fireflies had established inside the city walls. Port Wyckham's resident population was now over three thousand, plus another five thousand visitors at any one time. Many strange visitors from very distant planetary systems had told Wyckham that his city was the fastest-growing port they knew. Understandably, the British captain felt like a duke or marquis as he proudly surveyed the thriving port city over which the victorious League of Planets had proclaimed him master.

While there was abundant gold available on Draez, there was no saltpeter to make gunpowder for Wyckham's small squadron. Not a single one of the hundreds of bird and bat species on the planet even had the right kind of feces to make saltpeter. Even though there had been no hostilities for seven months since the defeat of the giant Draesh, other than the occasional skirmish with smugglers, Wyckham was uncomfortable with the low levels of powder and shot that the final battle had left him with. For shot he expected that one of the metals available on the planet would suffice, and he had some of the alien ants making molds for ball, grapeshot, and canister. But for saltpeter there was no alternative on the planet. He'd asked some of the various alien merchants that were bringing in goods to ship in some, but the race of Slicks that ran the League of Planets had banned the importation of any weapons or munitions to the newly designated planet of peace. How those stoic, idiot Slicks expected him to keep order on the planet without powder for his guns angered Wyckham whenever he thought about it.

Hopefully, today's testing would find a substitute for the gunpowder his guns needed. His first lieutenant, Pierce Rawlins, was walking about the battery, supervising the making of cartridges. Four barrels of different local substances with explosive properties had been brought up and placed behind the guns by the ever-industrious ants, while several of the crab-like Krag packed cartridge bags with various amounts of the candidates to be tested. Wyckham hoped that one of the muddy compounds would work at least well enough so they could start firing salutes again. Currently, when alien ships came to the planet or the brig *Scamp* returned from a visit to Earth, the time-honored Royal Navy tradition of greeting visitors had to be neglected due to the lack of powder. And that just wouldn't do!

But his doubts of success increased as he saw the Krag arguing among themselves over the task at hand. Their foreman, a particularly large and ugly creature, was clicking loudly in their strange tongue and shoving his workers rudely about. While Wyckham didn't know how the stupid creatures could ruin today's tests, he suspected they'd find a way.

After the planet had been won, thousands of the four-foot-tall Krag that the Draesh had brought to the planet as workers were left without a way to feed themselves. The leader of the Fireflies, the energy beings who had provided intelligence for the League of Planets, had explained that Krag were basically land crabs and could not live on this marshy planet without assistance. So Wyckham had decided to take them in and put them to work as well. While not particularly intelligent, they were obedient and could perform most menial tasks with their grasping claws.

The Krag leader was getting increasingly frustrated with one of his workers, which was having difficulty stuffing a cartridge bag with some malodorous black slime. Suddenly, he grabbed the worker with his powerful short claw, ripped one of his legs off, and threw it over the back wall behind the guns! *Well, that's a bit extreme!* Wyckham knew the crabmen could regrow severed limbs, but he still considered it rather rough discipline for whatever offense the worker had committed.

Somewhat at a loss for words, he turned to Rawlins to see his old friend's eyebrows raised in consternation as well. "Ah now, that was a mite harsh, what?" ventured Rawlins. "Makes our meanest bosun seem like a nun tending the wounded. I shall have a word with this big crab afterward. Perhaps we should proclaim a ban on dismemberment during work details? Won't get much work for weeks from any crabman missing an arm."

"As usual, your quick mind presents solutions that are both productive and based on British decency," responded Wyckham with a smile and a nod. "Might I also suggest you have some bosuns from *Righteous* distribute some rope starters to the Krag foremen and instruct them in the usage of that proven Royal Navy device?" Starters were lengths of knotted rope that bosuns would use to prompt laggardly sailors to get "started" on their tasks. "I warrant a good whack on a crab's arse will be just as motivating as those upon a sailor's. Definitely superior to ripping off appendages."

Rawlins nodded agreement as they watched several of the red, stork-size scavenger gulls that populated the shores of this aquatic world launch from their posts lounging on the walls, following the crab leg down, squawking and squabbling over the tasty treat. Krag meat was quite delectable. Many sailors from *Righteous* had objected to employing the beasts since they made for marginal servants but excellent dinner. Wyckham himself missed the crabmeat dipped in wolf-world butter that used to be common before they had saved the remaining Krag from starving to death. But when the leader of the Fireflies took the form of his childhood sweetheart Lady Brashton and asked him to adopt the silly little creatures, he had been unable to resist her entreaty. The fact that the issue was discussed while lounging in his bed aboard *Righteous* had made denying her particularly difficult.

Now there were sounds of more commotion from down below where the claw had fallen. The two officers walked to the parapet and looked down to see one of the mud-creatures blasting away in his flatulent voice at the aggressive birds that had flown down. The big gulls were now flapping about his market stall looking for the severed claw, causing considerable destruction.

As in medieval English towns, vendors had built little shops along the city walls to sell all sorts of goods. This mud-creature was selling the very popular aphrodisiac sticks that many of the British seamen used when visiting the local taverns. His tables were now overturned with much of his inventory scattered in pieces over the ground. The angry, six-foot-wide ball of mud, out for revenge, rolled over a bird and absorbed it into its center, to God knows what fate. This prompted the three other birds to change their mind about the importance of the claw and fly off to look for breakfast elsewhere.

"Yas…well, ah…matters down there appear to have settled themselves. No need for us to get involved," opined Rawlins.

"Um…no, no, certainly no need at all," replied Wyckham as they both drew back from the wall before the mud-creature looked up and saw them. He did make a mental note to reimburse the mudman in some way for the losses their gunpowder experiments had just caused him.

These mud balls were also employed in the Ruptured Krag, his favourite tavern, to keep order. There, they had saved him several times from drunken aliens trying to teach Wyckham a thing or two using their fangs, tails, claws, or the handy drinking steins. It definitely paid to keep these apparently indestructible fellows on his side.

Righteous's new gunner's mate, Fellows, approached and knuckled his forehead in salute. "Gunner Crawford's compliments, sor, an' ee wishes t' say that th' guns r' ready t' fire, sor."

"Thank you, Mister Fellows. My respects to Gunner Crawford, and he may begin firing."

Fellows scooted back across the bastion to Gunner Crawford, a big, red-headed cockney who had been aboard *Righteous* for years. Having fought valiantly in the struggle to take the planet, Crawford had been rewarded with the promotion to Sailing Master, the most important of all *Righteous*'s warrants. But his future in ship navigation had come into question when it turned out he was illiterate and couldn't read a chart, much less make one. However, he was the ship's best gun captain, and he had settled easily into the rank of *Righteous*'s Gunner.

Wyckham and his lieutenant remained a good distance away, having been warned by Lady Brashton that the compounds they were testing were not well understood and could do anything. Six-man gun crews from *Righteous* had the four guns loaded and ready to test. The guns had been run out until the muzzles of the nine-foot-long gun barrels protruded through the crenellations in the wall, their motion halted when their square wooden trucks bumped up against the stone walls. After aiming the guns down the empty beach north of the city, the four gun captains stepped back from their guns with lanyards in their hands, awaiting Crawford's signal.

Crawford nodded to the nearest gun. Its captain yanked his line, the firelock's hammer struck the frizzen, priming powder flashed, and…nothing. Wyckham and Rawlins shook their heads slightly, hoping for something at least from the second gun. It, too, was fired, but all they got was a long, whistling sound from the touchhole, sounding like a firework at a Westminster ball. The third gun actually did produce a low thump in its barrel, followed by a rolling sound as the six-inch round shot barely made it out of the barrel, dropping down to the beach to land with a dull thud.

Christ, I guess the next time I need to hit a foe with a thirty-two-pound ball, I'll just have to throw it at him, thought Wyckham. Disgusted, he started to turn to leave as the fourth gun was fired.

The huge retort was crisp and incredibly loud as a pure white flame erupted thirty feet from the gun's muzzle with not a wisp of smoke. Wyckham had never heard a gun's discharge anywhere near as loud. His hat was blown off as he watched the gun's breech explode in a full circle and the entire gun lift three feet into the air to fly back into its restraining cables. The stout cables held, but the long gun barrel broke free from its severed breech to go spinning over the back wall like a windmill blade in a stiff breeze. When it landed, the crash of the three-ton cannon barrel shook the entire tower.

Stunned and surprised, both Wyckham and Rawlins raised their eyebrows, for the moment at a loss for words. "Well, that was…impressive!" an awed Rawlins finally managed to spit out, and they both walked over to the parapet's edge to see where the gun had landed. And damned if it hadn't struck spot-on the same mud-creature, completely obliterating the big alien, blowing bits of his body all over the back side of the city wall. Yet before the hot gun barrel had even stopped rolling, the alien started to reform itself, all of its muddy bits moving back together and promptly reassembling as an apparently healthy mudman.

But without a doubt the alien was quite beside itself with the goings-on, as the two officers quickly learned when the speaking horn for its translator device emerged from inside the creature. Then it let loose with a tirade of strong curses in the English that it had learned from the British sailors with whom it did business.

Now, Wyckham and Rawlins had certainly heard lots of sailors swearing over the years, but this bit of oratory shocked even their weathered ears. "Bloody fookin' 'ell!" it rasped through the translator. "Firs' ye fookin' wankers oop there git th' guddam birds t' bugger oop me bizniz. Then ye drop 'iss big thing like a giant 'ot turd on me 'ed t' boot! By God ye mos' 'av right grand arses to shite this big!" The tirade prompted both Wyckham and Rawlins to step back from the wall, again hoping the thing hadn't seen them. "Ooever's oop there," it continued, "oye be cumin' oop right now t' straighten things oot! Mebbee oy'l drop a big turd on yer fookin' oogly faces, see 'ow's ye likes it wif a great big shite shoved down yer throats! N' mebbe I'll bloody bugger yer sodding fat arses as well!" And with that it started rolling toward the tower stairs.

Wyckham again raised his eyebrows and turned to Rawlins. "I say, rather some impressive choices of invective. Pierce, old boy, mayhap it's time for a glass at the Krag to discuss the day's tests? Certainly no reason to stay here any longer now that we've discovered the replacement for powder, hey? Give my compliments to Gunner Crawford, and might he join us as well? And might I suggest suggest the utmost rapidity?"

With that, he picked up his bicorn hat and walked briskly to the stairway opposite the one the furious mud ball was climbing, as Rawlins instructed Crawford to run like hell.

ANOTHER GLASS AT THE RUPTURED KRAG

"So that will be all, Mister Crawford. My compliments on a very successful day."

Gunner Crawford nodded, downed the last of his mug, and headed out the door of the Ruptured Krag. Wyckham leaned back into the magical chair, which conformed to his body as he moved. His special table, on a raised dais to give him a view of the entire officers' room, had several of the electrically powered chairs that one of the wolf-world's ships had brought in.

Over the last few months, the interior of the Krag had been steadily improved. The managing Fireflies had decorated the walls with paintings of various tranquil scenes from the English countryside. The "ladies," as they were referred to since they often took the form of human women known to the sailors, could also read stored facts in the sailors' minds and had found favourite scenes which they had other skilled aliens reproduce on canvas. The tavern also now had lots of quality wooden furniture made from trees cut down around the port. Wyckham's own table was made of some species that resembled cherry, beautifully lacquered and carved with intricate scenes on its mouldings of life aboard *Righteous*.

The three officers had spent two hours at Wyckham's official table, working out more detailed tests for the smelly black ooze that had been used in the fourth gun. They would beach a ship's boat and use its two-pounder bow gun for the tests. Firing tests would begin with a one-quarter-ounce charge, then increase by one ounce at a time, until it matched the range for standard British fine milled gunpowder. From what he had witnessed, Wyckham guessed that this new explosive had around ten times the force of British gunpowder, and he suspected the great guns could at most handle around one pound of the new charge. Wyckham wondered if some way could be found to use it to increase the range of British naval artillery without damaging his guns. A shame to have such an incredible explosive but be unable to take advantage of it.

Other matters from the morning's exercise had also been resolved. He had sent a sailor to the mud-being's market stall with a gift of distilled water, which mudmen craved. He hoped the sailor would return intact. Three of the British sailors present had been injured in the gun's explosion, hit by hot metal, but his Prussian surgeon, Shroeder, now under the tutelage of the incredible Slick surgeons, had reported that all would mend. Several Krag that had been milling about too close to the gun were not so fortunate. As a result, there would be fresh steamed Krag for the watch aboard *Righteous* tonight.

Now an ant whose name translated to "Queen's Most Favourite" walked up. He was the one that had been managing the effort to cast new shot for the British squadron. Wyckham's mood brightened further at the sight of some apparently weighty cloth bags it was carrying. Possibly another of his problems had been solved?

He stood and made a leg to greet this important alien. "Mister Favourite, your servant. I must say, I'm quite curious about the bag you are carrying. Perhaps we're about to have a little dog-and-pony show?"

The ant's antennae stopped their usual circling, which Wyckham knew indicated that their owner was puzzled. "Ah, don't concern yourself, of no importance." Wyckham had to remember not to use the upper class slang he grew up with when speaking to aliens. "So, my good man, please tell me, how have your efforts to cast shot been proceeding?" he asked.

Although the ant had a translator strapped to its head, its response was to tip up a bag and dump the contents on the table. Ants seemed to think communication was a needless exercise, when activity was all that counted. A brown round shot, obviously meant for a thirty-two pounder, fell from the bag to the table. But clearly it weighed more than thirty-two pounds, for when it landed, the stout wooden table top split right down the middle with a loud crack, the two officers' fresh drinks sliding down the newly created crevasse.

Wyckham bent down to pick up the ball. Even with both hands, it took almost all his strength to raise it. *Jesus, this ball must weigh at least five stone!* "By God, man, what is this material?" he asked the alien. "Are these balls easily produced?"

The ant reached into another bag, pulled out a crock, and dumped some brown liquid on the floor. Finally its translator came to life. "Brown lakes underground. Brown water dries quickly, very hard."

Sure enough, as Wyckham watched, the brown liquid started to sizzle and thicken. But in a few moments, the noise stopped and Wyckham gingerly bent down to pick up a frozen puddle about three inches long. It too was very heavy for its size. Wyckham whacked the thin sheet on the edge of the split table in an attempt to break it but only succeeded in gouging the wooden tabletop and jarring his hand.

Unbelievable! Some kind of wet clay that had perfect properties for making shot, easily worked—and there were lakes full of the stuff! But then it hit him—his guns wouldn't take the tremendous stress of propelling such weighty shot. To get a six-inch ball this heavy to fly straight for a mile would require a far larger explosive charge, one that the cast-iron breeches of his guns could not tolerate.

"Truly a wondrous material you have brought me, sir, and I must thank you for your industrious efforts," Wyckham said. "Unfortunately, these balls are too heavy for my guns. To shoot them any distance would require a charge that would violently destroy any British Naval artillery. Would it be possible to make these balls lighter? Maybe by diluting the liquid in some way?"

But the ant was ignoring him, looking behind him at some commotion coming from the Ruptured Krag's officer's door. As a crowd of labouring ants came through that door, the ant turned back to Wyckham and rasped, "Make guns too."

Although the dog-size ants were quite strong, the group coming through the door was struggling with something. Make guns? Could it be?

It was. About twenty struggling ants finally made it through the door carrying a ten-foot-long gun barrel, clearly cast in the magical brown liquid. God only knew how much it weighed. Even though one alien ant could hoist twenty stone, this burden was clearly a challenge for the group. Progress was slow, the ants were taking small shuffling steps to make sure their feet were planted for each forward movement. Finally, they stopped at some unspoken signal and dropped the gun with a loud clang to the Krag's stone floor. The group then backed off, their heads bobbing in what Wyckham thought must be the ant version of panting.

Wyckham walked over to examine the gun. While its bore was clearly for a standard six-inch, thirty-two pound ball, the wall thickness on the barrel was only around an inch and a half, far less than the six inches of cast iron that Royal Navy thirty-twos currently had. It looked ridiculously thin, but possibly this magic brown stuff was strong enough to make a practical great gun with such a thin casting? It better, because the ants apparently couldn't cast any reinforcing rings on it. The outside of the gun was smooth over its entire length. And maybe it could even handle large amounts of the new explosive they had discovered this morning? The bulbous breech was thick, about two feet in diameter as opposed to the barrel's nine inches. Good God, the range of such a weapon would be astounding! And loaded with a much heavier ball made of the new material as well? Wyckham again picked up the brown heavy round shot. He tried to imagine what would happen to a wooden ship hit with such a weight at the much higher velocity the black ooze would give the gun. Christ, it would probably go right through any ship afloat. It would probably go through anything!

But there were questions to be answered. First and foremost was whether the gun could handle the necessary charge to propel the heavier shot with such a thin casting, though Wyckham suspected that the miracle brown substance was up to the task. And what did the gun actually weigh? Hopefully, its thin casting kept its weight below what was practicable to mount in quantity aboard ship. *Righteous*, for instance, could only handle about thirty-five tons in armament and still be seaworthy.

"Mister Favorite, you astound me with your industriousness! Would you be so good as to join me for a glass here at my personal table here…ah…" Wyckham realized his official table was in splinters. "Well, actually at this table over here." He moved to a nearby table occupied by a pair of the serpent beings, who were known as the biggest smugglers in this universe. "Weren't you gentlemen just leaving?" he asked in a voice low with menace, giving them a steely glance, his right hand drumming the grip on his Moroccan sword. The two snakemen hesitated, then got up, and slithered off without a word. The malevolent look in their eyes clearly showed their hatred of the man who constantly harassed their business and had killed Lightning Fangs, one of their most revered captains, by thrusting the sword on his hip up through the snake's jaw right here in the Ruptured Krag.

Wyckham couldn't give a damn what they thought and was quite ready to run some cold steel through another one right now. He referred to them as Highwaysnakes and believed they were all pirates, responsible for the recent disappearance of two League merchant ships. Their recent embracing of Mediterranean corsair clothing angered Wyckham further. That these slimy buggers wanted to dress like human pirates was an affront to any seagoing man.

ABOUT THE AUTHOR

Vince Scully is a retired class clown, fencer, engineer, drag racer, furniture designer, and sales rep who lives in Long Beach, California, with his wonderful wife and two dogs. With his two children out of the nest, he spends his time writing, staying in shape, and tinkering with his treasured cars, a '32 Ford and a '31 Lincoln. He often pretends to be Dodger announcer Vin Scully in order to get better reservations at restaurants. His friends describe him as indescribable. This is his first novel.

Made in the USA
San Bernardino, CA
10 May 2018